The BLACKBIRDS of ST GILES

The BLACKBIRDS of ST GILES

LILA CAIN

SIMON &
SCHUSTER

London · New York · Amsterdam/Antwerp · Sydney · Toronto · New Delhi

First published in Great Britain by Simon & Schuster UK Ltd, 2025

Copyright © Lila Cain, 2025

The right of Lila Cain to be identified as author
of this work has been asserted in accordance with the
Copyright, Designs and Patents Act, 1988.

1 3 5 7 9 10 8 6 4 2

Simon & Schuster UK Ltd
1st Floor
222 Gray's Inn Road
London WC1X 8HB

Simon & Schuster Australia, Sydney
Simon & Schuster India, New Delhi

www.simonandschuster.co.uk
www.simonandschuster.com.au
www.simonandschuster.co.in

A CIP catalogue record for this book
is available from the British Library

Hardback ISBN: 978-1-3985-2657-0
eBook ISBN: 978-1-3985-2658-7
Audio ISBN: 978-1-3985-3770-5

Typeset in the UK by M Rules
Printed and Bound in the UK using 100% Renewable
Electricity at CPI Group (UK) Ltd

MIX
Paper | Supporting
responsible forestry
FSC
www.fsc.org
FSC® C171272

For Ileen Maisel

1955–2024

Prologue

1768: The Garnett Plantation, Jamaica

Above the trees, the sky pulsed with an eerie orange glow. Even the moon was tainted. Scuffed by clouds, it blinked like a bloodied eye over the turrets of The Salutation. The elegant plantation house straddled the hill above the estate like a great white bird, but tonight its wings would be blackened by fire.

Daniel pulled at the rag covering his nose and mouth and tried to call to the pale figure moving ahead of him on the stony path. Immediately his lungs filled with smoke. Around him, flames rippled through the undergrowth. The sparking threads shimmered like the golden lace of the parasol Mistress Isabella used to shield her ivory skin.

Over the crackle of scrub fire, Daniel was aware of the steady beat of the drums that had begun this night's work. The sound was measured, deliberate, insistent. They all knew the old rhythms and the messages they sent. The secret had been carried across the ocean. It was a call to arms. He listened, alert to another warning pounding beneath his ribs.

Adanna.

The path leading to The Salutation rose steeply. His brother was just visible. The grey shirt that strained across Jon's broad shoulders marked him out as he stumbled upward. Shadows flitted between

the trees; many others were heading up to the Great House. Even
if the alarm had been raised, there was a chance to take what they
needed. To take what they were owed.

Gulping a breath, Daniel quickened his pace. Jon hadn't thought
to muffle his face to ward off the smoke. He was gasping and coughing when Daniel levelled with him. Lunging for his brother's arm,
Daniel pulled him round to face him and ripped the rag from his
mouth.

'You swore to me that Adanna would be safe.'

It was the only thought in his head. Adanna was everything to
him. Their lives were bound together more tightly than the creeper
winding around the trees edging the path.

Jon's eyes slid to the top of the hill. Above them, the Great House
was silhouetted against a crimson sky. The tall windows that gave
a view of the lawn from the long wooden veranda glowed with a
light too fierce for candles. Jon frowned. Was that guilt? Daniel was
certain he saw it there.

'You knew it was tonight and you didn't tell me.' He rasped down
a breath before spluttering on. 'It was agreed. You said . . . you *promised* that I would be given time to warn her—'

'It was you who made promises.' Jon wrenched his arm free,
the sudden movement causing them both to lose their footing. In
a moment they were falling together, tumbling downhill in a hail
of pebbles. When they came to rest in a knot of limbs, Daniel was
aware of a sharp pain. Blood seeped through the coarse cloth of his
breeches where a stone had pierced the flesh. As he stared at the
darkly glistening stain, calls echoed from the woodland above. The
sound was harsh, guttural; almost triumphant.

What would they do to her?

He tried to scramble to his feet, but his brother caught him fast. Jon
had always been stronger; he resembled their stocky, muscular father
while Daniel had the grace and quick intelligence of their mother.

'Don't be a fool.' The blaze that hissed and snapped around them brought an amber glow to Jon's eyes. 'Go back down. It's too late.'

'Too late for what?' Daniel flinched as the yelping came again. 'What are they doing up there?'

When Jon didn't answer, Daniel twisted about. Above the treeline, fire rippled along the roof of The Salutation. One of the turrets was gilded with flames. The house servants slept in rooms directly beneath the eaves where the heat of the sun made the air thick as molasses.

'It's too soon!' He tried to free himself, but his brother pulled him so close that their foreheads touched.

'Listen to me.' Jon spoke slowly. 'You saw what Kemp did to Thomas this morning. We all watched a child beaten to death. And for what? For eating cane to fill his shrivelled belly. No, brother, it's not a moment too soon.'

Daniel's vision blurred. Unwilling to meet Jon's eyes, he looked down. There was a jagged rip across the left knee of his breeches where a livid red gash split his skin. He was aware of a stabbing pain and just for a moment he wondered if he'd be fit enough to work. If he was lame, Driver Kemp would use the whip on him.

Instantly, he was disgusted by the ingrained fear. Kemp was dead. He had seen the man's mutilated body hanging by the feet from a tree at the entrance to the path. His second, Riley, eyeless and broken, creaked beside him. It had been planned for weeks. The men had gone for them first. That was the message when the drumming began in the dark, and his brother must have known.

'You passed the word to raise them.' Daniel looked up. 'You knew and you didn't tell me.' His voice was thickened by smoke and by the ball of misery rising in his throat. He knew he sounded like a petulant child. But he was not a child. He was a man, with a man's responsibilities. Wildly, he stared up at the burning house.

The Salutation had many rooms. She of all people would know where to hide. All he needed to do was find her and make her safe.

'Daniel!' Jon shook him roughly. 'Even if I'd wanted to, I couldn't stop what's happening tonight. Thomas died today, last week it was Martha and her unborn child. How many others have we seen murdered by Kemp or Riley, or by hunger? Have you forgotten Father?'

It was a ridiculous question. Their father's death was seared into Daniel's every fibre like the 'G' branded on his arm. The flesh had puckered and healed, but the memory of that day still burned.

Late last summer a fever had swept the Garnett Plantation, but Driver Kemp and Riley gave no quarter to the sick. Slaves were expendable. It was cheaper to buy fresh stock in Kingston than waste time and expense on the weak.

At first when Adam – their father – fell ill, he had tried to hide it, but soon he became too frail to work or even stand in the rows. Riley accused him of indolence. He gave Adam thirty lashes and then, as an example to all, he had him stripped where he lay and manacled his feet and hands so that he could not crawl into the shade or even scratch at the bites of mosquitoes. For the rest of the day, Daniel and Jon were forced to work on, knowing that their father lay suffering nearby. They were powerless to help; Riley and his men had pistols as well as whips, but worst of all, Riley had a vicious mind. When the bell rang to mark the end of labour, he smeared Adam in molasses and ordered that he was to be left where he was. That night Kemp and Riley kept watch on the rows where the enslaved men, women and children of the Garnett Plantation were housed. Inside those fly-blown shacks no one slept; they all knew that the cane rats feasted in the dark. When the workers went to the fields the next day, Adam was dead. It was not the fever that took him.

'It cannot go on, brother.' Jon released Daniel from his grip. 'We brought the plans forward, that's all. It's better this way. The anger of the day makes us stronger. Besides . . .' he stood up, '. . . you lost Adanna a long time ago; we all did.'

Furious, Daniel sprang to his feet. 'They took her from us. Mistress Isabella wanted her because—'

'Because she was finer than the rest of us,' Jon interrupted. 'You have been blind to so much. You're clever, but you cannot see. Adanna was never for you. Forget her.'

Daniel's bellow of anger was ragged with smoke. He lunged at his brother and tried to force his way past, but as they struggled, a man emerged from the trees. Halting, he swung a hessian bag around his head before tossing it to the ground.

Something pale tumbled out. At first, Daniel took it for a white cat, but then the man prodded it with a foot. A head rolled on the pebbles. Daniel saw that he had mistaken a wig – still partially attached to short grey hair with silver pins – for fur. Watery eyes peered up at him. Jewels glinted at the ears; the stump of the neck was ragged and wet.

'Mistress Isabella will never cut my child again.' The man spat on the horror. 'I've taken her head to prove it to him.' There was a fierce triumph in his voice.

Daniel stared at the woman who had taken Adanna to be her maid. Isabella Garnett, mistress of the Garnett Plantation, was cruel and spiteful, worse if anything than Oliver, her fat husband. He didn't feel any pity, but his stomach churned with dread for the girl he had promised to protect, *no matter what comes.*

He heard Jon's question from a distance. 'What of the master? What's become of Garnett, Luke?'

Daniel tore his eyes from the grisly trophy, amazed that his brother recognised the man before them. The Luke he'd always known was mild and gentle. A loving husband, a good father, a friend. This version of him was forged into something terrifying and new by the heat of his fury. What had become of him tonight?

What had become of her?

'Dead.' Luke glanced at Jon. 'They had pistols up there but there were too many of us. There's still plenty to be had at the house. They're throwing everything out before the fire takes hold. We'll need all we can. The Maroons want payment. The rebels won't give us shelter in the hills unless we offer them something in return.'

He bent to the head and ripped away the diamond earrings.

'I don't need these. Take them, my pockets are full.' He offered them to Jon and jerked his head at the house. 'There's plenty more where these came from, if you're quick enough.'

Catching the head by the curling ringlets of the wig, he stuffed it into the sack and swung it to his back once more.

'I'll see you at the bay then. Make it sharp. The Maroons won't wait long.'

'Wait!' Daniel caught Luke's arm. 'What about the house servants? Adanna. Is she . . . ?'

'You mean that girl the mistress dressed in her cast-offs?'

Unable to speak, Daniel nodded.

'Then she's dead with the rest of them.' Luke shrugged. 'No one can serve two masters. Anyone in The Salutation tonight was our enemy.'

Daniel felt his brother's arms lock around him. A single gunshot cracked the night. Moments later a volley of shots sounded from below. Instantly the drumming stopped.

'They've raised the militia,' Jon said softly over his shoulder. 'Go on down, Luke. Gather your family and run to the bay.'

'You'd best take your own advice. They're on to us.'

Turning from the brothers, Luke skidded away down the shingle path.

Daniel struggled to free himself. 'Why didn't you tell me it was tonight? Didn't you trust me?'

There was a pause before Jon answered.

'It wasn't you I didn't trust.' He bundled Daniel about to face him. 'Mother is weak. She needs you now. And Pearl, what of her? Would you abandon them? One of us must help them. The only reason I'm going up there is to take something to pay our way. Luke is right, the Maroons won't shelter us for free. Find Mother and Pearl, and lead them to Kirtle Bay. It's been arranged – boats will be waiting. I'll join you as soon as I can.'

A flare exploded in the sky, bleaching the woodland with sudden cruel brightness. Daniel screwed his eyes shut against the brilliance. After a moment, he heard a sigh.

'Go to her then, if you must. I won't stop you.' Jon loosened his grip. 'All I ask is that you think of the future, not the past, brother.'

Daniel opened his eyes. Jon had taken a step back, leaving the way to The Salutation clear. Face hidden in shadow, he pointed at the stony track. 'You were a boy until this night, but now you must be a man. Up or down, it's a hard path. I'll not force you. You must decide. And then you must live with your conscience.'

Above them the broken backbone of The Salutation was blurred by smoke and flames. Even at this distance they could hear the dreadful groan of the timbers as fire engulfed the building. The acrid scent of charred wood filled the air. No one could survive the madness and the fury.

'She's dead with the rest of them.'

But his mother and Pearl lived. They needed him. Daniel swallowed ash and made the choice that left his heart a blackened cinder in the blaze. He could barely form his next words.

'I'll ... I'll go down.'

Jon reached out to smudge away the tears that streamed down his brother's face. 'Mother kept your secret all this time. Now you can repay her. Guide them to safety before it's too late.' Their eyes locked. 'If nothing else, do it for Adanna.'

Mute with misery, Daniel nodded.

'Save me a place on the boat.' Jon's voice was muffled by the strength of their embrace and the rough fabric of their shirts.

'Take these.' Something small and hard was forced into Daniel's hand – the jewels from the severed head.

'Use them to pay the boatman if . . .'

Unwilling, or perhaps unable, to finish, Jon released him and turned swiftly away.

As Daniel watched his brother begin again on the path leading up to the Great House he knew, with the certainty that told him the sun would rise every day, that it was the last time he would see him.

Gunshot maddened the dogs. They barked and strained at their tethers as Daniel ran through the quarters. Most of the crudely built shacks were already deserted, their plank doors swinging wide to reveal tiny cramped spaces. Some stragglers remained – mainly the old, the lame and the sick. A woman limped past carrying a crying baby in her arms, and a young man, his body twisted beyond use by Kemp's punishment, was slumped in a doorway.

Daniel ran on, hardening his eyes and his heart to the tragedies unfurling around him.

'Think of the future, not the past.'

Jon was right. He had to make sure that Pearl and his mother were safe. Moonlight cast a sickly glow over the dusty path and the shabby abandoned cabins. The crack of gunshot was nearer now and lights bloomed overhead, blanching everything to bone. In one of the sudden flashes, Daniel saw a brother and sister just a little older than Pearl outlined at a doorway. They didn't know what to do or where to go. When another flare went off, they cowered into the shadow.

He paused. 'Do you know the way to the bay through the fields?'

The boy nodded, his eyes huge with fear. Daniel knelt, awakening new pain from the deep gash in his knee. He tried to smile.

'Clever lad. Now, take your sister's hand and run. When you get
to the bay there will be people ready to help you. Give the boatmen
this.' He pressed one of the earrings into the boy's palm and folded
his little fingers tight about it.

'Will Father be there?' The girl stared at him.

'Yes.' Daniel hoped that the doubt didn't show on his face. 'He's
waiting for you. Go!'

Gripping his sister's hand, the boy began to walk. After a few
faltering steps, the pair broke into a run. Neither looked back.

Daniel loped on until he reached a shack at the furthest end of
the row. Relieved to find it deserted, he wheeled about determined
to go straight to the bay. Surely his mother and Pearl were there
already? The workers of the Garnett Plantation knew exactly what
to do and where to go if the rising came.

'It wasn't you I didn't trust.'

What did Jon mean by that? As Daniel ran, he realised with a furious conviction that his brother must have been talking of Adanna.
But she would never betray them. The only person who had committed an act of betrayal was him. Finally, the grief he had stoppered
inside since parting with Jon burst through. He halted on the track
leading to the cane fields as a choking sob wracked his body.

A small hand crept into his. The tiny girl looked up and the light
of another flare revealed her face. He was torn between relief and
anxiety. Why was Pearl here and not at the bay?

Tugging hard, she led him into the overgrown thicket beside the
path. In the milky light Daniel made out a shape huddled at the foot
of a dogwood tree.

'Ah! You found him. Good girl.' It was his mother's voice.
She looked up and he saw that her lean face was tight with pain.
Immediately he felt a pang of guilt. At thirty-seven, Sarah was old
for a field labourer and a wound on her leg, caused by Riley's baton,
had made her lame. His brother was right. They needed him.

'Where's Jon?' It was as if she heard his thoughts. Her eyes strayed past him into the gloom.

'He's gone to the house. He said he'd meet us at the bay,' Daniel replied, with a certainty he did not feel.

'And Adanna? Did you—' His mother's question was cut short by a new volley of shot.

'There's no time.' He held out a hand. 'The Maroons won't wait. We have to go.'

Sarah struggled to rise, gasping with pain at the effort. It was over a mile through the cane fields to the bay and then a scramble down the cliff to the sands. Daniel swallowed and turned to Pearl. 'Can you walk very fast?'

When she nodded, he forced a smile. 'That's good. I want you to follow me and stay close. Don't let me out of your sight, do you understand?'

Pearl nodded again. Daniel looked anxiously at his mother, who was supporting herself against the tree.

'I'll carry you on my back.'

Sarah snorted. 'You will not. I'll shift for myself, child. You'll take Pearl, not me.'

He knew her too well to argue. Instead, he took her hand and drew her from the tree.

'Can you do this?'

'Until I have a choice.' Sarah winced as she took a hesitant step. She met his eyes and he saw the truth.

Green-tinged flames flickered at the edge of the field ahead. The escaped workers had set light to the cane to destroy the crop and to block the way of the militia. Daniel looked back. Lanterns bobbed like fireflies through the rows.

They had to keep moving. He started off again, with Pearl riding on his shoulders. At two years old she was light as a bag of goose down. He felt her flinch at the savage barking of the dogs, but it was the gunfire that told him their pursuers were not taking prisoners.

'It's not far.' He tried to sound confident, but his mother was painfully slow. He turned to offer encouragement, but Sarah wasn't there. Several yards behind, a shadow lay across the path.

Releasing Pearl to the dust, he ran back, knelt and raised his mother to a sitting position. 'You must try, please,' he urged again. 'We're almost there.'

'I can't go any further.' She glanced at Pearl. 'Take the little one to the bay.'

'I won't leave you.' Daniel stood up. The lights were even closer now and the baying dogs were excited, sensing their quarry. He tried to pull his mother upright, but she struggled against him.

'Go now, Daniel!' Her voice was firm.

'I won't. I can't.' He could hardly say the words. Pearl clutched his leg and he felt the living heat of her body through the shredded cloth of his breeches. It was that more than anything that made his next choice.

His mother smiled at the terrified girl. 'You go with your brother now.' Her eyes met his. 'Take Pearl . . . and *live*.'

She spoke again gently. 'You two must live on for us, for our blood.'

A dog barked. A chorus of answering howls rose into the night.

Without allowing himself to think, Daniel snatched Pearl up and swung her to his back. He turned and blundered into the cane, eyes blinded by tears. From behind he heard his mother begin to hum an old lullaby. It was one he remembered – she had sung it to him and to Pearl.

He held the little girl tight and ran from his second betrayal. When gunshots split the air, he forced himself not to look back.

PART ONE

Inheritance

From *The London Courant,*
30th January 1776

NEWS come in from the American Colony – A PROCLAMATION given by His Excellency the Right Honourable JOHN Earl of DUNMORE, His Majesty's Lieutenant and Governor General of the Colony & Dominion of Virginia and Vice Admiral of the Fleet.

As I have ever entertained Hopes, that an Accommodation might have taken place between Great Britain and this Colony, without being compelled by my Duty to this moste disagreeable, but now absolutely necessary Step, rendered so by a Body of armed Men unlawfully assembled, firing on His Majesty's Tenders, and the formation of an Army, and that Army now on their March to attack His Majesty's Troops ...

... I do require every Person capable of bearing Arms, to resort to His Majesty's STANDARD or be looked upon as Traitors to His Majesty's Crown and Government ...

... And I do hereby further declare all indented Servants, Negroes or others, (appertaining to Rebels) free that are able and willing to bear Arms, they joining His Majesty's Troops as soon as may be, for the more speedily reducing this Colony to a proper sense of Duty to His Majesty's Crown and Dignity.

Chapter One

New Year's Eve, December 1781: New York

Daniel stared into the flames dancing in the hearth. Unlike most, he found it hard to take pleasure from a warming fire. The flickers of red and gold brought back too many memories and a pain that still, after all these years, twisted his heart. If he had kept his promise and Adanna had lived, she would be thirty. Older than him by a year, she was always one step ahead until . . . *until* . . .

He closed his eyes and tried to listen to the music. What would she make of him now? Would she be here with him and with scores of British army officers and their wives? On balance, he thought not.

The pitted road to freedom from the charred remains of the Garnett Plantation had led him and Pearl to a place that even Adanna's girlish sorceries could never have predicted. Opening his eyes, he reached to the mantel for his wine glass. Catching the fire-light, the silver buttons on the white cuff of his uniform glittered.

During the long and bitter struggle to retain America, the British had invited formerly enslaved men – those who had escaped from sugar estates on the islands and from the cotton fields of the south – to join the ranks of their army. The King himself had promised freedom in return for their loyalty. Five years ago, Daniel had answered that call and had proved himself worthy both on the battlefield and as a shrewd advisor. But now the time was coming when the King would have to honour his part of the bargain.

The buttons on Daniel's cuff seemed to wink mockingly.

The final notes of the country song lingered for a moment and then the cheerful group gathered around the harpsichord applauded the young officer. Acknowledging their appreciation with a shallow bow that combined both pleasure and embarrassment, he swapped places with a plump, pretty young woman, who began a lively tune.

From his place by the hearth Daniel studied the guests invited to celebrate the turning of the year at Major Fitzallen's temporary residence. Every man present was in dress uniform, their scarlet jackets and buttons glowing in the candlelight. The women – the handful of wives who had insisted on accompanying their husbands across the ocean when they were sent on the King's business – had put on their finest gowns. Jewels twinkled in their hair, from their ears and at their throats. Later there would be dancing in the large but sparsely furnished space. The Fitzallen's New York townhouse had been requisitioned by the army and in consequence had more of the camp about it than a home.

Tonight's merriment was a diversion. In the coming days difficult decisions would have to be made. Some of those present would return to England, others would fight on to an uncertain, untidy end.

Daniel knew the veterans were uneasy. He searched the room for Major Fitzallen and found him seated in a high-backed chair beyond the fire, deep in conversation with three of his fellow commanders. The serious set of the men's faces told him everything.

He watched the Major, alert to any sign of pain. The crippling leg wound that confined his friend to a chair had been sustained four years ago on the eve of the disastrous second Battle of Saratoga.

Under cover of darkness, Major Fitzallen had ridden with Daniel to a ridge high above the Hudson River to spy upon the massing

Patriot forces. The lights of the camp fires that twinkled across the plains below were numerous as stars fallen from the sky. It was obvious that the day would go against them; the British were outnumbered and outflanked but there was still time to warn the commanding officers and avoid a bloody massacre.

In desperate haste, they had abandoned caution and taken the most direct route back to the lines. In a moonlit glade of gnarled white oaks shots had rung out. The Major's horse had reared, throwing its rider into the twisted roots of a tree. Daniel's skill as a marksman ensured that the Patriot scout who had ambushed them would never rejoin the rebel forces, but Fitzallen lay trapped, his legs crushed by the weight of his dying horse.

After freeing the Major's mangled body, Daniel had strapped him to his back and then, lashed together, they had returned to the British lines on one sweating, panting mare. The perilous journey took them through four miles of dense, Patriot-infested woodland, but most dangerous of all was the arrogance and obstinacy of the British generals who refused to accept Daniel's warning of inevitable defeat.

Edward Fitzallen never forgot Daniel's bravery that night – both in the face of danger and in the face of his sneering superiors. But although Daniel saved Fitzallen's life, he could not save the thousands who fell or were terribly injured in a battle that proved to be the turning point in the war.

As for the Major, the encounter left him a changed man. His left leg was broken so badly in the fall that part of the shattered bone had burst through the skin. Even now, he wore a bandage and walked with a cane. He tried to disguise the pain, but Daniel knew him too well to be deceived.

As he watched him now through the New Year crush, he hoped Mr Jessop was right about London. The regiment's gloomy doctor maintained that the Major's last hope lay on the far side of the Atlantic.

'Do you think Edward looks tired?'

Daniel turned at the softly spoken question. Elizabeth Fitzallen had dressed with great care. The blue gown suited her pale complexion and her hair had been curled and powdered by an expert hand.

Most people in the room would not have noticed the shadows beneath her eyes, the rouge applied to her cheeks, the gape of the dress at her shoulders or the fact that the carefully arranged lace fichu could not disguise a throat strung like a violin.

Daniel pointed to the Major. 'He's talking to General Cley. That would exhaust anyone.'

Elizabeth laughed. 'You are quite right. My husband has introduced me to many dull creatures, but Cley is the most tedious man I have ever known. Poor Edward. Come, sit with me.'

Leading Daniel to a couch set before a tall window, she watched her husband fondly. A mischievous smile crept to her lips.

'I must tell you about the time when . . . Oh!' Whatever she was about to add about General Cley was instantly forgotten. Instead, she pointed her fan over his shoulder at the misted glass.

'Snow!'

In the islands it never snowed. In fact, Daniel had never known true cold – the sort that made your bones feel as if they might shatter – until he came north. Winters here were hard, brittle and long. Despite the heat of the room, he shivered and pulled at the braided collar of his uniform.

'Go back to the fire, Daniel. You do not have to sit with me.' Elizabeth smiled. 'I am quite well.'

It wasn't true. Elizabeth Fitzallen was as frail as her husband. In the last weeks the flesh had melted from her body like wax from a candle. Daniel knew that Pearl feared for her mistress. He smiled and hoped his eyes did not betray him. 'I am very comfortable where I am and happy to watch this fine celebration with you.'

'Forgive me for asking, but I imagine this . . .' Elizabeth gestured at the room with her fan, '. . . must be . . .' She frowned and began again. 'That is to say, I imagine that you and your sister never . . .' She stopped, embarrassed. 'I am sorry. I did not mean to be gauche or impolite and I did not mean to pry.'

Through the panes of the window Daniel saw the lights of a carriage travelling along the street below. Flurries of snow seemed to be pulled in its wake. The frond-like flakes reminded him of cane flowers battered by the wind. Elizabeth Fitzallen was a good woman, but she could never understand what he and Pearl had endured. He shook his head.

'Our lives were very different.'

The Fitzallens had shown them nothing but kindness, respect and gratitude. But they were unusual. Daniel knew he was a subject of gossip among many of the officers and their wives. Some were jealous of his relationship with the Fitzallens, others thought it preposterous that a black man should be allowed to move among them as an equal. He could count the number of his friends in the room tonight on one hand: the Fitzallens and Lieutenants Crawshaw and Murray who had fought alongside him at Saratoga and during the long and chaotic retreat to New York.

Once here, he had chosen to live by the docks because it was where other Black Loyalists who fought for the British were quartered. But it was not right for Pearl and he had been glad when the Fitzallens offered to employ her as a companion to Elizabeth. In truth, they treated her more like their child. Pearl was safe in their house and in their company.

Daniel envied her ease. The Black Loyalists regarded him with suspicion. He looked like one of them, but they knew he was different. Caught between worlds, he no longer belonged to his own past. At night, he muffled his ears to their songs because the ghosts they raised were too cruel and too bitter. Like him, the Black Loyalists all dreamed of sailing to England where the King would reward them. Unlike him, they were not officers.

Elizabeth spoke again. 'Does Pearl ever speak of the past?'

'Thankfully she remembers very little of the estate. She was so young.' Daniel shook his head. 'I am not so lucky. Our lives were harsh and the regime was brutal. Many thousands still suffer.'

Unable to find an answer, Elizabeth put down her fan and rested a hand on his. She looked back to the window. Snow was falling more heavily now and the street beyond the glass was obliterated.

'I was born here in New York. Did Edward ever tell you that?'

'I thought you came from England, with Edward ...' Daniel corrected himself, '... with Major Fitzallen.'

'It was such a long time ago.' Elizabeth reached to a low table for her wine glass, but her face creased with pain.

'Here, let me.' He passed her the wine, trying to blank anxiety from his expression. She took a sip and closed her eyes.

'My father was originally from the county of Buckinghamshire, but he came here as a young man, married and established a trading company. The house where I grew up was not far from this street. When he and my mother returned to England on family business, I went with them.' She opened her eyes and smiled. 'I had never met my English relatives and I thought them very grand. I was seventeen when I met Edward at a country dance. He was in his uniform. I'd never met anyone like him. My parents disapproved of his calling, but he is my first and only love.'

Her eyes strayed again to the Major. There was such an aching tenderness in her gaze that Daniel felt like an intruder. Embarrassed, he turned away. Unbidden, his own first love came into his thoughts – Adanna, bold, brilliant, beautiful; buried with his heart in the ashes of The Salutation.

'We were married soon after and vowed never to be parted.'

Daniel was grateful to focus on Elizabeth's story.

'At first, I missed this city and my friends, but now I yearn to leave. It has been too long.' She winced and altered her position. 'Moving with the army has been a trial. I have lived in so many places since I returned to America with Edward that I cannot remember their names.' She smoothed the fabric of her dress. 'When I was a girl the size of this land excited me, but now I have seen too much of it. Recently I have often dreamed of the rose garden I planted in Windsor. There is safety and a little world in those old brick walls and narrow paths. I fear that . . .'

Her eyes glassed with tears. Instinctively, Daniel reached for her hand to stop her naming that dread.

'You *will* see your garden again soon.'

Elizabeth's skin was cold and paper-like. He squeezed gently and her bones seemed to fold in his grasp.

He tried again. 'We sail in a few weeks. It won't be long.'

She nodded. 'We will be the first to leave, but not the last. The war is lost. Edward never speaks of it to me, but I know him too well. Freedom is a genie – once the bottle is unstoppered it can never be forced back.' She paused. 'You of all people know that better than anyone.'

Daniel took both her hands in his and rubbed gently. 'You are cold; perhaps we should go nearer to the fire.'

'You saved his life.' Elizabeth's voice rose a little. 'For that alone you will always have my gratitude, but in these last few years you and Pearl have become very important to us. Edward values your advice beyond all others.'

'Then I must be grateful too.' He held her hands a little tighter. 'If it hadn't been for the Major, we would not be sailing to England and to a new life.'

'And I pray it treats you well, Daniel.' He felt her body stiffen next to him at a new wave of pain. When it subsided, she took a square of embroidered cotton from her sleeve. She coughed into it, folded it quickly and tucked it away, but not fast enough to prevent Daniel seeing dark spatters of blood on the cloth. She turned to face him, her sad eyes searching his face for signs of discovery.

'I am so glad you are to sail with him . . . with *us*,' she corrected herself. 'My parents were Quakers. Some of our servants were black, but they were not slaves. My father thought it an abomination. There are many in England who feel the same, although I cannot pretend that your new life will be easy. Edward and I have always believed that men – and women too – should be equals. The colour of your skin means nothing to him. He sees your heart, Daniel, but there will always be those who are blind.'

She watched her husband and the men beyond the hearth.

'I fear for him. The journey will be hard. He is not a young man and six weeks at sea . . .' A new coughing fit stopped her. She produced the cotton square again, not troubling to hide it this time. Daniel knew she was dying, but he marvelled that her thoughts at such a time were all for her husband.

'My first and only love.'

Masking his sadness, he spoke firmly. 'We will all be with him on the voyage.'

Elizabeth nodded. 'Good Dr Jessop has assured me that by March I will be . . . quite ready.' She shivered. 'No. It is Edward I must think of. The wound never healed properly.'

Daniel recalled a recent conversation with Jessop who feared that amputation would be the Major's best and last option. He wondered if Fitzallen knew that. He tried a positive reply. 'Jessop is confident that a surgeon in London will be able to help. He says he trained with someone who is very skilled – a Scotsman, I believe.'

The only thing Daniel knew about Scotland was that it was north of England and that it produced brave and sensible men. His friend Lieutenant Murray was a proud Scot.

'Mackintyre, is it?' Elizabeth cast for the right name. 'No,

Mackintosh. That's the man. I believe he has served the royal household, so I am quite sure ...' Her words were choked by another spasm, the most violent yet. As she struggled to fill her lungs, Daniel sprang up to shield her from the room until it passed. At last, she sat back, a fine sheen of perspiration on her chalk-white face. The circles of rouge on her cheeks now looked strange, grotesque almost. A parody of health.

A look passed between them and Elizabeth smiled sadly.

'I am very much afraid that you will have to remember that surgeon, Daniel. Edward is so bad at names.' She moved the cushion at her back and sat straighter. 'Now, could I trouble you to bring me a glass of lemon water?'

Daniel made a small bow and turned quickly away, glad that she could not see his face. He picked a path through knots of chattering guests and waited for two officers to fill their wine glasses. The food laid out on the long mahogany buffet was simple, but plentiful. The Fitzallens were always generous hosts.

He reached for a jug and was about to fill a glass when he became aware of the conversation taking place next to him. It was obvious that the officers at the buffet had already helped themselves to many glasses of the Fitzallens' wine. The taller of the pair had discarded his wig and stuffed it into a pocket. The trailing ends hung grey and a little frayed over the golden braid and now his scalp glowed through thinning sandy hair. He spilled wine on the cloth as he filled his glass.

'Apparently, he's taking the black with him. Old Fitzy made him a lieutenant to bend the rules. Only officers are eligible, but that still doesn't mean we'll be out of here before summer and that's if we're lucky.' The man swayed and drawled again. 'Lucky bastard! I'd give my sister's virtue in exchange for a passage home.'

The other officer, smaller with thick dark hair made greasy by pomade, reached for a pie. 'There's the irony. It's not even his home.'

The man crushed the pie into his mouth before continuing through a crumbling cascade of pastry and meat. 'I hear he comes sniffing around this house every day like he owns it.'

The fair man nodded, spilling even more wine. 'Washington had the right idea at the beginning of this. He didn't want negroes in the ranks, so why did *we* take them in?'

Daniel concentrated on the dark wine stain spreading through the cloth. The aroma of the cloves scattered on the hearth suddenly came sharp and strong along with the other scents of the room: sweat beneath perfumed oils, the mustiness of fabric stored in camphor chests, brandy fumes.

'Because we were scraping the barrel, my friend.' The smaller man belched and carried on. 'Did I ever tell you about my grand-father? He inherited a cotton plantation in the south of this Godforsaken land and he even went over to see it once. Do you know what he said?'

'I do not, sir.' The other man shook his balding head slowly and stupidly. Propping himself against the table, his companion grinned.

'He said they were sly, lazy and thick as horse shit.' Reaching for his glass, he raised it with a wink. 'And that, my friend, is why Washington didn't want them in his army. Besides, Master George needs slaves to work his own estates.'

His attention wandered as three young women entered the room. 'Now what do we have here?'

Over the man's oily head, Daniel saw that Pearl was one of the neatly dressed girls making their way to the harpsichord. She was notable among them because her skin contrasted so strongly with the pallor of her simple muslin gown and the white cloth turban that bound her hair. He recognised the other girls as Dora and Susannah, two of Elizabeth's maids.

Dora sat at the instrument and glanced shyly round the room. Then she lowered her head and set to work. She was an unexceptional player but once her hesitant fingers established the melody Pearl and Susannah began to sing.

Immediately the babble of conversation died away. Both girls sang beautifully, but it was Pearl's clear soaring voice that brought a shiver of joy to everyone present. Surprised, Daniel almost forgot the conversation he had just overheard until the taller of the men in front of him nudged his oily companion and whispered loudly, 'And now the sister. Christ! What next, a talking dog?'

The small man shrugged. ''Tis a pleasant sight. Don't they say brown meat is sweetest? I'd give her a try – in the dark, mind.' He swung his glass at the pretty tableau and wine splashed everywhere. Swaying, the man tried to dab at the mess, but as he flailed about, he realised that Daniel was standing close by.

'Ah.' His eyes slid to his companion.

Placing the jug back on the table, Daniel drew himself to his full height, which was not inconsiderable.

'I believe you have been discussing me, gentlemen. And my sister.'

His voice was constricted by fury. The words a hiss of menace. He had always been aware of the insults that followed him, but they were never spoken openly to his face. It was shocking to hear these officers discuss him with such casual, arrogant contempt.

From the far side of the room, Pearl's crystalline voice rose and fell with the harpsichord. The purity of it served to stoke his anger. How dare these men insult her? He clenched his fist ready to strike, but instantly felt a restraining hand on his arm. Leaning heavily on a stick, Elizabeth moved to position herself between Daniel and the drunken officers. At the same moment, he was aware that Lieutenants Crawshaw and Murray had come to stand at his side.

Elizabeth studied the men's flushed faces. When she spoke, there was no trace of frailty in her voice. She was, once again, the wife of their commanding officer.

'My husband will hear of this, Bannister.' She turned to the small dark man who seemed to have shrivelled in her presence. 'You too, Turner. I will not allow our friends to be slighted under our roof. I suggest you leave now and go somewhere more suited to your low company. I have asked Crawshaw and Murray to escort you down to the hall.'

Daniel watched the men slink through the room, his friends herding them to the doorway. Only when they had gone, did Elizabeth loosen her grip. She opened her fan and batted it about.

'In truth, I am finding it a little hard to breathe in here. Perhaps it is because the air has become foul?'

Glancing at Pearl, she smiled.

'Your sister has been blessed with an extraordinary talent. When she has finished, will you bring her to me in the parlour? We must discuss her needs for the voyage and for London.'

Chapter Two

As the lantern swayed, the pool of light rolled around the cabin slicking the curved wooden panels with an oscillating glow. Experience had taught Daniel that ginger root was a remedy for seasickness, but in this confined, airless space where the walls shifted with both the swell of the ocean and the swing of the candles overhead, his stomach churned.

It was not only the movement that sickened him.

A stench of decay filled the tarry air as Mr Doyle unwrapped the bandage from Edward Fitzallen's leg. The Major groaned in the narrow bunk as the ship's surgeon carefully freed the last of the fabric.

Doyle shook his head a little too vigorously, dislodging the black ribbon that tied his neat sandy queue. Steadying himself against the roll of the ship, Daniel bent to retrieve it from the boards and in doing so caught sight of the Major's leg. Immediately he wished he hadn't. Chronic disease had eaten the dry shrivelled flesh to the bone, but now a raw and pus-weeping sore had opened over the knee. Even worse, the blackened skin above the lesion was fringed with livid purple veins. The mottling disappeared upward beneath a crumpled linen shirt hemmed with Elizabeth's neat sad stitches.

Daniel had seen gangrene many times before. It took the lives of nearly as many soldiers as bullets fired in battle. He looked away. The Major's grey cloak swayed from a hook on the cabin door like the ghost of the man who had worn it.

The surgeon tutted and dropped the soiled bandage into a bucket beside the low wooden bunk. More a shelf than a bed, it was suspended from chains attached to the wall. Fitzallen's only comfort was the thin, straw-packed mattress to which he had retreated two weeks into the voyage.

Doyle looked up and studied the Major's visitor with pale, watery eyes. Even though he was just a little older than Daniel, his freckled skin was already lined by salt.

'I'm sorry.'

Accepting the black ribbon, he retied the stub of hair. 'This should have been dealt with weeks ago, months even.' He glanced back at Fitzallen, whose face was sheened with perspiration, eyes moving fitfully beneath closed lids.

'It is good that he sleeps. A mercy.' Doyle frowned. 'It's a wonder to me that he walked aboard.' Turning from the bunk, he opened the large brass-bound box he had brought into the cabin. He lifted a tray of stoppered glass phials and sifted beneath it through rolls of bandage.

'This, I think.'

He selected a thick white clump and, bracing himself against the roll of the ship, cut a strip to length with a thin silver blade. 'It's clean at least. I'll try this, too.' Replacing the knife, he took a glass bottle from the tray and splashed clear liquid on the fabric.

'Alcohol.' Doyle replaced the stopper. 'Although at this stage it would probably be better to pour it down his throat.'

'Is there nothing else you can do?' Daniel watched the surgeon begin to bind the wound, seemingly oblivious to the moans of his patient.

'Beyond prayer, no. The leg should have been amputated. No point in that now, the disease has spread too far and his blood is poisoned. There.' He tied a final knot. 'I fear the Major will be dead long before we reach London.'

Daniel glanced anxiously at the bunk. Had Fitzallen heard that? Like all the medical men he had known in the army, Mr Doyle was curiously detached from his work.

The ship's surgeon studied his patient and reached into the box again. 'If he wakes, I can offer something for the pain, but that is the best I can do now.'

He pushed a tiny green glass phial into Daniel's hand. Catching the brass rings set into the ends of the box, he straightened up and squeezed awkwardly to the narrow doorway. 'I'll leave you now. I have others to see. Two of the ladies have complained of a persistent headache, although it is my belief that if they took a little more air above deck and a little less ratafia below they might cure themselves.' Doyle nodded at the phial. 'Laudanum, if he needs it. No more than five drops. Give him water if he thirsts, but hold his head high; you don't want to drown him.'

When the surgeon had gone, Daniel took a candle from a box on the panelled wall and lit it from the lantern swaying overhead. He blew out the lantern and, reaching to the railed shelf above the bunk, he retrieved a broad-based pewter chamber stick into which he pushed the single candle.

The light in the room was kinder now. He slipped the phial into a pocket and sat cross-legged on the boards. Waves pounded against the hull beyond the bunk, the steady beat reminding him of drumming from many years ago. The rhythm and the memory led him to words his mother had taught him, a prayer in her own tongue. An ancient appeal to the gods to accept the soul of a warrior had been quietly murmured by the men and women on the Garnett Plantation when one of their number died. Daniel's mother had been born far from the islands and that whispered entreaty had been an act of defiance and remembrance. Although he didn't understand all the words, he had felt their meaning.

He rested his head in his hands, fingers raking through his

cropped dark hair. Unlike the other officers on board the *Audentior*, he never wore powder or a wig.

If Doyle was right, and Daniel had no reason to disagree with the surgeon's blunt prognosis, the future was uncertain. He knew no one in London.

At a rasping cough, he looked up and was surprised to find Fitzallen staring at him. He was mistaken about the cough. The throttled laugh came again. 'I swear that man's breath will kill me before my blood does the job.' Fitzallen's voice was surprisingly firm as he continued. 'Bloody leech. Army, navy – they're all butchers.'

Daniel smiled, but then he realised Fitzallen might have been awake throughout the surgeon's visit.

'You heard what he said?'

'Of course I did.' A sudden heel of the ship filled the cabin with the alarming groan of massive timbers. The bunk swung heavily on its chains and bumped back against the wall where trickles of water seeped through the lime-washed planking. Fitzallen gasped. He tried to sit up, but the effort defeated him. Grey with pain, he fell back on the coarse striped pillow.

'I'm not a fool and neither are you. We both know this is a battle I cannot win.'

'Doyle gave me something.' Daniel pulled the phial from his pocket. 'Laudanum. It will ease the pain.'

Fitzallen shook his head. 'I have something I need to tell you and for that I need my wits.'

'Water then?' Daniel reached for the pitcher stowed beneath the bunk. Pouring a stream of brackish liquid into a tin mug, he held it to the man's cracked lips. Fitzallen gulped greedily, draining it to the bottom. His skin was cold and clammy to the touch, but when Daniel tried to pull up the rumpled blanket, Fitzallen stopped him.

'I'm burning. Molten lead is running in my veins.' He pushed the blanket away. 'Where's Pearl?'

'She's sewing in the women's cabin.' Daniel was relieved that the four English women on board had made Pearl something of a pet. He suspected it was as much for poor Elizabeth's sake as her own goodness. The army wives of New York had known how much Elizabeth doted on her pretty companion.

'Does she sing for them?' Fitzallen grimaced as the vessel lunged forward.

Daniel nodded. 'They enjoy listening to her and she is content in their company.' He didn't add that he was glad Pearl had found a circle of protectors. A ship was no place for a fifteen-year-old just coming into her beauty. He had seen the sly looks of the crew when they took air together on deck and he had heard the muttered obscenities.

'She brought my dear Lizzie such comfort in those last days.' Fitzallen smiled sadly. 'I wish I could hear her.'

'I'll bring her to you now. I know she would be happy to see you.'

Daniel made to stand up, but Fitzallen caught his arm. 'Stay. I need to discuss your future and there's little time left. We've both seen what happens at the end to the minds of men when . . .'

He didn't need to say any more. Daniel swallowed back words he knew to be a lie and turned his attention to the candle stub. He picked at the nubbled wax that had spilled to one side and watched the light dance on the studded wall of the cabin. He found himself wondering what happened to a flame when it was extinguished.

'You could have abandoned me and saved yourself that night at the ridge.'

Daniel looked up. 'And in the years since you have more than repaid me, sir. You gave me a chance to prove myself when others saw no further than the colour of my skin.'

'I am the lucky one.' Fitzallen gestured to the mug and Daniel helped him drink again. As he held the man's head, he saw that bruise-like mottling had begun to spread from the Major's shoulder to his neck.

Pushing the water away, Fitzallen clasped Daniel's hand. 'I have a confession to make. I questioned the sanity of allowing men like you to fight for the Crown. I did not believe that former slaves would feel any loyalty to our cause; quite the opposite in fact. I thought you might be spies sent to betray us. But I was wrong and I saw that early on. *You* opened my eyes, Daniel. It was a fortunate day when you came into the regiment. At first, I admired your courage, but then I came to value your intelligence, your judgement and your heart. The commission was a small thing in return for my life. My only regret is that it will come to an end before I can make sure that my debt is paid in full.'

'There is no debt.' Daniel gripped tight. 'If it wasn't for you – and for Elizabeth, who was a good, kind woman – we would not be travelling to England and to a new life.'

Fitzallen frowned. 'I hope you will not be disappointed.'

'I will be free. That is a good beginning.' The candle flame flared for an instant, making Daniel's shadow huge on the studded wall. 'My hope is that the King will keep his promise to me and to others like me and that in England we will find dignity and a home.'

'You will find more than that. I promise you.' Fitzallen released Daniel's hand and pointed to the corner of the cabin. 'Bring that box to me, please.'

The familiar rectangular chest was small, bound with metal and secured with leather straps. During the long campaign it had contained maps, plans and correspondence.

'Open it and bring out the first papers you find.'

Bewildered, Daniel did as he was bid. The scent of cedar rose as he lifted the lid. A folded document tied with black ribbon lay on the top of an ordered pile of papers. Taking it out, he showed it to Fitzallen.

'This one?'

Fitzallen nodded. 'That is the will I dictated yesterday to Captain

Benson. You and Pearl will always have a place in England. It will be your legal right set out in the document in your hands. When I die, my estates and interests will go to you.'

Dumbfounded, Daniel stared at the folded paper. 'But I cannot . . . surely, you cannot—'

'I'll do exactly as I wish,' Fitzallen interrupted him. 'These are the last commands of a dying man. My poor frail Lizzie carried so many babes, but none of them lived. I have no direct heir. We spoke of this before she died. It was her greatest wish and hope to see Pearl settled and you also.' He smiled at Daniel's confusion. 'You saved my life, man. This is the best way I, *we*, can repay you. My only regret is that my impending death has speeded matters to an early conclusion. I had hoped to introduce you to our circle and to ensure that my wishes were understood.'

Fitzallen gestured at the document in Daniel's hand. 'My family has been successful in trade for three generations. Despite my commission, as the eldest son I have retained a significant interest. This will pass to you. Read it and you'll understand.'

Loosening the black ribbon, Daniel unfolded the page. His hands shook a little as he gazed at the close-packed lines written in a slanting script. According to the will, he and Pearl were to inherit the bulk of Fitzallen's substantial estate with just a few small bequests and keepsakes entailed for friends and distant family members.

Fitzallen continued. 'There aren't many in the lower ranks who are literate – still less among the Black Loyalists. That marked you out from the start. I never thought to ask it until now, but who taught you to read?'

Utterly amazed, Daniel looked up from the paper. The question had caught him off guard. 'I learned many years ago. A . . . friend on the estate helped me. It was dangerous for both of us. If anyone found out—' He halted, unwilling to say more. Even now, so many years later, the secret times when Adanna had taught him the alphabet, and then, slowly, to put it together so that he might read and write like her were too painful to recall. He worshipped her memory, but like a holy relic, he locked it away.

He stared at the document. 'Your generosity touches me deeply, but I . . . *we* cannot accept so much.'

'You will and you must. If not for me, then for Elizabeth, who will not be happy with me in the next world if I do not secure your future in this one.' Fitzallen paused. 'I have one request.'

He groaned as the *Audentior* pitched sideways, crushing his leg against the ship's wall. Daniel went swiftly to help him. 'Listen to me.' Fitzallen patted Daniel's arm as he tried to move him to a more comfortable position. 'I know the name Garnett has a bitter meaning for you. If you are willing, I would give you a new name. The substance of my will does not depend on this, but it would please me to think of you and Pearl as the children we did not have. Will you take my name, Fitzallen, as a reminder of us?'

For a moment Daniel could not speak. Any attempt was choked by a leaden mass rising in his chest. At last, he managed a muffled reply.

'It would be an honour, sir.' He could think of no other answer. To refuse at such a time would be unforgivable. Besides, Fitzallen was right, Garnett was not his true name. It was a sign of ownership.

'It is settled then.' The Major smiled weakly. 'I am very glad, Daniel *Fitzallen*.'

After a silence filled only by the creaking of the ship and the thud of the waves, he nodded at the document in Daniel's hand. 'Would you bring Captain Benson and Mr Doyle to me now? The captain must write your acceptance into the will in the presence of a witness. For all his faults, Doyle is a gentleman and – as we have heard – scrupulously honest. Benson will be ready. He is a good man; we have discussed this.'

Drowning beneath waves of unfathomable emotions, Daniel was relieved to go to the door. He turned when Fitzallen called again.

'One last thing.' The dying man glanced at the chest beside his bunk. 'There is something at the bottom there, beneath the papers. The leather coin pouch is for you, the letter is for my brother, James. When you arrive in London put it into his hands yourself. I have made my intentions very clear so that there will be no mistake. You are my heir, Daniel. You and Pearl will have a name, a place and a home in England.'

Chapter Three

Fat-bellied clouds pressed overhead, their grey hides pierced by the steeples of churches visible across the stinking brown river. Filled with smoke and the metallic stench of industry, the air was also thickened by a downpour that came in waves of such ferocity that the churches were occasionally veiled from sight along with the naval ships tethered in rows across the Pool.

Despite the deluge, the docks teemed with life. Alongside men newly disgorged from the bowels of His Majesty's navy, the quay was choked with wagons and carrier carts. Blasphemies fell like the rain as drivers steered their horses through the mob. Nimble as rats, porters scurried between the drays trundling barrows piled high with goods and possessions. Street hawkers bawled out a pitch for their wares, and women, whose painted faces and garish costumes needed no vocal advertisement, sidled beside the huge black ships, winking and beckoning at sailors just come ashore with coin in their pockets and an urgent inclination to spend it.

Carried down the estuary, an east wind whistled through the cat's cradle rigging of the ships and rattled the spars, and, above it all, the discordant bells of London tolled for midday.

Daniel huddled Pearl to his side as a large leather-bound trunk thumped down on the greasy stones beside them. It tilted for a moment and then toppled flat into a puddle next to a smaller trunk delivered earlier by the same navy man.

'That's the lot.' The scrawny sailor waggled his dripping hand like a fish. It took Daniel a moment to realise that this was a sign.

'Here.' He dug beneath his cloak into a pocket and produced a coin. The amount was evidently acceptable as the man nodded. Grinning, he shot a furtive glance at Pearl. 'Good luck to you both.' But as he made his way back up the springing wooden gangplank to the deck, Daniel heard him mutter, 'You'll need it.'

The massive sides of the *Audentior* rose and bumped against the quay with the swell of the river. The ship's wide-studded timbers glistened in the rain and rivulets of water tumbled from the ropes and furled sails that loomed above them. The three-masted frigate had been their home for the last six weeks, but although it had carried them to a new life, it also carried their sorrow. Major Fitzallen had died mid-crossing and his body had been buried with full honours at sea. Now their entire world was packed into the two trunks beside them.

'What do we do now?' Pearl swiped at her face. The filthy water left dark smears across her nose and smuts on her wool-mittened fingers. Rain trickled from the brim of her plaited straw bonnet – a gift from Elizabeth – as she gazed anxiously at the crowd.

She had seen so much in her fifteen years. Daniel suspected that memory had drawn a veil across her early life on the Garnett Plantation and much of the fearful, turbulent time that followed their escape. He was glad to have seen her grow in confidence and assurance under Elizabeth's care. Tall like him, Pearl was fresh as a spring bloom just beginning to unfurl.

Now, she pressed closer, excited and perhaps – although she would never admit it – overwhelmed by the noise and the tumult. In truth, even he was a little shocked by the chaos. Scanning the jostling quayside, he was surprised to see numerous men and women whose skin and features spoke of lands far from London.

'So many people. I thought New York was the greatest city I'd ever seen, but this . . .' Pearl's eyes widened. 'I never imagined such a place. Where do we go?'

A wagon loaded with timber rumbled perilously close, splashing more dingy water over her cloak and the hem of her dress.

'Hey!' she called sharply to the driver. 'Watch where you're going!'

She stepped forward intent on attracting the man's attention, but Daniel pulled her back.

'Look at me!' Outraged, she pointed to the strip of rose-strewn cotton below her cloak and above her boots. The pretty fabric was now sodden and grey. 'This dress is ruined. I wore a good one today too, for luck.'

Daniel's amused grin angered Pearl more than the clumsy driver.

'If you think that's so very funny, I suggest you look at your own attire, dear brother.' Wrinkling her nose, she folded her arms and turned her back on him.

Looking down, he saw she was right. His own cloak was also spattered with grime.

The years they had spent living in the hills of Jamaica with the Maroons had been hard. The outlaws expected everyone to play their part. Even Pearl – a tiny child at the time – had been no exception. Daniel marvelled that hardship had never tarnished her fundamental optimism and tendency to see good in people. Except, it seemed, for careless wagon drivers.

'Well, what do we do now?' She didn't turn to look at him.

'I've arranged to meet Captain Benson. He said he would help to settle us.' Blinking away the rain, he looked back up at the empty deck of the *Audentior*. He felt in his pocket for Fitzallen's letter and searched the crowd again.

'He will be here somewhere.'

Releasing Pearl, he went halfway back up the gangplank for a better view, but it still was difficult to see through the rain and the surge of the crowd. For a moment, he thought he caught sight of Benson through a gap between two wagons.

'My, but here's a nice little puss. What's your name then, sweetling?' The voice was strident and coarse.

Daniel looked down. Two brightly dressed women were circling Pearl. One of them leaned forward and took the girl's chin between her fingers. Pearl's eyes sought his.

'Fresh in town, are you? We know someone who'd very much like to make your acquaintance, don't we, Kat?' The woman turned to her gaudy companion. 'Just look at her. Butter wouldn't melt, but you know what they say?'

'Hot as a furnace for it, Dol.' The other woman nodded and the damp green feather drooping from her tattered wig waggled like a fisherman's lure. Wrinkling her nose, Pearl drew back as she bent close.

'All alone, are you, my little tawny plum?'

There was no mistaking their uniforms. Daniel sprang down the ramp.

'And what do we have here?' The first woman took a step back and looked him up and down, her black-rimmed eyes sly and insinuating.

'They must come as a pair, like fire-dogs.' She shrugged, allowing the red bodice of her sullied dress to slip a little, revealing more of her damp crinkled breasts. Greyish powder had settled in the grooves. She winked.

'You her squire then? I reckon she snares you a mint. We don't see many such as you turned out so fine.' She clicked her fingers under his nose. 'Business brisk, is it?'

'I believe you are mistaken.' Pearl raised her chin. 'My brother and I have just arrived in London . . . from America.'

Daniel gripped her shoulder and pulled her away. He wanted nothing more than to steer Pearl into the crowd, but that would mean leaving their trunks unguarded. Instead, he tried to be civil.

'Leave us, please. As my sister says, you're mistaken.'

Hand on hip, the woman in red swayed forward. 'How about a little company then, 'ansome? We'd do you a good turn, wouldn't we, Kat?'

Her bedraggled companion grinned, exposing blackened gums studded with stumps. She edged closer and patted Daniel's arm with a broken fan. 'Tell you what, I'd give you a free ride the first time.'

Pearl was unable to suppress a sudden snort of laughter. Alarmed, Daniel forced her swiftly behind him. He jerked his head along the quay. 'You'll find what you're looking for that way, in the taverns.'

'I'm happy with what I've found here. You've got a lovely face and a voice to match. Where's that accent from?' Dol reached up to brush a stained index finger along his cheek. His nose filled with the unpleasant scent of gin, sweat and cheap cologne. No wonder Pearl had backed away.

'My old man always said it was lucky to touch a moor.'

Turning his back on the pair, Daniel attempted to shield Pearl from their hideous pantomime. He felt her body shaking with mirth as he stared down at the yellow-foamed gap between the ship and the quay.

'Too fine for us, are you?' Dol's wheedling voice was suddenly shrill. He heard one of them hawk something up into her mouth and then felt an unspeakable pellet hit the back of his cloak. Dol continued with venom. 'You won't get a sniff of good English cunny this side of Michaelmas.'

Kat chimed in. 'Not unless he finds himself a fucking black bunter in St Giles. Bad luck to the pair of yer. Come on, Dol, we can do better than this.'

Daniel held Pearl close as he watched the women strut away along the puddled quay. Business was not brisk.

Now Pearl laughed out loud. Her eyes danced above the mittened hands she clasped together beneath her chin.

'They were English whores, weren't they?'

Taken aback, Daniel opened his mouth to answer but nothing came out.

'Really, brother. How could you think I didn't know?' Pearl grinned at his appalled expression. She waved after the women. 'That's what they're *always* like. I've seen them in the army camps and when we first came to New York.' Beneath the dripping rim of her bonnet, her large eyes were full of mischief. 'Don't be so shocked. I'm not a child anymore. They were quite the rudest whores I've ever seen, I'll grant you that, but it might be because in London—' Before she finished whatever she was about to say, Pearl wriggled free from his grasp and pointed.

'Look! There he is.'

Captain Stephen Benson was not easy to mistake. Taller than most men, his distinctive red hair was caught in a long queue visible beneath his hat. Through a gap in the crowd, Daniel saw him walking away from the *Audentior* with another naval officer.

'Sit there.' He pointed at the larger of the trunks. 'If anyone talks to you, be polite but firm. And don't go anywhere with anyone, especially not those women.'

Pearl sighed and slumped down heavily. Folding her arms, she stared up at him. 'As I told you, I am *not* a child.'

But you are, Daniel thought as he pushed through the mass. When he was within earshot, he called out to the captain.

Benson turned. His ruddy face broke into an easy grin that dissolved to a frown as Daniel joined him. The captain dipped his head and a stream of water poured from the valley of his plumed hat. 'Forgive me, Lieutenant. My wife intends to greet me here. She is bringing our boys. In my eagerness to see them, I completely forgot our arrangement.'

Daniel smiled. 'That is understandable. How long has it been?'

'Two years.' Benson turned to his companion. 'This is my brother-in-law, John Faulds – also a captain in His Majesty's navy. He brought me Caroline's message.'

The younger officer made a slight bow in greeting and then, puzzled, he glanced at his relative. 'And this is . . . ?'

Benson laughed. 'Two years have done nothing for my manners. This is Lieutenant . . .' he paused for a moment and caught Daniel's eye, '. . . *Fitzallen*. He travelled with me from New York.'

Daniel returned the bow. 'And I still feel the world moving beneath my feet.'

'It will pass soon enough.' Benson patted him on the shoulder. 'Two days at least for a landman. For myself, I am confident the motion will be gone before I greet my family.' He looked back at the *Audentior*. 'According to the Secretary of the Admiralty, it will be six months before my mistress requires my attentions again. Unlike you . . .' He prodded the younger officer fondly. 'Next week, is it?'

Captain Faulds grimaced. 'We put out with the eastern fleet on Saturday next, if the weather changes.' He made another shallow bow. 'Excuse me, gentlemen. I am reminded that I should collect some documents from the warrant office.'

Benson smiled as he watched the young officer push through the crowd.

'It is his first command and natural for him to be anxious. John has been so good to Caroline and the boys.' He turned to Daniel. 'Where is your charming sister?'

Looking back down the quay, Daniel was relieved to see that Pearl was still sitting on the larger trunk and that she was alone.

'There.' He pointed. 'I have no wish to take your time, Captain, but I have a favour to ask.' Reaching into his stained woollen cloak, he drew out the letter addressed in a spider-like scrawl to:

James Fitzallen, Esq.
7, Scandrett Street,
Wapping,
London

Shielding the ink from the rain, he showed it to the captain. 'I have a message for Major Fitzallen's brother. Edward . . . the Major asked me to deliver it to him by hand.'

'Poor man.' Benson shook his head. 'It is a heavy responsibility you carry. I trust that you will describe our committal of his body as one of dignity and faith.'

'Of course. I hope that will bring comfort to his family.' Daniel studied the letter. The address was written in a frail, uncertain hand. He could not connect it to the man he had known. He swallowed. 'It is also my intention to make them fully aware of the respect Major Fitzallen inspired in all men who served with him.'

Benson's expression clouded. 'I know he valued you, Lieutenant, and counted you as a friend. More than that.' He paused. 'I imagine the Major's settlement will be a matter of some . . . delicacy.'

'I believe so, but he told me that he has made his wishes very clear . . .' Daniel indicated the letter, '. . . so that there might be no mistake.' After consulting his heart, he added, 'I cannot believe that the brother of the man I knew so well will be cut from different cloth.'

The captain seemed about to say something but instead he looked back along the quay at Pearl. They stood in an uncomfortable silence. Rain pelted their cloaks and streamed around their boots. At last Benson replied.

'Let us hope that is the case. A word of advice, London is a cruel mother and many of her children have hardened their hearts in her care. I must warn you that, away from those who know you, it may be difficult to claim the place that is due to you.'

Daniel baulked at this gloomy warning. 'But the King himself has promised—'

Benson raised a hand. 'The King has made many promises. He promised to keep America and yet . . .' His gaze locked on something beyond Daniel's shoulder. Turning, Daniel saw a woman and two small boys in matching naval uniforms beside a smart black coach at the end of the quay. The boys called out, jumping and waving, while their mother tried to calm them with little success.

Benson swept off his hat and waved it above his head – an exultant signal to his family.

'I have been promised six months with my wife and boys and I hope to God that is the truth of it. Two years is an eternity in a child's life. I wonder if I will know them?' He spoke quietly without taking his eyes from the joyful group. 'And if they will remember me.'

'I will not detain you.' Daniel pushed the letter into the shelter of his cloak. 'I merely wished to ask for your advice. I do not know London or its ways. Without Major Fitzallen, I am more adrift now than in all those weeks at sea. I do not even know where Scandrett Street is.'

At last Benson dragged his eyes from his wife and children. Daniel sensed his conflict. The captain was a good man, but at this moment his family took precedence over all.

'I must go to them, Lieutenant, but this is my advice. First take rooms and then make your enquiries for Scandrett Street when you and your sister are settled . . .' Benson smiled sympathetically, '. . . and *dry*. If you were to go direct to the Fitzallen house as you are, they would not open their doors. For now, go to the naval stores beyond the rails.' He pointed the direction. 'Ask for a man called Patrick Shersford, he's an old comrade. Tell him that Stephen Benson sent you and that you require lodgings in a clean, Christian house.'

The captain swept his hat back onto his head, oblivious to the rain that had collected in its crown. Reaching for Daniel's hand, he smiled encouragingly. 'I wish you well, Lieutenant. I wish nothing but good fortune for both of you.'

Chapter Four

Captain Benson's faith in Patrick Shersford was sadly misplaced. On making enquiries at the naval stores, Daniel was curtly informed that the man had died of bloody flux the previous winter. The bearer of this news was almost invisible behind piles of sail cloth, rope, oakum, lanterns, candles, pots of whale oil, rosin, tallow, twine, tar and all manner of metal tools. He shrank further back into the pungent depths of the chandlery when Daniel leaned across the counter.

'Stay back!'

The man's voice was cracked and breathless. 'I know who you are and I know who's sent you thinking to 'timidate a person with your size an' all, but it won't do no good. Shersford's dead and his debts have gone to earth with his bones. Take that back to your master and tell him not to trouble us again.'

Confused, Daniel peered into the cluttered corner to which the man had retreated.

'I know nothing of any debt. I was directed here to find Mr Shersford by Captain Stephen Benson. He said he was a former comrade.'

Daniel heard whispering from the shadows. After more muttering the old man came back into view accompanied by a sallow-faced youth as long and thin as one of the brooms hanging from the ceiling.

'Davy here tells me that the *Audentior* came in this morning.' The chandler, a sparse-bristled crumb brush compared to his colleague, wrinkled his pitted nose. 'Captain Benson's a small fellow with dark hair, yes?'

'He's as tall as me and his hair is red as that sign.' Daniel pointed to the flaking letters on a tin advertisement for linseed oil.

'Maybe he is.' The chandler scratched his chin. 'I've had to be very careful these last months since Paddy Shersford's passing. He were a decent worker and he told a good tale, but that was his problem, see. This ...' the man pointed at his nose, '... got 'im into a deal of trouble. That and his liking for cards. Paddy left debts whose papers could stretch from here to the dockside and back again twice over.' He sniffed. 'And you're just the sort his creditors send out to collect them. Boxer, are you? You've got the face and the frame for it.'

'I'm not here on anyone's business but my own.' Daniel's patience was beginning to wear thin as India muslin, but he pressed his case. 'Captain Benson said that Mr Shersford might be able to help us. As he's not here, I ...' He paused as the lanky youth bent low to whisper in his master's ear. The little chandler nodded, sniffed and squinted up at Daniel. Although wary, he seemed more convinced of his safety now.

'If it's a job you're after, there's nothing to be had. Davy and me cover all eventuals here.'

'I'm not looking for work. My sister and I arrived today on the *Audentior*.' Daniel pointed to Pearl just visible through the dingy panes of the chandlery's bow window. She was sitting on the larger of the trunks, hunched against the rain. Beyond her the dock was still seething with people and purpose.

'We need rooms,' he continued. 'Captain Benson sent us here for that reason.'

'Did he now?' The old man scraped at his chin. Daniel thought he saw something jump from the chandler's beard to the back of his hand. 'Paddy was always a helpful sort, that's true enough. He knew everyone and everyone's business. Even so, I can't imagine that finding a place willing to take you would have been easy.'

'What do you mean by that?' Daniel tried to keep his voice level and pleasant, but the man's changed attitude infuriated him. Having reassured himself that he was not being visited by a debt collector, the chandler had now adopted a superior manner shaded with insult.

'I'm not meaning anything but what's clear as the nose on your face.' The old man moved a lantern aside and stared brazenly at Daniel. He craned for a better view of Pearl and scratched again.

'You can't milk a pigeon. There's very few around here willing to take such as you into their homes. Once word gets about, they find that people don't want to lie in a bed where a black's been before them.' The chandler shrugged. 'Now, I could get you on a ship. The navy's not fussy about who's pulling on the ropes and it always needs a bit of muscle, but rooms is a very different matter.'

Daniel's first impulse was to grab the old man by the scruff of hair that remained and knock his lice-ridden head against the counter. Fighting the urge, his second instinct was to leave the store and the man's insolence. He glanced back at Pearl still huddled over the trunks; her hat was a sodden crumpled wreck and her grey cloak was now black and heavy with rain. Without Fitzallen to guide them, they were desperately alone and adrift in this new city, but at this moment, more than anything, they needed shelter.

At a scraping sound he turned back to see the chandler rolling a coin back and forth across the wooden counter top. The man caught his eye and winked. 'I can't promise anything, but I might be able to help – under the right circumstances.'

Mastering his contempt, Daniel smiled thinly. 'Surely our money is as good as anyone's?' He produced a small gold coin and held it up.

The chandler's furtive little eyes locked on the guinea. 'Now, that might go some way to ease things. What do you reckon, Davy?'

He turned to the youth, who bent to whisper in his ear again. The small man beamed.

'It seems like you're in luck. Turns out that Davy has an aunt who happens to have a room available.'

Widow Canty of Friary Alley wasn't clean and, as far as Daniel could ascertain, she wasn't particularly Christian. She was, however, willing to offer them a room in return for 'ten shillings in my palm, now'.

She dragged on the long clay pipe that dangled from the side of her mouth and thrust out a hand. The skin of her heavily ringed fingers was stained with tobacco and a faded black tattoo leached across the knuckles. The bodice of her grimy striped dress was cut so low that her large breasts threatened to overflow their whalebone confines. Every time she pulled on the pipe, fathoms of wrinkled flesh rose and fell.

The flick of her small dark eyes felt like flies crawling on Daniel's skin.

'Cat got it?' She spoke without removing the pipe from her lips. 'Perhaps you don't speak London?' She stared at her nephew. 'What you brought me here, Davy?'

The stringy youth from the chandlery whispered in her ear. He hadn't spoken a word as he led them through streets and passages of increasingly unsavoury aspect, although he had, at least, carried the smaller of the two trunks.

'I ain't got all day to stand here jawing. Do you want it or not?' The woman removed the pipe and tapped out the bowl on the wall. From the black marks on the plaster, it was evidently something she'd done many times before – an old she-cat marking her territory.

Daniel looked up at the crumbling three-storey house. Several windows were boarded over and others were blinded by rags. If he stood in the centre of Friary Alley, his legs straddling the gutter that burbled with filthy brown water, he could touch the walls on either side. It was a dismal place.

He glanced at Pearl. Shivering and exhausted, her head was bent low, eyes cast to the grimy cobbles. If they didn't get out of the rain soon, she would surely catch a chill. She was inclined to delicacy; two winters back when the regiment was newly stationed in New York, Pearl had developed a fever and a wracking cough. Elizabeth had nursed her like a mother.

'Can I see the room first?' Daniel edged closer to the door.

'Certainly not.' The woman blocked his way. 'Who do you think you are, the bleedin' king of Timbuctoo? It's as fine a room as any you'll find in Limehouse, with all amenities thrown in. Besides, being as you are, you won't find better. I'm only prepared to take you and the girl out of the kindness of my heart. Look at her, twitching like a foal.' She tucked a strand of lank grey hair back beneath her yellowed cap. 'Ten shillings, take it or leave it.'

She shot a knowing look at her nephew. 'Davy's got to get back to the docks, so if you decide against my accommodation, you're on your jacksie.'

Daniel cursed himself. Despite his years in the army, he had been outflanked and outmanoeuvred. Davy and his repellent aunt – and most probably the mangy old chandler – had ambushed them. She was right, they had no other option but to take her room no matter how foul. Judging from the stench in the alley it was likely to be as noxious as its owner.

The sound of Pearl sneezing made up his mind. He took Fitzallen's pouch from beneath his cloak. Looking up, he saw the woman hastily attempt to mask her interest.

'You said ten shillings.' He dropped the coins into her palm and she nodded at Davy, who slunk back along the alley without a word.

'Second floor back.' The woman delved into the chasm of her

chest and produced a large iron key. It was warm when she handed it over.

'You can carry the boxes up between you. My back's a martyr to heavy labour.'

She turned and went off down the peeling hallway, disappearing down some steps. The slam of a distant door was their greeting to her house, along with the smell of mouse, stewed cabbage and timber rot.

It wouldn't be for long, Daniel reassured himself, as he bent to take up the larger trunk. He and Pearl would spend a couple of days at most beneath Widow Canty's roof until the meeting that would change their lives.

Chapter Five

The hackney carriage clipped a sharp corner and Pearl tumbled against Daniel's side. Righting herself, she brushed at her skirt, plumping the green fabric beneath her cloak so that it might not crease or mark. The fresh colour of the figured silk was a pretty contrast to the pale pink petticoats beneath it – these made deliberately visible by looped panels held back with mother of pearl buttons.

This sweet floral ensemble was another of Elizabeth's gifts. Although it was now a little too tight in the bodice, the dress was still a favourite. Knowing the importance of the day ahead, Pearl had put on her finest gown and covered her hair beneath a lace-edged cap. The tiny earrings that shone like moons against her skin were another reminder of the Fitzallens' kindness.

Daniel squeezed her hand. The white lace gloves she wore today had been his New Year gift to her. It was the first time she had taken them from their tissue wrapping. His mother's hands had been calloused and scarred by work in the cane fields and Adanna's had been scalded by molten sugar. He was determined that Pearl should never know such hardship. Beneath the lace, her skin was smooth.

She smiled. 'Will I do?'

'You look perfect.'

'Good. I wanted to make the right impression.' Pearl brushed again at the dress half covered by her cloak, banishing an invisible imperfection.

Daniel knew she was anxious. In truth, he was also apprehensive. Captain Benson was right, it was a heavy burden to deliver the news of a death, but the terms of the Major's will added a layer of complexity to the meeting ahead. He wondered how he might feel under the same circumstances. No matter what had happened in the past, to James Fitzallen he would be a stranger.

'*When you arrive in London put it into his hands yourself. I have made my intentions very clear so that there will be no mistake.*'

The will and the letter were in the pocket of his coat. Daniel had never broken the seal. The contents of the Major's last message to his brother James were a mystery, but the character of the man he had known was not. This was reassurance enough that his family would be people of honour and integrity.

He glanced at Pearl whose hands were now clasped tight in her lap as she looked through the carriage window. The street beyond the glass was lined with tall red-brick houses whose wide stone steps curved to elegant doorways set high above the level of the street. It was very different to Friary Alley.

They had lodged in Widow Canty's house for two days now. Their room was almost as small as a cabin on the *Audentior*, but instead of tar and timber it stank of rot and rancid bacon. Rain crept through the bulging ceiling, knuckles of fungus bloomed in the corners and the single broken window overlooking a courtyard of singular squalor was partially boarded and stuffed with sheets from a newspaper. Instead of a bed, a stained, straw-filled mattress was pushed against the driest wall and a cracked china basin of dubious purpose sat next to it. A paper-blocked grate the size of a kettle completed the widow's 'amenities'.

The first night, too exhausted to do anything more, they had taken dry clothes from their trunks – which occupied most of the rest of the room – piled them on the filthy mattress and crawled beneath them. Sleep had been interrupted by the

return of Widow Canty's other tenants. Doors slammed, footsteps drummed on the narrow stairs and gin-cut laughter sawed
through the walls. Daniel had huddled Pearl close as he listened to
drunken rutting in the dark, taking consolation from the fact that
the key appeared to lock the door and that their trunks could also
be secured.

Next morning, giving strict instructions to Pearl to stay in the
room and speak to no one, he had gone out into the drab alleyways
of Limehouse to buy food and make enquiries as to the whereabouts of Scandrett Street. Once again, he was surprised to see men
and women who were not native to this city – or indeed to this
country – going naturally about their business. This glimpse of a
freedom he had not fully imagined struck a tinder spark of optimism
within him.

The baker who sold him a bag of seed-studded buns was black,
his arms dusted grey with flour. Although the man didn't know
Scandrett Street, he advised Daniel that the best way to find somewhere would be to take a hackney carriage.

'The drivers know all the ways,' the baker had said. 'As long as
you can pay.'

On his return to Friary Alley, they had eaten the buns with
cheese bought from a dairy cart, using the trunks as their table.
As they sat in dejected silence, weak sunlight seeped through the
smeared and broken window magnifying the deficiencies of their
dank accommodation. When something scratched in the walls,
Daniel determined that they would not stay under Widow Canty's
roof an hour more than necessary.

Unfortunately, that hour took some time to arrive.

With no assistance from the fireplace, which choked the room
with smoke when he tried to light the papers, it had taken a full day
for their sopping cloaks to dry, but even now in the confines of the
hackney carriage, the smell of damp wool still came strong.

The hack juddered to a halt and the driver thumped on the roof.

'This is Scandrett Street. The merchants all live in this row – near enough to the docks to take a close interest in their business, but far enough to keep themselves reputable. Number seven is there on the right.' He flicked his whip to indicate the direction.

Pearl bent forward to look up at the commanding double-fronted house. She turned to Daniel.

'It's very fine. Grander than I imagined.' She plucked again at her dress. 'I am sure they will be very fashionable people.'

Daniel opened the door on his side. The narrow, slatted steps clattered to the cobbles and the hack rocked as he stepped down to the street. He paid the driver and then he held the door open for Pearl to dismount. He took it for a good omen that the capricious April sun chose that moment to shrug off a cloud, bathing the street in the watery golden glow of a late afternoon.

They stared at the house as the hack rumbled off. Built from red brick, the doorway was approached by two flights of stone steps that curved from street level. Two sets of shuttered windows flanked each side of the heavily pedimented door and above them another row of arched windows reflected shreds of blue in the sky.

Pearl began to hum softly, something she often did when she was nervous. He remembered the song as one sung by the female Maroons when the working day was over and they sat around the fire. It was an old tune passed down from generations whose lives had begun very far from the island. Even without words, Pearl's sweet melodic tones gave it unusual beauty. As he listened, he was filled with gratitude at how far she had come. How far *they* had come.

Beyond a row of similar houses, a muscular square-towered church cast a block of shadow over a tree-lined churchyard. A richly dressed man and woman followed by a drab girl balancing a pile of brightly ribboned parcels walked past them. The woman stared at Daniel and then at Pearl. She tapped the man on the arm and tilted her head in a meaningful way.

The man peered at Daniel. 'Extraordinary.' He tutted and quickened his step. The woman turned back to address the girl, presumably a servant.

'Do keep up, Peggy.' The admonishment gave her another opportunity to study Daniel, who had thrown his cloak back over one shoulder to reveal the braided red coat of his army uniform. Her frank gaze lingered uncomfortably.

'Come.' He reached for Pearl's gloved hand and led her up one side of the curving steps. Grasping an iron ring hanging from a moulded lion's mouth, he knocked twice, the sound reverberating in the hall beyond the door. After a moment, footsteps sounded. The door opened, revealing a small man in a blue coat trimmed with gold. His eyes travelled from Daniel to Pearl and back again and his snub nose wrinkled in distaste.

'Is this the Fitzallen residence?' In answer to Daniel's question, the man began to close the door.

'Get back! Trade goes through the yard. Such impudence!'

Daniel put a hand to the panelled wood and pushed, but the servant resisted.

'This is an insult. How dare you.' The man's curled wig slipped to one side as he struggled to shut the door. The unseemly tussle was uneven. Wedging a boot in the gap, Daniel spoke loudly. 'I have a message for the brother of the late Major Edward Fitzallen.'

Instantly, a clipped male voice sounded from the hallway.

'Admit him.'

The footman continued to wrestle. 'But sir, he's—'

'I said admit him. For God's sake, Parkes, do as you're told.'

'Very well.' The servant muttered to himself and opened the door wider. He checked the street to reassure himself that these unusual visitors had not been noticed, adjusted his wig and stepped aside.

'You'd better come in then.'

Daniel allowed Pearl to go first. He followed her into a wide marble-floored hallway. A tall man in a long grey street coat stood at the foot of a sweeping staircase. From the lacquer cane on the side table, the hat on his head and the fact that a maid was midway through completing the buttoning of his left glove it was clear that he was about to go out.

'You have a message for me?' The voice was haughty and cold. A shaft of sunlight sliced through the door across the hall, illuminating the man's profile beneath the brim of his hat. The line of his long nose was interrupted by a prominent bump. Lazily, the man offered his right hand to the maid and watched her work at the horn buttons, giving no indication of interest in his visitors. It was, Daniel thought, a show. Beneath the studied indifference, there was something taut and alert about him.

'Well?' The stony voice echoed in the hall.

'I have a message for Mr James Fitzallen.'

'Then you have a message for *me*.' Now the man looked up. His face was pale and angular and his eyes were an odd shade of gold like those of a fox. Daniel could detect no resemblance between the Major and his brother.

'I have changed my mind. I will not be going to the Exchange.' James Fitzallen removed his hat and thrust it at the blue-liveried maid.

'Take them to my study, Parkes.' Languidly, he unbuttoned the gloves and cast them onto the table beside the cane. Spreading his arms wide in a gesture that seemed quite the opposite of welcome, he allowed the maid to remove his coat. Beneath he was clothed with elegant simplicity. The only concession to male vanity was the starched and complex white stock at his neck secured with a golden, arrow-shaped pin.

He smiled at Daniel but the skin around his close-set eyes did not move.

'I find there is a matter I must attend to before I hear your message. Follow my manservant; my wife and I will join you shortly.'

Chapter Six

Parkes led them through the hall to a corridor at the back of the house. He indicated a door to the left of a murky painting of a ship and stood aside to let them enter. James Fitzallen's gloomy panelled study smelled of leather, tobacco and smoke. A mahogany desk beneath a single half-shuttered window took up almost half of the space, its surface obscured by stacks of paper and piles of ledgers.

The servant went to prod at the remains of a fire. The embers crackled as he nudged them back to life with a poker. Next, he lit candles in brackets on the walls, one beside the desk and two either side of the heavy marble fireplace. The light revealed shelves crammed with more ledgers.

'You may sit.' He pointed at a stiff-backed couch covered in black chinoiserie silk. In the firelight, the jewel-tones in the embroidered fabric glowed like a starling's wing. He eyed them both suspiciously and sniffed.

'It's not my place to have opinions on who the master lets into his house but, just in case you've got any ideas, I know everything in this room, and its exact position.'

Adjusting his wig, Parkes squared his shoulders and went to the door. He slammed it behind him a little too loudly and they listened to the sound of his footsteps pattering away down the hall. When she was quite sure he was gone, Pearl unfastened her cloak and perched on the couch.

'He was insulting.'

'He was, but he does not know us yet.' Daniel took out the Major's letter and the ribbon-bound will and placed them on the desk in a space between the ledgers and the papers. 'We have every right to be here.'

He ran a finger along the spines of the ledgers; each appeared to be marked with the name of a ship.

The Sophia Charlotte

Swallow Tail

The Fair Venture

Shooting Star

Lysander

The White Horse

Lotus Flower

The Golden East

The Feather

If these were merchant vessels owned by the Fitzallens, business was thriving. Daniel turned as the door behind him opened. James Fitzallen entered the study, followed by a short, stout woman clutching a lapdog to the bodice of her vivid yellow gown.

Pearl rose. Smiling, she curtseyed to the woman, who ignored her. Uncertain what to do next, she offered her hand. Now the woman emitted a small squeak of outrage. Casting a confused look at Daniel, Pearl sat down again and folded her hands in her lap. His heart lurched as he watched her rub at the lace, fearful that she might have committed an offence.

James went to the chair behind the desk. He sat and studied them. Between the stacks of papers and ledgers, his face was half hidden in shadow. Grappling with the dog, the woman gathered the satin skirts of her sack-back dress and settled heavily on the couch, positioning herself as far from Pearl as possible.

Beneath the white cloud of her wig, her features were oddly

puckered into the centre of her face as if drawn together by thread. Despite the circles of carmine on her cheeks, her skin had the colour and texture of pastry dough; her tiny black eyes currants studded into the mixture.

She stared at Daniel without speaking and then, moving the dog aside, she pulled at a gold chain hanging from her neck.

'There is a peculiar smell in here.' Flicking open the cap of a little vinaigrette, she inhaled deeply and ostentatiously. The strong scent of lavender cologne battled the masculine aroma of the study.

Daniel remained standing, uncertain whether or not to take the chair beside the couch without invitation. Neither James Fitzallen nor the woman – presumably his wife – spoke. After a long and increasingly uncomfortable silence, he bowed his head a little and cleared his throat.

'Sir, I am Lieutenant Dan—'

James cut him off mid-sentence. 'I do not wish to know who you are. This acquaintance will be brief. At the door you mentioned my *late* brother.' He leaned forward, his sharp eyes catching the light from the candles and the fire. In that moment Daniel understood him. James Fitzallen was a man who, at a glance, could calculate the size of a meadow to the yard without seeing a single flower.

'Am I to understand that Edward is dead?'

The question was direct, untroubled by sorrow or any hint of feeling.

Daniel nodded. 'That is correct, sir. I am sorry to bring such news. I know this must be a great blow.'

James Fitzallen shrugged. 'Soldier Eddy died a hero, I suppose. In battle, was it?'

Surprised by the tone of the question – which was at once dismissive and patronising – Daniel replied, 'Major Edward Fitzallen was wounded in action, but he died sometime later during the journey back to England. I was with him until the end on board

His Majesty's naval ship the *Audentior*. I can assure you, sir, he was buried at sea with full honour and dignity.'

'So there'll be no burial?' James glanced at his wife. 'D'you hear that, Carrie, no funeral. He's at the bottom of the ocean.'

Daniel turned. Caroline Fitzallen was too busy petting her wriggling white lapdog to answer. This was a scene he had imagined many times and a speech he had rehearsed with care, fearing to trespass on the family's grief, but he had not expected such indifference.

Pearl frowned as she watched Caroline Fitzallen produce a sugar comfit from the lace at the sleeves of her dresses and tease the dog with it.

'What do I have here then?' Caroline dandled it above the lapdog's flat muzzle. 'Naughty Peruke – such a greedy little boy.'

Amazed, Daniel tried again, deciding that the Fitzallens' lack of sentiment was perhaps due to shock.

'I must tell you that the Major was revered and admired by everyone in the regiment and beyond. His loss will be mourned by many. He was a great man and I was honoured to know both him and his late wife.'

'Elizabeth too!' Caroline Fitzallen stopped fussing with her pet. 'She's dead as well?' Her small eyes sought her husband's. 'That is very interesting . . . I mean to say, that is very sad. Poor Lizzie.' She arranged her squashed features into something like concern but Daniel knew it was play-acting. So did Pearl, who had now settled into the furthest corner of the couch. Caroline Fitzallen's disgust at sharing her proximity was a stuttering candle to the bonfire of Pearl's contempt.

'Was she also consigned to the Atlantic?' James's question was almost brutal in its lack of feeling.

Daniel shook his head. 'Mrs Elizabeth Fitzallen died in New York a month before we left. She is buried there in the British military graveyard. We attended her funeral.' He indicated Pearl. 'She and the Major were always good to us. We are proud to have called them our friends.'

'Friends!' The word exploded from Caroline's lips.

'Yes, that is indeed a mystery.' James leaned forward. 'How did *you* ...' there was an edge to the word that Daniel could not misinterpret, '... come to be in my brother's regiment at all, let alone as an officer?'

It was a question Daniel had been asked many times. It was always best, he found, to keep the answer simple.

'I am sure you are aware, sir, that the British army in America is happy to admit men such as me to the ranks to fight against the Patriots. Perhaps you call them Yankees? Whatever the name, they are the enemies of the Crown. King George himself has promised that we will be welcomed here in return for our loyalty and service. In the years—'

'You are a slave, then?' James Fitzallen's interruption was freighted with insult.

'I was an enslaved man,' Daniel corrected him, careful to keep his voice even.

'Do not parse words with me.' The man flicked a hand. 'Continue.'

Stifling the urge to pluck Fitzallen bodily from his chair and smash him through the window at his back, Daniel glanced at Pearl. She was perched on the edge of the couch, face rigid with barely suppressed rage. He sent her a look she could not misinterpret and took a deep breath.

'In the years I was with the army I was honoured to serve under Major Fitzallen, who was a fair and good man. It was he who raised me to the rank of lieutenant.' He turned to Caroline. 'And yes, Pearl and I were glad to call the Major and Elizabeth our friends.'

'Extraordinary!' Caroline was too surprised to keep hold of Peruke, who slid from her yellow lap to the floorboards. The dog seemed happier beneath the couch and resisted her attempts to cajole him.

'Bleak times make odd bedfellows, my dear.' James Fitzallen watched his wife fish in her sleeve for a second comfit. 'This will be an interesting story when we dine at the Carterets tonight. I am sure Admiral Howe will have views on the matter. Perhaps Lord Detting will be able to tell us more. He has Rockingham's ear.' He studied Daniel. '*Friend*, eh?'

'That privilege was mine.'

James barked out a laugh. 'My brother was always too soft for his own good.'

Stunned by the man's discourtesy, Daniel looked again at Pearl. Knowing her as he did, he hoped she wouldn't say or do anything rash. Fortunately, she decided to lean forward to stroke the head of Peruke who was now curled on the boards next to her, presenting his fluffy white posterior to Caroline's wheedling endearments.

At a dull, clinking thud, he turned back to the desk.

'I must thank you for bringing us this . . . sad news. I trust this will be in order for services rendered.' James pushed a small leather pouch through the stacks of ledgers and reached for a handbell. 'I'll call Parkes to see you out through the back hall.'

'You are mistaken, sir. There's more.' Beneath his red woollen army jacket, Daniel felt the prickle of sweat between his shoulders. He pointed at the sealed letter and the will that still lay on the leather desktop. James had not noticed them between the stacks of ledgers.

Daniel pushed the letter forward. 'Major Fitzallen asked me to bring you this. It was his final command to me and his last message to you, sir.'

The crackle of the fire and Peruke snuffling in his sleep were the only sounds in the study as James Fitzallen read his brother's letter.

His angular face gave nothing away as his peculiar eyes slid along the close-packed lines. When he had finished, he held it out to Caroline, who rustled from the couch to retrieve it. He turned to the window while she read.

Unlike her husband, she did not digest its import in silence.

'Good God!' she cried out at one point, fluttering a fat hand to her throat.

'Be silent.' James's voice was flat and passionless.

When she had finished, her lower lip trembled and her tiny eyes flicked between Daniel and Pearl and then to her husband.

James rose from the desk and took the letter from her hands. Icily calm, he addressed Daniel.

'My brother mentions a will?'

'Here also.' Daniel reached to the desk and handed him the ribbon-bound document. 'I believe it is in order.'

'Indeed? And is there a copy?' James plucked at the black ribbon with the nail of his thumb.

'No, but I must tell you that the document in your hands was witnessed on board the *Audentior* by Captain Benson and Mr Doyle, the ship's surgeon. They will vouch for its authenticity.' He paused, aware of the significance of the moment, and bowed. 'Sir, I fully understand that this must come as a great surprise to you, as it did to me – to us . . .' Daniel smiled at Pearl, who was now sitting very straight and poised, her attention locked encouragingly upon him. Emboldened by her faith, he continued.

'But I give you my word that I will honour your brother's trust in me. It is my greatest, my *deepest* hope that, in time, I will also be able to earn your respect and regard.'

Caroline gasped, but James silenced her with a raised hand.

'I understand.' He smiled at Daniel. 'Edward was always a man of singular intent. I will not pretend that we always agreed, but his last wishes . . .' he placed the will carefully on top of the letter,

'... cannot be ignored. Let us drink a toast to my dear departed brother and to your good fortune.'

Once again, Caroline rustled. 'But James, surely—'

Her husband silenced her again with a flick of the hand and crossed the room to a small table where glasses and a decanter of amber liquid glowed in the firelight. He took up the decanter but paused.

'This calls for the finest brandy. I will ask Parkes to bring some from the cellar. You will excuse me for a moment.'

When James had gone from the study, Caroline's fury billowed like a storm cloud. Squat and yellow like a venomous toad, she stared at Daniel and then at Pearl, her small face compacted by hatred. As if sensing her foul mood, Peruke scuttled to the door and scratched at the timbers to be let out.

The silence was dreadful. At last, glancing warily at Daniel, Pearl spoke in a low clear voice.

'May I offer my condolences. I too felt the loss of Mistress Lizzie most keenly. She was always good to me.'

'I'm sure she was!' The words had detonated Caroline's anger. 'Elizabeth was a Quaker fool and easily tricked. Wretched Edward was the same and now I find that my own husband—'

She was interrupted by the return of her own husband. Seizing the chance, Peruke fled from the room.

James Fitzallen brandished a pot-bellied bottle. 'French – the very best. Although I despise them, I cannot find it in my heart to oppose their brandy. For the gentlemen only, I think.'

Ignoring Caroline's evident discontent, he went back to the table near the fire and poured two large glasses. Handing one to Daniel, he raised a toast.

'To my brother, Edward. May he rest in peace.' James tipped back the glass.

Unwilling to offend, Daniel copied.

James lifted his brandy once more. 'To the future.' He drank and again Daniel followed his lead.

'Good!' James placed his glass back on the little table. Daniel was surprised to see that it was still full when his own was almost drained.

'Will you leave us now, my dear?' Fitzallen smiled at his wife. 'The business of the day is concluded.'

'What on earth are you thinking!' Caroline's face was so flushed that the painted circles on her cheeks were no longer distinct. 'This is an outrage. They are charlatans!'

'Go, woman!' James's order was a bark of rage.

Mouth twisted into an ugly little knot, his wife rose from the couch and flounced to the door. Daniel was confused; there appeared to be two yellow-gowned women reaching for the handle. Suddenly, the floor beneath him seemed to rise and buckle. For a moment he thought it was a return of the motion sickness that had troubled both him and Pearl after leaving the ship, but then he realised with horror that it was something more. The meat of his head began to spin. His eyesight swam and a stabbing pain jabbed and jabbed again at his temples.

Struggling to stay upright, he attempted to focus on the two versions of James Fitzallen who stalked to the fire. Unable to move, he watched them cast the letter and then the will into the flames where they blackened and shrivelled.

'No!'

He tried to cross the room to retrieve them, but his legs wouldn't obey him. Instead, he buckled to his knees, head heavy as a cannon ball.

'Daniel!' Pearl rushed to his side. She knelt, but over her shoulder he saw James Fitzallen approaching. The man seemed to shiver and divide into a regiment of Fitzallens as he moved. He tried to warn her, but words tangled on his tongue. James caught Pearl by the wrist and pulled her upright.

'Stay where you are, brat. This game is at an end.'

She tried to fight. Daniel saw her small gloved hands – too many of them – pummelling away at the man's embroidered waistcoat. James caught one lacy fist in his own, but she lashed out with the other, catching him squarely on the nose. There was a crack and a yelp of pain. James Fitzallen swiped at the trail of red on his upper lip and examined the blood on his fingers in furious amazement.

'Bitch!'

Crushing the offending hand in his own, he twisted Pearl about and forced her arms behind her back. Dimly, Daniel was aware of her calling his name, but every second she seemed to be further away.

The study door opened and Parkes appeared; his outline was so blurred that a queue of other Parkes seemed to form behind him.

'The carriage is waiting, sir. As you requested.' The man's voice was as distorted as his form.

James Fitzallen released Pearl and pointed at Daniel.

'Get one of the grooms and carry this imposter from my house. Remove the girl, too.' He pushed Pearl roughly away and she stumbled to her knees. Before the blackness came, the last thing Daniel heard was a final instruction.

'Tell the driver to take them to the heart of St Giles and leave them there.'

Chapter Seven

Darkness pressed upon him like a weight. Daniel tried to move but he was caught fast, bound to the spot by invisible vines that circled his arms and legs. High above there was a dot of light – the tiny speck began to circle like a firefly. Confused, he watched it spin as it moved slowly towards him, before finally exploding into a ball of burning, blinding brilliance that made him want to cry aloud in agony.

'He's awake!'

There was a moment's silence, then the voice – a girl's – came again.

'Jen! Come quickly.' He felt a cool hand on his forehead. 'Daniel, can you hear me? Oh, you're burning up. Jen! He needs water!'

A hand caught his and squeezed. 'It's me, Pearl. I'm here. You've been asleep for so long.'

Pearl?

Now he struggled against the beguiling darkness, forcing himself to concentrate on the billowing grey form at his side. Slowly, Pearl's face revealed itself, her features sharpening and colouring as if rendered on canvas by an artist.

She smiled and clutched his hand tighter. 'You've come back.'

He tried to answer, but his jaw felt as if it was clamped in a carpenter's vice. His mouth seemed to be packed with salt that seared into his gums, carving pain to the roots of his teeth.

'Don't try to speak.' Pearl turned at the sound of approaching footsteps.

Daniel blinked at the low-arched ceiling above him. Gradually his sight cleared to reveal water leaking through stained bricks over-head. Green-tinged trails glistened in the feeble light of a candle that swam in a saucer of tallow. The regular smack of water on stone echoed in the tiny barrelled space like the ticking of a clock.

'I've brought water and bread.' A young woman carrying an earthenware pitcher stood behind Pearl. 'I don't reckon he'll feed, but I brought it all the same just in case. Here, hold this.' She handed Pearl a tin mug and filled it. 'I'll lift him.'

She moved from his line of vision. Suddenly an excruciating bolt of pain shot through his head, blinding him once again. He must have cried out, because the woman stopped trying to help him and stepped sharply away.

'Sorry.' Swimming back into focus, she held up her hands partly in apology and partly to prove that she wasn't touching him. 'But you must try to drink. Pearl, kneel beside him, that might be easier. Wet his lips until he gets the knack of it.'

Daniel heard rustling and then he felt gentle fingers dab water on his mouth. At first, it burned, but once the liquid found a way through his cracked, split lips and onto his tongue, he was possessed by thirst.

'Is it working?' the young woman's voice came again.

'I think so.' Water dribbled onto his lips as Pearl held the mug close and tipped it. It trickled down his chin, but soon, as it filled his mouth, he began to swallow, then gulp. When the mug was empty, he rasped for more. It was torture to speak, but at that moment his need was greater than his pain. There was a metallic clatter as the woman refilled the mug from the pitcher.

'Steady, you don't want to drown him.'

'He hasn't drunk anything for days. And he's feverish.' Pearl took the mug. 'Will he ... do you think he'll—' She broke off, unable to ask the awful question.

'I don't know, sweet.' The woman's voice was low and warm. As Pearl held the mug to Daniel's lips again, she continued. 'It was a terrible blow he took. I've seen men lose their minds for less. You've seen Knuckler Joe up top – the man who carries the barrels into The Mitre?'

Pearl nodded.

'When he went down in his last fight his wits never came up with him again.' Taking a hunk of bread from the pocket of her apron, the woman placed it on an upturned crate next to another lumpen candle and looked down at him.

'That's for later, maybe.' She frowned. 'Soak it first and see if he can take it.'

Daniel drank deeply and then Pearl brushed her fingers across his dripping chin. 'There, that's better.'

'Th ... thank you.' It still hurt to speak, but the water had eased the hellfire in his mouth and throat.

'Well, that's a fair start.' The stranger smiled encouragingly and then leaned closer to Daniel. She held up a hand.

'How many fingers?'

'Three.' He managed to croak a barely audible reply.

'There! I reckon we'll pull you through.' She grinned across him at Pearl. 'I'll send for Jerome again. He'll know what's best for your brother now.'

Pearl set down the mug and took the melted tallow candle from a jagged niche in the brick wall. Placing it on the stones beside her, she sat close to him, stroking his hand. Her eyes glowed in the flickering light, the intensity of her gaze willing him to life.

'Do you remember what happened, Daniel?'

The question seemed to come from a great distance. It was the last thing he heard before retreating once more to the darkness.

*

Daniel slipped in and out of consciousness. Mostly, he inhabited a feverish world populated by impossible women. The presence of his mother, Elizabeth and, more so, Adanna was vivid and real. He missed them when he woke to find drab, shadowy forms from the real world at his bedside. Apart from the reassuring presence of Pearl, a succession of strangers stared at him, prodded him, moved him and sat with him.

A young black man, whose eyes were made smaller by spectacles, changed the dressing on his head. He was gentle, but firm when Daniel cried out. A ragged old man read in silence. The age-marked skin around his eyes pleated as he strained to see the pages of his book in the dimly lit chamber. A thin-faced child with a shock of matted hair sat cross-legged at the end of the pile of rags that formed Daniel's bed. The boy peered closely at him, cocking his head to one side as if trying to unravel his secrets. He grinned and waggled his fingers when he saw that he was awake. An oddly familiar young woman in a brightly striped dress perched on a stool and hummed a tune he recognised. She tutted and freed his hands from the rags when they became bound up in the fabric. The woman – *Jane*, was it? – knelt on the stones beside him. He was aware of the brush of her fingers on the top of his arm where the mark of the Garnett Plantation had been seared into his flesh. She soaked a cloth in a bowl of warm water and gently washed his face, hands and chest, before carefully folding the makeshift covers back over his body.

He had no idea if hours or days passed while he lay amid the rags. Gradually the pain in his head began to fade and he was able to look about him at the stained, damp walls of this narrow, arched chamber. Small grey stalactites bristled in the corners and the air was fetid with the stench of stagnant water and earth. Occasionally there was a blast of foulness as if some hideous rot-riddled creature had opened its jaws to fill the space with carrion breath. Usually, a candle or two brought an eerie glow to the glistening walls, but once Daniel woke alone in darkness and thought himself buried.

His mind was muddled by fever and pain. When he was able to follow a thought rather than snatching at shadows, he wondered where he was.

'Do you remember what happened, Daniel?'

Every time he pondered Pearl's question, memories shimmered through his head like a shoal of parrotfish, but when he caught hold of one it slipped from his mind to join the whirling, formless mass.

A glove. A fox. A room lined with books. A dog. A woman in a yellow dress. A glass of amber liquid.

The images dissolved as quickly as they formed in his mind.

'I've brought down a stew.'

The young woman pulled a stool closer to Daniel's side and set down a bowl on the stones.

'You need to eat. You're spare as a sighthound.' She patted his hand and smiled. The cuffs of her dress were worn, her apron was stained and the lace at her neck was tattered and old. Her shabby appearance was improved by the red ribbon that held back her tumble of chestnut hair. He thought she was just a few years older than Pearl, around twenty at most.

'Do you think you can try some? It's mostly cabbage and scraps.' She held up a wooden spoon. 'I can feed you if you're not up to taking it yourself.'

Steam from the bowl rose between them, lacing the air with the scent of bacon. Suddenly, Daniel's mouth began to water. He struggled to sit up, but the movement sent fresh jolts of pain into his neck and back that made him gasp aloud.

'At least you've got an appetite. Here, let me help.' She adjusted the sacking pillow, gently raising him higher. As she leaned close, he caught the faint scent of roses.

'That's better. I'm Jen, by the way.'

Now she was close, he saw that her blue eyes were framed by long dark lashes that cast shadows on her freckled cheekbones. She sat back on the stool and took up the bowl.

'Maybe next time you can hold the spoon, but for now it's probably best if I help.'

Despite the pain in his jaw, Daniel found that, with Jen's help, the stew slipped down very easily and very quickly. He watched her scrape around the bowl for the remnants of goodness and found himself wishing there was more. Shepherding the last spoonful to his lips as if he were a child, she shook her head.

'It's not the finest, I grant you, but Ma Rumney was most particular that you should have it. Now, that's a rare generosity on her part, let me tell you. She's usually tight as a cork in a bottle. But after what happened you've got yourself a reputation.'

'Thank you.' Daniel's voice was still hoarse. He wanted to ask the girl what she meant, but she rattled on without giving him a chance.

'She's not all bad, once you get to know her. It's not everyone who'd take in a foundling. Ma Rumney's been very good to me. I wouldn't say she was like a mother exactly, but at least she gave me a place when my blood mother left me out on the steps of St Giles. All things considered it could have turned out a lot worse.'

Putting down the bowl, she bent forward to examine his bandaged head. 'Jerome's done a fine job. You're in good hands there.' She frowned. 'There's a strip come loose at the back. Lay still, I'll try not to hurt you.'

She took up a trailing end and tucked it carefully back into place, biting her full lower lip as she concentrated on the delicate task. At last Daniel found a space to speak.

'Where ... Where am I?'

Jen sat back and gestured at the small barrel-vaulted space. 'In The Maze, of course. This is my lodging, usually.'

She might just as well have been speaking in Dutch for all the sense she was making.

'The Maze?' He managed to croak out the question.

'That's right.' Jen nodded. 'It's what most people calls it, anyway, although some of them call it The Holy Land on account of the Irish. A lot of us live down here under the Rookery. Up top there's a spider's web of narrow streets, passages and courtyards. Down here it's just the same. And we all look out for each other. This is as safe a place as any to rest your head. The rooms aren't fine and the air is often foul, but it's better than the streets. These cellars all join up to run a quarter mile in every direction from beneath The Mitre Tavern. It's like a village.' She paused. 'Well, in truth, I've never seen a village, but I reckon it's the same, with less in the way of sky. Or sheep.' She shrugged. 'It's the closest thing to a home most of us will ever know.'

Daniel was completely baffled, but the warmth of the stew in his belly sharpened his mind and purpose.

'Where's Pearl?'

'She's up top in The Mitre, but don't worry, Ma Rumney's got an eye on her. She's rinsing the glasses out back. That's how I started too. She's a sweet thing, your sister — sings like a little bird. The customers like to hear her.' Jen placed her hand on Daniel's. 'Pearl told me how you came to be here in London. It's not right. What happened to you with the Jarvey boys — that's all down to them an' all. If I thought a magistrate would listen to such as me, I'd cant on the pair of them and see them carted off to Newgate. James Fitzallen don't sound like a gentleman, and his wife's no better.'

James Fitzallen.

The name turned the key to a door in Daniel's memory. Images that had been a jumbled patchwork rose, shuffled and gradually formed themselves into a discernible pattern: wide steps curved upward to a lacquered black door; a man lazily unbuttoned his grey gloves; a fat woman in a yellow dress billowed on a couch; a greedy white dog snatched comfits from her fingers.

Sharp golden eyes. A glass of French brandy. Papers charring and curling in a fire.

He sat upright. Pain ripped from his shoulders to the crown of his head, but it was nothing to the agony of betrayal. Scrabbling at the rags, he tried to stand but instead he lurched to the side and half collapsed onto the stone floor. Still clutching his hand, Jen knelt beside him.

'Put your arm around me and I'll help you back. It's too soon.'

He closed his eyes and choked out a bitter truth. 'You couldn't be more wrong. I need to see Pearl, now!'

Jen gripped tighter and grunted as she tried to haul him back into the bed. 'I told you she's working up top. We all need to pay our way. Medicine don't come free. Your sister will be back soon but in the meantime I'm here. Lean against me.'

'I need to see her.' Head throbbing, he repeated himself. Why couldn't she understand how important it was?

'You *need* to rest.' Jen tutted and shifted him about.

Daniel wrenched his arm from her grasp. 'Pearl and I have to leave this place. I must . . . I have to . . .' He faltered into silence. In truth, he had no idea what to do.

Jen stared at him. Ringlets of dark hair loosened from the ribbon moved about her shoulders in a sudden draught.

'Do you remember how you got here?'

When he didn't answer, she stood up. 'I'll fetch Pearl. Now you're back to something like yourself, you two need to talk.'

Chapter Eight

Pearl wiped her hands on her apron and tucked a spring of hair beneath her cotton cap. Daniel didn't recognise the plain dark dress she was wearing. Although modest, the cut emphasised her small waist, revealing her shape in a way he hadn't noticed before. A frown crinkled his brow as he gazed at her.

'Come now. It's not so bad. You look much better.' Pearl grinned encouragingly, mistaking his expression. 'We sat with you all through the worst. Jerome said that it might take a while.' She glanced at Jen. 'That's right, isn't it?'

The young woman nodded. 'He's the nearest thing to a doctor down here.'

'I'm sorry I wasn't here earlier when you properly came to yourself again, but Jen fetched me down immediately,' Pearl continued. 'It's good that you've eaten too. I was beginning to worry about that.'

'I've got to go.' Jen rested a hand on Pearl's arm. 'It don't pay to keep Ma waiting – besides, you'll want to be together for a bit.' She went to a low arch on the other side of the chamber. Pulling aside a flap of striped material, she dipped her head and disappeared into the passage beyond. Her footsteps echoed on stones and gradually faded away.

Daniel stared up at the curved ceiling above his bed. The bricks glistened in the light of several candles jittering in niches set into the damp and crumbling wall.

With difficulty he raised himself. 'Where are we?'

'This is Jen's room, usually.' Pearl sat on the end of the makeshift bed. 'She's been so good to us. I don't know what would have happened if she hadn't come along.'

Daniel screwed a corner of rag between his fingers. 'I can't remember what happened, Pearl.'

'None of it?' She frowned. 'Surely you recall Scandrett Street. How James Fitzallen tricked you? It was the brandy, I'm certain. He mixed something into it that addled your mind.'

'And afterwards? That's what I can't remember.' Daniel gestured at the dismal walls. 'How did I come to be here?'

'I told you – it was Jen who saved us.'

'Saved us from what?' The question came out more sharply than he intended, but he was on the precipice of his patience.

'It was horrible.' Pearl shuddered. She pulled at the raw edge of a rag blanket as if trying to pluck the memories from her mind.

'Tell me!' It was a harsh command. Aware of her distress, he softened his voice. 'Please,' he added more gently. 'What happened after I drank the brandy?'

The long grey thread pinched between Pearl's fingers unravelled from the blanket.

'You collapsed. I tried to wake you, but Edward's brother pulled me away and I hit him. Then his servant – Parkes – came into the room with another man, also a servant, I think. They took you between them and carried you out into the hall. That hideous man – I cannot think of him as the Major's brother – twisted my arm up behind my back and pushed me along after you. I'm glad I caused his nose to bleed so much.'

She fell silent and rubbed her wrist. Daniel reached for her hand. Fury cancelled any pain caused by the movement.

Pearl met his gaze. 'His fingers were like iron pincers. We didn't go to the front entrance with the steps. Instead, they carried you downstairs to a room at the bottom of the house that led out into a yard. Beyond the yard a carriage was waiting. It wasn't like the one we arrived in, it was grand and black with golden letters painted on the door. I think it belonged to the Fitzallens. The servants bundled you inside and then James Fitzallen forced me to follow. He almost threw me on top of you and slammed the door. The carriage started off immediately – the horses were going so fast that I crouched on the floor holding the edge of the seat to keep steady. The blinds were drawn, but it didn't matter because it was dark, and anyway, I had no idea where we were going.

'I felt for your heartbeat to make sure you were alive and I was so relieved when you began to wake up, but you started muttering to someone called Anna. I think it must have been the effect of the drug. It was only when I spoke that you recognised me.

'After a while – I don't know how long – the carriage stopped. The driver opened the door and ordered me to get out and then he dragged you down to the cobbles. He didn't say a word. He just climbed up again, whipped the horses and drove away.

'It was a terrible place, Daniel. Worse than Widow Canty's lodgings and all the alleyways around it. The houses were tall and narrow and they pressed so close together overhead you couldn't see the sky. Even though there were rags at the windows, it felt as if a thousand eyes were watching us. It was dark, but I could tell it was a sort of crossroads with narrow passages leading off in every direction. There was an open drain running through the middle. I saw rats feeding from it.' Pearl shuddered. 'It was cold too. So cold. My cloak was in Scandrett Street in that awful room and my green dress is so thin. I started to cry, but you managed to stand up and you wrapped me in your cloak. I'm sorry.' She lowered her eyes. 'I think it was the sound of me weeping that brought them to us. Do you remember now?'

Daniel shook his head. Every part of her account was completely unrecognisable, except for the fact that it served to demonstrate James Fitzallen's treachery.

'They came out of the passages,' Pearl continued in a small voice. 'There were six of them, mangy as foxes. One of them held a lantern and his face . . . Oh, Daniel, his face!' She swallowed. 'He didn't have a nose – there was just a hole where it should have been. And one of the others had a hook for a hand.

'They circled us slowly and they . . . they made comments about me; lewd comments – like the women at the docks, but a hundred times worse. It made you angry. I think that helped you throw off the last effects of the drug. You held me close and shouted at them to leave us, but they just laughed. One of them caught my hand and tried to drag me away, but you lashed out and he stumbled into the gutter. The others didn't like that.

'The man with the hook jumped onto your back. He tried to cut your throat but you were too strong for him, you shrugged him off like a flea but then the others fell on you. You told me to run, but I couldn't leave you. I backed against a wall and watched you fight them all. You were so brave and strong, Daniel! They couldn't better you. I felt sure that you'd beat them all, but I didn't see the seventh man who crept out from one of the passages until it was too late. He had a rock in his hand and he stole up behind you and smashed it into your skull.

'You fell to the cobbles and then they turned on me. The man without a nose pushed his face so close to mine I could smell his rotting flesh. He . . . he licked me and told the others I tasted sweet as sugar . . .' Pearl faltered. In the candlelight, Daniel saw the flutter of a vein in her throat as she fought against the memory.

'What did they do to you?' The whispered question was staccato with rage.

'Nothing.' She shook her head and continued so quietly that Daniel strained to hear her. 'Nothing . . . like that. He caught my arms in his and ordered the rest of them to "clean" you. There was nothing I could do. I watched them strip you of your cloak, your uniform – everything. When you were almost naked, they kicked you again and again where you lay – in the stomach, your legs, your face. There was blood, Daniel, so much blood. I thought that . . .'

Pearl swiped at the tears running down her cheeks.

'You thought I was dead?' Releasing her hand, he brushed the bandage on his head with the tips of his fingers. No wonder his head felt like a split apple.

She nodded. 'It if hadn't been for Jen, I don't know what would have happened. She saved our lives.'

'How?'

'I . . . I'm not sure exactly.' Pearl stared up at the barrelled ceiling. 'It was all so frightening. I was terrified and confused. All the time that man held me so close. I could feel his breath on my neck, and his hands were . . .' She shuddered again and flapped at the bodice of her dress as if to banish a swarm of flies. 'I couldn't wash the stench of him away for days afterwards. Sometimes I think I can still catch the reek.'

Daniel waited for her to continue. When he thought of what she'd been through, fury made his throbbing head feel that it might finally burst open. He reached for her hand again and willed her to finish her story. At last, frustrated by her silence, he prompted her gently.

'What did Jen do?'

'She called out to them to stop. And they did.'

She answered as if it was the most natural thing in the world, but the story made no sense. The girl who had fed him thin stew was hardly terrifying, and she was certainly no match for a feral street gang. Daniel squeezed Pearl's fingers.

'I know it must be hard, but please try to remember. Tell me exactly what happened. It's important.'

'She knew their names. She called out to them one by one. They were brothers – all called Jarvey.'

'Knowing a man's name is not a weapon, Pearl. There must have been something more.'

She frowned. 'There's nothing . . . except something I didn't understand. Jen came up close to the man who held me and said that anything within a quarter of The Mitre was the property of Elias and they'd be fools to forget it. That's when the man let me go. I heard them cursing and muttering as they disappeared into one of the passages.

'Jen told me to wait with you while she went to get help. I begged her not to leave, but she said no one would touch us now. She was right – no one came near while I waited, and it wasn't long before she returned with some men who carried you down here.'

Daniel stared at the dripping bricks arching above. Pearl's account contained more questions than answers. An all-too familiar prickle alerted him to danger – an acute sixth sense that had served him well in battle. Who was the woman who had clearly known these men and had brought them – with nothing left – to this stinking hole? And why? Suddenly he found it difficult to breathe. The place was close and narrow like a trap.

'We have to leave.' Flinging back the rags, he struggled to rise, ignoring the agony that blazed throughout his body. The army had taught him that in battle a mind can master any pain to survive. Gasping, he pulled himself upright.

'Where are my clothes?'

'I told you, those men took everything except your shirt and breeches. The shirt was ruined, but the breeches are here somewhere. Jen washed them.'

'Damn Jen, whoever she is!' The insult echoed from the stones. 'Don't you understand? We have to get out of this place. I have to find Captain Benson.'

At the sound of footsteps, he turned to the entrance to the chamber. Jen was framed in the archway. It would have been impossible for her not to have heard his curse. Even at a distance he could see the flint in her blue eyes.

'I'll leave this here.' She laid a tray on the stones. 'It's just some bread and cheese. Seeing as you did so well with the stew, I thought you might want more. I'd best get back up top before I hear you slight me again.'

'Where are my things?' Supporting himself on the wall, Daniel edged towards her.

Jen looked at Pearl. 'You've told him what happened?'

Pearl nodded.

Jen drew a sharp breath. 'They're a vicious set, the Jarvey boys, but you stood your ground. There's a deal of talk about what you did.'

'I don't remember what I did.' Infuriated, Daniel glared at her. If he expected further explanation, he was disappointed. Instead, unblinking, her cool eyes held his gaze. Daniel was the first to look away.

'Bring me my clothes. We're leaving.'

'Well, you can't.' Jen's voice was surprisingly firm. 'You're not strong enough to leave this room, let alone go up top. You need to rest and get your strength back before you can think about . . .' She paused and pushed the tray towards him with a foot. 'Here. The bread's cut with chalk most likely, but the cheese is good.'

Daniel took another faltering step towards her. 'I don't care about your food. It doesn't matter because we are leaving. Come, Pearl.'

'No!' Pearl rose from the bed and gripped his arm. 'Jen's right. You're still too weak. You must listen to her.'

'Listen to a thief?' Daniel shook her roughly away.

'Is that what you think I am?' Jen bristled. Stepping closer to Daniel, she raised her face to his. 'I've been called many things in my time, but never that. A thief would never go to the trouble of saving her mark. Or give him a bed. Or sit by him night and day to make sure he didn't die on her. Or keep his sister warm and fed and out of harm's way.'

A deep male voice continued. 'Or pay for his physic from her own pocket.'

Lowering his head, a young man stepped down into the room. His hair was cut short like Daniel's and a pair of metal-rimmed spectacles balanced on his nose. The candlelight brought a bronze patina to his dark skin. Although he was smart and clean, his patched frock coat had clearly seen better days. He glowered at Daniel.

'You would not be so insolent if you knew what she has done for you.'

Jen stepped between them. 'It was nothing, Jerome, just a few pennies.'

'And that's money you've earned fairly and decently.' The man laid an emphasis on the words that Daniel could not misunderstand. His accent was not of London, but something closer to the speech of the American colonies.

'I came to return these. You should not have left them for me. There was no need.' Reaching for Jen's hand, the bespectacled visitor dropped coins into her palm, then he turned to Daniel. 'How dare you abuse her. If it wasn't for this woman, you'd be wrapped in a shroud and lying in a paupers' lime-pit by now.' He pointed at Pearl. 'As for your sister . . .'

There was a long silence as the meaning of those words created a dreadful and sordid pageant in Daniel's mind. He put a hand to his forehead where a hammer seemed likely to break through his skull. Pain, confusion and desperation had mastered him. He was suddenly bitterly ashamed.

'Forgive me. The fault is my own.' He made a slight bow to Jen. Sinking to the bed, he glanced at Pearl. 'I must apologise to you too. I was harsh. I know that you will have done what was best. My anger was not for you; it was all for myself.'

The dripping from the walls was the only sound in the chamber as Daniel considered the wreckage of his dreams. He stared dismally at the damp stones and the smell of rot and decay filled his nose.

'How long have I been here?'

'Nearly three weeks.' The answer came from Jerome, but Jen added more. 'And you was out cold for the first six days.'

Horrified, Daniel looked up. 'That can't be.'

Jen folded her arms. 'Well, I'm afraid it's the truth and nothing can change it. You've been here in my room and in my bed for the last nineteen days.'

Chapter Nine

Jerome's coat was too tight. The fabric pulled across Daniel's shoulders and his wrists were visible at the cuffs where the sleeves of the clean shirt, also borrowed, fell short. Although the coat was not entirely shabby, it was far from the smart military uniform he had worn on the day he arrived in London.

Daniel was not proud or vain and he was grateful to Jen who had tried to find suitable clothes to replace those that had been stolen, but he felt the change in his circumstances in the dull patched fabric that rubbed his skin and constricted his movement.

It was the first time he had left the chamber where he had lain for so long. In three weeks, his bones seemed to have melted to marrow.

As he and Pearl followed Jen through the dripping passages of The Maze, he quickly came to understand that in London, apart from the streets, there was nowhere further for a man, woman or child to fall. A subterranean warren of dimly lit passages radiated in all directions. It was here that the poor and destitute had made their homes in brick-walled, barrel-roofed chambers that might once have been the wine stores of long-dead merchants or the sunken layers of buildings from an earlier time.

Every ten yards, light from a cheap tallow candle clenched in a bracket or melting in a niche puddled the damp stones beneath his feet. The air was earthy and sometimes thick with stagnant water.

Occasionally the putrid stench of human waste caused him to cover his nose.

It was not silent beneath the streets. The stones thrummed with the constant murmur of those who lived in The Maze. Hundreds of them. Daniel saw their candle-thrown shadows move behind the thin material slung against the entrances of chambers to afford some privacy.

Out in the passages, filthy rag-clad children, spindly as twigs, played games with stones on patterns marked out in the dust. Jen clearly knew them all by name and one of them, a small boy with a heart-shaped face and eyes as round as marbles, knew Pearl.

'Will you sing that song again?' He clutched her skirt as she passed and stared up hopefully. 'That one about the flowers. I heard it the other night when I was maundering outside The Mitre.'

Pearl grinned and bent to the child. 'I'm glad you liked it. That's a favourite of mine too.'

'Not now, Kip.' Jen scruffed the boy's head affectionately. 'Maybe later, eh?'

As they carried on down the passage, Daniel looked back. The boy waved. His skin was so dark he almost melted into the shadows. He had noticed, with despondent surprise, that many of the people living in The Maze were like him and Pearl.

The gaping arch of a half-collapsed cellar revealed a set of twisting brick steps that wound upward from the earth. The entrance to the underground warren was in the yard behind The Mitre Tavern where Jen, and now, it seemed, Pearl, worked. The timbers of the ancient inn were splayed and precarious and its plaster was cracked and blackened by smoke. Squat on a corner, it looked as if it might collapse at any moment.

For a moment, unaccustomed to daylight, Daniel shielded his eyes and took a welcome gulp of fresher air.

'We'll try for a ride but follow me close.' Jen signalled as she headed across the puddled yard. 'If you lose me, you'll never find your way to the Pool.'

'This is as far as I can take you. I'm to pick up a load of Baltic timber there.' The carter who had obliged them all with a place in the back of his empty wagon pointed his whip to a warehouse facing the river. The sharp clean scent of cut wood that filled the air here was not unpleasant. In fact, it suddenly reminded Daniel of the vast American forests. The man tipped his hat at Jen and stared with frank, but not unfriendly, interest at him and Pearl as they dismounted.

Although it was May, a sharp wind harried foam from the brown water of the Thames. The chill sliced along the quayside, but Daniel could not button the straining fabric of Jerome's coat against it. He tightened the scarf at his neck and pulled the dark, wide-brimmed hat lower to meet the collar. Beneath the battered felt, his head was still bandaged, but the wound was almost healed.

Jen had found Pearl another simple dress and a cloak that fitted her. As they were around the same height and build, he supposed that the garments were her own. Once again, he felt a stab of shame as he thought of the accusations he had made in the face of her kindness.

She was just a little way ahead of them. Her tawny hair was plaited and caught in a knot of red ribbon that bounced and swung on her back as she pushed through the crowd. The bright ribbon was the only colour in the day. As if she had heard his thoughts, Jen turned.

'Don't look so glum.' She had to shout over the hubbub. 'Once we find your captain, you can start to put things right. What's the name again?'

'Benson.' Daniel scanned the magpie vessels tethered along the quay and secured in rows across the river. Their massive hulls groaned as they rose and fell on the scum-flecked tide. One naval ship was very much like another, but he knew that the *Audentior* would be here somewhere.

Captain Benson had told him that it would be six months before his services were required again. If he could find Benson's ship, he could make enquiries as to the captain's address and prevail upon him to prove the truth of the will. And if not Captain Benson himself, then Mr Doyle, the ship's surgeon, had also witnessed Major Fitzallen's last wishes. They were both honest men. Daniel was certain they would support him.

He studied the lines of ships. Just as the last time, the quay was swarming with people and trade. Naval officers jostled for space on the stones with ordinary sailors, porters and harlots. It was a rough dance where partners switched places without elegance, grace or care.

Jen shouted again, but her words were muffled by the loud bleating of a goat. The roped and recalcitrant creature was dragged past them by a foul-mouthed youth. Perhaps it knew it was destined to provide fresh milk at sea from the lowest and darkest decks of one of His Majesty's ships of the line.

Gripping Pearl's hand, Daniel pushed closer to Jen.

'I said, the best place to go is the warrant office.' She pointed to a tall lime-painted building on the left side of the quay. A gaudy plaster coat of arms straddled the doorway.

'They'll have the lists. I reckon you might—' Before she could say any more, a covered wagon rumbled perilously close. Daniel stood back from its enormous studded wheels as the driver, oblivious to anyone in his path, ploughed a furrow through the crowd.

The wagon halted beside an ancient, ocean-bleached naval hulk some twenty yards off. Canvas flaps at the back were flung open and four armed men jumped down to the quayside. Forming a line, they dragged at chains attached to something inside. One of them cracked a whip on the stones. He barked out an order, but the only word Daniel heard was 'bastards'.

As he watched, the canvas flaps shuddered. A man lurched from the wagon and toppled to the quay. He lay blinking in the weak light as another chained man tumbled on top of him. Eventually four more prisoners – all of them black – were hauled from the wagon.

The quayside fell still and silent as people watched. The whip flailed again and the six chained men stumbled to their feet. Dressed in little more than rags, they bowed their heads as the armed men dragged them to a gangplank leading up onto the brooding ship.

'Judd!' A woman's voice broke the eerie silence and one of the stooped men paused on the shifting wooden slats. He raised his head and tried to look back at the quayside but a whip lashed across his back.

Daniel tore his eyes from the ship and searched the crowd. A tall woman carrying a small child had stepped forward. Raising the child, she called the name again, her voice thick with tears. A space opened around her as if those present could not bear to be associated with such misery. Balancing the child – a tiny girl – on her hip, she simply raised her hand, but the whip cracked again and the men shuffled upward. At the top, they disappeared from view onto the deck.

As if to cleanse the scene, at that moment the sun forced a way through the flimsy grey clouds, flooding the world with colour. The spell was broken. Nearby someone laughed and the spectators returned to their day.

'What was that?' Confused, Daniel turned to Jen. Grim-faced and silent, she had wrapped her shawl tight around her body.

'They're being sent to the western plantations. When a man . . .' She paused and looked directly at him. 'When a man like you is convicted of a crime in London, he – or she, it happens to women too – is most often sent to slavery.' Spots of anger flared on her freckled cheeks. 'Some have escaped and are being shipped back, but some are Londoners born and bred. There's money in it.'

Daniel stared at the dismal ship in horror and disgust. The men who had just been dragged on board would be locked in the darkness of the stinking hold. He knew that their crossing would be very different to the one he and Pearl had recently undertaken. His mother had often spoken of the living hell of the passage from Africa where infection, disease and despair were trapped below deck with the human cargo. Her wrists and ankles had borne the scars of the manacles that bound her. She was strong, but two of her brothers had died on the voyage. Adanna had barely survived the ten weeks that brought her to Jamaica. Unlike his mother, she had mentioned it once, and *never* returned to the subject.

He was so shocked that he was hardly able to speak. 'But I thought . . .' He held Pearl's hand more tightly. 'I thought there was freedom here.'

'Pah! That's a ripe myth.' Jen shook her head. 'I've got friends who'll put you straight on that – Jerome, for one. It's wrong, we all know it.' She took a step closer, rested her hand lightly on his arm and spoke in a low voice. 'Take my advice, Daniel. Keep yourself out of the way of trouble. By that, I mean the law. If you was ever to be unlucky enough to be taken like those poor men, you'd go the same way. Pearl too.'

'I don't care who you say you are, you're not coming in.'

The sour-faced clerk seated at a desk just inside the doorway peered up at Daniel. His horsehair wig appeared to have been made for a man with a larger head. 'I wouldn't give the particulars of a gentleman's private whereabouts to anyone without good reason, and certainly not to such as you.' He replaced his quill pen in the pot beside the ledger book and made a play of scrutinising his querent from head to toe. Evidently, he found much wanting.

'You could be a French *spy* for all I know.'

Heads turned at the incendiary word. The hallway of the warrant office was a slightly more ordered version of the quay. Aware that he had become a subject of interest, Daniel flattened his hands on the desk and said firmly, 'I am a lieutenant in the King's army, lately returned from America. I travelled to London on the *Audentior*. Captain Benson will confirm that. If you enable me to contact him, he will assure you of my rank and person.'

'Will he now?' The clerk sniffed and folded his arms. 'Been in a fight, have you?'

Removing Jerome's hat as a gesture of politeness had revealed the bandages. It was a mistake – the clerk was not a gentleman. The aroma of wet dog clung to his clothes and his person.

Daniel took the hat from the table.

'As I told you, I am a lieutenant in His Majesty's service.' He returned the hat to his head and tried to be civil. 'Come, sir. I asked a simple question.'

'Maybe, maybe not.' The clerk nodded, dislodging a slimy bulb that dangled from the end of his nose. He snuffled again. 'And I've got a question for you. What came first, the chicken or the egg?'

'I've no time for riddles.' Exasperated, Daniel thumped a fist on the desktop. The quill leapt from the pot. 'I must see Captain Benson.'

The clerk eyed the shining black drops that now spattered the crisp page of his ledger.

'Out!'

He pointed at the open doorway. 'Leave now, or I'll call for the officers. He tapped a yellowed fingernail on the stained ledger. 'This might be interpreted by a magistrate as criminal damage ... committed by a *foreign* spy.'

There was nothing Daniel could do. After Jen's warning he could not risk an encounter with the law unless he could prove his credentials. Suppressing the urge to take the man by the scruff of his grimy neck and roar into his face, he turned and stalked to the door. As he walked beneath the plaster coat of arms into the light, the pinch of Jerome's boots provided yet another reminder of the reversal of his fortunes.

Jen and Pearl were waiting across the cobbled yard. Jen had linked Pearl's arm with her own. As Daniel came closer, she raised her eyebrows.

'Since you went inside, we've had no end of trouble. You'll have to learn to take care of your sister. London can be a dangerous place for a pretty girl.'

'You saw them off easily enough.' Pearl grinned. 'I'd never heard half of those words before.'

'And that's just as well. A young lady like you shouldn't know London backchat. I'm ashamed of myself sometimes, but it comes with the territory. If you think I've got a mouthful of vinegar, you should hear Ma Rumney on a bad night.' Jen patted Pearl's arm and looked up at Daniel. He noticed that the blue of her patched woollen shawl was an exact match to her eyes.

'Well?'

'Nothing. The clerk threw me out. He accused me of being a French spy.'

Pearl was indignant. 'That's not true!'

'How can I prove it?' Daniel glared at the office. 'He won't help me find Captain Benson, but without Captain Benson . . .'

'What came first, the chicken or the egg?'

The clerk's riddle was insolent, but accurate.

'What about Mr Doyle?' Pearl's question was hopeful.

He scuffed the toe of a boot where the leather squeezed tight.

'Too late for that. The man threatened me with the magistrates.' He stared at the hulk that threw a vast shadow over the quay. 'I can't go back in.'

Jen turned to the scores of naval vessels moored across the Pool.
'If we can find your ship, perhaps there'll be someone on board who
can help. Surely your captain's left someone behind to keep an eye
on things?'

'But which one is it?' Pearl frowned. 'They all look the same and
to reach half of them out there on the river we'd need a row boat.
We could be bobbing around until nightfall.'

'Not necessarily.' Jen tossed her hair and adjusted the ribbon.
Brushing her skirts, she looked at the doorway to the warrant office.
A young man in full naval uniform stepped out beneath the lurid
arms and began to cross the courtyard. Polished buttons studded
his indigo jacket like stars in a midnight sky. From his swagger and
general air of great satisfaction it was clear that he held himself in
such high regard that it would be difficult for anyone, except possibly
his mother, to join him on that summit.

'Perfect!' Jen bit her lip and pinched her cheeks. 'Wait here.'

Head low, shawl clasped tight, her steps demure and small, she
approached the man and appeared to bump into him accidentally.

'Oh, sir!' Her hand fluttered prettily to her lips. 'I am so very
sorry to have put myself in your way.'

'Not at all. The fault was mine entirely, ma'am.'

The popinjay grinned and ran his eyes over Jen's neat form.
Immediately Daniel recognised his type. Just as Jen had done a
moment earlier.

She performed a dainty curtsey and the officer continued across
the cobbles.

'Sir!' Jen called once more and the man turned. She curtseyed
again, very deeply, and ran after him.

'I'm sorry to interrupt your business – and very important I'm
sure it is too – but I wonder if I might take a moment of your time?'

The officer doffed his bicorn hat, revealing a shock of golden
waves.

'I always have time for a lady.' Daniel caught the veiled mockery in his tone. He and Pearl were close enough to hear most of the conversation that ensued. The man's voice had a note that carried.

'I must find my brother who serves aboard one of these fine ships.' Jen gestured gracefully at the quay. 'Our dear mother has died and Tom should hear it from me and no other. I believe he is here, somewhere, only . . .' She faltered, allowing her voice to break a little.

Arranging his sly expression to one of concern, the vain man patted her arm. 'I offer my condolences, ma'am, but how may I assist you?'

Jen swallowed a sob. 'Tom serves aboard the *Audentior*. I need to find him, but it is hard to be a woman alone here without a guide. There are so many ships . . .' she lowered her head, '. . . and so many men.' When she looked up, her long black lashes glittered with tears that threatened to fall to her flushed cheeks. 'I don't know what to do.'

Pearl nudged Daniel and whispered, 'Mrs Kelly says she could be on the stage.'

He had no idea who she meant, but at that moment he had no inclination to question. As they watched, the effulgent officer reached into a pocket of his jacket. He produced a white handkerchief the size of a flag.

'No need for tears. Here, dry your eyes, m'dear. Come with me to the warrant office and we'll consult the lists together. I'm sure we can find your brother. The *Audentior*, you say.' He paused. 'The name is familiar.'

Dabbing at her eyes with the giant handkerchief, Jen seemed sweetly vulnerable as she walked meekly beside the officer. Daniel was not surprised to see the hand of the conceited young man creep to her waist. She allowed it to linger there for a while, before moving deftly and politely a little way out of reach.

'She's good, isn't she?' Pearl stifled a laugh.

Watching Jen evade the officer's unwanted attentions, Daniel found that he shared that admiration.

It wasn't long before Jen came scurrying back alone. Checking to see that she had not been followed, she produced a black ledger from beneath her shawl.

'I took it while he was jawing war to an admiral. At least I think that's what he was, given the size of his hat. Keep watch.'

The spine of the ledger cracked as she opened it to reveal densely packed lists of ships followed by names and dates. Finding nothing at first, she flicked over the pages until at last she jabbed excitedly.

'Here it is!' Indicating the place, she turned the ledger to Daniel, who followed a line of sloping black writing with a finger.

'*Audentior. Frigate. 32 guns. Captain E. Benson. Tea convoy.*'

He skimmed along the entry. '*Portsmouth. Lisbon. Benguela. Cape of Good Hope. Madras . . .*' he continued to trace the line, '. . . and so on to Canton.'

He looked up. 'China!'

'Ah, there you are. I was worried for you, m'dear.'

'Christ, almighty!' Jen smuggled the ledger back beneath her shawl. Smiling brightly, she whipped about as the spangled naval officer crossed the courtyard.

Daniel and Pearl stepped to a discreet distance and watched him come closer.

Too close.

'Damndest thing! But the ledger's not there. However, I made enquiries on your behalf and a queer do it was. I knew I'd heard of it. The Admiralty letters came through at short notice and the ship sailed on the next high tide. She'd been in London for less than a week. It's not the done thing. The Warrant was most put out.' He smiled sympathetically. 'I am sorry, ma'am, but if your brother is on board the *Audentior*, it will be two more years before you can tell him about your mother.'

'Beg pardon, sir?' Jen disentangled herself from the brilliantly buttoned sleeve that was trying to encircle her waist. 'I don't understand. Why would that be so?'

'Because two weeks ago his ship was sent out on the China route. Tea is a most valuable commodity. It needs protecting . . . Rather like you, m'dear.' The officer manoeuvred his constellated body even closer. His voice was a velvet purr as his hand slipped beneath Jen's shawl. 'Now, I believe you might be grateful for my assistance.'

The sound of the slap to his face cracked like a whip.

Chapter Ten

The painted dolphin creaked as it swayed in the wind. Rain dripped from its tail and from the end of its blunted nose. Daniel pushed at the peeling door below it and ducked his head to step down inside. As he peered into the gloom he wondered if this was the place Jen had meant. She had told him to come and find them at The Dolphin Tavern after his visit to Widow Canty, but this was a strange choice of meeting place.

Trapped beneath the low, beamed ceiling, the air was thick with tobacco smoke, gin and the press of unwashed bodies. Men and women huddled in booths or shoved for a place at the crude wooden counter where a server with ham-hock arms and cauliflower ears filled the pewter jugs and tankards of his customers. The man's face had the colour and texture of salted pork from the barrels on board the *Audentior*. It had begun to rain but that made little difference here. Sunlight could never penetrate the grimy diamond-shaped panes of The Dolphin's windows.

The dismal atmosphere compounded Daniel's sense of misery. His return to Friary Alley had not been successful. After a short, vicious exchange on the doorstep, the widow had slammed the door in his face.

Daniel searched the room. Perhaps he was mistaken and there was another Dolphin Tavern in the alleyways behind the docks? The place was rough and noisy and there was an edge to the raucous laughter that could easily tip into violence. The man behind the counter paused as he selected a pie assaulted by flies. He stared at Daniel and muttered something to his customer.

'Daniel!' He turned to see Jen waving an oversized handkerchief above her head. After slapping the young officer's astonished face, she had spun about and walked haughtily away, tossing back an insult to the effect that although she might not be a lady, he was most certainly no gentleman. A moment later, she had jettisoned the ledger into the Thames where it had floated next to the distended body of a dead cat before sinking.

Now, she and Pearl were in a booth in The Dolphin's dimmest corner, but they were not alone. Two men, one of them unusually tall and broad, leaned over the wooden panel that divided the booth from the room. Their long coats were worn and frayed, but oddly fine for such a place.

Daniel pushed through the crowd until he was level with the booth. Jen stood up. To his surprise she grabbed his arm, pulled him close and planted a kiss on his cheek. She smelled of rose and there was a tang of gin on her breath.

'There you are – come to meet us, like I said.' She smiled tightly at the giant leaning over the partition. 'I told you I was meeting my sweetheart – and here he is.'

The huge man stared at Daniel. His eyes were almost invisible beneath the thicket run rampant on his prominent brow and his nose seemed to have melted across his face. He smiled unpleasantly, revealing a churchyard of broken grey teeth, and spat into the sawdust.

'A sweetheart?' The question was ponderous as if it was difficult for the bear to string the beads of his thought. He scraped his stubbled chin with a shovel-like hand and nudged his thin companion, whose lank hair framed a face composed entirely of angles.

The other man wheezed out a laugh. 'Ain't it said that when a whore's cunny runs thin through use, she takes a black 'cos that's all she can get?' He stared at Daniel, hooded eyes filled with malice. 'And ain't it also said that a poor whore always prefers a black cock inside her 'cos the dirt don't show?' Unlike his friend, his insults came quick and sharp.

Pearl gasped. She half rose to her feet but Jen released Daniel and placed a restraining hand on the girl's shoulder. Daniel saw Jen's finger dig deep into the damp fabric of the borrowed cloak.

'My, you're a wit, Mr Janway. I could talk to you and Bill all day.' She smiled blandly and shot a quick warning glance to Daniel. 'But I'd very much appreciate it, *gentlemen*, if you'd leave us now. And so would my beau.'

'Beau!' The big man laughed, the sound ending in a belch. Detaching his bulk from the partition, he took a step closer to Daniel. The light of the single candle lantern lodged on a shelf above Pearl's head showed threads of tarnished silver embroidery in his coat. A fat tongue appeared at the side of his mouth.

'What's that, then? Something you've tied yourself to?' The man's pale eyes were strangely untethered beneath that mountainous forehead. They moved across Daniel's face without finding a place to focus.

'Look, Bill. Over there!'

Fortunately, his scrawny companion had lost interest in Jen and Pearl. His attention was now directed entirely at an obese older woman standing on a table just inside the doorway. He grinned and pointed.

'By my very life, it's Dirty Jude. I thought she was dead.'

The vast woman hoiked up her grey skirts and turned in a slow circle to reveal rolls of pasty, mottled flesh that swung low from her buttocks and thighs. The crowd whooped and catcalled as she twirled. Some of them pelted her with pennies.

The thin man caught Daniel's horrified expression. 'Quite the eyeful, ain't she? This'll be a rare show.' He winked and pulled at the bear's coat. 'Come on, we don't want to miss out.'

They moved away, the dull-witted man shambling obediently behind his sharper companion. From the way people stood aside, it was clear that the pair held some status in The Dolphin.

'Who are they?' Furious, Daniel rounded on Jen. 'Why did you let them insult you like that?'

'It was you I was thinking about.' Releasing Pearl, she sat down and pushed the handkerchief into her bodice. 'That's Bill Sankey the knuckler and Janway his business manager. Bill's got a brain the size of an acorn and what's left of it's been hollowed out, but he can still fight if Janway tells him too. Did you see his hands? If you counted the roaches scuttling under this table, you'd need a handful more to equal the men Sankey's sent into the next world, or left somewhere in between, which is worse.' She reached for a tin mug. 'Besides, I don't think it was me they were interested in. It was this one. She's a peach in a sack of crab apples.'

She turned to Pearl who was rubbing her shoulder where Jen's finger had gouged deep.

'You need to learn when to hold your peace, girl.'

'But he . . . he was insolent!' Pearl was furious. 'I couldn't allow him to talk about you like that.'

'Yes, you could.' Jen shrugged and swirled the contents of the mug. 'You've got spirit and that goes a long way, sweet, but you've got a lot to learn about London. If you'd given mouth to Janway just now, you wouldn't be sitting pretty next to me.'

Tipping back the mug, she grimaced. 'Gin's cut – who'd have thought it?' She swiped her lips and pushed the mug away.

'You said you'd keep her safe while I went to back to Widow Canty.' Daniel glared at Jen and reached angrily across the table for Pearl's hand. 'Come. We're leaving now. This is no place for you. Either of you.'

'It didn't used to be like this when it was run by Mother Clegg and her daughter. It was more respectable then and they looked out for the women who came here.' Jen lifted her chin defiantly. 'I thought it would be better to bring your sister here than to drag her to Limehouse.'

From behind him came shouts followed by the slow clapping of hands. Daniel turned. Most of The Dolphin's clientele were now pressed around the table where the dancing woman was flagging. Despite the yelping of the crowd, she swayed uncertainly, her breasts rising and falling like a pair of foundry bellows. There was a bleeding cut on her thigh where a coin had nicked the flesh. He could not understand how this sordid display passed for entertainment.

'Truly I didn't know the Cleggs had gone. I wouldn't have come if I had.' Jen tugged at his sleeve. 'It's changed and I'm sorry, but we won't be here long. Besides,' she said, looking across the room, 'Janway and Sankey have forgotten us now.'

She pushed a tankard towards him across the sticky wood. 'I bought it for you. It's ale not gin, so that's a mercy. From the look of you it's raining so you might as well sit down and tell us what happened.' She frowned. 'Where are your things?'

Chapter Eleven

'Widow Canty said she had never seen me before in her life. I didn't raise my voice . . . not at first. When I challenged her, she barred the door and refused me entry. I tried to push past and go to the room, but she started to scream out to anyone passing by. She called me a thief, and worse, and begged them to fetch a constable . . .' Daniel faltered. In his mind six chained men repeated that awful shuffle to the deck of the transport ship.

'Those trunks held everything.' He looked up at Pearl. 'Everything – apart from the dress you wore on the day we went to Scandrett Street – has gone.' He stared into the ale. 'I have nothing but the clothes I am wearing. And they are not even mine.'

'The old cow!' Jen folded her arms. 'Those trunks and everything in them will have been sold at the Rosemary Lane Rag Fair by now. This Widow Canty – whoever she is – has made herself a packet out of you. If only . . .' She bit down on her lip. After a moment she sighed deeply. 'The past is shifting sand. Never stand on it too long or it'll take you under. What's done is done.'

She seemed to be speaking to herself rather than her companions. *'Think of the future, not the past.'*

His brother's words on the night of the fire came back, but there was little comfort in the memory. Daniel drank deeply and felt the ale pool in his belly. Unlike the gin, it was true but still he was sickened. He stared at the candle lantern above the bench and swallowed.

'The theft is not the worst of it, don't you see?'

Jen shook her head, but Pearl sat forward. 'Without the army papers, you have no proof of the past. Of our past?'

He nodded, unable to meet her eyes. 'I have nothing to prove my years of service, my station, and what was promised to me.'

'Then what can we do?' She continued firmly without waiting for a reply. 'You'll think of something, brother. I know you will.'

Daniel looked up. He struggled to keep desperation from his voice but his words were choked with emotion.

'I'm sorry, Pearl. So very sorry to have brought you to this. There is not a soul in London who can vouch for me or the inheritance. I am no one. The *Audentior* has been sent on the China route and will be away for at least two years.'

Jen nodded. 'It left on the high tide exactly two weeks ago today, according to the date in the ledger I took.'

'And that was less than a week after I met James Fitzallen.' Daniel froze as a memory slotted into place. If it was a drawer made by a master cabinet maker, it could not have fitted more perfectly.

'I see it now!' He thumped a fist on the table. The blow was so hard that the sound made people turn towards them. Jen's tin mug jumped, spilling the last of the gin. Despite her doubts, she had managed to drink most of it.

'Hush.' Scanning the tavern, she tightened her shawl. 'It's not wise to draw attention here. What do you mean?'

'James Fitzallen is a merchant with friends in high places.' Daniel's voice was filled with sour understanding. He appealed to Pearl. 'Do you remember what he said about our visit being an interesting story to relate at dinner?'

Pearl nodded. 'I thought he was trying to impress us.'

'As did I.' Daniel laughed bitterly. 'But think of those names. I knew of them in America – Admiral Howe and Lord Detting are two of the most powerful men in the navy. And Rockingham is the Prime Minister. If James Fitzallen wanted anyone to be sent far from these shores, *they* would wield the influence he desired. Where better to send the only living men who know the truth of his brother's will than to the other side of the world?'

A shadow fell across the table. Daniel looked up to see the meat-faced owner of the tavern. The man wiped his hands on a gruesome apron and jerked his head towards the doorway.

'Out, all of you. I've had complaints from the gentlemen over there.'

He stood back to indicate the table where the woman had danced. Now, surrounded by jugs and bottles, she was slumped between Sankey and Janway, who was staring back at the booth. The man's angular face was sharp with spiteful interest.

Daniel recognised the type. He had served in the army with men who took delight in discord. During the long, dull winters they found diversion in setting man against man, stealthily, assiduously stoking minor quarrels to something lethal. Usually, such devils were clever. Frustrated, they used their talent as a confirmation of their worth and for sheer pleasure. It was always best to avoid their traps.

'My money's as good as anyone's.' Jen's face was flushed in the candlelight.

'It's not your money my friends take exception to, it's your company.' The man flicked a stubby finger at Daniel and then at Pearl.

'Out!'

A silence had fallen on The Dolphin. Again, Daniel felt the prickle on the back of his neck. It was a silence that clanged with expectation, the silence before battle.

'We have every right to be here.' Jen bristled and he realised with some alarm that the gin had fired her. Now it was his turn to advise caution. He caught her eye and shook his head – a small warning gesture.

He reached for Pearl's hand. 'We are just leaving, all of us. Come.'

Jen stood and edged mutely around the table. Together the three of them walked slowly to the door. Daniel measured the pace, knowing with a soldier's instinct that any sign of fear would unleash the rabble. They were almost at the door when someone spoke.

'They're so dark the pair of 'em you could hardly see 'em in that corner. God knows what they were up to – all three of them.'

The knife in Janway's voice cut through the silence. He grinned at Daniel, his eyes dancing with excitement. Standing up, he turned slowly about to be certain of his audience.

'Leaving us, are you? Good riddance, I say. Good riddance to the whores and their black pimp master.'

It was too much. Janway had trespassed to a point far beyond Daniel's pragmatism.

Forcing Pearl behind him, he took a single step forward.

'You will apologise.'

'Will I now?' Janway made a show of taking Daniel in. 'My but you're a big one, ain't yer?'

His clothes were almost that of a gentleman, but the stock at his neck was yellowed. Without turning, he clicked his fingers and his bear–like colleague shuffled to his feet.

'I reckon you might care to try yer luck with my friend, Bill.' Janway clicked his fingers again. Obediently, Sankey took off his coat. There was something childlike in the way he folded it neatly and laid it over the back of his chair.

'I have no quarrel with your friend.' Daniel's voice was low. 'It is you who cannot hold your tongue.'

Janway grinned wider. Raising his arms, he spun about, his coat flying around him.

'Let's see if *you* can hold your own with champion Bill Sankey,' he barked, like a fairground showman. The clients of The Dolphin whooped and catcalled. Dirty Jude had been a sideshow, but this was the main attraction. They backed away, creating a ring around Daniel in the sawdust.

'No, Daniel! Don't!'

He turned to see Pearl caught in Jen's arms. She squirmed to free herself, but Jen held her tight. She shook her head slowly, her freckled face taut with fear.

'Let's just go. Please!' Pearl called again and Jen huddled her closer. She soothed the girl's hair and whispered into her ear as Sankey lumbered forward into the makeshift ring.

'I will not fight this man.' Daniel stepped back, but Janway moved to stand beside his pet. He raised his right hand.

'Coward, are yer?'

'I fought for the King beside better men than you will ever know.'

'Did you now?' Janway clicked again. 'On him, boy.'

Sankey lunged. The blow came from nowhere, knocking Daniel almost to his knees and his borrowed hat to the floor. Head ringing with pain, he staggered back, but the man came at him again like a wall. The second blow fell short, catching his right shoulder rather than his head.

The bear moved fast, his movements and his senses awakened by Janway's command. There was a precision and competence in his attack that was lacking in his speech.

Daniel tried to parry the third blow, raising his arm and dodging to the left, but Sankey's huge fist still caught him in the stomach. Bent double with pain, he was aware of yelping and jeering. Coins spattered around him and now he saw blood in the sawdust from the newly opened wound on his head.

'If you counted the roaches scuttling under this table, you'd need a handful more to equal the men Sankey's sent into the next world.'

James Fitzallen had drugged him and abandoned him and Pearl on the streets. He had been attacked and left for dead. Today he had discovered that he had lost everything and now he was reduced to brawling in a backstreet tavern hardly worthy of the name.

Was this his inheritance?

A rush of anger flooded his mind and body. With a roar, he straightened, clenched his left fist and swung. The blow landed on the side of Sankey's head and the man staggered back, surprised by his opponent's recovery and ferocity.

Pressing his advantage, Daniel lunged again, catching Sankey's face full on. There was a crack and a great spurt of blood gushed from the man's squashed nose as he fell backwards. His shaggy head met the side of the table where Dirty Jude had danced and it collapsed, legs straddled wide.

The Dolphin fell completely silent. Janway scuttled to Sankey's side.

'Up! Get up, d'yer hear me!' He prodded his man's arm with the toe of a boot, but the bear grunted and shuddered. Blood from his shattered nose spread in the sawdust.

Incandescent with fury, Janway rounded on Daniel. 'Look what you've done!'

'I did what you wanted me to.' He breathed deeply. The tavern seemed to be bathed in a reddish light. Gradually he understood that it was his own blood clouding his sight.

'Bastard!' Janway spat at him.

Wiping the spittle from his face, Daniel bent to retrieve his hat.

'We will leave now.' He signalled at Pearl and Jen.

'Scum!' Janway aimed a kick at Daniel's leg, but it missed its mark. The lank-haired man lost his footing and collapsed in a heap of grubby coat and impotent rage.

'Perhaps *you* would like to continue where your friend left off?' Daniel balled his bloodied left fist and crouched beside Janway. The skin of his knuckles was split, but at that moment – every sense raw to continued danger – he felt no pain. There were cheers and shouts of encouragement, but the tavern owner intervened.

'Enough. We don't want trouble. It wouldn't be good for trade if the law were to take an interest. Or the Excise.' He scowled. 'Take your women and go.'

The disappointed crowd parted as the three of them went to the door. Daniel stood back to let Jen and Pearl go first. Once outside, he gripped Pearl's hand and walked swiftly along the winding narrow alleyway. It was raining hard now but he didn't care. He didn't know where he was or where he was going, but he was certain they needed to leave The Dolphin far behind.

'I'm sorry.' Jen almost had to run to keep up with them. 'I shouldn't have taken Pearl there.'

Grim-faced, Daniel ignored her and strode on in silence. From the corner of a bloodshot eye, he saw Pearl turn her head and mouth something to her friend.

'We need to go right at the end, and then straight on.' Jen's voice came again. 'When we get back, I'll see to that wound. It's not as bad as it looks, it's just come open again and blood's seeping through the bandage.' She paused to catch her breath. 'I've never heard of anyone besting Bill Sankey before. He won't forget that in a hurry ... and neither will Janway.'

Daniel stopped and turned to her. 'Do you think I will forget it, Jen? Forget how you took Pearl to a place like that where God knows what might have happened? I don't care about this ...' He gestured to his head. 'I care about *her*. How can I trust you? I don't even know who you are, not truly.'

Jen's hair was stuck to her head and her face was streaked with rain. 'It wasn't my fault that Janway and Sankey were there.'

'She's right.' Pearl wriggled to free her damp hand from Daniel's. 'When we arrived, Jen said The Dolphin had changed for the worse, but it was too late because we'd agreed to meet you there. That's why we sat in the darkest corner so that no one would notice us. I really think that—'

Daniel never found out what Pearl 'really' thought. At that

moment the sound of pounding feet echoed from the walls of the alleyway. Behind Jen a pack of men rounded a curve and thundered towards them.

'Stay with me!' Jen yelled. Darting past Daniel, she pelted along the alleyway and disappeared into a side passage. They followed her lead and quickly found themselves splashing and skidding through a warren of stinking alleyways and slivers between buildings. At first their pursuers kept pace – Daniel heard their shouts and the echo of their boots on the cobbles – but as Jen led them deeper into the heart of the fetid labyrinth the sounds vanished.

At last, they came into a courtyard, blocked by lopsided timber-framed buildings on three sides but open to a square of Thames-grey sky. Channels frothing with filth bubbled from each corner to a central pit. The air was foul with the stench of human excrement. The mouldering walls, which had never seen sunlight, were coated with greenish slime. It was the bleakest place imaginable, but worse, because Daniel had never imagined himself or Pearl in this version of London.

His head was ringing now. Closing his eyes – fearful that the women might see his tears – he leaned back against a damp wall. Sodden plaster crumbled and pattered at his feet.

'I'm sorry, Pearl.' Daniel's voice was barely a whisper. 'I didn't think it would be like this. I thought London would be our home – a new start, a new world, but—' He broke off, his voice choked with misery.

When Pearl's hand crept into his, the tears leaked from his eyes and ran with the rain on his cheeks.

'There is . . .' Jen's voice was unusually hesitant. 'There is some-where you might find a home. If Elias agrees.'

Chapter Twelve

In their bedraggled, beggarly state, no one was willing to give them a ride. The trio trudged back west through the city in a rain-sodden, dejected silence. Jen led them along Cheapside where canopied shops and sparkling arcades sold gold and silver, fine cloth, ribbons and trinkets to the better classes.

The customers emerging from these elegant establishments were beautifully attired. From the feathers in their hats to the silken tips of their buckled shoes, they possessed a lustrous sheen that whispered of wealth. Even the ribbon collars of the women's tiny lap dogs were studded with jewels. As these pampered sons and daughters of London mounted the steps of smart monogrammed carriages, their clipped voices carried the braying certainty of their absolute right to exist.

For Daniel, the sight was a bitter reminder of all that was lost. And worse, the sound brought back the humiliating memory of James Fitzallen's contempt.

But even here, money was no defence against the reek of the streets — a noxious, sulphurous blend of smoke and ripe horse shit that lodged at the back of the throat. The women pressed dainty jewel-studded vinaigrettes to their noses while men flapped away the foulness with handkerchiefs drenched in citrus cologne.

They cut from the Strand into Covent Garden just as dusk was falling. The stench was worse here. Pearl and Jen raised their skirts to avoid open sewers leaking from the shadowed ginnels surrounding the square.

Traders were packing up their stalls, loading anything still possessed of a nodding acquaintance to freshness onto their carts and trolleys. The stone arcades rang with their strident calls and, underfoot, the paving slabs were slippery with fallen vegetables trodden to a pulp in the rain. The pungent miasma of rotten cabbage mingled with the putrid stink of poverty.

As the costermongers' working day ended, for others a new one was beginning. The beggars, pimps and whores who shifted for a living in the darkening alleyways were a grim reminder to Daniel that London was a city of two faces. The face she now presented to him was pitiless.

Yet Covent Garden was a paradise compared to St Giles just a few streets further away. Here, sickness, disease and deformity seemed to be a badge of belonging. Pearl gripped Daniel's hand as a legless man trundled from the mouth of a dingy passage on a small wheeled tray. Jen knew the beggar's name and crouched down to talk to him. There was a flash of silver as she dug into the pocket of her skirt and folded a coin into his grimy outstretched palm.

When they came to the entrance to The Maze in The Mitre's yard, he was almost relieved to descend the broken, jagged steps to the warren below. Exhausted, soaked to the skin and utterly wretched, he trailed Jen and Pearl along the low winding passage that was now depressingly familiar.

Jen paused before a shrouded archway.

'Harry. Are you there?'

She called again and a pallid youth with a birthmark covering one side of his face twitched the rags aside. He stared at Daniel suspiciously, but his gaze softened when it alighted on Pearl.

Jen held up another silver coin. 'I need you to take two messages for me tonight. I'll give you this in return. Are you willing?'

The lad eyed the sixpence and nodded.

'Good.' She whispered into his ear and the only words Daniel caught were familiar names: Jerome . . . and *Elias*.

'Is that clear?' Jen stepped back and showed the coin again. 'This'll be waiting for you.'

The youth retraced his steps. He disappeared behind the curtain of his cell and emerged a moment later in a threadbare coat and shapeless woollen hat. Sliding another admiring glance at Pearl, he squeezed past Daniel and went back towards the entrance of The Maze.

Jen chewed her lip as she watched him go. Daniel saw her cross her fingers before she twirled about.

'This way. It's easy to get lost down here, but you'll soon get used to it.'

As far as Daniel was concerned, that day would never come. He watched Pearl's slim frame moving just ahead and made a silent vow.

Once they reached Jen's chamber, she lit two candles and handed one to Pearl, who was drooping from exhaustion.

'You need to rest, lamb. Take this and go along to Sally's. I'll join you there when I've seen to your brother.'

'Daniel?' Pearl sought his agreement.

He agreed wearily. 'Jen's right – go. Take off those wet clothes and sleep.'

Since coming to his senses again, he had slept alone in Jen's chamber while she and Pearl shared quarters a little way along the passage with a buxom, good-natured redhead. Sally Scattergood slept through most of the day, which made it possible for Pearl and Jen to share her bed at night. Daniel had not objected, openly, because he had assumed the arrangement to be temporary.

Pearl shivered beneath the dripping cloak. 'The rain feels as if it's seeped into my bones. Tomorrow, Daniel? We'll talk then, yes?'

He nodded, but he didn't know what to say. Tomorrow nothing would have changed.

When Pearl had gone, Jen examined the blood-stained bandage. She pursed her lips as she removed it.

'You'll always carry a scar but I was right. It's not as bad as it looks – just crusted blood.' She tutted. 'And it was already healing nicely. Sit on the bed. I'll see to your hand as well.'

'You don't need to.' Irritably, Daniel tried to evade her ministrations. 'I was ... I *am* a soldier, remember? I'm used to dealing with wounds. This is nothing.'

I am nothing.

The words insinuated themselves into his mind.

'I've helped Jerome in the past and he didn't complain and neither did his patients.' Jen was undeterred. Turning from him she doubled over. There was a ripping sound and she held up a strip of cloth from her petticoat. 'This'll do for your hand too. There's fresh water in the jug.'

Kneeling beside him on the makeshift bed, she went to work. Daniel stared at the red ribbon in her damp hair and remembered the hope he had felt when he had followed her at the docks. He took up the jug from the floor and poured cold water over the torn skin of his knuckles. The fresh wound stung, but the chill roused him a little from the lethargy of despair.

'Who is Elias?'

Jen ignored the question and started to bind his hand.

'You said we might find a home if *Elias* agrees. What did you mean?'

He remembered Pearl's description of his assault by the Jarvey gang. They had apparently vanished into the night when Jen reminded them *anything within a quarter of The Mitre is the property of Elias.*

That name again?

'Well?' he prompted.

There was a notable silence, before she spoke.

'Ma won't be happy. I've missed a whole day up top. She's mean as a country curate's wife, that one. Did I ever tell you about the barrels of gin she split with turpentine? That's how I knew the slop in The Dolphin was gut rot. Ma was lucky the law didn't find out or she'd be in Newgate with her sister. If Nora's still alive, that is. Two years she's been in there and all for taking a pair of ruby drops from her mistress. And there's more to that story than meets the eye, let me tell you. When is a gift from the master not a gift? When the mistress finds out about it, that's when.' She paused to draw breath and rattled on. 'Thinking about it, that gin today might not have been cut with turpentine. I've heard it can lead to blindness and I can see what I'm doing perfectly well, even in this light . . .'

This torrent was nothing new. Daniel had come to understand that Jen's constant chatter was a shield. She rarely spoke about herself, deflecting questions with a fanciful story or an anecdote about Ma Rumney or one of her customers.

He stayed her hands.

'Stop, please. Just tell me.'

Releasing her, he reached to tilt her face towards him. Jen was suddenly still and silent. The candlelight brought a soft glow to her skin and the pupils of her eyes were stretched and dark. The only sound in the chamber was the tick of water dripping from the bricks and his own breathing. He was aware of the warmth and the natural scent of her body close to his. Beneath his fingertips, he felt the pulse of a vein in her neck. Shocked by the intimacy, he swiftly removed his hand from her jaw.

Jen swallowed and looked down.

Unsettled in a way he could not – or more accurately would not – allow himself to examine, Daniel sat back, folded his arms and interrogated her again, brusquely.

'You said "*if Elias agrees*". What did that mean?'

'You'll find out tomorrow.'

The answer was as brief as it was evasive.

'There – you're done.' Rising, Jen went quickly to the canvas-draped doorway. Before stepping out into the passage she spoke without turning to look at him.

'Jerome will take you. I've asked him to collect you first thing.'

Daniel did not call her back to ask more. As her footsteps disappeared along the passage, he was aware of the lingering scent of roses.

That night he dreamed of Adanna. She walked ahead of him through woodland threaded with striped hibiscus flowers. Her dress was blue and her hair was bound in a red cloth turban. When he called, she didn't answer, instead she faded from view. Suddenly, cannons blasted, horses screamed and lines of red-coated men toppled beside him, limbs torn from their bodies, eyes open to a vast grey sky. He ran among the fallen, searching for the Major in the blood-churned mud. Rearing above him, the rutted earth crashed down as a wave, flooding the world to the limit of his vision where a single frail ship – so small against the sea and the sky it was hardly a speck on the horizon – carried all his hopes further and further away.

When he woke in the early hours, the strands of the dream weaved through his mind; a tangle of fury and despair. It was the tradition of his mother's people, the Yoruba, that dreams should be told to an elder so that their meaning could be explained, but Daniel did not need help to unravel what he had seen. Everything represented some part of a future he had lost.

He did not see Pearl or Jen next morning. Instead, Jerome arrived early at the chamber to serve – as far as Daniel could tell – as some sort of escort. He was not an easy man to talk to. As they walked away from The Mitre side by side and along the shabby street dominated by the tower of St Giles Church, Daniel was not sure if his companion was deaf or sullen. He had wondered if their connection as young black men in a largely white city might provide common ground, but so far, he had been discouraged by Jerome's indifference.

The passages of St Giles were dismal, but overhead, in gaps visible between jutting roofs that almost kissed high above the cobbles, there was a thread of blue.

Daniel tried again. 'I must thank you for this coat.' Feeling the pinch of the boots that were also borrowed, he added, 'In fact, I believe everything I am wearing came from you. I will repay you when I can.'

The answer was a noncommittal shrug.

Stepping to one side to avoid a girl pushing a wheeled crate piled high with turnips, Daniel studied his guide. Jerome was a little older than him, shorter and more compact. His black hair was cut close to his head, but threads of silver were already visible. The thickened lenses of his metal-rimmed spectacles made his eyes appear smaller than they really were, but also disconcertingly alert.

Earlier, Daniel had detected judgement in that stern gaze. At Jen's request, Jerome was taking him to Elias, but it was clear that he did not intend to make small talk.

At a tap on his shoulder, Daniel turned to see a young woman standing in the half-shadow of an open doorway. She grinned and moved aside, revealing a lamplit flight of stairs at her back.

'I can help you spend a shilling if you've got the fancy.'

Daniel raised a hand, half as greeting and half to ward her away. Her painted lips twisted into a moue of disappointment. 'It's a clean establishment, if that's what bothers you. We all bathe regular as sparrows here.'

'Not today.' Daniel shook his head and returned his attention to the bustling street. Jerome was several paces ahead now. Sunlight brought a sheen of wear to the back and elbows of the faded green velvet of his frock coat.

Pushing through the throng, Daniel drew level once more, but

Jerome didn't acknowledge him. Irritated, he now decided to abandon any attempt at building a conversation.

'Who is Elias?'

When no answer came, he pulled on Jerome's arm and repeated the question, shouting it aloud over the hubbub.

The effect was immediate. His guide spun about and the burble of voices around them died to a whisper. Jerome batted furiously at Daniel's hand as if he had been stung by a wasp. Behind the bottle-glass panes of his spectacles, his brown eyes flicked nervously from side to side.

'Never speak that name aloud.' He hissed the words. 'Not in the street where anyone could hear. Do you understand? It could bring...' He swallowed. 'It could attract the wrong sort of attention.'

Daniel stood his ground. 'At least tell me where we are going.'

They were now the focus of attention. An old man with a wooden cage full of tiny brown birds slung across his back paused and pretended to fiddle with the leather straps that secured the door of his trap. A woman of similar vintage laden with so many brushes and brooms that she might almost be mistaken for a monstrous bristled beast of the forest turned with such haste to eavesdrop that her wares swung out. A broom clouted a boy with a tray of oysters, most of which skittered to the cobbles.

Jerome scanned the street and then walked swiftly on. A flick of his hand indicated that Daniel should follow.

'I won't move another step until I know what's happening,' Daniel shouted at Jerome's faded back and bent to retrieve some of the fallen oysters. 'Here.' He handed them to the boy, who was as interested in the exchange as the bird seller and the brush woman and a dozen other idlers.

When a pair of scuffed, brass-buckled shoes appeared next to an oyster Daniel looked up. Jerome had retraced his steps and was glowering down at him.

'I do not wish to become involved with your troubles. The only reason I am helping you is because of Iphigenia. She asked me to take you to see ...' Jerome's face creased as if with pain. He seemed to be struggling to find the words, but at last he continued. 'An old friend.'

A coarse voice rang out. 'What you done to me?'

Lumbering from a doorway, a large woman surveyed the scattered shellfish. 'I've got forty pie crusts to fill and these are all spoiled.' She clipped the oyster boy round the ear. 'I'll be taking the cost from your wages, goosepaw.' She lashed out again, but the boy ducked to avoid the flat of her hand.

'They'll serve.' He dodged aside as the woman rounded on him. 'After all, you've used worse in your pastry, Mrs T.'

'He's not wrong,' another voice chimed in. 'I was shitten meself for a week last time I bought one of your beef and oysters, Nelly Triskett.'

Mrs Triskett was not amused by this contribution. Puce-faced, she turned upon the speaker, a tall shabby man accompanied by an absurdly well-dressed dog.

'I'll thank you to keep your thoughts to yourself.' Sputtering with rage she added, 'The only way a street beggar like you would get a taste of one of my fine pies is if he stole it!'

The dog began to howl and then, sensing an audience, it jumped up onto its hind legs and twirled about. Sequins sewn into its ruff and its braided red coat sparkled in the sunlight.

By now, everyone in the street had lost interest in Daniel and Jerome. The prospect of a brawl between the pie cook and the beggar offered entertainment of the most diverting nature.

With a wink, Daniel handed the last of the oysters back to the boy and stood up.

He turned to Jerome. 'Who is Iphigenia?'

'Jen, of course.' Jerome rolled his eyes. 'It is her true and most beautiful name. Given to her by the curate who found her on the steps of St Giles Church. He wondered at the sacrifice of such a perfect child. I would not do this for anyone else.'

It was a reply of such earnest devotion that at last Daniel understood his companion's antipathy.

'I believe you are mistaken, my friend. I do not have feelings for Jen, other than gratitude for the kindness she has shown to me and to my sister.'

Jerome scowled. 'It is not *your* feelings that trouble me.'

Daniel shook his head. 'I hardly know her. And she does not know me.'

Unbidden, a memory of wide dark eyes, glittering in the light of a single candle, stole into his mind.

'I am nothing to her,' he added firmly.

'You sleep in her bed.' It was a statement, but there was a question in Jerome's voice.

'Jen sleeps elsewhere – with Pearl. For a short time, I have commandeered her lodgings. At present, my sister and I have nowhere else to go. I have nothing to offer except for my thanks.' He stared intently at the young man. 'May I ask—'

'You may not.' After a moment Jerome sighed. 'There was a time when I thought that Iphigenia and I . . .' He shook his head. 'Perhaps one day I might . . . *we* might . . .' He stared dejectedly at an oyster beside his foot. He kicked it and it clattered into the gutter.

Daniel did not question his companion any further. He had heard enough.

The tolling of a church bell indicated that half an hour had passed since Jerome had collected his unwelcome charge from Jen's room. Dull and heavy, the notes lingered over the street.

Daniel folded his arms. 'Has a time been appointed for this meeting?'

'He doesn't work like that.' Jerome pushed his spectacles up his nose and peered myopically over Daniel's shoulder. The escalating war of words between the pie cook and the beggar was now attracting a circle of spectators. The excited dog was performing somersaults. Satisfied that no one was paying them attention, he continued. 'It will make no difference when you arrive. Elias doesn't keep time like others.'

'Then I have a suggestion.' Daniel pulled at the sleeve of his coat – Jerome's coat – where his wrists extended several inches from the cuff.

'As a soldier I learned never to go into battle unprepared. I need to know the lie of the land. Before you take me to this . . . Elias, perhaps we should talk together. I would be most grateful.'

Jerome stared at Daniel's face. At last, he seemed to find something satisfactory in his unwanted companion. Nodding slowly, he pointed along the street. 'I know of a place where we may speak with some freedom. It's this way.'

Chapter Thirteen

Jerome knocked four times on an inconspicuous black door set low into an otherwise blank wall. He waited for a moment and then he rapped twice again. The door opened and a small but muscular man in a neat grey coat corded with golden thread peered at them both from beneath a powdered wig. Its extraordinary whiteness was startling above a face brown and rutted as a field of turned earth. The man leaned forward to examine the Stygian alleyway and once he was satisfied that they were alone, he moved aside to allow them to enter. Daniel found himself in a long hallway where candles burned in brass and silver lanterns set at intervals along the red-painted walls. The air was filled with the scent of wax polish and coffee.

'Always a pleasure, Mr Jerome.' The man closed the door behind them and sat down in a padded leather porter's chair positioned by the door. He pointed along the hallway. 'It's a slow afternoon at The Apollo. You'll find seats in the salon and the parlour.'

'Thank you, Cyrus. It's still early in the day. I'm sure that business will improve later. Besides . . .' Jerome turned to indicate Daniel, '. . . a quiet corner will suit us well.'

'Oh, you'll find plenty of them.' The small man waved a hand to usher them forward. The leather creaked as he settled himself more comfortably and returned his attention to the door, which was fortified from within by stout iron bands.

Jerome led the way down the hall. He moved aside a heavy

tapestry curtain and allowed Daniel to go first into a large, high-ceilinged, rectangular room where a fire crackled in a broad brick hearth. Painted in a darker russet shade than the hallway, the lantern-lit space was comfortable and well furnished. Several men sat at tables or sprawled in chairs and couches arranged as if in the salon of a great house. From their smart livery, it was apparent that some of them were servants. Two men had removed their wigs, which now sat on the table beside their elbows like small white lapdogs. As he followed Jerome across the room, Daniel saw that these men were playing chess.

He also saw that every man at ease there was black.

The pleasant scent of rich coffee and good tobacco was a contrast to the evil fug of The Dolphin and the murmur of conversation was low and convivial. It did not stop when Daniel and Jerome entered, although one of the seated men – old, with a portly figure barely contained by a fine embroidered waistcoat – put down his pipe and raised a hand in greeting.

'I must pay for the tincture, Jerome. The fever broke just as you said it would and now Alys is almost herself again.' His voice was deep and firm. It carried the accent Daniel had come to recognise as the speech of London.

'I am glad to hear it.' Jerome crossed the room to shake the old man's proffered hand. 'Your wife is a strong woman. I'm sure it was your care and her own will that brought her through.'

'Never.' The stout old gentleman gripped harder. He had a shock of white hair – plainly his own – that was a stark contrast to his creased brown skin. ''Twas all down to you, 'pothecary. You must believe in your talents as we all do. Send me the bill as we discussed and for now let me stand you and your friend ...' he glanced at Daniel, '... whatever you're taking this afternoon. I won't be resisted on this.'

'There is really no need.' Jerome tried to free himself but he was caught fast.

'Tolly!' The old man signalled to a boy carrying a tray. 'These men are my guests. Don't let them pay a farthing this afternoon – d'ye understand?'

'Yes, Mr Richardson.' The boy nodded and continued across the room, disappearing beneath an archway. The corpulent elder pointed to the bench opposite his own large and comfortably appointed chair. 'Join us?'

A young man dressed in a blue frock coat stood to acknowledge them. His face was broad and his eyes danced with amiable intelligence. The perfectly tied stock at his neck was very white and he wore his hair naturally, the abundance caught back in a queue.

'Sit with us a while, both of you, won't you?' Mr Richardson grinned at Daniel and pulled Jerome closer, still clutching his hand in a bear-like paw. 'This is my friend Mr Cugoano. I would very much like him to make your acquaintance, you have much in common.' He turned to his companion. 'Ottobah, this is the 'pothecary I was telling you about.'

'Delighted to meet you, sir.' The smart young man bowed. 'Mr Richardson has already recommended you. We were discussing the merits of London's artists. I am afraid to say that my employer does not meet with our host's approval.'

'Damn tiny things!' Mr Richardson's belly quivered as he laughed. 'Cosway's a painter for dolls' houses. A man would need a microscope to see his work clearly.'

'The miniature is a much-prized form of portraiture.' The young man raised his hands in a show of mock exasperation. 'Cosway's client book proves that.'

'Pah!' Mr Richardson snorted. 'I doubt your man could capture this mighty corporation ...' he patted his belly with the hand that was not gripping Jerome's, '... in such an impoverished space.'

'And what do you say, sirs?' The genial young man appealed to both Jerome and Daniel. 'Please join us, if only to convince this philistine of the error of his ways.' He grinned at Mr Richardson. It was clear that the two were friends. Now that Daniel looked closely, he noticed tiny spots of red and blue paint in Mr Cugoano's hair.

'Another time, most surely.' At last, Jerome managed to regain his hand. 'Today we would be dull company. My friend has ... an appointment to keep later this afternoon and we must prepare. Cyrus said there were tables free in the parlour where it might be a little quieter.'

Mr Richardson took up his long clay pipe and waggled it towards a doorway beyond the hearth. 'There's room aplenty back there. Trade's softer than a coney's belly.' He looked shrewdly at Jerome and then at Daniel, his protuberant brown eyes creasing with mischief. 'Is it business or women?' Without waiting for an answer, he slapped his ample thighs and laughed loudly. Jerome did not.

'I assure you that it is the former, sir.'

He made a shallow bow to the elegant young man. 'I hope we will meet again another time.'

Mr Richardson grinned. 'You will, Jerome. I have persuaded Ottobah to come to our next meeting.'

Jerome sent a meaningful look at the younger man. 'That is good news. You will be welcomed.' He turned again to Mr Richardson. 'Please give my regards to your wife.'

'That I will.' The old man grinned and sucked on his pipe. 'Remember. Not a penny to be paid.'

Jerome dipped his head again. Turning, he led Daniel through the tables to the door indicated by Mr Richardson's pipe. Two stone steps led down to a more intimate, square-shaped room where the walls were hung with panels of faded blue silk. A speckled mirror hung over a marble mantelpiece and embers glowed in a small grate. As Mr Richardson had said, they were alone here.

Jerome went to a table in the furthest corner and sat down. Daniel took the chair opposite him. He studied the room, which, although scrubbed clean, was a little worn. The tables and chairs were ill-matched and deep grooves in the wooden floor showed the passage of many feet. It was clearly a place that was well frequented. He turned back to his companion.

'Where have you brought me?'

'The Black Apollo is a coffee house, much like any other.' Jerome smiled. It was the first time that Daniel had seen him do so – it made him look younger.

'You have just met its owner, Mr Inigo Richardson. He inherited it from his father, who named it to honour the Greek god of the civilised arts and for the inspiration that coffee awakens. For more than sixty years The Black Apollo has served people in London who wished to find a place where they will be among friends and treated as equals.' Jerome pushed at his spectacles. 'In that respect it is *not* like any other coffee house. Many of its clients are servants like Mr Cugoano. You saw the men playing chess by the fire?'

Daniel nodded.

'From their silver livery, I'd hazard a guess that their master is the Duke of Southminster.' Jerome's grin widened at Daniel's puzzlement. 'Even footmen are allowed some time to themselves. When they can escape from their duties they come here for an hour or so. There are others, too. Men of respectable trades and means whose families have roots in London but who have never felt entirely welcomed. There are also Africans – mainly people from the lands in the west – who were, perhaps, farmers, blacksmiths, rice growers, carpenters before they were taken. Men who were proud of their work and their skill. Most who find themselves in London now are freed or escaped from enslavement, and those,' Jerome jerked his head at the door through which they had just come, 'like the footmen back there who occupy a territory somewhere between those states.' His expression grew serious. 'There are many people like us in London, Daniel, but we live beneath its skin. The Black

Apollo has always served those of our race. It is not a secret place, but it does not advertise.'

Daniel remembered the way the porter, Cyrus, had examined the street when they arrived. He also thought about the sturdy iron-banded door. Even if you knew where it was, it would be difficult to force an entry. From his brief experience of London, he could easily imagine times when such protection was needed.

Jerome continued. 'Have you read any Shakespeare? *Othello*, perhaps?'

Daniel shook his head. 'I've never read any of his plays. Pearl, now that's another matter. In America she . . . *we* had a friend who encouraged her interest.'

'Then she might like to meet Mr Richardson. One of his ancestors supplied cloth and costumes to the theatre in London where William Shakespeare's works were first performed. Generations of Richardsons have lived here. People like you and I have walked these streets for hundreds of years, but the evil of slavery has marked us now in ways that go beyond the wretched scars of ownership.'

It was the most that Jerome had ever said to him. More than ever, Daniel heard the accent of the American colonies in his companion's low, passionate voice. He saw Jerome's right hand creep unconsciously to a patch on his left sleeve just above the elbow and was suddenly certain that he bore a brand like his own.

He leaned forward. 'Your accent is American.' The statement of fact was followed by a soft-spoken question. 'And you were enslaved?'

Jerome's fingers stilled on the velvet. After a moment he nodded. 'You are right on both matters.'

They sat in silence. The only sound was the faint murmur of conversation from the russet salon. Daniel waited patiently. Experience had taught him that the best way to encourage a confidence from another – be they friend or enemy – was to make a space and wait for them to fill it. For the first time in a long while, he felt bonded to another man and wondered how far Jerome's story mirrored his own.

For his part, Jerome stared at Daniel across the table, his eyes very small behind the panes of his spectacles. At last, he seemed to make up his mind.

'I was born in Virginia as a property of the Purbright family. There were a hundred and forty of us working on the estate. Anthony Purbright was a cruel man who followed the old ways, but his son Philip was different. He was ashamed. When he inherited, he freed us. Some continued, quite willingly, to work for the family, but Philip also bought apprenticeships for those, like me, who showed intellectual promise and an aptitude for skills beyond those required in the cotton fields. I was bound to an apothecary in Boston – a distant cousin of the Purbrights and a fair man – but he could not afford to keep me beyond my indenture.' Jerome peered at Daniel. 'At the beginning, the war made many men poor. It did not seem likely that the Crown would be defeated, but ...'

Shrugging, he took off his spectacles and began to polish them on the greyish cuff of his shirt.

'How did you come to be here?' Daniel prompted.

'In Boston I had a good friend who bought a passage to London.' Jerome continued to rub at the thickened glass. 'Like me, Matthew was a freed man. He had an affinity for figures and worked as a clerk for a timber merchant. But the woman he loved was employed as a servant to an English family living in the city. When the war sent them back to London, he decided to follow her. It wasn't hard. He was able to pay his way and he had papers to prove his freedom. We continued to correspond and his letters persuaded me that there was a future here. So, six years ago, I made the same journey.'

Jerome returned his spectacles to his nose. 'The street air smears the glass.' He stood up. 'I will go to find Richardson's boy. I fear he has forgotten us.'

'Wait!' Daniel caught his arm as he turned from the table. 'You didn't finish. What happened when you came here? Your friend — was he ...'

'He was dying.' Jerome looked away. 'He died a pauper in the St Giles Rookery and his body was buried in an unmarked grave along with forty others. His wife and child followed him there shortly after. His letters were a lie ...' He frowned and shook his head. 'No, that is harsh. Matthew's letters were full of dreams. Perhaps he thought that writing them down could make them real — but the truth was he could not find work because no one would employ or trust a freed black man as their secretary.'

He smiled sourly at the question in Daniel's eyes.

'I was more fortunate. London is a place rich with poverty and disease. There is always call for apothecaries here. I am far from wealthy, but unlike poor Matthew, I am able to support myself. When my friend's widow died, I vowed that I would use the skills I had to help those who had fallen as low as they.'

Jerome pushed at his glasses again. 'There — you have my story. In return, perhaps you will tell me yours. Now, where is Richardson's boy?'

As Daniel watched his companion walk back across the uneven floor and up the steps, he felt a chill draught in the parlour. Pulling Jerome's ill-fitting coat about him, he rose and went to the hearth. After poking the embers back to life, he took a dry log from a pile next to the fire surround and added it to the sparks crackling and snapping in the grate. While he nurtured the flames, he thought of those letters filled with Matthew's hope.

An image blazed in his mind — a will curled and crumbled to ash in the heart of a spitting fire.

The coffee was rich and strong. It enabled Daniel to order and relate his account with an unwelcome clarity. Jerome listened in silence, but when Daniel reached the treachery and deception of James Fitzallen, he rose from the table and went to the fire, hands clenched tight behind his back.

Jerome stared into the spotted glass over the mantel as Daniel described his last encounter with thieving Widow Canty. The more he spoke, the more he felt the injustice of his situation and its hopelessness. Anger and despair wrestled for control as he reached the awful conclusion, in both his story and his complete comprehension of his position.

'I am adrift. I have no papers, no army commission and no fortune. I do not have a single penny, a rank, a profession or a home. When James Fitzallen burned the will, he obliterated my future and then he made certain that anyone who could swear otherwise would be unable to do so. Apart from Captain Benson and Mr Doyle, no one can prove that the Major's last act on this earth was to make me his heir.' Daniel's voice finally cracked with fury and misery. 'There is an irony – is there not? – in the fact that Edward Fitzallen asked me to take his name, but now I am no one.'

Overcome, he buried his face in his hands, unwilling to show the tears of humiliation and rage that blurred his vision. It was Pearl who occupied the centre of his shame. The thought that he was the cause of her destitution was more than he could bear. Was he always destined to fail those he loved most? The fabric of the borrowed coat tightened across his shoulders as he breathed deeply again and again, struggling to subdue his emotions.

Though his head was bowed, he was aware that Jerome had returned to the table. The apothecary waited without comment until the storm subsided and then he refilled Daniel's china can from the silver pot provided by Richardson's boy.

'I see now why Iphigenia asked me to take you to Elias.' He poured out the last dregs for himself and swirled his can around. Daniel blinked in confusion, but then he remembered that his companion was referring to Jen.

Jerome examined the sticky dark liquid at the bottom of his coffee can.

'The Rom hold that a man's fortune may be divined from a cup. It is a superstition with no basis in fact or science, but I confess that I wish I had the skill at this moment so that I might advise you.' He looked up. 'The St Giles Rookery is the place where those who cling to the edge of the world find themselves when every other door has been slammed in their face. Elias is the King of the Rookery. Every man, woman and child living within a quarter mile of The Mitre is his subject. In return for their loyalty, Elias offers protection. The poor are housed and they feel a sense of community that they have probably never known, but more than anything they are bound together by his authority. Elias's rule is law – he *is* the law. No one disputes that, not even the magistrates or their runners who fear the Rookery more than the shadow of their own headstones. The question is, are you willing to live under such a master?'

'Are you?' Daniel frowned. 'Is that how you live?'

Jerome stared into the depths of his can. If he discovered any pattern or meaning in the dregs, he did not share it. After a long moment he replied.

'I have lived on the fringes of Elias's kingdom for such a long time now that I no longer know if I am a subject or a free man. I do, however, know that there are many forms of slavery, Daniel. Today, you will have to make a choice.'

Chapter Fourteen

Jerome led him from The Black Apollo through a series of twisting alleyways, arriving at last at a stone-paved courtyard with a crumbling well at its centre. Three of the walls that enclosed the yard were blind, but the fourth was punctured by rows of small barred windows above a black, nail-studded door.

Jerome halted some way before the well and pointed across the yard. 'Behold the fortress of Elias. Many years ago, it was a private debtors' prison. In consequence, it is still a place difficult to enter or leave without its master's consent.'

Disgust and fear were easy to read on his face as he stared at the building's mottled wall and banded windows.

'This is where I take my leave. I'll go no further with you, brother.'

The use of the word 'brother' was as welcome as it was unexpected. But it was true that their shared confidences at the coffee house had kindled a bond. At last, Daniel felt he had met someone in London he could trust.

'I hope ...' A muscle below Jerome's left eye twitched as he stared at the shuttered building. After a moment he continued. 'I have always trusted Iphigenia's instincts, but in your case, I fear they may have clouded her judgement. Take great care, Daniel.'

Without another word he spun about and walked back to the arched passage from which they had emerged into the yard. Bracing himself against whatever lay ahead, Daniel faced the black door. Behind him, Jerome's retreating footsteps echoed from the stones. Suddenly they stopped. A moment later they sounded again more loudly. Daniel turned to see his guide striding back towards him. Pulling Daniel close, he whispered a warning.

'When he affects the manner of a gentleman, he is at his most dangerous. Remember that.'

Jerome's spectacles had slipped down his nose. Without them his eyes were large, owlish and loaded with meaning, but before Daniel could interrogate him further, he bowed and walked quickly away.

The courtyard was eerily silent. The early promise of the day was banished. Now a leaden square of sky overhead weighed heavy, pressing the air from the dismal enclosed space. Weeds sprouted from gaps in the cobbles and from the crumbling stones of the well. Any plant that grew here in the shade and the dirt was a desperate, blind and ragged thing.

Yet Jen had implied that Elias could secure their future in some way. In a world of vanishing options, this meeting was, at least, a chance.

Breathing deeply, Daniel stepped forward. Taking hold of an iron ring on the door, he knocked once. Immediately a grille slid back. A large bloodshot eye blinked behind the bars and the door swung open. When no spoken invitation was forthcoming, he stepped into a hallway. The door slammed behind him and he was enveloped in deep shadow laced with the scent of rotten wood and, surprisingly, good tobacco.

It took a moment for his eyes to adjust, but soon a panelled hallway revealed itself. Ahead a broad wooden staircase, the newel posts formed by huge carved grotesques, rose into the gloom. Looking up, Daniel saw square, heavily balustraded galleries that turned upon themselves as they climbed higher and higher. Candlelight glowed from the lower floors, but the upper storeys were lost in darkness.

He turned to the man who had admitted him. Squat, bow-legged and dressed in a coat as ill-fitting as his own, he had turned his back on the visitor and was now watching the courtyard through a sliver of the grille. Despite his lack of stature, the man was powerfully built with shoulders as broad as the door he secured. He was bald, but there were tattooed marks on the folded pink skin of his neck. A black-inked sun with many rays covered the dome of his pallid head. It was clear from the set of his broad back that he did not intend to waste words. Instead, he flicked a hand upward, indicating the way.

With no other option, Daniel started to climb.

Six closed doors lined the walls of the first floor. From their huge locks and sturdy construction, Daniel understood them to be former debtors' cells. He peered over the balustrade to the hall below. The bald man had not moved an inch. Hands on hips, he still faced the door, guarding the entrance like a one-headed Cerberus.

He returned his attention to the deserted gallery. From somewhere above a trilling woman's voice was answered by a deep male laugh. A door slammed and the woman's voice came again. Although Daniel could not hear words, her tone was gentle, coaxing almost.

He ascended to the next floor. In an alcove along the wall two young, well-attired men lounged on straight-backed chairs, booted legs barring the way. Their sprawling, muscular confidence was that of the dandy and the bully. Candlelight brought a ruddy glow to the half-empty decanter on the table between them and it sparked off the silver pistols laid ready beside it. The scent of brandy sweetened the air.

Lazily, one of the men leaned forward to take up a pistol. He cocked it and rested it on his knee, the muzzle pointed at Daniel.

'You the fighter then?'

Confused, Daniel shook his head. 'I have an appointment. I am expected.'

Ignoring this, the man turned to his companion. 'Don't look much, do he now? What you think?' His accent was closer to that of the islands than London. Daniel recognised the speech of his youth.

The other man shrugged. 'I'm not paid to think.' Although he too was black, this was a London voice. Taking up the decanter, he poured himself a brimming glass of brandy and settled back. He studied Daniel with little interest and waved a large hand glinting with many gold rings in his direction. 'Wait there for your turn.'

There was rustling from the stairs and the soft wheedling female voice came again.

'Would you like a jelly, kitten?'

Daniel looked up to see a woman and girl descending. The woman was wearing a dress striped with vibrantly clashing shades of red and violet. Her lilac wig shimmered with sparkling powder, which also dusted the fleshy mounds of her breasts. In contrast, the girl gripping her hand wore a modest white muslin gown, her dun-coloured hair tied back in a simple blue ribbon. Head low, she walked very slowly.

The woman tugged at her hand. 'You've been such a good little thing, I'm sure Mr Foljambe will let you take your pick of the sweetmeats when we get back.'

As they stepped onto the landing, the men hissed at each other. The child looked up and Daniel saw that her pretty face was as pale as her dress. The fingers of the hand that was not held fast by the woman drummed in turn against the muslin, as if she was counting over and over. She was younger than Pearl, perhaps twelve at most.

'Come along now. Don't dawdle, kitten,' the woman chivvied again.

She was of middle years, but time had not been her beau. Chalky powder sat heavily in the lines around her waxed scarlet mouth and darting eyes. Beneath the flamboyant dress and glitter there was something rodent-like about her.

She slid a cold appraising glance at Daniel and then she approached the men, dragging the girl in her cheaply perfumed wake. They pulled in their legs to let her pass.

'Master is pleased. Very pleased indeed. We're to come back this day fortnight.'

She lingered a moment and then Daniel heard a jingling thud on the wooden boards. From his position, he could not see what had happened but he guessed that a payment had been made.

The woman bent forward to retrieve whatever it was that had been flung at her feet. Straightening up, she pulled the girl to the staircase leading down to the hall. As they passed beneath a candle set in a sconce, Daniel saw that the child's large eyes were glazed with unshed tears.

His stomach twisted.

In New York he had known of establishments that catered to particular tastes. The clients were army officers as only they could afford to pay for their sins. The girls they used were the same age as Pearl and often younger. And like her, many of them were black. At his instigation, Major Fitzallen had tried to have these houses closed, but he was overruled by his superiors on the grounds that 'recreation', as long as it was discreet, was harmless.

It was the only time he and Edward Fitzallen had argued.

Daniel was not a saint. Although his heart would always, *always*, belong to Adanna, he had paid whores for their company and in some cases that transaction had become a friendship – but they were women, not children. Until this moment, Elias had been nothing more than a name, but as Daniel watched the woman lead the girl down to the hall, he wondered about the nature of the man he was about to meet.

The guard with the pistol leaned forward and looked into the shadowy throat of the house. His heavy-lidded, wide-set eyes narrowed as he watched the descent. When he was certain that the woman was at least a floor down, he spat into the air. Daniel saw a ball of saliva arc over the balustrades.

'Bitch!' The man turned to his colleague. 'You ever been to Foljambe's place?'

Raising the brandy glass, his companion gulped down several mouthfuls and swiped a cuff across his lips. 'Why would I? I have no taste for jellies – or mollies or children. That's what they serve there. If you ask my opinion on the matter, Mother Foljambe's worse than her husband. Unnatural, she is.'

The armed man grinned. Most of his teeth were gold. 'And didn't I just hear you say that you weren't paid to think?'

A handbell rang from somewhere above. Keeping the weapon trained on Daniel, he flicked his eyes to the staircase.

'Master's ready for you now.'

Chapter Fifteen

Two more guards were stationed at the head of the stairs. The men were built like dray horses. Although they too were armed, their presence alone was enough to discourage any thought of revolt. They regarded Daniel in sloe-eyed silence and then one of them twitched his pistol to point the way to a half-open door at the end of the gallery.

The scent of fine tobacco mingled with the faint trace of Mother Foljambe's sickly cologne. As he walked, that familiar prickle kissed the nape of his neck. Daniel squared his shoulders against it. Fear was the soldier's greatest weakness. Once doubt crept into the ranks it spread like wildfire, burning brighter in every heart until hope was obliterated. Battles were lost that way before they had even begun.

A door slammed below. Hesitating, he looked over the balustrade into the hallway four storeys down. He assumed that Mother Foljambe was now gone. The thought of the blank-faced child brought him to Pearl. Was that why Jen had been so evasive? Surely she would not intend him to barter his—

'Next!'

The command came from beyond a half-open door at the far end of the gallery. The aroma of tobacco was strong here, spiked with rum and cloves. There was something else, too. Beneath the scents of good living, there was the trace of something acrid and musky.

Daniel walked slowly to the doorway. A pool of light spilled through the gap, gilding the toes of Jerome's boots.

'Come.'

Pushing the arched door, he stepped into the room. For a moment he was astounded. Although he had not expected the 'King of the Rookery' to live like a beggar, he was not prepared to find himself in the most opulent place he had yet encountered in London, or, indeed, anywhere else.

Candles blazed in wall brackets and in gilded sticks set about a graceful octagonal chamber. Overlapping Turkish rugs made a crazy mosaic of the floor. Where the walls were not lined with books, paintings in ornate golden frames were clustered in groups according to size. In the furthest corner, a Chinese screen – the red lacquer and golden figures glinting in the candlelight – formed a partition before a curtained archway.

A man sitting behind a vast gilded mahogany desk looked up from a book and indicated a chair in front of the desk. As Daniel crossed the room, he was aware of being scrutinised. Once seated he returned the favour.

The man was of middle age. His long black hair – streaked with silver – was partly arranged to cover half his face. Tied with a length of black silk, it hung over his left shoulder in a fat gleaming coil. In the candlelight, his beaten copper skin glowed and a golden ring winked in the ear that was visible. It was a match for the jewels that were strung about his neck and stacked upon his long brown fingers.

Elias, for surely this was he, was dressed in a black velvet frock coat, trimmed with silver and pearls. The crisp white shirt beneath it was unfastened and the stiff embroidered collar of the coat strained across broad shoulders, revealing a muscular neck. Under the shirt and the golden chains, sinews pulled like hawsers.

Now he was close, Daniel saw why the man wore his hair in such a singular way. His left eye was sealed by a membrane of puckered skin, yet despite this disfigurement, his features suggested a weathered nobility. His appearance spoke of a lineage woven from the strands of many continents. It came to Daniel he was in the presence of one who was at once both something *more* and something *less* than a gentleman. Remembering Jerome's warning, he gathered his wits.

Elias closed the book and studied his visitor.

'I have been curious to meet Iphigenia's discovery and here you are.'

The voice was deep and rich. It rolled with the familiar rhythm of the Caribbean, sharpened by the edge of London. It was both beautiful and dangerous.

In the winter before the disastrous battle at Saratoga, the regiment had camped in the Hudson River Valley. Snow had begun to fall in November and never ceased. By January supplies were low and the men grew mutinous without meat. Daniel was charged to lead a party into the hills to hunt game. The first animal they killed was a buck deer. The shot was long and by the time they came to the carcass a mountain lion was tearing at the buck's flesh. Daniel had fired another shot to scare the animal away, but it was starving and refused to leave the kill. A pool of red spread around the creatures in the snow as Daniel raised his gun. Above its blood-soaked muzzle, the cat's golden eyes were defiant and deadly to the last.

Daniel thought of that beast as he sat across the table from Elias. The man's single eye was deepest amber flecked with gold.

'You seek my protection.' It was not a question.

Elias placed the book on a pile on the desk. A single word, *Voltaire*, was embossed along the spine.

'Those who come to me generally have no other option. Is that true of you, Daniel?'

Disconcerted by the casual use of his name, Daniel was caught off guard. He resented the man's condescending tone.

'I am no pauper. In time, I hope to establish myself. But for now—'

'Now you are destitute,' Elias interrupted. 'I hear that you were set upon by the Jarveys who took everything from you, including your breeches. Further, I understand that your remaining possessions are likely to have been sold by now at rag markets across the city.'

The man's patronising smile widened. Anger that had steeped within Daniel at the injustice of his situation simmered. Beneath the desk, he balled his bandaged hand to a fist and struggled to find a civil answer. He knew it would not be wise to provoke.

'You are mistaken. I have prospects and in time I expect to establish myself.'

He heard the words ring hollow. Aware of Elias's amusement, he swallowed and continued.

'I came to London as the heir to a good man, but I was tricked. While it is true that my current situation is not . . . as I would have hoped, this is a temporary condition. I *will* find a way to make things right.'

Elias arranged the lace that frothed from the embroidered sleeve of his velvet coat. The scent of cloves filled the space between them as he shook out the fabric.

'Then why are you here?' He spoke indifferently, without looking up. 'If you are so certain of your future, you do not need my assistance. Perhaps it would be best if you were to be escorted from The Maze this evening. You are clearly eager to establish yourself and I would not wish to stand in your way.'

Elias rose from his chair. He was strikingly tall. Candlelight sheened the black velvet of his coat as he reached for a golden hand-bell on the desk.

'I will ask my man to accompany you back to the tunnels and to make sure that you leave with . . .' he smiled again, '. . . *everything* you possessed on your arrival.'

At the jangle of the bell, one of the men from the landing loomed at the doorway.

'My visitor is leaving.' Elias's gold-flecked eye did not leave Daniel's face. 'You will go with him to The Maze, Cuffee, and there you will—'

'Wait!' Daniel hated the desperation in his voice, but The Maze was their only shelter – for the time being at least. He remembered Jerome's friend, buried with his wife and child in a pauper's grave.

'The truth was he could not find work because no one would employ or trust a freed black man.'

What would they do? How would they live? Despite the fact that every instinct sang out to him that Elias was deadly, he could find no other option. He needed time. Time to think, time to plan, time in which Pearl would be sheltered from the cruelty of London, until . . .

Until what?

Cuffee walked slowly towards him, but Elias raised a hand.

'I believe my visitor has something more to say. You will return to your post.'

When Cuffee had disappeared back into the gallery, Elias sat down again.

'Perhaps you have reconsidered your "prospects" and now find them wanting, Daniel?'

His voice was smooth and dark as the fabric of his coat.

'I want to hear you beg for my protection. It is the custom of the Rookery.'

Elias settled back into his carved chair, a look of enjoyment on his pitted face. Fury took control of Daniel's tongue.

'I have seen the custom of the Rookery for myself. The girl I saw leaving here just now with her keeper. How old was she? Eleven? Twelve?'

Elias laughed. 'Oh, brave Daniel. Did you want to protect her? Did you want to save her from a life of depravity?' His expression hardened. 'I *am* protecting her. She is an orphan, a foundling. I am paying for her education and for her board and lodging. She was not a virgin when she was taken in by Foljambe, her father had seen to that. The loss will affect her value, but she will, I assure you, possess many accomplishments. When the time is right, she will be auctioned to the highest bidder. The girl will benefit from that transaction, as will her keeper. And as will I. After that she will have a trade and I will have made a continuing profit on my investment.'

Elias shifted his hair to conceal his disfigurement.

'Tell me, what would you have me do with her? Should I return her to the streets where she would soon find her way to a more brutal version of the trade for which she is being carefully prepared?'

When Daniel didn't answer, Elias took up the volume he had discarded and flicked through the pages. For a moment, he seemed to forget his visitor, but then he spoke again without looking up.

'Of course, there is your dainty sister to consider. Pearl, is it? Dark, exotic but still innocent, I believe. Now, she would fetch a high price.'

'You go too far.' Daniel stood up so abruptly his chair clattered to the floor. It was just as he had feared. Jen had betrayed him – betrayed them both.

'You will not have her.'

There was a long silence.

'Then we find ourselves in a difficult position, do we not?' Elias snapped the book shut and whistled softly.

There was a rustle from behind the screen and then a ticking sound. A large spotted cat with a striped muzzle rubbed its head against the edge of the lacquered panel. It stretched and yawned, revealing a set of spiked white teeth and then, slowly, tail swaying from side to side, it crossed the room towards Elias. The cat was long and sleek, framed like a hunting dog. It prowled with a lazy grace. When it moved onto the rugs, Daniel realised that the ticking was the sound of its claws on the wooden boards. As it came closer, he understood that the faint but unpleasantly musky scent in the room was that of a captive animal.

'My princess.' Elias reached out to fondle the creature's head. It nuzzled his hand and butted its ears against the flat of his hand. He glanced across the desk.

'Infanta is a cheetah, a native of Africa. Like us she is far from home. When I found her, she was in the hold of a Spanish ship off the coast of Cuba. Her mother was weak and her three sisters were already dead. The animals were intended as a gift for a great noble in Havana. I took Infanta from the dark and the stench of death and now she is devoted to me.'

As if in answer to an invisible command, the cat turned to Daniel and narrowed her eyes. The fur at the humped base of her long neck rose and her striped muzzle wrinkled as she bared her teeth.

Elias plucked at her ears. 'She cares for no one but me. And she is loyal because she knows I saved her life.'

'Is that why you're showing her to me? Is that what you see your-self as, a saviour?'

Elias's hand stilled in Infanta's fur. 'Now, it is *you* who go too far.'

The cheetah and her master stared at Daniel, their eyes a savage match. Elias released his pet and she settled at the side of the desk licking her paws.

Steepling his hands, he leaned forward.

'You are in no position to judge me. You do not have a penny to your questionable name. You have nowhere to go and no trade to support yourself or your sister. You do not even own the clothes in which you stand before me. You are a poor strategist indeed if you do not understand the gravity of the position in which you find yourself.' He twisted a ring set with a huge red stone. 'However, I think we might come to an arrangement that suits us both.'

'Not Pearl.' Daniel stood his ground. 'I would rather beg on the streets than that.'

'She is irrelevant.' Elias waved a hand – a lazy dismissive gesture. 'If you agree to my terms, she will not be touched. Despite your pride and your insolence, I am prepared to offer you the protection of the Rookery. I offer it to your sister also without consequence or hindrance. I give you my word on this.'

'*When he affects the manner of a gentleman, he is at his most dangerous.*'

Daniel's neck prickled again. 'And what is your price?'

Candlelight glowed in the depths of Elias's single eye.

'It has come to my attention that not only did you fight the entire Jarvey gang, but also that you recently defeated William Sankey.'

'Who told you that?'

'I hear everything.' Elias shrugged. 'Sankey is a name. He has rarely been bested. His defeat at your hands has acquired a notoriety on the streets, although it seems that you were injured.' He pointed at Daniel's head.

'That was not Sankey.' Daniel raised his rag-bound hand. 'But this was.'

Elias seemed pleased.

'You favour the left hand?'

Daniel nodded.

'Good.' Elias fingered a golden coin strung on a chain about his neck. It glittered in the candlelight.

'Have you fought with your fists in contest, man to man?'

'A long time ago in America – in the army.'

'How many fights?'

'Six, maybe seven.'

'Why did you fight?'

The question prompted uncomfortable memories. When Daniel had first enlisted with the British army, the colour of his skin had set him apart. At first, he was the butt of jokes and a target for insults, but he had found a way to change that. He rubbed the bandage where the linen from Jen's underskirt pulled tight across his knuckles.

'It was a way to prove myself, to win respect. I suppose I

wished . . . to belong.' The answer was spoken mainly to himself. If Elias noted this introspection, he ignored it.

'Did you win?'

Daniel nodded again. 'Every time. But that's long past. It was not my fists that brought me to the attention of my superiors. I proved myself again and again to be the equal of any officer. I do not see what this has—'

'You do not have to see anything; it's what you can *do* that interests me.'

Rising, Elias crossed the room to a trestle table piled with silver- and glassware. Above it a strange decoration – a confection of tall black feathers mounted in a golden collar – stood at the centre of an ornate shelf. Taking up a squat brown bottle, he poured out a single measure of dark liquor, rum by the scent of it. Turning, he raised the glass to Daniel.

'You have my protection. I am happy to welcome you and your sister to The Maze and to St Giles. You will be presented at the next Tribute. Iphigenia will arrange it. In addition, I will make arrangements for your training. You will await my instructions.'

He made the low whistling noise again and Infanta pricked up her ears. Rising gracefully, she stretched and padded from the desk to his side. Black and gold, they made a strange and imposing couple. Murmuring an endearment, Elias scratched her ruff and the cheetah began to purr. The odd, high-pitched throb of pleasure was almost like the trill of a bird.

'I do not understand. You have not named your price.' Confused, Daniel stepped forward. The purring deepened to a growl.

Elias took a mouthful of rum. 'When Rafael Safardi arrives in September, I will win a fortune. He has won every bout in Portugal – the land of his birth – and now he is fighting his way across the Continent to London. A great deal of money will be wagered on the success of O Touro. Of course, we will have to find an apt name for you. Over the years I have found that success demands an element of theatre along with skill.'

He smiled at Daniel's bewilderment.

'I did not expect to find you a simpleton, but I see I must make it plain. You will fight The Bull.'

He raised the glass in a mockery of a toast.

'You will be my challenger and my champion; the champion of the St Giles Rookery.'

Chapter Sixteen

'It's not that bad. Truly, it's not.'

Pearl tucked an escaped coil beneath her plain white cap and turned slowly about to survey their new lodgings. The brick-arched space was similar in size to Jen's, but the chamber that had been assigned to them by Elias's man Cuffee was deeper in The Maze. It smelled of earth and brackish water. Light from the brass candle lantern in Daniel's hand brought a queasy gloss to the greenish walls.

'At least there's a window.' Crossing to the far side of the chamber, she gathered up her skirts and scrambled onto a jutting ledge in the stonework to examine a small grille set like a grimace at the top of the arch.

'No. It's not a window after all. I'm not sure what it is.'

'Take care. The stones are damp.' The candle flame quivered as Daniel raised the lantern to shed more light on the wall. 'What can you see?'

'Nothing.' Pearl jumped down. 'It's just black – a channel for air perhaps.' She wrinkled her nose and glanced at the fluttering light. 'Not fresh air, though. It smells foul and there's a draught. We'll have to block it or we'll freeze in the winter months.'

'We won't be here then.' Daniel gritted his teeth and turned away, unwilling for her to see his face. He placed the lantern on the stones at his feet, casting light on the deficiencies of the cracked and rutted floor.

'Do you think this room is bigger than Jen's?' Pearl's clear voice rang from the walls. 'I do.'

More than ever, he was grateful for her unfailing optimism and unquestioning trust, but the fact that this noxious cavern was now the only shelter he could provide hammered another nail into the coffin of his pride. If she caught any of his bleak mood, Pearl chose to ignore it.

'Look!' She darted back to the entrance. The jagged hole in the brickwork was shielded by a square of canvas. Metal-rimmed eyelets suggested its past as part of a sail.

'There's a sort of shelf here that we can use for crockery and such, almost like a dresser. And over there,' she pointed at a long niche set deep into the wall, 'a place for one of us to sleep. We can make another bed by the far corner where the stones are raised.'

Beneath the cotton of Jerome's cast-off shirt, Daniel's heart ached at her determination to make a home from a hovel. He watched her swipe a hand along the place she had designated as a dresser and was reminded of the old oak dresser in the Boston house of the Fitzallens. Elizabeth had been proud of its gleaming rows of blue and white porcelain. For an all-too-brief year – before Saratoga – it had been the home he could never have hoped to provide.

'Jen said she'd bring us some things.' Pearl turned to Daniel and smiled. 'And Sally said she'd let me have two or three dresses that don't fit her anymore. When she came back this morning she gave me this.' Delving into a pocket, she produced a small comb made of bone.

'Sally said all the girls at the theatre have them. They're gifts from admirers. It's a pretty thing. See.' She brandished it towards him. Above the teeth, flowers were carved into the bone. In the petals and leaves tiny colourful gems – paste – sparked from the light of the candle. It was a cheap trinket.

'What do you think?'

When he didn't answer she pushed the comb back into her pocket.

'I know this isn't what you want, Daniel. It's not what either of us imagined. But we have each other and at least we have a chance. When those men set upon you in the street, I thought you were dead. After that ... *anything* after that ...'

Shaking her head as if to dislodge the appalling memory, she came to him and took both his hands in her own. Her head was level with his shoulders, but when she looked up, he saw her mother in the shape of her eyes and the frame of her face. Sarah's determination was there too.

'Take Pearl and live. You two must live on for us, for our blood.'

Squeezing his hands, Pearl took a deep breath.

'I don't remember anything from the island. Or if I do, I can hardly make sense of it. Sometimes I ... I have a dream – a nightmare really – where I'm being hunted by dogs. I can hear them howling in the dark and I'm running, but the path is surrounded by flames. My feet are bare and the stones are hot and sharp underfoot. It's so clear and real that when I wake, I can smell burning and my eyes are wet with tears. Do you recognise that? Is it something that really happened?'

Daniel was unable to speak. He nodded, eyes suddenly blurred.

Pearl reached up to brush his cheek. 'When I have that dream, all I know is that I have to keep going because whatever is behind me is far worse than whatever lies ahead. *We* have to keep going forward, Daniel.'

'Think of the future, not the past.'

Jon's words came to him again as he looked down at Pearl's earnest face. In the soft light her eyes were huge. Twin flames flickered in their depths.

'You're right, we won't be *here* forever. But it's where we can make a start. In time you'll be able to claim our inheritance from that man and his wife. I know it, here.' Releasing his hands, she brought a small clenched fist to her heart. 'And in the meantime, I will do whatever I can to help support us. Jen says I can work at The Mitre and she'll watch out for me. Oh, don't look so grim, Daniel, I'll be safe with her and besides, we need to earn our keep.' She paused. 'That man who brought us here, Cuffee? He said that our first months will only be free if you win. What did he mean?'

Daniel thought about the paper he had been forced to sign before being escorted from Elias's room not two hours earlier. There had been no other option. In return for the protection of the Rookery, he had consented to the King's terms. Not only had he agreed to fight, but unwittingly he had entered a legal trap. While the signature dried on the page, Elias had sat back and rested a hand upon the book he had been reading when Daniel first entered the lavish octagonal room.

'I have learned a great deal from my rational companion here . . .' Elias had tapped his ringed fingers on the book's leather cover, '. . . the greatest misfortune is dependence.'

The rope of hair had fallen away from his disfigured eye as he leaned forward. The healed socket was dark and empty.

'Freedom is always an illusion. Your bond is set at four hundred guineas. For each bout you win, I will reduce that sum by twenty guineas. By my reckoning it will be five years before you can repay my kindness – if you are successful. My friends in the legal profession will uphold any case if you defy me. The Marshalsea is full of debtors, but most of them are milk-faced. It will not be difficult to return you to the islands as an escaped slave, leaving your sister alone and unprotected. Be in no doubt that under such circumstances she will be sent to Mother Foljambe for tuition . . . or to a similar establishment, perhaps one dealing in *exotics*. From this day forward, you and your sister belong to me. You will be watched day and night.'

Elias had scratched Infanta's head. The sound of the cat's pleasure reverberated around the room as he reached for the handbell. 'So, now you see, I am not a saviour. I am a captor.'

'What did Cuffee mean?' Pearl repeated the question. 'What do you have to win in order for us to stay here?'

Daniel rubbed at the bandage around the knuckles of his left hand and wondered what to say. At last, he gave her part of the truth.

'I have agreed to fight for Elias. In return, he will allow us to stay here.'

Her eyes widened. 'Does Elias have an army at his call – is that why he wants you?'

He shook his head. 'I'm to fight another man. A pugilist. If I win, Elias will win a great deal of money.'

Pearl frowned. 'Like before in Boston?'

'You remember that?' Daniel was surprised. He had taken care to shield her from such knowledge. 'I had no idea you knew about the fights.'

She shrugged. 'It was just after you joined the army. You'd left me with a woman who smelled of fresh-baked bread. She was like us. When she laughed her whole body quivered like a bowl of junket. I liked her.' Pearl concentrated on the memory. 'But the first time you went off, I ran away. She chased me through the camp, but she couldn't catch me. I heard men shouting your name and that's how I found you. I was so little you wouldn't have noticed me in the crowd. Patience – that was her name – tried to drag me away, but I wouldn't go. I wailed when the other man hit you and she hid me in her skirts. And she scolded me afterwards and told me not to tell you what I'd seen.'

Daniel smiled. 'Patience was one of the Fitzallens' servants and she was kind to us both from the moment I joined the regiment. She often gave me sweetmeats for you.'

'Little cakes soaked in honey.' Pearl nodded. 'I can almost taste them now.'

'And it was Patience,' Daniel continued, 'who introduced you to Elizabeth.'

'Yes! I remember that day in the kitchen. You were busy as usual and she was looking after me.' Releasing his hands, Pearl sat in the long niche she had nominated as one of their beds.

'Elizabeth came down to ask the cook about something and I hid under the table. I thought she was so very grand and I was frightened, but her dog found me. Do you remember Hector? He was such an odd little creature, but he took a liking to me, and Elizabeth said I could play with him.'

'She took a liking to you too that day.' Daniel sat down beside her.

'I miss her.' Pearl stared at the scuffed toes of the shoes that dangled beneath the hem of her dress. A mouse — eyes glinting like tiny diamonds — sprinted in front of them, following a crazy path between the broken stones.

'Do you think she knew about James and Caroline, how awful they are?' Pearl spoke softly and rested her head on his shoulder.

He put an arm around her, drawing her closer. 'Elizabeth hadn't seen them for years. People change. Besides, she thought that the Major would survive the crossing. She hoped that a skilled doctor in London might be able to help him. Even if she had doubts about James and Caroline, she believed Edward would be here with us.'

'I wish he was.' Her reply was almost inaudible.

'So do I, Pearl.'

They sat in silence watching their shadows bulge and flicker on the curved brickwork.

At last, she spoke again. 'What will happen if you lose, Daniel?'

He concentrated on her shadow. At first, he couldn't find an answer, but when the shape that was the dark mirror of Pearl turned to him, the silhouette of her delicate profile filled him with a fierce and furious love.

'I won't. I *won't* lose again. That's my promise to you.'

Huddling her tighter, he kissed the top of her cap.

At a noise from beyond the canvas hanging, they looked up.

Footsteps echoed on the stones outside and then a pool of cloth cascaded across the threshold.

'Welcome to the Rookery.' Jen grinned at Daniel's startled expression. She gestured at the muddle of fabric. 'It's all for you. And that's just the beginning. There's plenty more where that lot came from, and pots and crockery as well. None of it fine, but all of it serviceable. The Maze can be generous when it sees fit.'

She turned to Pearl. 'There's enough there to keep you decent in The Mitre, but I'll bring you something else for the Tribute. It'll be for the best. There'll be outsiders from up top there too and you'll be notable.'

Daniel stared at the heap of rags at her feet. Tattered sheets tangled with threadbare shirts, yellowed petticoats, creased skirts and coats patched with old repairs. *More charity.* He knew he should be grateful, but he could not find it within himself to acknowledge these gifts or Jen's cheerful welcome. The meeting with Elias had sown seeds of doubt about her.

He stood up. 'What is the Tribute? Elias mentioned it during our meeting today.'

Jen bent to sort through the clothing. 'How did you find him?'

'Dangerous. As I'm sure you'll know.'

Her hand stilled. 'I don't know anything except that he's given you permission to stay here. At least you're not on the streets.'

The truth stung.

'This chamber's bigger than yours,' Pearl cut in swiftly, her voice light and teasing. Daniel knew she had sensed his mood and wanted to avoid confrontation.

'Well, there are two of you.' Jen looked up from the rags. She winked. 'And your brother's not exactly a mouse, is he?'

But he was trapped in a hole.

Biting his tongue, Daniel stalked to the furthest wall. Pearl was right – the air from the grille was foul. He turned and watched them pick through the clothing. Jen seemed to be insinuating herself into their lives. Leaning forward to pull at something, her bodice gaped to reveal freckled skin beneath. Embarrassed, she clasped a hand to the fabric. Glancing up, she caught his eye and realised that she had been observed.

Daniel looked quickly away. There was something about her that troubled him. Elias seemed to know her well. Too well?

He pressed again. 'You didn't answer my question. What is this Tribute?'

Jen tugged at a ball of striped cloth. 'Elias has called a meeting of the whole Rookery for two nights' time – it's called a Tribute. You two have to be there now you've joined us.' She held up a dress and turned to Pearl. 'This looks like a good fit for you. Mrs Jenkin's girl has grown too long in the back for it.'

Daniel moved closer.

'What happens at the Tribute?'

Jen looked up. Her pale face flickered in the candlelight.

'You'll see for yourself soon enough.'

She turned away and continued to sort through the puddle of cloth on the floor, but he knew he had seen fear in her eyes.

Chapter Seventeen

The noise was faint to begin with, a low rumble like the sound of waves on a distant beach, but as they made their way along the passage the sound of voices – many voices – swelled to a roar. At a lantern-lit fork in the way, Jen turned and motioned for Daniel and Pearl to keep up. The arched ceiling pressed so low that Daniel had to stoop. Compressed into the tight space, the booming sound was almost deafening. Pearl, who was just behind Jen, paused to make sure that he was still close. She said something, but he couldn't hear and he could hardly make out her face beneath the brim of her large brown cap.

Jen veered left into another passage. They followed her for a few yards more until they emerged onto a wide stone platform at the top of a flight of steps. Grateful to straighten up at last, Daniel was astonished by the scene that opened below him.

The platform was high above a pillared cavern the size of at least two churches. The vast space was deep beneath The Maze. To Daniel, it seemed partly a natural formation of rock and partly something sculpted by expert hands.

Light from a galaxy of crude grey candles pierced the murky gloom, filling the air with black smoke and the stench of burning fat. The smell of cheap liquor was strong too, but it was preferable to tallow and the reek of unwashed bodies.

At the bottom of a twisting stone staircase cut into the wall, scores of men, women and children were gathered in the smoke-blurred space. Some sat on benches drawn up along makeshift tables. Others were gathered in shadowy knots beneath deep-set arches that lined the walls. From his vantage point, Daniel saw people drinking, playing cards or tossing coins as part of a simple gambling game. Although the cavern rang with voices, there was little laughter.

From the platform, Jen searched the crowd. Evidently, she found what she was looking for. Holding up her skirts, she began to descend the steep stairs.

'There are some people I want you to meet.' He heard her quite clearly. Away from the confines of the echoing tunnels, the sound of the gathering was free to rise and spread like the smoke that gathered like dirty wool in the vaulted crevices overhead. The blackened plaster bore witness to many such meetings.

He let Pearl go first and watched her negotiate the steps easily in breeches. Earlier, he had been angered by Jen's insistence that she should dress as a boy, but now, as he became aware of the faces turned towards them, he began to understand why the disguise was necessary.

Gathered beneath one soaring stone roof, the inhabitants of the Rookery were the lowest of the tribes he had yet encountered in London. He felt the rake of their eyes like bony fingers digging into his pockets.

As he made his way down the stairs, he heard an accent familiar from his days in the army. Several men he had fought beside were Irish, as fiery and wild as their thick red hair. The conversation rising from a clump of dishevelled men at the foot of the steps carried the same rhythm and passion. He scanned the rest of the crowd. Some were almost respectable in their dress and manner, but others were draped in rags and covered in sores, their bodies emaciated to a point just above starvation.

The most shocking and bleakly depressing realisation was that so many of the people gathered in the cavern were like him and Pearl – their skin a living collage of every shade that could not be described as white.

Jen waited for them both at the bottom of the steps. Signalling that they should follow, she turned and started to walk away. Daniel tapped her shoulder.

'Where are we?' he shouted above the clamour.

'Under the church.' She pointed upward. 'This place was found beneath St Giles's crypts years back. Some say it was a temple once, but not to a god any of us are on kneeling terms with.' She reached out to adjust Pearl's cap. 'Keep your head low and make sure this stays tight. There's plenty here who'll get ideas – bad ones – if they see you true.'

Taking Pearl's hand, Jen spun about, but her path was now blocked by a boy whose oversized coat trailed behind him on the stones. With its multitude of polished buttons, it was an oddly fine thing for such a scrawny, smut-faced scrap.

The boy stared frankly at Daniel and darted a suspicious look at Pearl before shifting closer to Jen.

'This 'im, is it? The man you found at the boundary?' He pushed a grubby hand through a cloud of black hair matted with grime. 'I heard he took on six of the Jarveys before he fell. Sankey too, at The Dolphin. And I hear that him and his sister ...' keen brown eyes returned to Pearl, '... have taken on old man Gudgeon's place. God rest 'im.'

Jen pursed her lips. 'News got wings, ain't it? You've clearly been a busy little bird. Eyes in the back of your head as usual.'

The boy grinned and tapped his nose. 'It's all here. I sniffs things out – that's my business, innit?'

'Well, business must be good if you can afford a coat like that, Sparrow. You look like a proper little prince.' Jen leaned forward and traced the tip of her finger down the glinting buttons. Daniel saw a faint flush spread across the boy's smutted cheeks.

'Get off!' He huddled the coat around him and stepped back. 'This comes from a gentleman, only where he's gone, he don't need it.' He scowled at the look on Jen's face. 'I didn't touch him. It's come to me in payment.'

'Let's hope you grow into it someday.' She peered over his head. 'If you're so observant, tell me where Octavian is tonight.'

Sparrow turned and pointed to the shadows beneath the alcoves. 'He's back there with Marcus.'

'I thought so.' Jen dipped a mock curtsey. 'We'll be on our way then, with your permission, sir.'

The boy slid another look at Pearl. 'Who's this?'

'New pot boy at The Mitre,' Jen answered without hesitation. Immediately Daniel knew that she had practised this story.

Sparrow examined Pearl and sniffed. 'He don't look like a pot *boy* to me.' He turned back to Jen. 'So, you're going to introduce this one, the fighter,' he jerked his thumb at Daniel, 'to the family.'

She nodded. 'Not me personally, but it'll be tonight.'

The boy grinned. 'I'd better pass word that he's here then. There might be a coin in it.'

Without another word he scuttled away into the crowd, the fine coat trailing behind him in the dust.

'Who was that?' Pearl pulled the brim of her hat lower and raised the collar of her coat.

'A nuisance.' Jen watched Sparrow's progress. 'I knew his mother. Poor Annie died a few years back. No one knows who his father was, but that's not surprising given the line she was in. He's not all bad.' The wry expression on her face was balanced somewhere between exasperation and affection. 'But that doesn't mean I'd trust him any further than I could flick a farthing. Come on.'

Moving in the opposite direction to the one taken by Sparrow, they rounded a table where a group of silent men shielded the dog-eared playing cards in their hands like flames from a tinderbox.

Beyond them, Daniel caught sight of Jerome kneeling before a small child. The boy's eyes were so purple and swollen that they bulged like plums in his tiny grey face.

As they came nearer, they heard Jerome talking to a rag-clad woman, presumably the child's mother.

'Bathe them with clean warm water at least four times a day. I'll send a salve to your lodging, but you must use it, do you understand?' The woman – hard-faced with grimy fingers that twitched at her sides – nodded sullenly. Grasping the boy's hand, she backed away. Jerome stood up and caught her arm.

'I mean it. Don't sell it for pennies. It's worth more to you, and to him, than that.' He lowered his voice and spoke urgently. 'If you don't use the salve, he will go blind.'

Daniel saw her eyes slip to the stones at her feet. Jerome watched the woman and child melt away into the mass of people. He turned, still frowning, when Daniel clasped his shoulder.

'The salve will be free of charge, but I do not think she understands its true value.' He spoke as if Daniel had been there all the time.

'Can the boy's sight be saved?'

'Perhaps. In truth, I do not know.' Jerome sighed. 'One eye is less infected than the other so that might heal, but only if she does as I ask. I know she'll sell it or swap it for a loaf of bread. A bad bargain when her boy's future depends on it.'

He studied Daniel through the smeared lenses of his spectacles. 'You agreed to his terms, then?'

'I had no choice.' Daniel glanced at Pearl. Catching the meaning of that look, Jerome nodded.

'I hoped that you might . . .' He faltered. 'Don't listen to me. I am tired. I don't know what I hoped for.' He slipped the spectacles from his nose. There was a pale band across the bridge where the frame had pinched the skin. Rubbing the glass, he peered sourly after the woman and child.

'I cannot force her. She must decide for herself.'

After a moment he turned to Jen, who was standing beside Pearl. It was unlike her to be so quiet.

'Do you understand what you've done?' Jerome replaced the spectacles and stared at her, his eyes very small and piercing beneath the glass.

'They had nowhere else to go. They needed a place. I just ... I thought ...' She shuffled uncomfortably beneath his stern gaze.

'What did you think, Iphigenia?' He gestured at the teeming cavern. 'That this was a refuge?'

'They haven't got a chance anywhere else, Jerome.'

'Look around you,' he hissed. 'As long as Elias holds court in the Rookery, none of these people have a chance — you know that as well as I. When we—'

'No!' Suddenly Jen lashed out. Daniel was certain that she was about to strike, but instead she put her fingers to Jerome's lips.

'Not here.' She shook her head. 'Not now. Please.'

Despite their intimate stance, Daniel sensed the chasm between them — a space haunted in the way that an empty room retains the presence of a person who has just departed. Recalling their conversation in the street, he watched his friend struggle with a depth of feeling that Jen did not share, or shared no longer.

Jerome looked away. 'I'm sure you did what you thought was best. I'm sorry.'

The short confrontation had roused some interest in the crowd, but Daniel saw that most of the attention was focused on him and on Pearl.

'I know what I'm doing.' Jen rested a hand briefly on Jerome's arm. 'I'm taking Daniel to see Octavian. He could be the one.'

Their skin was dark as Daniel's own, but the contrast between the two men in the shadowed alcove could not have been more marked.

One was almost birdlike while the other was built like an ox. In the half light, his shoulders cast a brooding shadow on the wall. The tiny man seated – perched would be more accurate – on a jut of masonry raised a twig-like arm in welcome. He was so small that he seemed almost lost in the vastness of his shabby, but beautiful clothes.

'Lovely Iphigenia.' He smiled and nodded at Daniel. 'And this must be the one we have heard so much about. The Maze is alive with gossip.' The man's voice was educated, playful even. Although his body was frail and painfully contorted, his face – a curious mixture of delicacy and strength – was handsome. As he examined Daniel, his eyes were bright with humour and intelligence. Without looking away he spoke again.

'It has been a while since you came to a meeting of the Brotherhood, Iphigenia. We thought . . .' He paused. Now he turned back to her, cocking his head to one side. '*Jerome* thought you had abandoned us.'

'He can think what he likes.' Jen was dismissive. 'Anyway, I've just been talking to him. He's gone to see about Jemmy Quinton's leg. Did you hear about that?'

'The accident with the dray?' The tiny man nodded. 'Let us hope that Jerome can help him – and his family. A bad business.'

He stretched his back and neck and shifted to a more comfortable position.

'Will you introduce us, Iphigenia?'

'It's why I came over here!' Jen pointed. 'Daniel, this is Octavian. It's time you met. And this,' she indicated the other man in the alcove, 'is Marcus. They live up top down by the garden end.'

Daniel was tall, but when Marcus detached himself from the wall, he towered above them all. Like Octavian, his clothes had once been very fine. He smiled but did not speak.

'And who is this?' Octavian glanced shrewdly at Pearl.

'His name's Barnaby. He's a new pot boy at The Mitre.' Jen

spoke very loudly. She looked about to make sure that she had been heard. Then she leaned forward and whispered, 'I thought it was for the best.'

'You are wise as well as beautiful.' Octavian smiled.

He stared past Daniel into the cavern, his gaze moving from group to group. The humour in his eyes faded to sorrow.

'*Terribilis est locus*,' he murmured to himself.

Although he did not understand, Daniel felt something of his meaning. He turned to take in the scene.

'Behold the court of the King of the Rookery.' Octavian raised a child-sized hand and made a sweeping gesture. 'If you wish to stay here with us, you must pay homage . . . and more.' He turned to Jen. 'What have you told him?'

'I . . . I thought it best if he saw for himself.' She looked away, unwilling to catch Daniel's eye. 'They say there's to be a trial tonight.'

'Then our new friend will soon understand.' Octavian nodded. 'Tell me, Daniel, what do you make of us?'

Daniel did not know how to answer. Truly, this was a desperate place. The men, women and children gathered beneath its vaulted ceiling were hardened by poverty, by experience and by despair. The cavern was a bustling market where all the goods were damaged.

'What do you see?' Octavian's voice came again.

'Outcasts.' A muscle in Daniel's jaw twitched.

This was what he and Pearl had become.

'I see those who live in the darkest shadows of the city, but I did not think that there would be so many people here like—'

'Like us?' Octavian interrupted. He twisted uncomfortably on the stones and Marcus bent to ease him to a new position.

When he was settled again, he looked up at Daniel. 'People *like us* have lived here for centuries, but enslavement has now made us invisible.' He smiled. 'We are, in the most literal sense, a caste aside. But we are not alone in our fall; the Rookery is full of those whom

London chooses not to see. Have you never heard of the Blackbirds of St Giles?'

Daniel shook his head. 'I have been here for barely a month.'

'Then let me enlighten you.' Octavian swept the cavern with a spindle-thin arm. 'Here we are flocked together. The lame, the sick, the maimed, the destitute and the abandoned. Many here have good, honest hearts; some have turned bad through experience; and some, I am sorry to say, were vicious from birth. Of course, not all of us are truly *black* birds; poverty has many shades, but we are all – as you rightly say – outcasts. And you and this young man . . .' he slid a quizzical look at Pearl, '. . . have come to join us.'

Before Daniel could find a reply, Jen rustled forward and knelt before Octavian.

'Will you make the introduction tonight?'

'I know nothing of this man.' Octavian turned to Daniel. 'Forgive my blunt speech, but it is a fact.'

'You know I can't bear his eyes on me and you'd do it better than anyone,' Jen pleaded again. 'Please. There's time before the Tribute.' She stood and plucked Daniel's sleeve.

'Tell Octavian how you came to be here.'

'There are other black men here who fought against independence as you did, Daniel. All of them disappointed. Did you find irony in the fact that you supported a tyrant against a peoples' desire for freedom?'

'It was my own future I fought for.' Daniel considered Octavian's words and saw an uncomfortable truth. 'Everything I did was for us.' He glanced at Pearl, who had shrunk into the shadows of the alcove. Huddled in a boy's jacket, she watched the squalid, seething crowd from beneath the lowered brim of the cap.

'And so, you were betrayed?' Octavian linked his hands together and rocked forward. His shoulders were hunched beneath the fine cloth of his coat. He concentrated on a pebble in the dust as Daniel concluded his story.

'James Fitzallen destroyed the will. I have no proof other than my word. The only men who can vouch for me are not likely to return within two years. And now my papers are gone. We have nothing and nowhere to go.'

'I ache.' Octavian raised a hand. 'Please.'

Marcus lifted him bodily from the jut of masonry. He cradled the tiny man in his huge arms for a moment, allowing him to stretch like a cat and then he set him down again.

Wincing as his twisted bones settled back into place, Octavian saw Daniel's concern.

'I was not always like this. Once I was a pretty ornament in a grand house. I was a pet, an amusing plaything. My master ...' the word dripped with contempt, '... dressed me in the finest cloth and taught me to read and declaim so that I might shine for his friends. He had ... a great regard for the classics.

'When I was not yet ten years old, he began to teach me other things. One night I resisted. He beat me so hard that he broke my spine. If it had not been for Marcus here, who was also a servant in that house, I would not have survived.'

Octavian placed his hand on that of the silent man beside him.

'Marcus had already been punished. When he was six, our master cut out his tongue for insolence. That night, nearly thirty years ago, he carried me here and we have lived as children of the Rookery ever since.' Octavian looked directly at Daniel. 'Is this what you want for yourself and the girl ... your sister? This is a wretched place.'

'What am I to do?' Daniel tried to swallow shame that rose like bile in his throat. 'I have no money, no family, no connections in London. Perhaps, in time, I might be able ...' He looked out into the dismal cavern and faltered, humiliated and unable to find any hope in a future that had already betrayed him.

'In time you will still be here. There are very few who fly free from the Rookery.' Octavian's cultured voice was gentle. He looked up at Daniel and an odd expression flickered across his face. Just for a moment, he seemed confused and then, shaking his head, he smiled.

'In your case, I may be wrong. I hope so. Perhaps it was providence and not Iphigenia that brought you to us.'

A single drum began to beat loud and slow. Instantly the hubbub of the cavern faded. Jen reached for Octavian's hand.

'It's time,' she whispered. 'Will you do it?'

The frail man nodded. 'If it is Daniel's wish.'

Chapter Eighteen

As the monotonous beat continued, the crowd at the far end of the cavern melted back to the walls and into the alcoves, revealing a square dais raised several feet above the stones. A black chair carved in the old style with rolled arms, clawed feet and a scroll-topped back sat at its centre. Neither had been visible earlier through the crush of bodies.

Daniel watched a thickset man mount wooden steps to light four candles – one at each corner of the dais. As the flames sputtered to life, he recognised him as one of Elias's guards.

When all the candles were lit, the man took up a position to one side of the platform. Folding his arms, he scowled ferociously at those who had not been able to shrink into the shadows. Through the smoke, Daniel saw fear etched into the faces of the silent men, women and children.

At a single blast from a horn, the drumming ceased and four young men armed with pistols and nail-studded cudgels sauntered from the back of the cavern. Arrogance and menace clung to them as cloth carried tobacco smoke. As they took up places around the dais Daniel realised that two of them were familiar from his visit to the house of Elias. Candlelight sparked off the silver pistols tucked into their belts and from the golden rings in their ears and stacked upon their fingers. One wore the skin of an animal across his shoulders. His hair had been shaved in jagged lines close to his scalp to echo the stripes of the pelt. When he turned to face the cavern, Daniel saw that he carried a red cushion on which sat the feathered collar he had seen in Elias's room.

The horn sounded again. All eyes turned to the platform. The air was filled with such a weight of expectation that Daniel imagined he could almost reach out and catch it in his hands. Suddenly, Infanta sprang from the shadows onto the dais. Her golden eyes narrowed as she gazed at the crowd. Unfazed, she yawned and stretched before prowling the perimeter of the platform, tail sweeping from side to side. Her claws ticked on the wood as she lazily measured the space.

At the third circuit, a yowl of delight signalled the arrival of her master.

Like Infanta, Elias appeared from the deepest shadows. Pausing to scratch the cheetah's head, he walked slowly to the chair and sat down. The long gown that pooled around his boots served to emphasise his height and muscularity. His fingers glinted with gold and the wine-red of his robe accentuated the multitude of jewel-studded chains draped round his shoulders. Just as before, his hair was arranged to shield the missing eye.

Resting his hands on the curved arms of the chair, Elias surveyed the silent cavern. Far from reducing the impact of this inspection, the single eye served to magnify his scrutiny. As his gaze moved from face to face even those in the deepest recesses seemed to cower.

It was a display of power. Now Daniel understood why Elias was called the King of the Rookery, and yet he also knew that this was a façade.

'Over the years I have found that success demands an element of theatre.'

He remembered those words as he watched the king survey his tawdry empire.

Confident of her territory, Infanta stopped marking the boundary of the platform and went to her master's side. Settling at his feet, she began to lick her forepaws. Elias ruffled the fur at the ridge of her neck, smiling down at his pet like an indulgent father. Without looking up, he snapped his fingers.

'Bring him.'

There was a scuffling from the direction of the stone steps that led down into the cavern. Everyone turned to see two more of Elias's guards dragging a bound man whose head and shoulders were covered by a sack. When they reached the platform one of the guards kicked the man's legs from beneath him and he crumpled, whimpering, to the dust.

'Tell them what you did, Zachary.'

Elias's voice was threaded with menace – a deep rolling tone, pitched to reverberate from the stones.

'Tell them,' he commanded again, but the prisoner curled into a ball. The whimpering rose to a wail.

Elias tapped his fingers on the arms of the chair as he stared impassively at the hooded man. He nodded to one of the guards.

Without a moment's hesitation the guard kicked the fallen man in the stomach. Zachary cried out. He lay still for a moment and then, dragging himself to his knees, he tried to shuffle away. It was a pathetic and dreadful sight. When Daniel glanced at the people around him, he saw that those who could bear to watch were careful to set their faces into masks of impassivity.

The guard went after the hooded man. Catching him by the hands bound behind his back, he plucked him up and swung him towards the dais, dropping him in front of the steps like a sack of flour.

It was unbearable. Daniel stepped forward, but someone caught hold of his hand. Jen stared up at him.

'Don't,' she mouthed, gripping tight.

Zachary lay motionless on the stones. His stillness and silence were worse than the wailing. Infanta stopped washing her paws and looked down at him. Her nostrils twitched and she rolled back her upper lip, exposing a row of tiny white daggers.

The guard went towards the fallen man again. He glanced up at the platform for instruction, but Elias raised a heavily ringed hand.

'If Zachary won't speak for himself, Carney will. Let him approach.'

There was a commotion as the crowd parted and a tall man clutching a hat scuttled towards the dais. His lank red hair fell below his shoulders and he walked in an ungainly way, veering from side to side as if his long thin legs found it difficult to keep to a straight line. Nearing the platform, he stepped carefully around the hooded man and bowed deeply to Elias.

'What would you have of me, master?' The man's voice was high and reedy like a broken flute.

Elias waved a hand at the crowd.

'Tell them.'

The man turned to the cavern. The skin of his face was raw and pockmarked, his pale eyes lost beneath a tangle of reddish brows. He held a battered tricorn hat between black-stained fingers. Daniel saw the prominent lump of his Adam's apple bob above the collar of his stained shirt as he swallowed.

'Zachary French is a thief.'

For a moment there was silence, then someone laughed. Within seconds, more laughter rippled through the crowd. Gradually it strengthened until the sound echoed from every corner and crevice.

Uncertain, Carney turned to look at Elias. His pitted face brightened when he saw that the King of the Rookery was amused. Bending double, Carney let out a bark and made a great play of hugging his baggy coat to his sides as he rocked with mirth.

Daniel recognised that hollow sound. In the army men had laughed loudest when they were scared. As he watched Carney and listened to the crowd it was desperation he heard. He turned to Jen, who still gripped his hand. She was staring at the stones. He looked over her shoulder to Octavian and Marcus; both were silent in the deep shadows of the alcove. Pearl had withdrawn to stand with them.

At last Carney straightened up. Wiping his eyes, he raised his hands for silence.

'Hear me out. Hear me out, I say. Zachary French is a thief.' He grinned, revealing crooked yellowed teeth. Flailing the hat in his hands as if to dampen a fire, he finally managed to subdue the crowd.

'And so are many here. I know that well enough. But there are different sorts of thieves, as I trust we all understand. Yesterday Zachary stole from *me* – from my premises in Goat Alley. My apprentice Ephra saw him do it while I was tending to a customer. He took three very valuable books that were marked for an acquaintance of . . .' He turned and bowed once more. Elias smiled.

Emboldened, Carney continued.

'You all know me. Vincent Carney deals in publications designed to satisfy the most particular tastes. The volumes Zachary took could be dangerous for me if the wrong type were to see them. And more than that, it could bring unwanted attention to the Rookery.' He paused before adding significantly, 'And that, my friends, would bring trouble to *us all*.'

'The skinny red fella makes a fine point there.' This observation was made by an Irish woman in the crowd. Murmurs of general agreement followed.

Comfortable with his audience, Vincent turned the tricorn between his fingers and grinned.

'Besides, two thirds of the payment for those books – and as I said, they were very fine pieces of art, created with great skill and attention to detail – was due to the King who cares for us all like his very own children.' He simpered at Elias once more, before facing the cavern again.

'What I say is this. Zachary French has stolen from every one of us.'

This accusation was greeted by stamping. Carney bloomed at the attention. Pulling his gangling frame to its full height, he waved the hat above his head.

'But it was a lucky thing that Ephra saw what he did and followed him. He took the books direct to a gentleman's residence in St James's.' He sniffed and looked at the man on the stones. 'Didn't you, Zachary? Why don't you tell us all about it?'

The hooded man was silent.

Carney turned to Elias.

'No matter, sir.' He tapped his head with a blackened finger. 'The current vicinity of those precious volumes is safely lodged here.'

Elias scratched Infanta's ruffled neck. 'Then they will be retrieved. Barlow . . .' he called to one of the guards. 'Take Cuffee and Smith with you later tonight. Do whatever is necessary.'

He stared at Carney. 'Give Barlow the particulars. You are dismissed.'

'Thank you, sir.' Vincent Carney contorted his bony frame into a cringing obeisance. 'And may I say—'

'You may not.' The King of the Rookery flicked his hand. Carney puckered his thin lips to a dowager's coin pouch and sidled back into the crowd.

Elias leaned forward.

'*Now* do you have anything to say, Zachary French?'

The battered creature curled on the stones keened again. A pitiful noise.

'Speak, man, don't mew like a woman.' The roar of contempt echoed from the walls.

The cavern fell completely silent. If there were vermin scuttling through the cracks in the stones, even they froze at the sound.

'I . . . I am sorry. Forgive me. It won't happen again. I give my word.' The stuttered reply was muffled by the sacking.

Elias smiled.

'Good. That wasn't so difficult, was it?' Now his voice ran smooth and rich as coffee served at The Black Apollo.

He stood and walked to the front of the platform. Infanta watched him for a moment and then she sprang into the empty seat. Alert and disdainful, she sat up straight, but soon she became mesmerised by the skeins of smoke weaving above the heads of the crowd.

Elias snapped his fingers and the young man wearing the animal pelt turned from his post. Mounting the steps, he knelt and presented the object on the cushion.

Daniel had wondered if it was a collar for the Infanta, but now he knew what it was. He watched Elias take up the golden band studded with tall black feathers and raise it to his head. In the candlelight, his crowned shadow fell huge across the stones.

'What do I ask of you?' His voice rang from the cavern walls and as one the crowd replied:

'Loyalty.'

'And what do I give you in return?'

'Protection.'

'What else?'

'Shelter.'

It was a litany. Daniel understood that all those present had responded to these questions before. He watched Elias raise his arms.

'What is there between us?'

'Trust.'

Elias nodded. 'And when that trust is broken the consequences must be borne.'

He pointed at the hooded man cowering before him.

'Zachary French, you have broken that trust and now you will hear my judgement.'

Daniel felt a jolt run through the crowd. Some melted deeper into the darkest corners, others pressed forward, their eyes alight with anticipation.

Aware of the moment, Elias paused and scanned the cavern.

'You will be taken from this place to the river. Your feet will be bound like your hands and your body will be weighted with stones. Your mouth will be filled with salt to remind you – at the end – of the bitter taste of treachery. Finally, your busy lips and your covetous eyes will be sewn shut, for they sinned against me and against us all.'

'Mercy. Please . . . I didn't mean . . .' Zachary attempted to crawl towards the sound of Elias's voice. Blind and wounded, he wriggled across the stones before finally bumping into the edge of the platform. He butted his head against the wooden slats and wailed.

'Great lord, I beg you for mercy.'

Elias watched him writhe like a worm in the dust and then he raised a hand.

'Take the traitor away.'

Two of the guards fell upon Zachary. Catching his feet, they dragged the wretched creature the full length of the cavern to the stairs at the furthest end. Losing control of his bowels at the last, he left a smear of degradation on the stones.

Daniel felt a pressure against his shoulder. Pearl had left the shadows and now she pressed her head against him. Pulling his hand from Jen's grasp, he comforted her, appalled by the silent sobs that wracked her body. He wanted to say something, to offer some words of reassurance, but it was too late. He knew that nothing could erase what she had seen from her mind.

The horror that had just played out before them had woken his own long-buried memories of the cruelties of the Garnett Plantation, but his greatest fear was that it might have unlocked a room in Pearl's mind too. He held her close and prayed he was wrong.

When Zachary was gone, Elias turned to his throne, for that was the nature and purpose of that great black chair. He hissed at Infanta, who jumped obediently back to the platform, and sat down. After casually arranging the fall of his robes and adjusting the rings on his fingers, he settled back and smiled.

'The law of the Rookery, my law, is absolute. Zachary is no loss. Besides, tonight, we are to welcome a new friend.'

Jen nudged Daniel's arm. He glared at her. How could she ever have imagined that this was a place of refuge? Every instinct told him to take Pearl's hand and lead her from the cavern, but it was too late.

Elias's voice rumbled again. 'Where is he? Where is my soldier, my pugilist?'

At this, there were murmurs from the crowd. Daniel heard the word 'fighter' and the names 'Jarvey' and 'Sankey'.

Jen stepped back. 'You have to go to him.' She spoke softly without looking up. 'It's the way of the Rookery.'

Reaching for Pearl's hand, she prised her gently from Daniel's side. 'I'll keep her close. Go now. You *must* do this.'

Pearl looked at Daniel and then at Jen. Her face was tight with anxiety. 'He will be safe, won't he?'

Jen stared at Daniel and nodded. He knew the answer was meant for him.

'I am waiting.' Reaching over the edge of the chair, Elias allowed Infanta to lick the tips of his fingers. 'Such a sweet, *innocent* creature. *Exotic* pets like my own dear Infanta are always desirable.'

It was a threat meant for Daniel.

'*There is your dainty sister to consider. Pearl, is it? Dark, exotic but still innocent, I believe. Now, she would fetch a high price.*'

He looked back to the platform to find Elias's eye fixed upon him. Candlelight glinted on a ruby the size of an egg as the King of the Rookery beckoned him with a twitch of a single ringed finger.

'Approach.'

Daniel stepped from beneath the arches and out into the light. The blackbirds flocked beneath the vaulted cavern rustled as they craned for a view.

Without looking away, Elias moved his hand to caress Infanta's tufted ears. The cheetah chirruped with pleasure and batted her head against the flat of his palm.

'It is customary for a new child of the family to be formally introduced. Who speaks for you?' Elias scanned the cavern.

Daniel was aware of a movement behind him. A moment later Marcus lumbered by, carrying his friend as if he were made of glass. As they passed close, Octavian brushed Daniel's arm with the tips of his fingers and whispered, 'There will be no going back. This moment will change everything. Is it what you want?'

Marcus paused. Over his wide shoulders, Daniel sought Pearl in the gloom. In her boy's clothes she was coltish, young and terribly vulnerable.

He nodded.

'So be it.' An odd smile spread across Octavian's face as he raised a hand – the gesture like a benediction.

'There is more to the Rookery than this, Daniel. *We* can offer you so much more. I promise that. Listen well, when I speak.'

For a second, the tiny man's dark eyes locked on his. Confused, Daniel watched Marcus place him on the lip of the platform, settling him with a delicacy and gentleness quite at odds with his giant frame. He stepped back and Octavian turned to look up at Elias, head cocked to one side.

'I will propose this man.'

'I might have known.' Elias rolled the chains around his neck between his thumb and forefinger. Bending forward, he spoke so quietly that only Daniel and Octavian could hear his next words.

'You are a pebble in my shoe, little puppet, but I tolerate you for the keenness of your wit and the elegance of your speech.' His eye slid to Daniel. 'You are fortunate indeed to have the most eloquent of blackbirds as your sponsor.'

Sitting back, he addressed the cavern in a lazy drawl.

'Octavian will make the address.'

Seated at Elias's feet, Octavian seemed like a doll. Taking a breath, he surveyed the crowd and then he began to speak in a beautiful, cultured voice that soared like a dove to the vaulted roof. The cavern fell completely silent, the savagery of the place soothed by his words.

'Dear friends, the paths that lead here are many, but all are strewn with rocks and jagged stones. When we bleed – and it is the same blood that flows in the veins of every living soul – no one weeps for we are the forgotten, the unwanted, the outcast, the hunted . . . the lame.

'Some of us barely remember the lands of our birth: the colour of its earth, the caress of the sun on our skin, the cooling rain, the scents carried by the winds. Neither can we recall the faces of our mothers or the strong arms of our fathers. Our past was taken from us, just as we were taken from those blessings.

'There are others here tonight who remember their birth lands only too clearly. For them the memories are not sweet, they are bitter. These are not the places to revisit in dreams for they are filled with nightmares. There are those among us who still feel the smart of the whip, the weight of the collar, the blow of the club, and we will always bear the marks of that cruelty.

'The Bible tells us that we must build our lives on faith, hope and charity. The Lord knows as well as you or I that these have been denied us. But He also tells us the greatest of these is charity. For the benefit of those here who are not scholars, in Latin the word charity is *caritas* – it means love.

'I put to you all that it is love, not charity, that sustains us. It is love that makes us strong. When you feed your neighbour, allow them to sit at your fire, offer them clothing, medicine or comfort, that is love. Above all things, love binds us and together we are strong.

'Tonight, I ask that we welcome this man, Daniel, to our number.

'Once enslaved, like many I see here, he fought in the Americas for the British Crown. He came here as a free man; a man of fortune and position, but he has been betrayed. Promises made to him have not been honoured. The rewards of the Crown he fought for are hollow. I know there are many here who feel that injustice, many who share that pain.

'Yet here we have found refuge. Here we build a life that is our own. Here we have … a freedom. Tonight, I ask that we offer Daniel those privileges. I ask that we give him shelter and welcome him as a brother.

'I ask humbly that we offer him our love.'

There was a moment of silence and then the cavern erupted with echoing cheers and whoops of approval. Hats were thrown into the air and the floor vibrated with the stamping of feet. Suddenly, Daniel was caught up by a ripe-fleshed blonde who planted a kiss on his lips.

'There's a proper Rookery welcome for you.' Twirling him about, she winked at Octavian. 'I didn't understand the half of it, mind, but you made a right 'ansome speech for a right 'ansome man.'

Kissing Daniel again, she spun him around in a dance without music. As he whirled, he saw that Elias was watching the crowd.

There was no love in his single amber eye.

PART TWO

A Dark Comet

From *The London Courant*

Who is She? That is the Question on the Lips of all London. Last nighte at the Drury, the lovely Lady M ... appeared in the Box of His Grace the D of C ... impressing those present with her Exotic style and Moste graceful manner. Forsaking all other Titled Ladies who have, hitherto, Enjoyed his Attention, the D was seen to Favour her company. It has also come to the ears of your faithful Correspondent that the D and the Lady later tooke Supper together at Vauxhall Gardens in a Private Bower.

Truly, this season, the Colourful Lady M ... blazes across our Drabbe Scene like a Dark Comet.

Chapter Nineteen

Melkie Trimm was a small man with dark, clever eyes and a clipped grey moustache that stretched from ear to ear. His hair was shorn close to his scalp, except for a plaited pigtail that dangled over his neat clean collar. Although his olive-green coat was not of the most fashionable cut, it was made from good cloth and fitted his compact, wiry frame in a way that suggested it had been made for him – and him alone – by a skilled tailor.

Taking a small leather pouch from his pocket, he filled the bowl of a clay pipe and lit it from the taper he extended to a candle on the desk. The bowl of the pipe glowed as he leaned back in his chair, closed his eyes and sucked in a meditative reverie. Occasionally he pursed his lips and allowed a circle of smoke to float up into the rafters of the training hall housed in an old warehouse by the Thames.

Good tobacco mingled with the masculine aroma of sweat and the faint but putrid tang of the river. The dozen or so men who had watched the trial were silent. Arms folded, they leaned against the slatted wooden walls and waited. Almost a minute passed before Mr Trimm opened his eyes.

'There's not many who can best Big Jake first time.' He waved the pipe at the huge man lying flat in the middle of a square marked out in chalk on the boards. 'You did well.'

Panting, Daniel nodded and went to retrieve his borrowed shirt and coat from a chair just beyond the marks. Before taking up the shirt, he rubbed his left fist. Although wrapped in thick material that Trimm had called a muffler, the final blow had probably hurt him as much as the man he had just floored.

Within the first thirty seconds of the trial, Daniel realised that his opponent was strong but slow. To begin with, he parried the blows, blocking the man's giant fists with his arms or body, but Big Jake had been relentless, lumbering after him with a determination that matched his solid frame. At last, he caught Daniel's right shoulder and knocked him off balance.

As he stumbled, the fury that had been simmering within boiled over. Staggering to his feet, Daniel turned again to his adversary. It was not Big Jake he saw now, but the King of the Rookery – the man he despised with every sinew of his being. Elias was the reason he was here. Elias was responsible for the pain that gripped his shoulder.

Raising his fists, he advanced again.

They were not evenly matched, but that was an advantage. After deftly avoiding the big man's lunges and darting beyond range, Daniel finally landed two head blows in quick succession. The first disoriented his rival, the second – a sharp, left-hand jab to the right temple – knocked Big Jake senseless to the boards. The bout was over in less than five minutes.

Daniel pulled Jerome's shirt over his head and went to his oppo-nent, who had now managed to draw himself up into a kneeling position.

'Here.' He extended a hand to help the fallen man to his feet. 'I'm sorry if I hurt you.'

Big Jake grinned amiably and waved the hand away. 'Get away with yer. It's what I'm here for. I'm Melkie's punch boy. Ain't that right, sir?' He raised a swaddled fist in a parody of a salute, stood up and ambled off to join the other men. One of them patted him on the back.

'None better, Jakey,' the older man called after him before shifting in his chair to face Daniel. 'I always try a new face with Big Jake to get a prospective of their mettle.' He blew another smoke ring into the air. 'There's many who'd be 'timidated by Jake. He's got height on you for a start and I'd hazard he's carrying at least thirty pounds more. But I liked what I saw. You've done this before, I reckon?'

Daniel nodded. 'In America.'

The older man stared frankly at him. There was interest, not judgement, in his keen brown eyes. 'Cotton or sugar?'

'Neither ... in the end. I fought for the Crown. I was promised a legitimate place here in London, but ...' Daniel stopped, bone-weary of his own story.

'It didn't work out?' Melkie Trimm offered.

'Not exactly, no.' Daniel began to unwind the striped fabric from his left fist. When his hand was free, he stretched out his fingers. 'I wouldn't be ...' Again, he faltered. He turned to study the hall around them. Now the trial was over, most of the young men had started to spar with each other within the bounds of the squares marked out on the boards.

The older man knocked the ashy contents from the bowl of his pipe into a brass tray on the desk.

'I believe you were about to say something like "I wouldn't be here if it had". Am I right?'

Daniel nodded.

Melkie shrugged. 'And somehow, you've fallen in with the King of the Rookery. I won't ask any questions and I don't expect any answers. It tends to be safer for all concerned that way. I'd trust this lot,' he waved at the men, 'most of them, with my dear daughter's life.' He reached to the collar of his shirt and caught a golden star on a chain between his fingers. 'But a badly placed word or a mis-understanding can lead a man to a midden of troubles. What I will say is this. It's a snowy day in hell when His Majesty sends me a good prospect.'

Elias's message ordering Daniel to present himself at Trimm's riverside premises had arrived the morning after the gathering in the cavernous crypts beneath St Giles Church. It was for Pearl's sake and hers alone that he had followed the grubby dark-skinned boy in the oversized coat – Sparrow, was it? – to the warehouse beside the Thames where men learned to fight from the old master.

Melkie Trimm unfurled the tobacco pouch and filled his pipe again. He sniffed. 'Has Elias told you why he sent you to me?'

'I've only spoken to him properly once.' Daniel remembered the meeting in Elias's opulent octagonal room. Compared to the gruesome theatrics of the previous evening, their first encounter now seemed briskly business-like – an interview for the position of a junior clerk.

'He said something about a fight with a man called The Bull. He wants me to be his challenger.'

'Does he now?' Melkie jabbed the stem of his pipe at the wall behind his head. 'That's The Bull. Calls himself O Touro in his native lingo.'

Daniel looked up at a large red-printed bill poster pinned to the slats. Although he wasn't close enough to read the words, he could see a crude drawing of an extravagantly bearded man with unusually broad shoulders. Legs spread wide apart and hands planted on hips, the exaggerated image was a challenge.

Melkie sucked on the pipe and continued. 'Rafael Safardi – that's his real name – has knuckled his way round Europe. He's won famous victories all the way from Lisbon to Amsterdam, via Madrid and Paris and a lot of other places in between. Now he's coming to London. He's issued a general challenge – well, his people have – and there's a lot of money to be won on the back of that game. Thing is, he's never been beaten.'

Without taking his eyes off the bill poster, Daniel frowned. 'Then why would Elias imagine that I could succeed where so many others have failed?'

'That's a good question. And when I was watching you earlier, I was asking it to myself.' Melkie spoke from the side of his mouth without removing the pipe.

'And it came to me, like a visitation you might say, that you could be just the right man. There are six things to consider. First off, you're light on your feet, but Safardi now, he's slow and steady. That can work to your advantage if you know how to use it. Second, you favour the left hand. That's always good, especially where The Bull is concerned as he swings right. Third, you're well put together. You have balance and your limbs are long. One might even describe you as graceful. You've got the reach, lad. Fourth – and this is not to be underestimated – you'll have the element of surprise on your side. No one knows you … yet. No one will have studied your game and I can be very sure my boys here won't report what they see.' He paused. 'Do you play chess?'

Confused by the unexpected question, Daniel shook his head. He knew of it; Edward Fitzallen had promised to teach him the complicated rules, but there had never been time.

Melkie raised a feathered eyebrow. 'You should. It's an old game, very old. And it's a game of strategy much like pugilism. Most people imagine it's all about strength, but that's not true. It's about thinking ahead; planning your moves in advance. Now, Safardi – he's such a big fucker he doesn't usually need to think much beyond the next punch, but that's where we might have him.' He stood up and straightened his shoulders. 'Look at me. I'm not tall and I don't carry weight like Big Jake, but twenty years back there wasn't a man – or woman for that matter – who hadn't heard of the pugilist Melkie Trimm. You're like me, Dan, you fight here …' He tapped the side of his head. 'Most often, that's where a bout is won. And that's the fifth thing. Taking all matters into account, I concede that Elias might be right. You *could* be the one to take on the Portuguese.'

'Are you saying you'll train me?' Daniel spoke eagerly, surprised by the sudden and overwhelming realisation that he *wanted* this. Even though he was coerced by Elias, the thought of working, training, doing something useful each day brought him closer to the man he had been before he had arrived in London. For the first time in many weeks, he would have a purpose, an identity.

If he had been inclined to self-examination, he might also have discovered that his very recent victory over Big Jake had brought him the greatest satisfaction he had known in a long time.

Melkie rolled his eyes. 'I thought you were clever. Of course that's what I'm saying. You need guidance, but I can see potential.'

Daniel grinned. 'You said there were six things to consider, but you've listed just five.'

'You'll have *me*.' Melkie sucked loudly on the pipe. The pale clay bowl was moulded as the head of a woman. Suddenly her hair glowed like a furnace.

Pearl handed Daniel a bowl. The stew was thin and although she said there was bacon in the pot, its most notable quality was its absence. But at least it was hot and savoury and there was coarse white bread too, which he was grateful to dip into the broth, imagining the chewy crust to be meat.

In the meagre light of two tallow candles, Pearl's shadow fluttered on the curved brick walls as she filled her own bowl and sat down on a stool. Daniel noticed that several items of furniture and more bedding had appeared during the hours when he had been away.

The stew pot bubbled over a small fire at the back of the chamber. Although smoke curled upward and blackened the bricks, it wound its way to the grille in the wall that they had mistaken for a window.

Their eyes smarted a little in the confined space, but it was bearable and the warmth was welcome.

'And you are to train with him?' Pearl chased something around her bowl with a crude wooden spoon.

'I begin tomorrow. I am to go every day except Saturdays. He says I have the making of a good prize fighter. He thinks I'll do well.'

'Of course you will!' She looked up. 'You can do anything you put your mind to, Daniel. I've seen it a hundred times. What is Mr Trimm like?' She frowned. 'Is he ... is he like Elias?'

'No.' He shook his head. 'Not at all. In fact, I got the impression he is no friend to the King of the Rookery.'

'Then why did he take you on?'

It was a question that Daniel had asked himself. The first answer that came to him was pride. If he won, he knew that Melkie Trimm would revel in his role as the trainer of the man who defeated The Bull, but he also wondered if Trimm was, in some way, caught like himself in Elias's web. After witnessing the barbaric trial beneath the church, he could easily understand the nature of Elias's power.

He watched Pearl take up a misshapen ladle to fill his bowl again and silently vowed that he would use everything that came his way to make a better life for her, for them both.

'I think there are some chicken bones at the bottom.' She stared dubiously into the stew before handing it back to him. 'I'm glad he accepted you. But it's not quite the same as choosing a path for yourself. Do *you* want to do this?'

Chewing a lump of gristle, he nodded slowly. 'Yes, I do.'

After the trial with Big Jake and the conversation that followed, Daniel had been invited to stay on at the warehouse to watch the sparring. He had spoken to a couple of the men and soon realised that the old pugilist was regarded with something between affection and awe. As he watched the training, Daniel understood why. Melkie was firm, sometimes alarmingly so, but he was also fair.

Behind the glowing pipe and those sharp brown eyes, he was a good soul.

He thought about him as he scraped the last nubble of bacon rind from the bottom of the bowl. He had found two people in London he trusted: Jerome and now Melkie Trimm.

'This was excellent.' He smiled at Pearl.

'It wasn't.' She snorted. 'It was horrible – the dregs of the day. But there is something else.'

Rising from the stool, she went to the niche she had chosen as her bed.

'Look!' She pulled back the blanket. 'A whole cheese! Jen gave it to me today when we were at The Mitre. Ma Rumney won't miss it – there are dozens stacked in the cellar. It's not stealing, Jen said it was more like fair wages. She gave me the stew too. It comes from the big pan they keep going all day.'

Daniel didn't answer.

Jen again. It was always Jen with Pearl. The young woman seemed to have a hold on her and now she was making her a petty thief.

If Daniel had looked more deeply into the matter, he might have discovered a flicker of jealousy beneath the simmering pot of his antipathy; after all, Pearl had never had a friend close to her own age. It is quite possible that he might also have found something even more uncomfortable, but he did not allow himself the luxury of introspection. It was not the soldier's way. Instead, he blamed Jen for the predicament they now found themselves in. If it hadn't been for her, they would not be living in squalor and he would not be Elias's creature.

When he thought of Jen, which was something he tried not to do because it infuriated him, he was confused. After the Tribute they had not parted on good terms. He'd accused her of leading him into a trap, which led to an escalation of insults. Their heated argument in the passages of The Maze had attracted attention and several of the women had emerged from their lairs to take Jen's side. Eventually she had turned her back on him and stalked away. Her final volley, tossed over her shoulder – 'It's time you thought a little more about your sister and a little less about yourself!' – had been maddening.

But was it also true? If she had not found them that day on the street, what would have become of them both?

He stared at Pearl, who was unwrapping the small round cheese from its coat of brown paper.

Today she was wearing a shapeless, high-necked, blue cotton dress and her hair was bound in a length of wide dull ribbon. She began to hum as she pulled at the paper, a pretty sound for such a dismal place. Far from soothing him, it made him angry.

Irritably, he jutted the spoon in her direction. 'I suppose that dress is another of her cast-offs?'

Pearl nodded. 'It's for The Mitre – good and plain. Jen says that's best.'

'It's best that you don't go to work there at all.' He could not keep bitterness from his reply.

Pearl glared at him. For a second, there was an aching family resemblance in the jut of her chin, the fire in her eyes and in her sharp reply.

'What else am I to do all day? Do you expect me to sit here in the dark, alone? If you can't see that I'm working for *us*, you're not as clever as I thought, dear brother. Without this . . .' she thumped the cheese down onto the table and gestured at the pot and the remains of the bread, '. . . we'd have nothing to eat. You didn't think to bring anything back, did you?'

Embarrassed by the truth, and by the echo of Jen's words, he turned away to stare at the fire. A moment later, Pearl knelt beside him.

'I'm sorry. That was unfair. But you've no reason to worry. Jen always looks out for me and I'm careful. Mostly I work out at the back where no one can see me. There's honour in The Maze, that's what she says. No one would dare come near me down here, but up top it's a different matter. This old thing,' she plucked at the high collar and grimaced, 'is like a shield. It's a disguise, like the clothes I wore at the Tribute.' She cocked her head, eyes glinting merrily in the candlelight. 'Do you remember all those times when you dressed me as a boy? I wore breeches for a year when you worked our passage to Boston.'

'That was a long time ago. Now you are ...' Daniel broke off and took her hand in his. 'You are *very* precious to me. If anything were to happen ...' He shook his head. 'Many years ago, I made a promise to ...'

'To our mother. Yes, I know.' Pearl stared up at him. 'I wish I remembered her as you do. I'm certain that if she could see what you've done, she would be proud.'

As Daniel stared into the sputtering flames of the fire his eyes began to water from the smoke. He wondered if Pearl was right.

Chapter Twenty

Days at the warehouse were long but rewarding. The sour lethargy that Daniel had begun to fear as much as the dawn diminished with each training session, and soon he found himself waking each morning with an enthusiasm and appetite for the hours ahead. Pearl was right: this was not a path he would have imagined or chosen, but for now, at least, he had found a place in this new world.

In the evenings when he returned to The Maze sore but satisfied with his progress, Pearl was waiting for him and so was a meal from her day at The Mitre. Mostly it was stew or something pretending to the name. Just occasionally she managed to smuggle back a mutton pie and once there was half a chicken. The broiled creature was scrawny and tough as an old leather bag, but Daniel remembered the rich taste of the grease he had licked from his fingers for several days after the carcass was picked clean.

He didn't challenge Pearl again about working with Jen. She had been right to rebuke him. How were they to eat when he earned nothing? And what was she to do all day while he was away? Grudgingly, he knew that she would be safe. In fact, he was almost glad to think that Pearl was with Jen during the hours when he trained with Melkie Trimm.

The old fighter was a harsh master but where a pupil combined talent with the ability to listen he proved to be fair, affectionate even. By the end of the first week, he had taken Daniel under his wing and into his confidence.

Melkie lived in the city above a tailor's shop with his wife Hannah and daughter Abigail. One day, when Daniel asked about the golden star that hung about his neck – an object upon which he swore often in fluent Anglo-Saxon – the old fighter explained that he followed, 'in a light-footed manner', the Jewish faith of his father and of his 'grandfathers' fathers'.

His name was a contraction and a confection. Trimm was taken from the first ever description of his physique and pugilistic style to appear in *The London Courant*:

Do not be Mistaken, Gentlemen, by his trimme Figure for this neat Challenger could certainly trimme the Hopes of the moste Experienced and Weighty Adversary.

The newsprint was yellowed and creased, but Melkie had produced it from the depths of his tobacco pouch with the reverence due to a holy relic. Although he did not allow Daniel to touch it, he had flattened it carefully on the little desk where a candle burned constantly to feed his pipe and allowed his pupil to bend close to read the tiny print.

'"Trimme". I liked that, see,' Melkie said. 'It had a cut to it; a swagger. To speak fair, it was nothing but the truth. And it was better than Drabkin.'

His true first name was Melchior. 'I didn't mind that,' he explained, 'but it had to be shortened to Melkie to fit on the bill posters when I was starting out, and it stuck.'

Melkie's approval meant that it didn't take long before Daniel was accepted by the other regulars at the warehouse. Most were ordinary men from humble beginnings eager to improve their lot. Just occasionally, the older man deigned to coach a gentleman or introduce him to a suitable sparring partner. They all knew what Melkie really thought about 'fucking amaturds', but a rich man's silver was always welcome where his person was not.

There were two fighters in particular whom Daniel was always pleased to see: Rowson, a former navy man whose arms and back were covered by extraordinarily detailed tattoos of women, ships and writhing sea creatures, and Musa. London-born, Musa – a former page – had been cast onto the streets at the age of eleven when he was discovered playing in the walled garden with the daughters of his master and mistress.

'We were chasing a frog,' he explained to Daniel. 'It made us laugh. But one of the housemaids heard us and told the steward. Then he told the mistress, who told the master. I don't think he liked the thought of his daughters playing with a black servant boy.'

Rowson reminded Daniel of the bluff, plain-spoken men he had served alongside in America. There was something solid and dependable about him. Although he was no strategist, he was a strong and relentless sparring partner. Melkie used him as he used Big Jake, to test stamina and perseverance.

Musa reminded him that London was a city of many faces, races and chances. Despite his past, the young man was charming and light-hearted. Daniel enjoyed sparring with him above all others, learning much from his playful, intelligent generosity. When they talked, it was easy to imagine the boy punished for daring to amuse those above his station.

The tiny bird distracted him. Trapped with no means of escape, it flitted between the rafters high above and then it swooped low over Musa's head to a patch of sunlight on the slatted wall, mistaking it for a window. It was a pretty thing, delicate with bright black eyes. The tilt of its head and its inquisitive expression reminded him of Pearl.

The blow caught him under the chin. Toppling backwards,

Daniel just managed to curve his shoulders and roll to prevent his skull cracking against the boards.

'What the fuck was that?' Melkie's contempt was loud. 'You left yourself wide open. Get up and come over here. You can take a rest, Musa.'

Gathering his body and his wits, Daniel winked at his sparring partner and obeyed the command. He knew what would come next.

The bowl of the pipe glowed dangerously.

'That was a fucking pig's breakfast.'

'I'm sorry. It was the bird.'

Wiping the sweat from his brow, Daniel pointed. The bird was now perched at the top of a beam just where the ceiling began to arch above a row of narrow shuttered windows. It fluttered its wings as it watched them.

'I don't care if it's fucking Queen Charlotte with her tits out. When you're in the game, you're in the game. Nothing else exists except you and the bugger you're trying to bring down. Do you understand me?'

Daniel nodded.

Melkie's moustache rippled with disapproval. He pulled the pipe from his mouth. 'Just when I was thinking how well you were looking there. You could have taken him down in another minute. Less maybe. Musa's good, but you're better. Usually. What do I always say?'

'A fight is won here.' Daniel tapped his head.

'Exactly. What were you doing looking at a bird?' Melkie wrinkled his nose. 'It takes a second, that's all. The other fella's searching for a moment when you're not thinking about him, not working him out and then he'll take you. Musa just did that to you. Never underestimate him. He's a clever one, too.'

'I don't.' Daniel shook his head. 'He's good. Very good. In fact, I sometimes wonder why you don't train him to take on The Bull. I know that's why Elias sent me here, but you already have someone. Musa's fast, light and, as you said, he's clever. I know *you* want to win as much as Elias – why not with Musa instead of me?'

Melkie was silent for a moment and then he jabbed at Daniel's chest with the end of the pipe.

'Because you have something else. Something more valuable.'

Daniel frowned. 'What? What do I have that Musa doesn't?'

The older man closed his eyes and drew again on the pipe. 'There were two things I liked about you when you came to me. One of them was the fact that you're gracious. You went to help Big Jake that first time. People will like that – especially the ladies. Mind you . . .' His eyes flicked open. There was an amused, appraising look in them. 'They'll like you, Danny.' He sniffed. 'That first time, I was sitting there watching you giddy around like a French dancing master and I got to thinking that maybe the King had sent me a pup. I won't deny it, I was irritated. There's no point in wasting my time, I thought, I'm not a fucking charity.

'But then, all of a sudden, a fire went off in your belly. I saw it strike like a flint in your eyes. Next thing I see is Big Jake flat on the boards. It was anger that put him there – your anger – and I thought to myself, you can use that, Melkie. Anger is a very powerful weapon if you know when to call on it.' He glanced over at Musa, who was leaning against the furthest wall talking to two of the other men. 'He doesn't have it. He's good, mind, very competent and all, but he's not angry. I reckon you got a rage in you, Danny, that's barely kept on the leash.'

Daniel scratched his head. He recognised a truth in the assessment, but it was a hard thing to hear, still less to admit to.

'You make me sound like a dog.'

Melkie shrugged. 'I make you sound like a winner. All the great fighters are angry. The trick is to know when to use it.' He licked his thumb and forefinger and extinguished the candle flame at his elbow. 'Gone. But I can bring it back whenever I want if I know what to strike.'

Daniel frowned. 'What were you angry about?'

'Life.' The older man shrugged. 'London's not a good place to be different. I've made a living and I'm satisfied with my lot, but I still hear the voices at the fights, especially if one of my boys wins. Thirty years back, it wasn't easy for the likes of me, even though I was born three streets from St Paul's – not that I've ever been inside. My guess is that it's not easy for you either.' He emptied the contents of his pipe into the brass tray by the dead candle without taking his eyes from Daniel's face. 'And at least I didn't stick out like a liquorice in a box of comfits.'

'Are you insulting me?' He glowered at the older man.

'No. I'm testing your strike points and I reckon I just found one.' Melkie winked. 'Go and find your friend Rowson and let him chase you round the square. Sailor Jim's getting lardy and needs the exercise. If he spent less time on his arse and more on his toes, he might win more often.'

Dismissing him with a wave of the pipe, the old fighter reached into a pocket for his tinderbox. As Daniel turned away, he heard the sharp chip of flint on metal. A moment later, the air was filled with the distinctive woody scent of Melkie's tobacco.

At the far end of the warehouse, Rowson was playing cards with three other men, the whale tattooed across the lower half of his back sagging over the belt of his breeches. Daniel suppressed a grin. Melkie was right, as usual: his friend was growing flabby.

He tapped him on the shoulder.

'We're to spar.'

'I just need to finish here first, Dan.' The former sailor allowed him a fleeting glimpse of a promising hand. 'There's a crown in the pot. Sit with us. It won't take long.'

While the men finished their game, Daniel studied the warehouse.

Melkie was now watching a bout between two of the younger regulars. The boys were skinny as tent poles, their prominent ribcages jutting over hollowed bellies. Neither showed great promise, but they were present most days and always went home with a hunk of bread and some cheese or a meat pie.

'*I'm not a fucking charity.*'

Daniel smiled and returned his attention to the game of Brag that Rowson was hopeful of winning.

'Don't you dare!'

He turned at the unusual sound of a woman's voice. Beyond the sparring bouts taking place in the chalked-out squares, he saw an unexpected flash of colour by the doorway, but two men blocked his view.

The woman's voice came again. 'No! I told you, get your greasy hands off me.'

Daniel stood and began to walk slowly back down the length of the warehouse. Although there was defiance in that voice, there was also fear. Most of the men had ceased their practice bouts now, their attention focused on the scene at the door. When he was closer, he heard low, threatening male voices.

'Outside. Or we can do it here in front of everyone if you prefer.' One of the men laughed unpleasantly. 'It makes no odds to me and I'm sure my friend here won't disagree.'

'Indoors, outdoors, in my lady's chamber.' The second man leaned forward. 'Pretty thing, ain't yer? Come here.'

Daniel heard a yelp.

The two men closed ranks and moved together to herd the woman back through the doorway. Now he saw who they were – Coppin and Lynch. He was not surprised. Of all the men who frequented the premises, they were the only ones he distrusted. Coppin was a sullen, slab-faced bully and Lynch was his weasel-eyed ally. Occasionally he had wondered why Melkie tolerated their presence. The only answer he found was that Coppin, according to Musa, was a faded champion.

'Can't you take no for an answer? Perhaps you don't understand the King's English – too many knocks to the head – is that it? Let me through!'

The voice was familiar. The men parted for a moment and Daniel saw Jen standing between them, her feathered hat knocked to a precarious angle. She pulled at the neck of her dress where the lace around her shoulders had been torn. Coppin caught her wrist.

'Let's have a look at the goods.'

The delicate fabric ripped again as Jen struggled to retain her modesty.

'Leave her!' The strength of Daniel's voice surprised everyone, including him.

Coppin turned. He grinned, revealing the one broken tooth at the front of his mouth.

'Want some for yourself, do you? Well, we saw her first.'

'That's right.' Lynch's small eyes glinted with malice. 'But we'll get her nice and ready for you.'

Striding forward, Daniel pushed between them and stood in front of Jen. He heard the rustle of her brightly patterned skirts as she backed away.

'Didn't you hear what I said?' He stared at Coppin, who scratched his thick, dirty neck. The man's pouched, mud-coloured eyes were threaded with tiny red veins and his broken nose spread like lard across his face.

'You going to fight me for her?' The scent of liquor was on his breath.

Lynch grinned. 'Why not? It's about time you took on a real man instead of dancing with Musa.' He jerked his head at Daniel's friend. Both Musa and Rowson had come to stand nearby. Musa flicked a look at Coppin and shook his head. A warning.

'You don't scare me.' Daniel balled his muffled left fist and cradled it in the palm of his right hand. He nodded at Coppin. 'I'll take you on, if that's what you want?'

'Enough! No one's taking anyone on.' Melkie pushed forward to stand in the midst of the men. Taking a drag on his pipe, he exhaled. A perfect smoke ring rose into the air to float above his head.

'If you want to continue at my establishment, gentlemen, I strongly suggest that you leave this young woman alone.'

He straightened his shoulders and stared up at Coppin. Although the man towered above him, the old fighter held the authority.

After a long moment, Coppin swore. Pushing past Rowson, he lumbered away. His companion twisted about, hoiked up a ball of spittle that landed on the boards at Daniel's feet and sauntered after him. When they had gone, Melkie plucked out his pipe and waggled it at Jen.

'D'you know her?'

Daniel nodded. 'She ... she's ... a friend.' From the corner of an eye, he caught a look that passed between Musa and Rowson.

Without looking at her, Melkie waved the pipe in Jen's direction. 'It's fucking stupid to bring a woman here.'

'He didn't ask me to come.' Gathering together the torn lace at her breast, Jen dipped a curtsey to Melkie. Daniel noticed that a single glossy ringlet coiled like a fat spring had escaped to her bare shoulder from beneath the skewed straw hat.

'It's not his fault, sir, truly it isn't. I've brought a message for him.' She glanced at Daniel. 'It should have been Jerome, but he was called to a sick bed and there was no one else. I couldn't send Pearl, could I?'

'Spit it out and be on your way, there's a good girl.' Melkie sucked loudly on his pipe.

'I won't take any more of your time than necessary.' Jen turned her attention back to Daniel.

'There's to be a meeting tonight at The Apollo. Octavian would like you to be there. He said it's important. I'm to take your answer back.' She moved closer and the scent of roses bloomed between them. 'What do you say?'

It had been a fortnight since he had last seen Jen. Their paths had not crossed since the night at the cavern. Although a part of him regretted his anger, he still had the uneasy feeling that she had invaded his life. As he stared at her now, he noticed the way the freckles across her nose and cheeks merged to bring a flush of gold to her fair skin. Today she had applied a little colour to her lips. Her dark lashes were so long that they cast a fringed shadow.

'Well?' she asked again, tilting her head a little to the side in question. As she did so, the tip of the feather in her hat brushed across the exposed dip at the base of her throat where the lace had been torn away. She was wearing a string of twinkling red beads.

Suddenly, he was aware of the attention of the men around him. For once they were all, even Melkie, uncharacteristically quiet as they enjoyed the exchange.

Ambushed by embarrassment and an acute desire for Jen to go, Daniel replied gruffly, 'Tell Octavian I'll be there.'

'Good.' She smiled. 'I'll let him know then.'

Still clasping the lace at her neck, she bobbed again for Melkie's benefit, turned and walked slowly back down the passage to the wide warehouse entrance where a shaft of sunlight made a shimmering rainbow of her skirt. At the last moment, the bird that had distracted Daniel earlier made a swooping bid for freedom, following her out into the cobbled lane running up from the river.

They stood in silence and then Melkie sniffed. 'That's two things that shouldn't have been in here today. Still . . .' he looked shrewdly at Daniel, 'she's a decent piece. You got yourself a nice girl there.'

'She's not my girl,' Daniel said with a frown.

'Isn't she?' If there was a smile on Melkie's lips, it was hidden by his moustache. He removed the pipe from his mouth and nonchalantly inspected the bowl. 'It's my experience that when a girl curls her hair, puts on a pretty necklace and dresses herself in her best to deliver a message, she's got aspirations.'

The air was suddenly close and overly warm. Daniel pulled at the collar of his shirt.

'I told you, she's a friend. No, she's less than that really. Jen's nothing to me . . . just an acquaintance.'

Melkie sniffed again. 'And I thought you were clever.'

'Was that your pox-riddled whore?'

The blow caught him in the small of the back. Daniel staggered forward, but then he twisted sharply and struck out just once. His fist caught Coppin square in the centre of his ugly flat face. The man swayed for a moment. His dulled eyes rolled in their sockets like chipped marbles and then he crashed backwards to the boards. Daniel stood over him.

'Jen is not a whore.'

Melkie bent to examine the fallen man. He prodded him experimentally with the toe of a polished boot, the fine leather figured in the Spanish style. Blood and mucus streamed from Coppin's flattened nose. He was out cold.

The old fighter straightened up. Before lifting the pipe to his lips, he nodded at Daniel.

'I think we've found another strike point, lad.'

Chapter Twenty-one

Pearl was absent when Daniel returned from the warehouse, but she had left a note on the rickety table – another item of furniture that had recently appeared – along with half of a small pie stranded at the centre of a battered pewter dish.

Her handwriting was large and untidy. Elizabeth Fitzallen's patient lessons had not been wasted, but there was still something childlike about her pupil's work. Daniel shook his head in fond exasperation as he took up the folded paper addressed to him.

As you will be away at The 'Pollo tonight, Jen has asked me to keep her company at The Mitre where there is a great deal of work to keep me occupied. <u>You must not worry for me</u>. I promise to be always watchful. Jen will be with me and she is the best friend I could have hoped to have found in London. Besides, I am very sure that you will find me in my bed when you return. The pie is oyster and kidney. I am sorry that it is so little.

The words that Pearl had underlined twice were easy for her to say, but not an easy thing for Daniel to do. At nearly sixteen years of age, she was no longer a child. She was developing a strong will and a notion of herself as a fully separate being that he found difficult to accept. Jen, however, seemed to encourage it.

He read the message again and tried to see it through Pearl's eyes. The thought of her sitting alone in this miserable chamber while he was at the ''Pollo' was almost enough to convince him that an evening working in the tavern was preferable. At least she would be with others.

Torn between vexation and a grudging feeling of gratitude that Jen had thought to look out for Pearl while he was gone, Daniel sat at the table and reached for the pie. It was rich and the pastry was good, but it was a poor meal after a day of Melkie's rigorous training.

Before leaving the warehouse, he had endured more comments and insinuations about his 'lady friend'. Even Melkie had joined in. It was a ridiculous notion. The best way to ensure that they forgot about Jen as soon as possible was to ignore their mockery.

Daniel thought about her now as he chewed, furiously, on a scrap of gristle. What was she thinking coming to the warehouse like that? Didn't she realise how foolish she had made herself look, and him too? What's more, she had almost tricked him into this meeting with Octavian. He had been glad to see the back of her – walking away down the passage, the sunlight slanting across the back of her patterned dress, the crimson bow tied at her neat waist and that ringlet of chestnut hair bouncing on her shoulder.

Cramming the last remnant of the pie into his mouth, he rose and went to douse his face in cold water from a cracked china bowl, before changing his shirt. As he passed Pearl's bed in the niche, he noticed a rounded lump beneath the blanket. The thought came to him that it might be another cheese and perhaps some bread too. It was typical of Pearl to play tricks. She had even hinted as much in her note.

'*I am very sure that you will find me in my bed . . .*'

His stomach grumbled appreciatively as he pulled back the blanket. It was not a cheese.

Adorned with feathers, ribbons and tiny jewels that glinted in
the candlelight, the dainty green headpiece was a pretty thing. The
scent of jasmine rose from the circle of tissue paper packed beneath
it. Pearl was not secretive by nature; there was surely an explanation,
but he frowned as the thought occurred that this might be a gift
from a customer at the tavern, an admirer.

'Daniel!'

Still frowning, he turned to see Jerome at the entrance to the
chamber. The apothecary smiled.

'I thought we might walk together to The Apollo.' Catching
the look on Daniel's face, Jerome adjusted his spectacles. 'You *are*
coming, I trust?'

St Giles was an ill-favoured place at the best of times, but at night
a sense of menace crept like a fog through the lanes and alleyways.
Every legitimate business and trading enterprise had closed its doors
and shuttered its windows and now the shadows were filled with
pinched faces and huddled shapes. Where light showed at a doorway or through grimy panes of glass, it served only to advertise the
nature of the transactions taking place within. When a woman, or
man, beckoned from the steps of one of these dingy buildings, the
goods on offer were corrupted.

Daniel remembered that the entrance to The Black Apollo was
hidden in a passage leading off the web of streets at the eastern edge
of Covent Garden, but as he had only been there once before, he
was grateful for Jerome's company.

As they walked, he listened to his friend's account of the patient
he had visited earlier. The man – a tanner working at Bermondsey –
suffered the most excruciating pain from a bladder stone the size of
a hen's egg. Several times in past weeks, he had begged the apothecary to remove it, but Jerome had refused. He was not a surgeon,
he explained, and quite apart from any deficit of skill, if it were to

be discovered that he had performed such an operation he would be deemed to have committed an offence.

'What did you do?' Ignoring the hiss of a woman from the shadows, Daniel kept pace with his companion.

'In the end I had no choice. He was in agony.' Jerome shook his head. 'Will could not afford a surgeon but without excision he would have died. Infection was already setting in. In Boston, the apothecary who took me on as his apprentice supplied several medical men, a surgeon among them. Occasionally he allowed me to watch him work. I have no fear of cutting living flesh, and no concern of betrayal – Will's wife is a good woman. No, my only fear now is that I may have killed him. I believed I knew enough, but now I recall what Mr Pope said of a little learning. It is, indeed, a dangerous thing.'

Jerome stopped and pushed his spectacles back to the bridge of his nose. They had come to a crossroads lit by a brazier. The firelight carved hollows in his face that made him seem much older than his years.

'But what was I to do? They have four small children. If he died of the stone then his family would surely follow him to the grave.'

Daniel remembered the handiwork of the army surgeons in America. The men called their rows of tents 'the shambles' because of the blood spattered on the canvas. He suspected that the brutal ministrations of the physicians were often more lethal than a bullet wound, but he could not believe that his friend would treat life in such a callous way.

'How was he when you left him?'

'I gave him brandy – lots of it – but the pain robbed him of his senses long before the liquor numbed his mind. I told Jemima, his wife, that I will come to him again tomorrow. If Will Carter survives the night, he may live. I pray to God that he does.' He peered anxiously at Daniel. 'Did I do the right thing?'

'I believe so, yes.' Daniel nodded slowly. 'You have given him a chance. The alternative was a miserable death. If he lives, you have saved more than one life.'

'And that will be payment enough.' Jerome smiled sadly. 'Truly, Daniel, I am not made to be a businessman.'

'But you are made to be a healer, not a pauper. Can they afford to give you anything?'

'Jemima takes in sewing. She has promised to mend my clothes.' Jerome raised a hand to reveal the fraying cuff of his black frock coat. The material was old and threadbare and the seam of the sleeve was split, but once – many years ago – it had been a fine coat. A glittering band of tiny black stones sewn into the fabric swirled and looped above his wrist. In the light from the brazier, Daniel saw that the collar and pocket flaps were adorned with similar elaborate decoration. For all its wear, this was not the coat of a poor apothecary.

Jerome smiled at Daniel's puzzlement. 'Two years ago, I was given this in payment by an old gentleman fallen on hard times. He was once a courtier and he told me that he had worn this coat in the presence of the King. It is the finest thing I possess – my only vanity. If Will lives, I will ask Jemima to mend it.'

The winking beads reminded Daniel of the strange discovery he had made in Pearl's bed. The unexpected arrival of his friend had interrupted an unwelcome train of thought with regards to the mysterious headpiece, but he returned to it now as the cracked bell of St Giles began to toll, its distinctive flat note ringing from the cobbles.

'Come. We don't want to be late.' Jerome reached out to Daniel's shoulder. 'I am very glad that Octavian has invited you to join us.'

The question of the hat was immediately replaced by another in Daniel's mind.

'What is this meeting tonight, Jerome? I would be glad to visit The Apollo again and I would be happy to see Octavian, but why would he invite me?'

The apothecary glanced warily at the shadows before answering. 'It is better if you see for yourself. I know there is something he wishes to discuss with you.' He frowned. 'Did Iphigenia tell you anything?'

'There wasn't time. She . . . she left the message at the warehouse door, that's all.'

Jerome nodded. 'It was good of her to go for me. She is a true friend to the Brotherhood. Come.'

As they walked on together, Daniel wondered why he had not told the truth about Jen's visit. Troubled by an obscure sensation of guilt, he questioned Jerome further about his patients.

The Black Apollo was quite different tonight. As Mr Richardson's boy Tolly led them through the crowd, Daniel hardly recognised the coffee house from his previous visit. Scores of men were seated at the tables and in the wooden booths lining the russet walls. More stood talking in animated groups while others craned for a view of the cards in the hands of those seated at tables in the centre of the room. Elsewhere, Daniel counted three games of chess under way in the booths, all of which had attracted knots of spectators.

Many of those present had removed their wigs, some of which had slipped to the floor. While the men's natural hair shone in the candlelight their wigs curled like cats on the boards beneath the tables. As Daniel followed Tolly, a small fluffy cloud with a flicking pigtail sailed past his ear. He turned to see several young footmen in identical livery taunting the unfortunate owner of this flying head-piece. Tossed from hand to hand, the wig eventually came to rest in the metal branches of a candelabra overhead. Luckily, its owner scrambled onto a table to retrieve it before it burst into flames.

Over by the hearth, two high-backed benches positioned to face each other were occupied by a sprawling group of handsome men who stretched their long legs out across the boards. Their chestnut leather boots glowed in the light from the flames. Two of them smoked long clay pipes and nodded as they listened to the conversation. From their clothing, Daniel recognised them as coachmen.

The atmosphere was warm and convivial, the air laced with tobacco and spiced rum. With a notable exception quite peculiar to the premises, Mr Richardson's patrons were as various in age, appearance, temperament and station as the customers of any London tavern.

Tolly held back a thick curtain to reveal a narrow flight of wooden stairs. The hubbub was so deafening that he simply motioned for Jerome and Daniel to go upwards, before slipping back into the merry chaos.

At the top of the steps, three doors formed a gloomy box of a landing. Jerome knocked twice on the left-hand door. After a moment, it opened a little and Marcus peered out into the dimly lit space. A smile spread across his craggy face as he recognised them. Standing aside, he ushered them into the room.

'Ah! We are almost complete.' Octavian's cultured voice welcomed them, although Daniel could not locate his person. It was only when Mr Richardson stood up to indicate their places at the oval table filling most of the room that he saw the delicate man. Octavian's wooden chair had arms and his frail body was guarded between them by a nest of cushions. He looked almost like a doll propped up in a nursery, although no toy could match the intelligence that sparked in his eyes.

Taking his allotted place next to Jerome, Daniel looked at the other men around the table. He recognised four of them – Octavian, Marcus, Richardson and the young man he had met the first time he had come to the coffee house.

There was one other – an older man whose mass of silver-streaked hair was barely contained by the black ribbon of his queue.

'You'll be the fighter then?' He grinned as he reached for Daniel's hand and pumped it up and down. The man was open-faced and large of frame with all the enthusiasm and finesse of a puppy.

'We've heard a great deal about you, lad.' He turned to Octavian and winked. 'If his grip is anything to go by, we have a champion in our midst.'

Octavian tutted. 'You have run ahead, as usual, Meriday. We have not even made introductions. Our guest deserves that courtesy.'

Admonished, Meriday seemed about to say something, but Octavian raised a hand to stop him and turned to Daniel.

'You know our host Mr Richardson, of course.' He gestured at the portly proprietor of The Black Apollo seated to Daniel's right.

'A pleasure renewed.' Richardson smiled broadly as Octavian continued.

'I believe you have already met Mr Ottobah Cugoano.'

Daniel nodded to the smart young man seated opposite. 'You were here with Mr Richardson when I came that first time with Jerome. You were discussing art, I believe?'

'You have a good memory.' Ottobah pulled his shirt sleeve from beneath the edge of his elegant cuff. There was a green stain on the cotton. He made a wry face. 'I do indeed work for an artist and my shirts bear the scars. Although today I have had the chance to work on pieces of my own. It is good to see you – this is also my first visit.'

'And we trust it will not be your last.' Octavian smiled at Ottobah and then he pointed at the man who had shaken Daniel's hand with great vigour. 'Mr Colly Meriday has already made free with your person, but I trust you will forgive his lack of etiquette.'

Meriday harrumphed and folded his arms in feigned affront. 'If it's manners you want, you'll rarely find them in an ostler.'

Octavian's eyes gleamed. 'Come, you diminish yourself, my friend. You are the proprietor of one of London's most successful livery stables.' He glanced at Daniel. 'And beneath that bluff exterior you will find a good soul.'

The sound of London was present in the speech of both Richardson and Meriday, but Ottobah had acquired a sheen of refinement.

'And finally . . .' Octavian pointed to a dim corner on the far side of the room by the door. 'May I introduce Mr Lemuel Darke, who joined us a few moments ago.'

There was a movement in the shadows. A tall man Daniel had not noticed arrive stepped forward to take the final seat at the table. He wore a long grey riding coat spattered with mud. The head that rose from the high-turned collar of the coat was hatless and wigless. The man's black, close-cropped hair emphasised the lean austerity of his profile.

Removing fine leather gloves, he nodded to Octavian, who darted a questioning look at the new arrival.

'I worried that you might not come, Lemuel.'

'So did I.' Darke's voice was deep and husky with tobacco. 'Let's just say there were some people I had to avoid on the way.'

Octavian grinned. 'Mr Darke is a journalist. They rarely have friends.'

He settled back into the nest of cushions.

'And so, we are finally gathered, Daniel.' His face hardened. 'Do you remember the promise I made to you at the sham court of the counterfeit King of the Rookery?'

Daniel nodded slowly. 'You said . . .' He tried to remember the words that had confused him. 'You said there would be no going back, but that you could offer me more. You asked if it was what I wanted.' He frowned. 'I did not understand what you meant.'

Octavian raised a twig-like arm. He encompassed the table in a sweeping motion.

'This is what I meant. Welcome to the Brotherhood of Crows.'

Chapter Twenty-two

After the introductions had been made, Octavian explained that there were others who attended meetings whenever their particular skills or contacts were needed. The group's full complement included clerks, tavern owners, engravers, stewards serving in prominent households (who were often privy to the conversations of their masters) and several long-established businessmen like Mr Richardson. Some of their number were women, and some were not black. Although the tiny man did not elaborate, Daniel understood that there were also members of this society who operated in what Octavian enigmatically described as 'the grey seas that lap upon the shores of the law'.

In the hours that followed, Daniel came to see that the men gathered in the panelled, smoke-filled room above Mr Richardson's coffee house worked covertly to rectify the injustices experienced by those whose skin set them apart. The interests and influence of the Brotherhood went further than London.

As he listened, he realised that the schemes hatched or discussed in the stuffy panelled room above The Black Apollo were part of a greater, ambitious vision. The Brotherhood dared to imagine a world where slavery no longer existed. That radical aspiration made them a threat to those whose vast fortunes were built on human misery, but more than that, it made membership of this secret society dangerous.

Daniel felt honoured by their trust.

The men in Mr Richardson's upper room took it in turns to bring an issue to the attention of the group or to pass on information. Their reports were uniformly bleak and riddled with cruelty and inequity, none more so than that of Lemuel Darke.

When Octavian invited him to speak, he took a deep pull on the long clay pipe he had been smoking.

'I will begin with the worst.' He set the pipe down.

'One of my ... acquaintances is employed as clerk to John Shoolbred of the African Company of Merchants. We have long known him and the business of that company.'

'It is slavery,' Jerome whispered at Daniel's side.

'My clerk has learned of a Guineaman which, last August, sailed from the Gold Coast to Jamaica with more than four hundred captives on board – twice the number it was designed to carry. Plagued by bad weather and navigational errors, that voyage took longer than expected and eventually water supplies ran perilously low. I believe that to be a lie.' Darke studied the faces round the table. 'I have it on good authority that there is doubt on the matter of the water. What there is no doubt on, however, is the fact that the crew cast one hundred and thirty men, women and children into the ocean – all of them living. All of them enslaved.'

There was a dreadful silence as each man present conjured the horror of that bald statement. At last, Darke spoke again. 'They were thrown to their death. It was a massacre.' He allowed that word to linger for a moment before continuing coldly. 'It has lately come to my attention from the same source that the vessel's owners had insured their cargo and now expect full compensation.'

'How can that be?' Daniel turned to Jerome, who had removed his glasses and was pinching the bridge of his nose.

Meriday snorted. 'I'm afraid you have much to learn of London.'

Daniel gripped the edge of the table. 'But how can a claim be made under such circumstances?'

'Too easily.' Darke stared at him. His angular face was a mask of fury. 'Many of us know that a higher price is paid for healthy slaves on the quays at Port Royal, but in this case, the journey had made the captives weak and diseased. How could they be otherwise after a dozen weeks in the stinking hold of a ship?'

He looked at the appalled faces round the table.

'Is it not obvious, gentlemen, that those people were worth more dead than they were alive? That is why the crew threw them into the ocean. Lack of water had nothing to do with it. By insuring their property, the owners of that cursed ship reduced those men, women and children to mere chattels. And now, *they* expect to be recompensed for *their* loss. It is monstrous.'

Ottobah rested his forehead in his long fingers. In the dim light, the green paint stains on the cuff of his shirt looked dark as blood.

'What can we do, Lemuel?' Octavian asked softly.

'The claim is disputed. There is to be a court case. I do not yet know when. Shoolbred is bound to be involved and my friend in his office has offered to make as much information available to me as he can without risking discovery.' Darke leaned forward. 'But know this: when the time comes, we must speak for our dead brothers and sisters. I can tell their story on the printed page, but that is not enough. We must ensure that this infamy is heard in every quarter.'

Octavian nodded. 'What is the name of that ship?'

'It is the *Zong*.'

'Then we will make it known.' Octavian nodded. 'We will pass this truth among our friends and we must make very certain that when, as you say, the time comes, that name will be reviled.'

Mr Richardson's boy Tolly deposited a pewter tray piled high with oysters on the centre of the table. It sat next to a dish of crumbling, heavily veined cheese and a large blue and white punch bowl. The briny smell of the oysters mingled with the faintly rancid stink of the cheese, the spice from the liquor and the smoke from Darke's pipe. Daniel's stomach protested, but not with hunger.

He and Pearl were but one generation from the horror of the Middle Passage. His parents could have been jettisoned alive into the ocean, as could have Adanna. Darke had moved to a new subject now, but the thought of that ship and the terrible fate of those men, women and children obliterated his appetite. Darke had called it 'a massacre'; another word for it was murder.

'Fresh from the market today, sir. The knives are there too.' Tolly nodded at his employer before leaving the room.

'She is like us.' Taking up where he had left off before the arrival of Richardson's boy, Darke tossed a printed sheet into the middle of the table. 'Read it closely and you'll understand.'

Richardson reached for the crumpled paper and squinted at the close-packed print.

'My eyes aren't what they were. I'll need more light to see it.' Silver buttons pulled at the embroidered fabric of his waistcoat as he stretched across the table for a brass candlestick. Placing it at his side, he peered at the article.

'Read it aloud, Inigo.' Octavian tapped the arm of his chair. 'If we all digested that piece in silence, we would still be here at breakfast. I cannot fault your hospitality, but I confess I long for my bed.'

'It will still take better eyes than mine. You do it, lad.' Richardson handed the sheet to Daniel. 'I'll warrant your sight is sharper than Jerome's. The man's a damned mole.'

Glancing apologetically at Jerome, who did not appear to be insulted by the slight, Daniel found the place marked on the print by Darke and began to read aloud.

'*Who is she? That is the question on the lips of all London. Last night at the Drury, the lovely Lady M . . . appeared in the box of His Grace the*

D of C . . . impressing those present with her exotic style and most graceful manner. Forsaking all other titled ladies who have, hitherto, enjoyed his attention, the D was seen to favour her company. It has also come to the ears of this correspondent that the D and the Lady later took supper together at Vauxhall Gardens in a private bower. Truly, this season, the colourful Lady M . . . blazes across our drab scene like a dark comet.'

He looked up. 'This is gossip – tittle tattle to amuse the gentry. Why do you assume she is like us, Mr Darke?'

'Because I know the true meaning of the words set down there. It is a code. Let me enlighten you.' The journalist reached across the table for the newsprint and read it aloud again, placing emphasis on several of the words. When he finished, he jabbed at the paper.

'The writer calls her "exotic" and "colourful". Not descriptions generally applied to the whey-faced beauties of the court.'

Instantly, Daniel recognised Elias's description of Pearl.

'"Exotic" alone would hint at debauchery,' Darke continued, 'although I think the writer here is referring to the lady's skin rather than her morals. That will come later, I'm certain. The word "colourful" is weighted with meaning that points the way to the clearest description in the last line.' He waved his pipe. 'She "blazes across our drab scene like a dark comet".' The prose is execrable.'

'I agree.' Octavian nodded. 'On both counts. The writer is a hack, but it is very clear that the lady is unusual. It is a rare thing for a man of our race to be taken up by society, but a woman . . .' He pursed his lips. 'It is unheard of. She could indeed be a useful friend, or at least sympathetic to our cause.'

There were murmurs of agreement around the table.

'Do we know anything of this mysterious lady?' Octavian gasped and shifted painfully in the chair. Jerome stood to help him, but Marcus was already at his side. Daniel was struck again by the

tenderness between them. The huge man tucked and folded the cushions supporting his friend with the gentleness of a mother soothing
a child.

Octavian patted Marcus's paddle-like hand and smiled up at him,
then he returned his attention to the newsprint. 'Do you know any
more, Lemuel?'

'A little.' Darke pointed at the print with the stem of his pipe. 'I'd
hazard that the gentleman is the Duke of Calne. He keeps a box at
the Drury for visits with his mistresses. There have been many of
them. The man's a notorious rake. The lady now ...' He shrugged.
'This piece only came to my attention this afternoon.'

'I think I can find out who she is.' Discreetly, Ottobah pushed
the pungent dish of oysters away. 'There are men who collect
butterflies and pin them in glass cases where they can admire their
beauty at their leisure.'

The table juddered as Richardson turned his great bulk to look at
him. 'It is a most curious thing to do, but I cannot see a connection
to the point under discussion.'

'Ah, but nevertheless there is one.' A sly grin spread across
Ottobah's face. 'As Mr Darke says, the Duke of Calne has enjoyed
the company of many women. And he has commissioned my employer Mr Cosway to paint them. There is a drawer in the dressing
room of Calne's great house in Piccadilly where the ladies he has ...
known are pinned to black velvet, just like butterflies. My master
has recently received a new commission ...' he paused for effect,
'... from the Duke.'

Octavian clapped his hands. 'Can you find out more?'

Ottobah nodded. 'In time. Cosway is much in demand, but I
always accompany him to Piccadilly to take note of the Duke's
instructions. He has particular requirements for works added to
his private collection and Cosway doesn't mind as long as he pays.
When the details have been noted, I am generally banished to

the company of the servants while the Duke and my employer seal the commission with a glass of Marsala. I have found Calne's servants to be both convivial company and extremely informative when it comes to the peccadillos of their master.'

'Good man.' Meriday ladled a fresh serving of punch into his glass. 'This is a mite heavy on the clove, Inigo, but the rum is good.'

Richardson took up his own glass and made a mock toast to the ostler. 'It's my own mother's recipe. I'll not change it a jot to please any but myself.'

Octavian stared into a corner where he appeared to see things invisible to the rest of the gathering. 'It would useful indeed to find an ally in the Duke's circle.'

'He's a good friend of the Prince of Wales, that I *can* tell you.' Meriday stood up. The boards creaked as he went to stand behind a screen next to the hearth. 'The pair of them have taken horses from my stables when they've been out carousing and have not wanted to be identified.' His voice came again from behind the leather panels as he relieved himself into an echoing porcelain pot. 'He's a wild one, Calne, and so rich that nothing can touch him. He wouldn't care who he had on his arm as long as all London talked of it.'

Meriday emerged, sat at the table again and reached for an oyster. 'Whoever she is, the Lady must have a rare beauty.' Taking a knife, he prised open the shell and tipped the glistening flesh into his mouth. 'Calne chooses his doxies as if they were thoroughbreds. Only the best will do.'

Octavian nodded. 'Then we must make it our business to find out all we can about her. Now, finally . . .' He turned to Daniel. 'I am interested to know what you make of us.' He smiled. 'Speak freely. You are among friends.'

'I hardly know what to say.' Daniel looked from face to face. 'It is a privilege to be admitted to your company and to know that you . . . *exist*. The work you do is honourable. No, more than that, it is wonderful and most needful. This evening has been a revelation and a cause for pride. You have shown me a world I have been unable to imagine since I came to London.' He smiled. 'Forgive my clumsy speech, but you have shown me hope. If you require me to pledge myself to your cause then I will happily take any oath.' He flattened his hand over his heart. 'You will think me naïve, gentlemen; when I came to London, I hoped for many things but—'

'You've been disappointed?' Interrupting, Richardson pulled the dish of oysters to him. 'You're not the first and you certainly won't be the last. This is a cruel city if your face don't fit it. Six generations of my family have lived here, maybe more. I'm a well-set man, prosperous you might say, yet there are still those who wouldn't allow me to cross their threshold.' He plunged a knife into a flat gnarled shell and began to cut with vigour. Flipping the oyster open to expose the meat, he pointed the knife at Octavian and then at Jerome.

'No need to give us your life story, lad. These two have already told us a great deal about you. We know you were a soldier in America and now you're down on your luck.' He pitched the moist gobbet of oyster flesh into his mouth and swallowed without chewing. 'I've no doubt that you'd make a fair speech, but to be frank, it's not your past that interests us. It's your future.'

'Inigo! You are as blunt as Colly,' Octavian admonished their host and turned to Daniel. 'I must apologise again, but our friend is right.' Tilting his head to the side, he regarded him with eyes as bright and dark as those of an inquisitive sparrow.

'How go your sessions with Mr Trimm?'

Daniel was confused. 'You know him?'

Octavian nodded. 'In his time, the pugilist Melkie Trimm was the toast of the city. He is now the most skilled and admired tutor in London. I also know – as do we all – that Elias intends you to fight Rafael Safardi and profit from your victory. There are not many who could take on The Bull and win.'

'I have no choice on the matter.' Daniel took up his glass. The scent of rum reminded him of his first meeting with Elias in that fine octagonal room. He gulped down a mouthful and felt its warmth curl down his throat to his belly. Richardson's punch was sweet and powerful.

'How does your game progress?' Octavian pressed again.

'I did not imagine that you would be interested in prizefighting.' Daniel's answer was sour. Instantly he regretted it. 'Forgive me, that is not because of your . . . because . . .' He stumbled, fearing that his words might have offered even more offence.

Clearly none was taken.

'I am indeed most interested.' Octavian smiled encouragingly. 'We all are.'

'Mr Trimm seems to think that I will do well.' Embarrassed, Daniel stared at the cheese. A crimped grey maggot wriggled from its crumbling surface. As he watched, a knife sliced it in two.

'Will you win?' Colly Meriday spoke through a mouthful of mottled cheddar.

When he was at the warehouse in the company of Melkie and the others, Daniel found it almost easy to forget why he was there. Now he thought of Elias's hold over him, not just the four hundred guinea bond, but of the threat to Pearl.

'*She will be sent to Mother Foljambe for tuition . . . or to a similar establishment, perhaps one dealing in exotics. From this day forward, you and your sister belong to me and you will be watched day and night.*'

Darke was right about the insidious meaning in that scrap of newsprint. He would never allow Pearl to be sullied.

He looked up. 'I can defeat The Bull.' Turning to Meriday he nodded. 'In answer to your question, sir, yes, I *will* win.'

'Good.' Octavian smiled. 'The St Giles Rookery is a foul place, do you agree?'

Bewildered by this change of tack, Daniel agreed. 'It is. But I, *we*, had nowhere else to go.'

Confusion was swiftly replaced by anger as he understood a new truth. 'It was you who spoke for me at the meeting, Octavian. Your words helped to make me a part of that place. Why did you do that? Surely it would have been better to advise me to leave.' He stood abruptly. 'From what I have heard this evening, you could have helped me. The Brotherhood could have helped us both.'

Jerome reached for his arm, but Daniel pulled free.

'Why am I here?'

The room was suddenly silent. All eyes turned to the man at the head of the table. After a moment, Octavian answered.

'The Rookery is a place of infinite despair. Those who live there are trapped into a life of hardship and poverty. Many of them are criminals, not by nature, but of necessity. Hope has died in their hearts to be replaced by fear. The King of the Rookery relies on that to ensure his rule. We ...' he gestured at the men around the table, '... have many brothers and sisters in The Maze. They deserve better, as do all those who pay homage to Elias. Now, his time has come. At last, we have found someone worthy to take his place, someone who will lead the Rookery in a new and better direction, perhaps even to a freedom that is true.' Octavian's eyes gleamed in the candlelight.

He raised a hand to stop Daniel from speaking. 'Let me explain. The people of the Rookery need someone to look up to, someone to follow. We know that in the past you have been a leader of men. Your promotion to the rank of lieutenant is extraordinary and tells us that you have already won trust and respect in the most unexpected quarters. Others have seen something in you, something that I too recognise. You are honourable – you have a nobility of spirit and person that cannot be learned. *When* you conquer The Bull, you will be hailed as a hero.' Octavian paused. 'People follow heroes.'

It was so absurd that Daniel almost laughed out loud, but as he looked from face to face, he realised that all the men gathered in Mr Richardson's upper room were in deadly earnest.

He turned back to Octavian. 'I have heard you speak. You are a true orator. I have seen the way they listen to you. You are more of a leader than I could ever be. Why not you?'

The small man smiled. 'Perhaps you have not noticed, Daniel, or perhaps you are too courteous to mention it, but this ...' he pulled his hands to his tiny concave chest, '... is not a form that inspires confidence. It is not the body of a challenger, still less a leader. Besides, there is more.' He glanced at Jerome. 'Tell them.'

Pushing his spectacles up the bridge of his nose, Jerome blinked hard. 'Surely it is not for me—'

'Please,' Octavian interrupted gently. 'A man cannot pronounce his own death sentence.'

'Very well.' Jerome took a breath. 'Octavian, our dear friend, has a canker of the spine. He is gravely ill.'

'Can nothing be done, 'pothecary?' Richardson's great jowls quivered.

Jerome shook his head. 'The condition is incurable.'

Seated across the table, Darke stared at Octavian and then at Marcus. He removed the clay pipe from his mouth and placed it beside his half-filled rummer.

'How long do you have?' It was the question in every mind, but the blunt journalist was the only man brave enough to ask it.

Octavian smiled brightly. 'I believe my friend's prognosis runs to months.'

The scratch of a mouse in the panelling was the only sound in the room until he spoke again.

'And so you see, Daniel, you have come to us in good time. To succeed against Elias, we must offer a credible candidate to take his place. We need the people of the Rookery to choose a better way and a better man. Who is more fitted to lead them than one of their number who is a true champion? For that reason alone, you *must* defeat The Bull.'

Chapter Twenty-three

'My lodgings are that way.' Jerome indicated the narrow street beyond The Mitre. Light from a single flaming torch bracketed on the side of the tavern made little impression on the gloom. 'I'll bid you goodnight then.'

When Daniel did not answer, he removed his spectacles and polished them on the cuff of his shirt.

'I hope you will forgive me for not telling you more. It was not my place.' He continued to rub at the glass and did not meet Daniel's eye. 'Octavian has searched for a long time to find a way to challenge Elias, but illness has hastened his hand. What you said about him was quite true. He is a leader, but in thought rather than deed.'

Richardson's punch swilled in Daniel's empty belly and sat heavily upon his teeming head. He had taken too much, but not enough to deaden the warning that had stalked alongside him since they had left The Black Apollo. In America he had often sensed, rather than seen, trackers sent by the Patriots. Ignoring the unwelcome prickle, he tried to focus on Jerome.

'How long does Octavian have?'

'Months, most likely. A year at most. I believe the canker is slow and has been with him for a long time. Perhaps it is the result of the harm done to his young body all those years ago. I have seen such injuries turn that way. Death has made him determined. He is certain that you can help us.'

'That is a thin strategy.' Daniel stared up at the sliver of moon that seemed to balance on the eaves of one of the houses pressing close over the street. 'If I defeat Safardi, what then? I have no wish to be the King of the Rookery, and even if I did, Elias will not give up his place. This isn't a plan, it's a dream.'

'You are wrong.' Replacing his spectacles, Jerome spoke quietly. 'Elias does not have the support of the Rookery. He rules by fear and that does not inspire loyalty or even respect. Octavian is a dreamer, yes, but he is also far-sighted – a visionary. What he has seen is a way to mount a successful challenge, and that will need a leader.'

'What if I refuse?' Daniel stepped back as a rat the size of a cat scuttled between them. Half its tail was missing and its coat was patched with sores. He barked out a bitter laugh. 'There goes one of my subjects.'

'It is not a jest.' Moonlight silvered the glass of Jerome's spectacles. Suddenly, Daniel's head swam with an image of the coins placed on the eyes of Major Fitzallen before he was sewn into a canvas shroud and buried at sea. He reached for Jerome's shoulder to steady himself.

'None of this was meant to happen, my friend. Before I left America, I was promised a name, a home, a fortune even, but look at me. If there is such a thing as fate, I believe it laughs at me. I am not a saviour, I am cursed. If you place your hopes in me, you will be disappointed. As I am.'

Behind the glass, Jerome's eyes were small and disapproving. 'We will not discuss it now. You grow . . . maudlin and need rest, but you must know that when the time comes you will not be alone. Octavian has worked towards this, he is pulling the strands together.'

'You are a pebble in my shoe, little puppet.'

Jerome's words reminded Daniel of the sour, whispered exchange between Elias and Octavian that night at the cavern. The potency of Richardson's punch was slow to reveal itself, but now questions battered like waves beneath his skull. He fought to marshal his words.

'Does . . . does Elias know about the Brotherhood?'

Jerome put a finger to his lips and looked over his shoulder. Turning back, he shook his head. 'If he does, he does not understand its true purpose. In truth, I imagine he despises our desire to seek the company of our own kind. He would see it as a weakness. That is why he has no fear of Octavian, although he should.'

'Why does Elias tolerate him?' Daniel forced himself to focus on the glinting glass panes of Jerome's spectacles. They seemed to multiply.

'There is no one in the Rookery whose mind is a match for Octavian's. Elias relies on him to read and interpret the documents of law and ownership connected to his interests.'

'Are you saying the King of the Rookery cannot read? I saw him with a book – Voltaire.'

'That was an act. He is barely literate.' Jerome's voice fell to a whisper. 'And he is ashamed of it. He cannot abide weakness, and that is his. He despises Octavian for his frailty, but his prejudice has blinded him to our friend's strength. Plans have been made. When Iphigenia told Octavian about you, he knew immediately—'

'Ah! Lovely Iphigenia,' Daniel interrupted. 'Jen – that's who you mean, isn't it? If it wasn't for her, I'd be—'

'Dead.' Jerome cut him off. 'Dead in a gutter, that's where you would have been. And what would have become of Pearl?' He paused and looked up at the moon. 'I am a man of science, but I believe that there is an order to the universe that cannot be denied. Fate led you to us.'

Daniel thought of the inheritance that had been snatched from his hands and burned before his eyes. Clenching his fists, he growled.

'Then fate has made another poor choice. If fate was here now, I'd—'

He halted mid-sentence. From the corner of his eye, he detected a metallic glint in the shadowy depths of a passage running alongside The Mitre, but this was no rat. He whirled about, his automatic response to danger honed and co-ordinated by years of army manoeuvre. His head was suddenly quite clear as he dragged a hooded figure from the darkness.

'Ow! Gerroff!' The voice belonged to a boy. It came again. 'Let go of my arm. You're hurting me.'

Pulling at the hood, Daniel revealed a thin dark face that was familiar. Jerome came to his side.

'Sparrow! What are you doing here at this hour?'

'Nothing.' The boy's eyes slid to the cobbles. 'I might ask the same of you two.'

'You've been following us, haven't you?' Daniel tightened his grip on the boy's arm. 'Why?'

'Because I gets paid to, that's why.' Sparrow wriggled and tried to break free.

'Who pays you to watch us?' Daniel dragged him further out into the street. Moonlight gleamed on the buttons of the coat that drowned his scrawny frame.

'I'm not watching both of you. Just you.' Sparrow jerked his head in Daniel's direction. 'The King likes to know where his investment goes of an evening. I'm paid to be his eyes and his ears. I've not done anything wrong, just kept a look out.' He stared up at Daniel. 'First time you've been out late, ain't it? They say the coffee at The Apollo is the best in London. Wouldn't know meself as I haven't been inside, even though I could, if I wanted to . . .'

Jerome glanced warily at Daniel and gave a small shake of the head.

'That's right, Sparrow. Inigo Richardson's coffee is excellent. I invited Daniel to accompany me to The Black Apollo tonight because he is my friend. When you report to your master, as I know you will, he will not be surprised to hear that after a day training on his behalf, Daniel sought convivial company in a place of safety and acceptance.'

Sparrow nodded. 'That's what I'll tell him then.'

The Maze was quiet. Where people were still awake, candlelight showed at the edges of the canvas sheets and patched blankets that served as doors. Just occasionally low voices echoed in the torchlit passages: a woman crooned a lullaby, a couple argued in voices squeezed by the confines of their lodgings, old men rattled out snores and lovers murmured endearments.

Daniel's head was heavy again, the sudden clarity that had come with danger now replaced by a dull, muffling throb. Minutes earlier he had watched Sparrow scurry away, his coat trailing behind him in the muck of the street.

'I've known him since his mother died,' Jerome had said as the boy disappeared into the shadows. 'There's no real harm in him. He likes to think he's important, but he's just a child.'

Daniel wished he was as certain of that as his friend. One thing was clear, however. The King of the Rookery *was* watching him, just as he had promised.

Turning the corner of the passage leading to the chamber he now shared with Pearl, he heard Jen's voice.

'... impressed her tonight. I could tell from her face she was pleased. As a rule, she keeps her cards close, but not this time.'

He had no aspirations for Pearl to be a tavern maid. Nevertheless, he was pleased to hear that she had acquitted herself well, and grateful to think that Jen was still with her at such a late hour. Pushing at the canvas, he stepped down into the stone and brick-lined room.

Jen was seated on Pearl's bed. The light of two tallow candles glinted on the beads and fine green fabric of the object in her hands.

She was talking to a plump woman who stood with her back to the entrance, but when she saw Daniel, her eyes widened in warning.

Immediately, the conversation stopped. Sally turned and smiled. Matching dimples appeared in her prettily rouged cheeks, but there was a wary look in her black-rimmed eyes. The women were alone together.

'I'd best get going. I'll leave you to tell him.' Sally's boldly patterned skirts – vibrant even in the dim glow of the candles – swirled as she moved past him. The sound of her footsteps tapping along the passage quickly faded away.

Daniel stared at Jen and a hundred horrible possibilities jostled for space in his head.

'Tell me what?' His throat was so constricted by fear and anger that he could hardly ask the next question.

'Where is she?'

Jen scanned his face and looked swiftly away. 'Pearl worked hard today and long into the evening too. I know how you feel about her being alone so I came back to The Maze with her. On the way we ran into Sally – she likes to talk, that one. Tongue enough for two sets of teeth, she has. Pearl fell asleep on her bed and we didn't have the heart to wake her. She's quite safe. I was waiting here to tell you so you wouldn't worry.' She swallowed. 'And now I have, so I'll be on my way.'

Still clutching the headpiece, she stood up. Daniel lunged for her arm. Richardson's punch made him more forceful than he intended.

'If any harm has come to her . . .'

Jen pulled herself free, but instead of backing away, she held her ground.

'Why don't you go along the passage to Sally's room and see for yourself? Your sister's sleeping like a babe and she deserves to. If you knew how well she did tonight, and all on your account I might add, you wouldn't dare . . . you wouldn't . . .'

Her eyes slid away once more. She was hiding something, he knew it. He forced her back towards the furthest wall.

'Tell me the truth.'

'I am. She's asleep in Sally's room.' Jen was not intimidated. The scent of her rose cologne filled the air as she stared up at him. Unsettled by her direct gaze, he looked away. Sensing an advantage, she continued. 'Pearl's a gem, but she reached her limit today. If you want to wake her up and drag her back here, go ahead. But it would be a cruelty.'

There was a rustling sound. Daniel turned to see that Sally had returned. She took in the scene from the doorway.

'I forgot.' She pointed at the feather- and jewel-encrusted band crushed between them. 'My head's a sieve. That's what I came here for in the first place.' She stepped down into the chamber and asked pointedly, 'Everything all right?'

'It's fine.' Jen smoothed her skirts as Daniel took a step back. 'He was worried about Pearl.'

'She's in my bed, lost to the world.' Planting her hands on her hips, Sally jutted her chin in Daniel's direction. 'And if you want my opinion, it does your sister good to have some friends looking out for her while you're away all day. A bit of female company doesn't go amiss. Now, about that bandeau.'

'Catch!' Jen tossed it across the room. As it spun through the air, flailing green ribbons brushed Daniel's cheek.

Sally clutched it to her generously scooped bodice. 'If you're sure?' She flicked a wary glance at Daniel and then at Jen, who nodded.

'Tomorrow then? I'll let you know what she . . .' There was a slight pause before Sally continued. 'Well, I'll tell you what's what.'

The metallic thread in the brilliant fabric of her dress shimmered in the candlelight as she twisted about and went back into the passage.

'Now do you believe me?' Jen took a step towards him. 'Or do you need to see her for yourself before you're satisfied? Pearl is safely asleep in the bed of a friend.'

'The bed of a whore!' Daniel growled.

The slap to the side of his face was as swift as it was unexpected. *'Jen is not a whore.'*

Remembering Coppin's vile insult at the warehouse, Daniel was immediately disgusted with himself. And the memory stirred other uncomfortable recollections from the afternoon.

Uncertain, he raised a hand in apology.

'Forgive me. It was Mr Richardson's punch speaking. That was—'

'A bleedin' insult, that's what. How dare you!' Jen's eyes blazed. 'Sally is no such thing. She's not so very different to you, although I very much doubt that you'd understand the similarities. She's an actress and you're a fighter. You're both paid to put on a show.' She prodded his chest. 'You're so prim and proper it's a wonder to me that you don't disappear up your own backside.'

'What was I to think?' Daniel caught her hand to stop her, his fingers completely encircling her small wrist. 'I came back here to find Pearl gone and the two of you discussing her.'

'Sally came for her bandeau, that's all.' Jen flicked back the dark curls that had come loose from the ribbon in her hair. They tumbled around her face and over her shoulders in wild and extravagant abandon. 'We got talking.'

Unable to hold her gaze, Daniel pointed at Pearl's bed. 'That's another mystery. I found that thing hidden beneath the covers earlier. What was it doing there?'

'Are you spying on your sister?' Jen tried to yank her wrist free, but he held tight.

'Why did she have it? Did a man give it to her?'

Jen's eyes flitted to the bed and then back to Daniel. 'If you must know, Sally lent it to *me*, specially. Pearl offered to dress it up. She was adding some beads and ribbons. Your sister's a rare seamstress.'

It was true that under Elizabeth's tutelage Pearl had become a skilled needlewoman, but the words didn't ring true.

'I've never seen you wear anything like that.' He frowned. 'It's very fine – a lady's piece.'

Twisting her hand free, Jen glared at him.

'Are you saying I'm *not* a lady?' The candle flames danced dangerously in the depths of her eyes.

'No. I . . . that is . . . You are not . . . you *are* . . .' He stuttered to a halt. They were so close he could smell the sweet muskiness of her skin beneath the scent of her cologne. Again, the space between them was filled with the heat of their bodies.

'When a girl curls her hair, puts on a pretty necklace and dresses herself in her best to deliver a message, she's got aspirations.'

Melkie's unwelcome observation leapt into his head.

Jen took a shuddering breath. 'If you must know, I was planning on wearing it to meet a gentleman.'

'Who? Who are you meeting?' The blunt question flew out before Daniel fully understood what he was saying. As it hung between them, its meaning unfurled and fluttered like a bright pennant in a breeze.

Reaching out, he wound the fingers of one hand into her dark curls. The other traced the contours of her waist, pulling her closer.

She wrinkled her nose, but she didn't push him away. 'You stink of liquor.'

'You smell of roses.' He tried to catch her hand once more, but she held it behind her back.

'They've got thorns, or haven't you noticed?'

'When you came to the warehouse with Octavian's message, I noticed . . .' Daniel faltered, realising with a clarity that fought through the effect of the strong rum punch that her unexpected appearance earlier had delivered a different kind of despatch.

'I'm sorry.' He stepped back. 'You should go.'

Jen stared up at him, her blue eyes suddenly very dark.

'Is that another order?'

He looked away, but she reached up and caught his face in her hands.

'Kiss me.'

Unable to resist, he obeyed her.

Chapter Twenty-four

Half awake, Daniel took in the faint scent of roses. Grinning, he turned in the muddle of sheets to wrap Jen in his arms again, but she was gone. Only the ghost of her cologne lingered now. Disappointed, he frowned and murmured her name. Suddenly, comprehension and memory shot through him like a bolt of lightning. Sitting up so sharply he bumped his head against the wall, he looked around the chamber.

A fresh candle burned on the table and a small fire had been lit. Tendrils of smoke wound upward to escape through the grille in the wall. The clothes he'd been wearing last night were not scattered around the narrow bed now, but gathered into a neat pile on a chair. The dress, petticoat and stiffly boned bodice that had been shed along with them were gone, along with their owner.

But his senses were full of her. Along with rose, he could smell Jen's skin, taste it almost. The scent of her hair enveloped him. He could still feel her body pressed close, her mouth on his.

He looked to the niche where Pearl slept. For a moment, he was relieved it was empty and then he was ashamed to have forgotten her so easily and so completely. If she had returned and found him with Jen, what would she have felt? Freeing his legs from the sheets, he sat on the side of the low wooden box that formed his bed and cradled his head in his hands. Pearl's feelings on the matter were one thing, but what of his own?

There had been women since Adanna, but none of them had
made him feel quite like this. He had always believed that his capacity to love another as he had loved her had died that night at the
Garnett Plantation. The truth was that he had never felt worthy of
another. He had punished himself for betraying Adanna by making
quite sure that no one ever took her place. But now ...

A bell rang in the passage beyond. Daniel heard the shuffle of
steps and then the waker's cry.

'Five of the clock. Five of the clock.'

It was the same every morning. In return for stale bread and the
occasional coin, an old man whose coat stank of poverty and piss
patrolled the passages with his bell and his dog to call The Maze to
a new day. Those who had work often had to leave before sunrise.
Above the dingy passages, there were ovens to be filled, pots to
scour, hearths to be tended.

Jen had tidied his clothes, lit candles and set the fire before she
left. Suddenly he felt naked and exposed in a way that had never
troubled him before. He stood and went to the chair to pull on his
breeches and shirt. Jerome's coat tumbled from the pile to the stones.
He stared at it for a long moment, before taking it up and hanging
it carefully over the back of the chair.

Next, he splashed water onto his face, rubbing it into his neck and
into his hair to sharpen his wits. If he had hoped to wash Jen from
his mind, he was unsuccessful. Reaching to refill the bowl with stale
water from a china jug, he caught sight of a red silk question mark
curled on the stones at the foot of his makeshift bed. Jen's ribbon.

'Daniel!'

Pearl's greeting echoed from the barrelled ceiling and her shoes
clattered on the steps at the entrance to the chamber. Swiftly he
took up the ribbon and pushed it into a pocket of his breeches. He
turned and smiled, hoping his guilt – *was that what he felt?* – was
not apparent.

'I came as soon as I heard the waker.' She nodded at the candles and the fire. 'But I see that I needn't have worried. Look here ...' She set a cloth bundle on the table. 'Jen came to Sally's room a little while back, just after the waker passed. She gave me these.'

The scent of fresh baking rose into the air as she peeled back the cloth. 'They're still warm. Sally took a couple, but there were half a dozen. Jen said I should bring some to you.'

Pearl handed him a golden, currant-studded bun and took one for herself. Tearing it apart, she crammed a chunk into her mouth. 'Delicious. Try it.'

Daniel watched her loosen the old patched cloak around her shoulders with one hand. Beneath it, she wore her usual dull work dress – frayed at the cuffs and stained with London mud at the hem. Kicking off her scuffed shoes, she sat on her bed and attacked the rest of the bun.

'I'm so hungry this morning.' Grinning up at him, she continued between mouthfuls. 'I didn't even realise until I woke up that I'd fallen asleep in Sally's room, but Jen said she'd told you I was safe. Oh, these are so good!' She reached for a second bun. 'If you don't eat your share immediately, Daniel, I swear I will. It was very kind of her to think of me – to think of us both. Jen said to tell you it's to keep your strength up. You're going to the warehouse again today, aren't you?'

He nodded. Wondering what more to say, he tore the bun in two. The spiced dough was sweet and warm. The dusting of sugared flour coated his fingers as he raised it to his mouth.

'How was your evening?' Pearl tucked her feet beneath her skirt and leaned back against the wall. 'I want to hear all about it.'

'You've got a furnace in your belly this morning.' Melkie prodded the tattooed arm of the man stretched out at Daniel's feet with the finely worked toe of a Spanish leather boot.

'Get up, Rowson. He's winded you, that's all.'

When there was no response, the old fighter clamped the pipe between his teeth and stomped away to collect a tin bowl from a nearby bench. Flinging water over Rowson's head, he knelt to pat his cheeks. Finally, the big man spluttered and opened his eyes.

'That's it!' Melkie ceased his ministrations and stood up. 'You should have been paying attention to his left, not shoving and pushing. If you reckon that's the way to win, you need to take lessons from my good lady. There's no one to match her in a draper's sale. On your feet.'

Rowson blinked, puffed and struggled to his knees. Daniel reached out a muffled hand to help his dazed friend.

'I'm sorry.' He smiled ruefully. 'You nearly had me.'

Rowson shook his head slowly. 'I've got the ring of St Paul's going off in here. If you land a punch like that on The Bull, he won't stand a chance.'

Melkie sniffed. 'Let's hope that fortune telling is another of your distaff skills. Now, off you go. I need to have a talk with this one.' He waggled the pipe at Daniel. 'In my office.'

They walked through groups of sparring partners to the back of the warehouse where the battered desk of uncertain provenance served as Melkie's office. The old fighter took up the chair that afforded the best view of the space and indicated that Daniel should take the seat opposite.

Pulling out a drawer, he produced a dented silver tin and proceeded to replenish his leather tobacco pouch. While he did so, Daniel scanned the ancient bill posters pinned to the wall behind him. Several featured versions of the old fighter in his prime. Twenty years back an engraver had delineated muscles on Melkie's bare chest that were no longer displayed, but his wiry frame, combative stance and distinctive moustache were still instantly recognisable. Above him there was a row of more recent contenders. Outlined in red,

The Bull glowered at the centre. Daniel had found his eyes drawn to that menacing figure many times in the last weeks.

Melkie extended a taper to the candle on the desk and lit his newly filled pipe. As the scent of his tobacco fugged the air, he sat back and stared at Daniel, eyes almost invisible beneath the coppice of his brows. Three smoke rings rose and dissolved in the rafters overhead before he spoke.

'I've never seen Rowson laid out cold before. That was quite a blow you dealt him.'

'As you said, I caught him off guard.' Daniel shrugged and began to unwind the stiff protective fabric from his knuckles. 'It was lucky.'

'Luck my arse.' Melkie snorted. 'In my considerable experience, when a fighter comes alive like you just did, there's either a war or a woman at the heart of it.' Eyes never leaving Daniel's face, he sucked on the pipe. 'In your case, I reckon it's the latter of those two evils. Or maybe both?' He raised a hand to stop the answer his pupil was not about to give.

'I'm not complaining, lad. And I don't want details. It's just good to see the finished article, so to speak. You're a prospect, Dan, don't get me wrong. But until five minutes ago, I didn't think you were complete. Not quite. All this time you've been holding a part of yourself back and now . . .' he leaned forward, '. . . you're unchained. And that's a very good thing, because I have some news.'

Daniel stopped unravelling the muffler. Looking up, he caught sight of the red poster above Melkie's head again. As smoke wreathed about it, the crudely drawn figure at its centre seemed to move. He felt that prickle of apprehension on the back of his neck.

'Is it about The Bull?'

'You must be a mind-reader, lad.' Melkie twisted about. Removing the pipe, he pointed it at the bill poster. 'He's in Paris now, celebrating I imagine. Four days ago, he nearly killed Emmanuel Martel, poor sod. Now, Martel was good, rarely beaten.

He went by the name of Le Baril – The Barrel – so that gives you the measure of him. Big fucker, he is. Anyway, it won't be long before The Bull's on the move and Paris isn't far.'

Releasing his hands from the last of the fabric, Daniel rubbed his knuckles. 'Are you saying he's coming here next?'

Melkie nodded. 'In three weeks' time. The date's been set – you'll meet him on the fifteenth.' He eyed the fabric in Daniel's hand. 'You'll meet as nature intended– no mufflers for a prize bout.'

Putting the pipe to his lips again, he closed his eyes and drew in the tobacco. Until this moment, the fight had been an abstract event in Daniel's mind, but the date made it solid as a wall. In the same way, The Bull suddenly ceased to be a creature of myth, but a real, flesh and blood opponent. Rafael Safardi was coming to London, for him. Was he ready?

'Did you choose the date, Melkie?'

The bowl of the pipe flared. 'That was chosen by Elias. He's the one putting you forward, not me. I won't lie to you. The King of the Rookery doesn't make polite requests and he's not a man to cross. I didn't agree to train you up – I was forced to.'

'What do you think now of your unwanted pupil?' Daniel scowled. 'Would *you* put me forward?'

The old fighter opened his eyes. 'This is what I think. Fortunes will be lost and won that night, but neither you nor I will see much in the way of gold.' He paused. 'But what I will see, and take the greatest pleasure from, is the man I trained taking on the Continent's greatest fighter and laying him out cold, just as you did today with Rowson.'

Daniel sat up straight. 'Then you think I can beat Safardi?'

Melkie nodded. 'You can beat anyone, if you put your mind to it. What have I always said?'

'A fight is won here.' Daniel tapped his head. 'But am I ready? Three weeks is—'

'Time enough. Any longer and you'd miss the ripe spot, and

from what I've seen today, you're just about to hit it.' Melkie sniffed. 'Besides, the fifteenth makes sense. It's the beginning of the season so the gentry will be back from their estates and looking for entertainment. Word's already gone around about a new challenger. There's to be an auction.'

Seeing Daniel's puzzlement, he plucked the pipe from his lips and leaned across the desk. 'No one knows who you are yet, but you're already famous – a draw. There's a lot of prestige attached to a fight. The richest men in London are bidding for the honour to host the meeting between you and The Bull. Which reminds me, we need to think up a name for you, although ...' he tapped his nose, '... I've had an inspiration.'

During the rest of the day, Melkie set up a series of tests with the best of the men, instructing them not to hold back. Daniel's confidence increased with every blow that landed true, and with every victory. At the end of the session, the old master gathered everyone together and announced the date of the fight against The Bull.

The room erupted. Musa and Rowson – who had recovered and harboured no ill will – hoisted Daniel onto their shoulders and carried him around the warehouse. Only Coppin remained silent. Sour-faced, he lounged against the furthest wall and turned his back when they came near.

Before Daniel left, the men lined up by the door to pat him on the back, shake his hand or ruffle his hair. Touch was lucky according to Melkie, who was the last to shake him by the hand.

'Remember what I said, lad.' He winked and gripped tight. 'If I'm right and that fair piece who came here is waiting for you, then you can thank her from me.'

At the warehouse in the company of men it had been almost easy to forget the night that had gone before, but now as Daniel walked back through the lanes and passages leading up from the river, Jen filled his thoughts. Last night they had given themselves to each other with a furious passion. At first, her hunger for his body matched his own and he had delighted in her abandon and audacity. Gradually their love had become more delicate. Her moon-pale face had glistened in the candlelight and her wide eyes had locked on his as they moved slowly and luxuriously together.

It was not a pleasure to remember. Instead, he wrestled with his conscience and his guilt. Most particularly, the thought of Jerome. The fact that he still wore his friend's coat seemed to wrap him in duplicity. The pull of the fabric across his shoulders was a torturous reminder of the decent man's innocent devotion to Jen. The poor fit rebuked him for the wrong he had done.

How could he have allowed it to happen? He was a man of honour, not a traitor.

Although he could no longer shy away from the truth about his feelings, the more he concentrated on Jerome rather than Jen, the more he resolved to end this betrayal before it went any further, no matter what it cost him.

By the time he reached the southern end of Covent Garden, where the stones were slippery with the mush of fallen vegetables and where the raucous flower girls of the day bloomed into very different specimens at dusk, his mind was set.

Entering the yard behind The Mitre Tavern, he decided to go directly to Jen's chamber and explain himself. He would be brief, kind, regretful, but firm.

The air in the passage just outside her lodgings was threaded with the faintest scent of rose. Immediately Daniel realised that this was not a good strategy. The response of his body to her fragrance betrayed his convictions. He froze for a moment and then took a couple of steps back. It was too late.

'Sal? Is that you?'

Footsteps sounded behind the canvas panel. Long slim fingers parted the edge of the fabric and Jen's face appeared.

'Daniel!' She smiled, unable to hide her delight. Light from the torch in the passage glowed in her eyes. The delicate ring of blue that framed her large dark pupils matched the ribbon in her hair. She was different in every way to Adanna. Two women could not be more unalike.

'I'm sorry.' Daniel moved away and back into the gloomy passage. 'It was a mistake.'

'Do you mean last night. Or now?' She raised a brow. Her smile widened.

'Both,' Daniel whispered. 'I shouldn't . . . we shouldn't . . .'

'Don't I get a choice in the matter?' Taking his hand, Jen led him through the doorway and down into her room. Defeat was inevitable.

Chapter Twenty-five

'When, exactly, were you going to tell me?' Pearl folded her arms. The steam rising from the iron pot at the centre of the table obscured her face, but Daniel hoped he heard mischief rather than anger in her voice.

'Well? I'm waiting,' she said again. 'Apart from anything else, I would have thought it a courtesy. You're my brother and she's my friend after all. Hearing it accidentally from Sally wasn't quite the same.'

It had been nearly two weeks since that first night. Now he and Jen snatched every moment to be together. Daniel had tried to be discreet, but Pearl's next jibe proved him mistaken.

'Did you honestly imagine I didn't notice you sneaking out of here when you thought I was asleep?' She reached for a large metal spoon and stirred the contents of the pot. More steam rose along with the smack of cabbage and bacon.

'I lay in my bed watching you wash your face and primp your hair. The sight of you taking up your shoes and tiptoeing in case I woke up almost made me laugh out loud. It was only because Sally had already told me about the pair of you that I didn't worry.' She filled his bowl with a dollop of something pink and grey.

'I wish you had, though.' Her tone was solemn now. 'I kept telling myself that you would, eventually, but you didn't. Why not?'

'I ... I meant to. At the beginning I was ...'

Wasn't sure, Daniel had been about to say, but, in truth, his surrender to Jen had been complete from the night in her chamber. There had been something exciting, intoxicating almost, about their trysts – an echo of those passionate, long-ago years with Adanna, when they struggled to keep their dangerous secret.

'I was . . . waiting for the right time,' he corrected himself. 'But it never came. I was worried you'd be angry.'

'Why?' Pearl spooned out a bowlful for herself and sat down. She frowned across the table, her eyes huge in the candlelight. 'That makes no sense. I'm delighted for you. For both of you. Why on earth would you imagine otherwise?'

Daniel stared into his bowl where a lump of bacon glinted amid the flaccid leaves. It was the remnants of another stew from The Mitre, but this time Pearl had managed to scrape more meat from the giant pan that bubbled all day in the tavern's hearth. Suddenly, he was filled with a fierce tenderness at the thought of how hard she worked to care for him.

'I'm sorry.' Putting down his spoon, he reached for her hand. 'I should have told you. Jen thought the same from the start. She said the only one you should hear it from was me. I just couldn't find the moment.' He squeezed her fingers. 'Whatever happens, *you* are the most important thing in the world to me.'

In her neat striped dress, Pearl looked very pretty. Her features were still balanced between the child she had been and the beautiful woman she would become. She was poised and self-possessed, but there was still something painfully young about her. Just for a second, he caught a bittersweet glimpse of the past and smiled sadly. 'After all we've been through together, we have a special bond. I didn't want to do anything that might weaken it.'

She pulled her hand from his. 'Such nonsense! I'm very happy for you. It's delightful that the two people I care about most in the world – my brother and my dearest friend – should love each other.

Really, Daniel, you are such a goose sometimes. I just wish I hadn't had to force it from you.' She pointed at the bowl. 'Now eat that before it goes cold.'

Justly upbraided and grateful for the apparent end to her inter-rogation, he dug his spoon through the layer of cabbage and found another sizeable chunk of bacon. It was mostly rind but there was some meat there too and it tasted good.

'I know you want to protect me,' Pearl continued, 'but I'm a grown woman and you must treat me as one.'

'You are still a child,' he answered between chews.

'I am sixteen next month.' She flattened a hand to her bodice and continued theatrically, 'There are plenty here in The Maze who have a child of their own by that age.'

Daniel almost choked. A kaleidoscope of dread circled in his mind. Unable to speak, he stared across the table. Smirking, Pearl pushed a tin mug towards him.

'Here, drink this. I'm not talking about myself. I'm merely point-ing out a fact. I'm an adult and Jen and Sally, at least, treat me as one. I only found out about the pair of you because Sally let the cat out of the bag. She made a passing remark about how it was good to see Jen truly happy at last. At first she was embarrassed, and then surprised that you hadn't said anything. I don't blame Jen, because she is quite right. It should have come from you.' Pearl stared at him through skeins of steam rising from her bowl. 'But now we have talked about it and that's an end and a beginning ...' she grinned fondly, '... for both of you.'

Starting on the stew, she paused in surprise. 'This really is quite good. Ma Rumney stopped me on the way out tonight. At first, I thought she was angry because I'd taken too much, but instead she marched me back to the pan and fished out more bacon.' She looked up. 'It was for you, she said, to "put some meat on your bones for the fight".'

Daniel smiled at Pearl's accurate impersonation of the old woman's rough voice, chafed by years of bawling at customers.

'I know it's supposed to be a secret, but everyone in The Maze is talking about it.' She took another mouthful. 'Well ... talking about *you*. Ma Rumney said something about it being "not long to go". Is that true?'

Nodding, he scraped the last of the meat from the depths of his bowl. 'The last thing to be decided now is where it will be held.'

Pearl stood up to prod the metal spoon into the grey-green sludge at the bottom of the pot. 'There's still plenty here. You're already famous beyond The Maze apparently, even if the gentry don't know who you are yet. Ma Rumney said the fight was to be the opening event of the season. Will Jen and I be allowed to come?'

Daniel shook his head. 'I don't imagine so. If it's held in a private house, it will be by invitation. The fight is set for the fifteenth.'

The spoon clattered from Pearl's hand onto the table beside the iron pot and clanged to the floor.

'You mustn't worry about me.' Daniel bent to retrieve it and handed it back to her. 'Melkie, Mr Trimm, says I'm ready.'

'I'm not worried about you. Not at all.' Pearl concentrated on cleaning the spoon with her apron. 'But thinking about it, Daniel, it's for the best if I'm not there. Even if you're going to win – and I'm sure you will – I ... I wouldn't want to see you hurt.' She paused and rubbed furiously at the tarnished metal without looking up. 'I'm quite sure Jen wouldn't want to see it either for the same reason.'

The old man with the ship on his head waved at Jen. With his long, tattered coat sewn from patches of sail cloth, his great carved walking stick and the full-rigged frigate swaying in the place of a hat, he was an extraordinary sight. Even though it was stained from long wear and from the dirt of London's streets, the pale fabric of his coat was a contrast to his dark leathery face. The old man raised a hand in a final friendly salute to them and then, whistling, he hobbled away down an alley leading to Flitcroft Street. The jaunty tune echoed from the walls. Daniel recognised it from the days when he lodged in the naval quarter of New York.

Bemused, he turned to Jen. 'You know him?'

'There's not many who don't round here. Old Sam was a navy man once, but a cannon shot took off half his foot. A cripple can't climb the rigging, or do much else on a ship come to that. Now he's a beggar.' She leaned out from the step where they sat, but the old man had gone.

'Poor Sam.' She shook her head. 'They didn't give him a pension because he was foreign-born, so there was no option for him but the streets. He gets by with his hat and his songs, but I worry about him in the winter months. He's always refused a place in The Maze. Sometimes I give him food, although I think he'd prefer rum.'

'Does he live on the streets?'

'There's no other option for him.' Jen turned to look at Daniel. 'If I hadn't come across you both that night, you and Pearl would have found it hard too. That's if you'd lived.' She raised a finger to his lips to stop his reply. 'I know you might disagree. But it's the truth and I reckon you know it.'

Daniel forced himself to swallow his anger. The one thing he *did* know for certain was that he was the legitimate heir to a fortune. His only chance of proving that fact was en route to China at the behest of James Fitzallen. Who would believe him? He had truth on his side, but truth was not evidence.

In bleak moments he tried to imagine ways to prove his claim. He'd even wondered if he could take a party of Melkie's best men to Scandrett Street in order to force the Major's brother to admit his crime.

It was a dangerous fantasy, of course. Fitzallen had proved the value of his connections in the highest places and it would be reckless – the act of a fool – to put his friends at risk. There was Pearl to consider too. If he challenged James Fitzallen and lost, what would become of her?

The more he thought on the matter, the more desperate his situation appeared.

Most days it was a relief to forget, or at least subdue, his anger by throwing his mind and body into the physical demands and routine of the warehouse, but Jen's words were an unwelcome reminder of his fall.

'*Think of the future, not the past.*'

His brother's advice from so many years ago rang hollow now.

The flat bell of St Giles began to toll. The notes fell like metallic rain on the stones around them. Daniel looked up at the plain square church. Evening sunlight glinted on the panes of the arched windows set along the sides, but it presented a stern, almost mournful aspect. They were sitting on the steps leading up to an iron-bound, slab-like door.

'Why did you bring me here, Jen?'

'It's where I was found. I come here to think. Most often I think about the woman who left me by the rails over there.' She pointed to a row of rusted spikes separating the church from a muddle of stained marble monuments. 'I imagine her as younger than me. She's wearing a plain blue dress and a bonnet. She's got my face, my hair, my figure and she's frightened.' Bending forward, Jen brushed the pointed toe of the shoe that poked from beneath the hem of her dress. Daniel remained silent while she worked at a grey smut on the crackled leather.

Taking a breath, she continued. 'Truth is, I don't know who my mother was other than that she cared enough to leave me where I'd be found. Mrs Kelly swears she must have been Irish on account of my looks.'

'Mrs Kelly?' Daniel was puzzled. He vaguely remembered the name from somewhere.

'She's the sole proprietor of a theatre on the edge of the Garden.' Jen smiled. 'That's quite a thing for a woman, but if you were to meet her, you'd understand. Juno Kelly is Sally's employer. She came over from Dublin thirty years ago with nothing but a pet canary and an ear for a tune. She always says I remind her of the girls back home. That's why she thinks my mother was Irish.'

'And what do you think?' Daniel reached out to tuck a stray curl behind her ear.

'I reckon she might be right. Irish servant girls are two a penny in London. Perhaps my mother was a maid in one of the new buildings.' She gestured to the smart townhouses across the street. 'They went up just before I was born.'

With their clean brickwork and crisp lines, the elegant houses opposite the church were very different to the tottering, ramshackle dwellings of the rest of St Giles.

'She might even be working in one of them now.' Jen rested her head on Daniel's shoulder. 'I know it's foolish, but when I sit here, I like to think that she might look out of one of those windows and catch sight of me. That would be a fine thing, wouldn't it?'

Tonight, she was very different to the bold young woman he had come to care for. Her words didn't tumble like a stream and her melancholy revealed a vulnerability that surprised him. He tried to imagine her life as an orphan raised in the Rookery.

'Has it been hard?' He stroked her hair.

'Not as bad as it was for you. I know about the sugar trade. Octavian opened my eyes to the evil of it a long time ago. It was Jerome who introduced me to the Brotherhood. I've even been to some of the meetings with him, but that was back when he—' Breaking off, she shook her head. 'Poor man, he was mistaken about some things, but not about how I'd feel about people forced into slavery. This is a city built on blood and we should be ashamed.'

She looked up at him. There was doubt in her eyes. '*I am*

ashamed, Daniel. It's partly why I brought you here. There are things you should know about me before we go any further. Things about the past.'

Her face caught the glow reflected from the arched windows as he stared at her.

'I . . . I know I am not the first, if that's what you mean to tell me?'

She looked quickly away. A smart red-lacquered carriage drawn by two greys rolled past on the street. Its lamps were already lit for the night ahead. Through the window, Daniel saw that the woman inside sat at a precarious angle to protect her towering wig. The edifice of powder and curls was as strange as Old Joe's ship.

Taking Jen's hand, he raised it to his lips. 'It doesn't matter.'

'If we're counting, you're the second.' She didn't look at him. 'There's been no one else. I promise that on my mother's life. I never wanted a man to rule me ever again and I swore I'd never let it happen. I didn't want complications, and besides, I've learned to look out for myself perfectly well without needing a man to do it for me. But then . . .' Now she smiled at him, her eyes glassy with tears. 'I won't lie, I wanted you from the moment I laid eyes on you – even with your head cracked open – no matter what I told myself, I couldn't stop you from strolling into my dreams like you owned the place.'

'I don't think anyone could own you.' Daniel turned her hand to stroke the skin of her palm. He traced the lines and remembered the fortune tellers who made a living from the soldiers during the endless American winters. Men would pay well to hear that a long life lay ahead.

'This line is supposed to represent love.' He followed a line on her work-roughened palm and looked up questioningly.

'There's not been much of that.' A single tear traced its way down Jen's cheek. 'The first . . . I was twelve years old. He forced me and then he made me a plaything until he grew tired of me. He prefers them young, see, and I grew too old. When I look back now, it's confused. Sometimes he was good to me, almost like a father, others . . .' She swallowed. 'It was Elias. I wanted you to know. It's why I fear him and why I hate him. I never knew it was possible to wish so much harm to a living thing as I wish upon him.'

As Daniel brushed the tears from her face, he remembered the pale-faced girl he had seen on the stairs when he was first summoned to meet the King of the Rookery. Then he thought of Elias's threats to Pearl.

'You were a child,' he whispered through clenched teeth. 'You have nothing to be ashamed of, Jen. Nothing.'

She nodded and swiped at her cheek. 'Even now he thinks he owns me. Sometimes, at the gatherings, I've felt his eye on me and it makes my innards curdle. He looks at me like he knows me, and the worst of it is, I suppose he does.' She took a deep breath. 'If you want to end it now, Daniel, I'll understand.'

He didn't answer. Instead, gathering her close, he kissed the top of her head and inhaled the scent of her. They sat in silence for a long while until she spoke again. 'Octavian thinks you can replace him. Elias, I mean. I heard it from Jerome.'

'I have no desire to be the King of the Rookery. Besides, it's not a plan, it's a wish. And I know better than anyone that they are not to be relied on.'

Jen linked her fingers with his. 'Octavian believes you're the one. If you win the fight, you'll win the heart of the Rookery. He's thought it all through.'

'Then I'll be grateful when he shares his thoughts with me. I cannot see how I will make that leap. I am entirely Elias's thing in this. He gave me no choice in the matter.' Pulling his hand from hers, Daniel scraped his fingers over the stubble of his hair. The day before, Melkie had clipped it close to his scalp.

'Pearl and I live on charity. We are paupers, like Old Joe. We owe the roof above our head to the King of the Rookery, and he has trapped me. Beyond the fight, I have nothing.' He closed his eyes. 'Sometimes I grow dizzy with the weight of expectation laid upon me – not just by Elias.'

'I believe in you.' Jen took his hand again and gripped tight.

He looked up. The setting sun burnished her hair with licks of copper.

'You know the match is set for the fifteenth?'

She nodded. 'And it's to be a private event. Well, not private if you've got money or a title, but as good as.'

Daniel threaded his fingers with hers. 'I wish that you could be there. You'd bring me strength.'

'No!' She sat back. 'I . . . I couldn't bear to watch. I know Pearl feels just the same.'

The bell in the plain tower above them struck the quarter. Immediately Jen sprang up. Scanning the cobbled lane running alongside the church, she frowned. 'He's late.' She peered into the thickening dusk. 'That's not like him.'

Brushing the dust from his breeches, Daniel stood up too.

'Who do you mean?'

Jen pushed back the curls that had come loose from her ribbon. 'I wanted to be honest with you today, Daniel. I brought you here because this place,' she looked up at the church, 'is special to me. I come here when I want to work things out. I met . . . a good friend here earlier. There was something I had to tell him. Ah . . .' She raised a hand to signal to someone in the lane.

Daniel turned to see Jerome walking towards them.

Chapter Twenty-six

'I do not blame you.' Jerome stalked two paces ahead. 'But I do not wish to discuss the matter. Iphigenia and I have spoken, and I wish you well.'

It was clear from the strained tone of his voice that he was very far from content.

They had walked through St Giles Churchyard and along several passages in an ominous silence until Daniel had spoken. Now he regretted his faltering apology and protestation of friendship. As the words had stumbled from his lips, they had sounded treacherous and hollow. But he could not deceive himself; in gaining Jen, he had lost a friend. He stared at Jerome's squared shoulders and knew that there was nothing he could say to make things right. His only hope was that time might heal the rift between them.

He didn't know what Jen had said earlier, but he hoped she had been kind. Worst of all was the fact he was grateful to her. It made him feel ashamed and cowardly. So much for the champion of the Rookery, he thought, as he plodded gloomily in Jerome's wake. He should have had the courage to be honest days ago.

Ahead of them lay a meeting of the Brotherhood. In his only clipped exchange, Jerome explained that Octavian had called them together at short notice and hoped for Daniel's presence. From the rigid set of his neck and the prickliness of his person, it was clear that Daniel's presence was something the apothecary wished to avoid.

As they turned into the narrow passage where a torch blazed above the heavily banded door of The Black Apollo, Daniel was glad that there would be others in Mr Richardson's upper room. At least it would spare him Jerome's silent censure.

Lemuel Darke, Colly Meriday, Ottobah Cugoano, Mr Richardson and Marcus were already present when they arrived. Nestled between the arms of the chair at the head of the table, Octavian seemed smaller and frailer than ever. His eyes, however, were bright with anticipation.

'Your message was intriguing. Tell us what you have learned.' He smiled at Ottobah, who was seated to Daniel's right. It was clear that the young man had come straight from his employer's studio. There was a streak of white paint in his hair and, rather than his usual neat attire, he was still dressed in drab working clothes.

'First, I must agree with our friend here.' Ottobah nodded across the table to Darke. 'The lady mentioned in the newspaper is, indeed, like us. I have seen her and heard her speak. Her accent is French, but I hazard that France is very far from the land of her birth. Her skin is darker than that of any man seated at this table. It must be said that she is a beauty – tall, elegant of frame and manner with the finest, most extraordinary eyes. The Duke of Calne is quite besotted. In the short time I spent in their company with my master, Calne's eyes never left her face and his hand never left her waist.' He smiled, impishly. 'As I told you last time we met, gentlemen, the most impeccable information is always to be found in the lowest quarters and yesterday I spent an hour in the company of the lady's little companion.'

Ottobah paused. Taking up his glass of port, he swirled it around. The ruby liquid glowed in the candlelight.

Richardson thumped the table. 'And what did you discover, man?'

'A great deal. Some of it pertinent to our friend here.' Ottobah raised the glass to Daniel before taking a mouthful.

'It seems that the mysterious lady *is* titled.' He arched a brow as he looked at their astonished faces. 'Yes, I too thought it unlikely, but it appears that the Marquise de Notaille, for that is her name, is the widow of a French noble. When he died three years ago, she inherited his estates in Aquitaine and America. Celeste, her companion – a reduced version of her mistress – told me that the Duke and the Marquise met in Naples this spring, and since then they have become inseparable.'

'So much for gossip.' Meriday folded his arms and sat back. 'Will she be useful, do you think?'

Ottobah shook his head. 'Sadly, that is where my informant disappointed me. Although one cannot always trust the word of a servant, it appears that the lady has only one great interest – and that is the acquisition of money. My pert new friend does not believe her to care for the Duke, beyond his wealth, his title and his property.'

'She'd have to marry him for that!' Richardson snorted. 'And I very much doubt he'd ask her.'

'I'm not so sure.' Ottobah shook his head. 'Having seen them together, it is very clear that the Duke is completely in thrall to his dark lady. We all know Calne's reputation. He would not care if such a union scandalised society, in fact he would revel in the notoriety. Besides, his closest friend is the Prince of Wales. If *he* were to approve of the marriage, very few people would dare to criticise ... in public at least.'

'This would be extraordinary.' Octavian frowned. 'Are you quite sure she would not be sympathetic to our cause, Ottobah?'

The young man nodded. 'I am. My new friend tells me that although her mistress did not gain a fortune on the death of her husband, she inherited a large cotton plantation near the city of *Nueva Orleans* – New Orleans. The men, women and children who work there are not free. It is an uncomfortable fact that she does not like to be reminded of. Celeste tells me that the plantation is the lady's prime source of income. The old Marquis – and he was, apparently, very old – died in debt. But as we know, the Duke of Calne is exceedingly rich.'

The room was silent as they digested this information.

'You said that you'd learned something about me?' Frowning, Daniel leaned into the circle of candlelight. 'Forgive me, I cannot see a connection.'

'Ah, but there is.' Ottobah took up his glass again. 'While I was in the presence of the Duke, he and my master discussed your fight against The Bull. It is already a sensation. As are you – the unknown contender.' He raised the ruby port in a toast once again. 'I must tell you, Daniel, that Calne's bid to host the match outstripped every other. It will be held at his fine house in Piccadilly.' He grinned over the rim of the glass. 'When you win, you will be the most famous man in London.'

Octavian clapped his hands. 'And that will be the beginning!'

Daniel and Jerome walked from The Black Apollo in an awkward silence. Daniel tried to talk, but his companion's responses were curt and unyielding as a locked door. When they parted two streets from The Mitre, Jerome carried on without a pause. He raised a hand in farewell, but he did not speak or turn back.

As he watched him go, Daniel felt wretched. There was nothing he could do about his feelings for Jen, or Jerome's for that matter, but he deeply regretted that she had come between them. It was a bitter irony that the price of his own happiness was the misery of his friend.

Confused and despondent, he sunk his head into the collar of the tight bottle-green coat and turned into the cobbled lane leading to the heart of St Giles. High above in the gap between the gabled roofs, stars twinkled in a sliver of inky sky.

His mother had told him of the lights that danced in the night

above the land of her birth and of the legends her people had attached to the patterns formed in the sky. Over the years he had
taken comfort when he looked up and remembered her soft voice
and her arms around him. Tonight, he did not feel comfort. Instead,
he recalled the look of accusation on her face when he had first
told her about Adanna. There had been something of that look in
Jerome's eyes too.

As he passed the shadowed mouth of a narrow alleyway, he heard
a hiss. A woman, naked to the waist, stepped from the gloom into
the puddle of light cast from a street torch and smiled. There were
no teeth in her blackened gums and her flattened breasts drooped to
her waist where her ragged bodice had been folded down. Once she
might have been pretty, but her gaunt face was pitted with sores and
lice moved in the mat of her hair. Above the hollows of her cheeks,
her eyes were filled with a feverish desperation.

Reaching out a claw-like hand she clutched at his sleeve and whispered, 'Is your cock hungry?' She pointed at her mouth. 'Here or
wherever you want to put it. Yours for a penny. I never disappoint.'

Horrified, Daniel pulled away.

'Please.' The woman stared at him. She was young, but her sallow
skin, ingrained with dirt, stretched like paper over the bones beneath. 'A ha'penny then?'

Stepping back, he started to walk quickly on. He heard a noise
behind him and turned to see that his accoster had slumped untidily
to the ground by the wall at the corner of the alleyway. She scrabbled
at the bodice to cover her naked torso and then she cradled her head
in her hands, her scrawny body jerking with silent, heaving sobs.

The pitiful sight cut like a knife. If he had died that day when
Jen found him, what would have happened to Pearl? Alone and
penniless in a hostile city, would her fate have been so very different
to this woman's?

Although he had no coins, there was something he could give her.

Shrugging Jerome's coat from his shoulders, he went back.

'Here.' He held out the coat. 'I don't have a penny, but I do have this.'

The woman stared up at him uncertainly. 'Is this a trick?'

He shook his head. 'Take it, please. Sell it if you can, or at least use it to cover yourself.'

After a moment, she blinked and reached up for the coat. Her hands were black and her nails were torn and bloodied. 'I . . . I have a baby, a boy. I'd do anything to feed him.'

Daniel nodded. 'Then use this. It should fetch a shilling at the rag market.'

As he walked away, he hoped that was true, but he also knew that guilt had prompted his charity. Even though Jerome's cast-off coat no longer pulled across his shoulders, he still felt the weight of his betrayal.

A torch burned above the cramped passage leading to The Mitre. Just as he was about to duck his head, a shadow joined his on the wall. Daniel spun about swiftly, fists clenched and ready.

'No need for that.' Sparrow raised his hands. 'I've got a message. The King wants to see you. He told me to fetch you to him.'

'It's late.' Daniel scowled. 'Tell him I'll come tomorrow.'

Sparrow's eyes widened. 'He's not one to be told anything. I'd have thought you'd know that by now.'

Daniel shook his head. 'Tomorrow – take that message back.'

And even tomorrow he would not go willingly. Tonight, however, he could not be sure to trust himself with the man who had caused Jen such pain and shame. He had taken more of Richardson's punch and that was dangerous. Although he had no ambition to wear the crown of black feathers, his anger had congealed to a weapon.

'Tomorrow.' Repeating the dismissal, Daniel turned to the passage but Sparrow called out.

'I don't think you understand. It's not an invitation.'

Daniel looked back and saw dark shadows circling the boy's eyes. 'Do you ever sleep, Sparrow?'

'Not much.' He shook his head. 'But luckily I don't need it, see.'

'Well, I do.' Daniel sighed heavily as the bell of St Giles struck just once. Above Sparrow's head a bill sticker which had partially detached itself from the crumbling plaster swayed in the breeze. He recognised the familiar outline of The Bull crudely printed in red, but as the paper moved, he saw another figure, feet apart and hands raised in a pugilistic stance, depicted in silhouette. Instead of a shadow, the second figure cast a question mark. It was him.

Following his gaze, Sparrow sniffed. 'They're all over the place. Everyone's talking about it — the fight, I mean, not you in the specific. They know what would happen otherwise. The King wouldn't be happy. And he won't be happy now if you don't come with me. Please. It won't take long, I'm sure.' He pulled his ridiculous coat around him, the buttons glinting in the light of the flames overhead.

'What does he want to see me about?'

'I don't know. He's not one for conversation, not with me at least.' The boy chewed on his lower lip. 'But I do know this. If you don't come with me now, it won't go well for you.'

He paused and scuffed the holed toe of one of his boots on the cobbles. 'It won't go well for me, neither.'

He held up his left hand. The smallest finger was missing.

'Elias took this last year when I disappointed him, but it still makes a fair point. I'm asking you to do what he says, for my sake.'

Chapter Twenty-seven

A hundred beeswax candles burned in the octagonal room, filling the space with golden light. The sweetness of honey was in the smoke that coiled to the domed ceiling.

'Sit.' Elias pointed at the chair before his desk. He was dressed as a gentleman at leisure in a gold silk banyan robe secured at the waist with a wide embroidered band. His oiled hair was held back from his face, tied at the neck with a length of thick black ribbon. Tonight, he wore a jewel-studded patch over the missing eye.

Several books lay open on the desk, but Daniel reminded himself that the King of the Rookery was almost illiterate. This was all part of the theatre he created. It was a performance.

As a confirmation, Infanta stirred on the velvet cushion beside the desk. Raising her head, she studied Daniel with eyes that resembled that of her master. After a moment, she rose and stretched her long limbs before settling once more, this time with her back to him. He felt that he had been dismissed.

'She does not like you.' Rising, Elias went to an alcove beyond the fireplace. He pulled at a mound of dark velvet to reveal a large, exquisitely wrought golden cage. Opening the door, he clicked his fingers twice. Immediately the cheetah stood and padded to his side. He clicked again and she stepped delicately into the cage, arranging herself upon a cushion. Baring her teeth, she hissed at Daniel from behind the bars.

'My princess cares for no one but me.' Elias bent to ruffle her speckled head and then he closed the door and re-covered the cage with the length of velvet. Daniel knew that this too was a display of power and control. Infanta was a wild and dangerous creature, yet she obeyed her master's every command.

Returning to the desk, Elias smiled. 'When she was a cub, I allowed her to sleep in my bed, but now, usually, we are both more comfortable this way. She has her uses, but tonight she will not disturb us. Infanta has learned the consequences of disobedience.'

He regarded Daniel with his single tawny eye.

'Mr Trimm tells me that you are ready.'

Uncertain what to say, Daniel remained silent. Elias sat again and adjusted the loose sleeves of his robe so that they spread like golden wings. The movement filled the air with his distinctive fragrance – rich with spices, heady and feral. Daniel could not tell if the animal scent woven into the cologne came from the man or his beast.

'No doubt you are wondering why I asked you to come here at such an hour?'

'Asked? I was given the impression it was an order, not a request.' He tried to keep his voice neutral, but it was difficult to disguise his contempt. He could not block Jen and what she had so recently told him from his mind.

'Let us not quibble over words. You are here, that is all that matters.' Elias stared across the desk. Daniel could almost feel the man's eye trace across the skin of his face.

'Sometimes, at the gatherings, I've felt his eye on me and it makes my innards curdle.'

He understood what Jen had meant by that. The King of the Rookery exuded a power that was almost tangible. It was not merely his size and presence that were intimidating. His soul, if he had such a thing, seemed to reach beyond the confines of his body – an invader.

Daniel did not flinch from the man's gaze. He knew that was important.

Several seconds passed before Elias looked away. It felt like a victory.

'I hear you visited The Black Apollo again this evening. It is a singular establishment, is it not?'

Daniel examined this question before replying.

'I do not find it so.'

'How do you find it?' Elias reached for a book and flicked, pointlessly, through its pages.

Where was this leading?

Quite suddenly, Daniel thought he understood why he had been summoned. Elias intended to question him about the Brotherhood. Perhaps, somehow, their hopes of rebellion had come to his attention? He answered carefully.

'From the little I have seen, it is a place of companionship. I am sure you know that The Apollo is owned by a man whose skin is as dark as yours or mine. That is a rarity in London. I am grateful to have been introduced to its society.'

'Ah yes!' Elias tossed the book back on the pile. 'Your dull friend the apothecary, Jerome, he took you there, didn't he? I wonder how he feels about you and dear Iphigenia?' He raised a ringed hand to stop Daniel's furious answer. 'I merely asked about your visit to Mr Richardson's premises this evening to prove that I have you watched. You are a valuable asset, Daniel, it would be remiss of me not to take a close interest in my investment. Obviously, I also know about your affair with the whore.'

'Jen is not . . .' Daniel struggled to bridle his fury. To lose control now would be a mistake. Time and again in battle counsel, Major Fitzallen had demonstrated the wisdom of cool pragmatism in the face of provocation by his superiors. The titled commanders of the King's army were infuriated, a little intimidated even, by Edward's calm refusal to rise to their insults. It was a powerful card to play. Nevertheless, he could not stop himself.

'I know what you did to her.' His voice was low, but the tone was unmistakable. 'I know what you do. I saw that girl with the painted woman when I first came here.'

Elias shrugged. 'Mother Foljambe is pleased. Little Kitty is very happy with the trinkets I give her. As Iphigenia was, once. Where do you think . . . *Jen* would be now if I had not taken an interest in her? She would not be the blessed lady of The Maze – on that I am quite certain.'

'You are the one who should feel shame.' Daniel's throat was constricted.

'From that, I deduce that *she* feels shame?' Elias leaned forward. 'Take my advice – young flesh is sweeter and less likely to conceal rot. I will not make that mistake again.' Stroking the edge of the eyepatch, he stared into the flame of a candle on the desk.

'I have not called you here to discuss morality. I have a request.'

'Another.' Daniel simmered. 'I assume that this will also be a request I cannot refuse.'

'Not if you want to keep your pert sister from the brothels of Covent Garden, although I have also received an alternative offer for her.' Elias smiled. 'Do you recall Vincent Carney from the night you were admitted to The Maze? I must tell you that my tame printer has taken quite a liking to your Pearl. He has watched her in The Mitre. A premium is added to books of engravings that include . . . shall we say, birds of paradise? I know he will be very keen to add such a fresh prize to his collection of models. Her skin would produce very well on the plates.'

Daniel's thoughts were crowded by horrors. He recalled Vincent Carney's lank red hair, stained fingers and his reedy fluting voice. The thought of the man merely watching Pearl was bad enough, but the idea of Elias giving her to him – for that was surely what had been implied – was intolerable.

'You cannot have her and neither can he.' The clenched fist Daniel slammed onto the desk caused several books to topple to the floor. Immediately he regretted his loss of discipline, but Elias smiled, satisfied that his goading had found its mark.

'Calm yourself. You will disturb my princess.' He gestured towards the shrouded cage. 'As long as you do as I ask, it will not be necessary to take your sister from you. You have my word – a gentleman's agreement.'

'You are no gentleman.'

There was a moment of silence before Elias replied, in a voice velvet with menace, 'You walk on dangerous ground, Daniel.' He raised a hand to indicate the opulent room. 'If I am not a gentleman then what are you? Let me tell you, so that you are in no doubt on the matter. You are completely my subject. Mine to do with as I wish.' He tapped one of the books. 'Monsieur Voltaire has much to say on the matter of free will. He does not believe it truly exists and neither do I. At this moment, I control you in ways that you cannot even begin to comprehend. Now you will listen while I tell you what you are about to do.

'As I'm sure you know from Trimm, you are to meet The Bull on the fifteenth. Six days from now. It has become a carnival. Every rich man in London has made a bid to host this fight.' Elias twisted the ring with the large red stone. 'I learned today that the Duke of Calne made the highest offer. It will be held at Rutland House in Piccadilly.'

The fact that Daniel already knew this gave him the smallest satisfaction as Elias continued.

'Although you are untried, it seems word of your prowess has spread. A great deal of money has been placed on your victory. This means we must alter our plans.' He grinned at Daniel's confusion. 'Come now, you must see why this changes everything?'

He waited for a reply that didn't come.

'Then let me explain – it is quite simple. You will fight well. You will exhibit every element of Trimm's excellent instruction, but ultimately you will submit to The Bull. Five rounds and no more. You will lose this fight and I will gain a fortune by wagering against you.'

The brightly lit room swam before Daniel's eyes. The heady scent of the candles and the cologne was suddenly nauseating. He wanted to lash out at the man, but instead he linked his hands tightly in his lap. Even if he landed a blow, Elias's men would be on him before he could follow through.

'I can't.' He shook his head. 'I won't do it.'

Elias stared at him in much the way that a cat might study a mouse before biting off its head. 'Oh, I think you will. I know you too well. But let us consider sweet-voiced Pearl. How well do you really know her? Do you imagine, for example, that at this moment your sister is sleeping soundly in her little stone bed?'

For the first time in many nights, Daniel did not go to Jen. Instead, when Elias dismissed him, he ran through the dark streets and alleyways, certain that Pearl had already been taken from him and given to Carney.

Elias's meaning had been plain. She would be held as a hostage to ensure his subservience.

Blundering along the torchlit passages of The Maze, his heart pounded beneath his shirt and his breath caught in his throat. When he came to the chamber they shared, he was almost too afraid to pull back the sailcloth flap, but when he did, he was flooded with relief to see her curled in the niche beneath a pile of blankets.

Her head was wrapped in the pale cloth she wore at night. In the light of the single candle on the table it looked fragile as an egg against the grey fabric of the bolster. Dimly aware of his presence, she shifted and sighed a little. Then, half asleep, she turned away from him to face the wall.

Daniel went to his own bed and sat down. For a long time, he watched her as she slept and then he stared at the candle flame. Its jaunty fluttering was a rebuke.

Cradling his forehead in his hands, he thought, desolately, of his next betrayal.

Chapter Twenty-eight

'*You are to meet The Bull on the fifteenth. Six days from now.*'

To Daniel those days had seemed both an eternity and a matter of seconds, but now the sand had run to the bottom of the hourglass.

Torches burned away the darkness along Piccadilly. From the shadows, he watched a line of smart carriages await their turn to deposit passengers at the steps to Rutland House. Released from having to keep pace with the horses, link boys idled beside the wheels. The flames they carried etched their reflections in the lacquered paintwork of the conveyances they had recently chased. Wigged and dressed in livery, the boys were facsimiles of their masters in all but one respect – most of them were black.

A carriage rolled to the front of the queue. One of the two footmen standing at the back dismounted. He went to open the door and a woman whose many jewels glittered in the torchlight alighted to the street. Raising the skirts of her wide, pale dress from the cobbles, she waited for her companion, a small rotund man, to join her and together they mounted the steps to the glowing entrance above. Before entering Rutland House, the woman turned to survey the scene. Beneath a gem-scattered wig, her face was hidden behind a circle of black velvet.

Daniel turned to Melkie, who sat beside him in one of the two small plain hacks the old fighter had hired for the occasion.

'I didn't think society women would attend.'

'Oh, you'd be surprised.' Melkie delved into the folds of his uncharacteristically bulky, long dark coat and produced a small silver box shaped like a boot. 'In my experience, they're often the worst. There's something about the sweat and the blood that drives 'em mad.' Flicking open the lid, he tipped a tiny quantity of black powder onto the back of his hand, raised it to his nose and inhaled sharply.

'Snuff. Only for special occasions, mind.' He grinned. 'Mrs Trimm gets it mixed for me by a tobacconist in the 'Change.' Leaning forward, he looked over Daniel's shoulder and through the window. While the exquisite carriages of the gentry rolled to the lighted steps, their own shabby hacks loitered in the shadows on the far side of Piccadilly.

Melkie sniffed. 'It's like Bartholomew Fair out there tonight.'

'It has become a carnival.'

Daniel swallowed at the echo of Elias. He turned sharply away, but not before the old fighter saw his expression.

Melkie nodded at the shimmering stream of arrivals. 'They're like a flock of fucking parrots – squawking, squabbling, puffing up their feathers – nothing to be frightened of there.' He smiled almost affectionately. 'And you needn't worry about Safardi. You're ready, Dan. If my name's not truly Melchior Drabkin, this'll be your night.'

As the bell of St James's tolled for the ninth time, Melkie rapped on the roof.

'It's time we got you inside.' The hack jerked about as the driver climbed down. A moment later the door opened and the steps rolled to the cobbles.

'We're to go in round the back. I brought this.' The old fighter pushed a bundle onto Daniel's lap. The scent of lavender – presumably the result of Mrs Trimm's laundering – rose from the folded sheet. Melkie prodded the cloth. 'Over your head. No one's to see you before the appointed time.'

Hidden beneath the sheet, Daniel allowed himself to be guided around the carriage and across the street. As he walked, he heard the footsteps of the men who had ridden in the second hack. Melkie had asked Musa and Rowson to act as his seconds and attendants. The thought of his friends from the warehouse, particularly Musa, cut deep when he contemplated what he was about to do.

He heard the clang of a metal gate and then he was aware of a narrowing of the space around him. In confirmation, his steps and those of the men who accompanied him echoed from stone walls. They turned into a gravelled area and Melkie warned him that a flight of steps lay ahead. At the seventh step, they crossed a threshold; Daniel was aware of the distant sounds of music, conversation and laughter. The area was evidently lit. Now from under the sheet, he could see polished stone beneath his feet.

'This way.' He heard a new, clipped male voice. 'A room has been prepared. Master is very particular that the men shall not meet beforehand.'

'That's to be expected,' Melkie replied evenly. 'Lead on.'

Daniel was guided up another flight of stairs and along a passage with wooden boards. A door creaked open and the voice yapped again, 'You are to wait here until you are summoned. The Duke has informed his guests that the tournament will begin at ten. Refreshments have been set out, should you require them.'

The door closed. Immediately Daniel pulled the sheet from his head. He had not expected to find himself in a cloakroom, but that was plainly the use to which this space had been put. Although furnished with a table, a settle and several wooden chairs, three of the walls were lined with racks of coats, numbered tickets pinned to their sleeves. The air was fugged with the fatty smell of wool.

Glowering, Melkie stared at the hanging garments. 'Bloody

insult, that's what this is. You'd imagine that in a house this size, they might have found somewhere else. They always know how to put a man in his place, mind. Now we know ours – a fucking wardrobe.'

He stalked over to the table where two candles burned in a pewter tray alongside a bowl of fruit, a large brown jug and some ill-matched glasses. There was also a pile of rounded black discs.

Melkie picked one up and raised it to hide his face. His eyes glinted through two holes. It was a mask like the one Daniel had seen worn by the woman outside.

'Watch.' Melkie held his hands away, but the eerie black velvet circle stayed in place for several seconds before dropping to the floor.

The old fighter reached down and turned its inside face to Daniel. 'It's called a moretta. The ladies – and some of the men – keep them on by gripping this between their teeth.' He flicked at a small mother of pearl button sewn into the lining. 'It's supposed to keep a person's identity secret if they want to be private about their affairs, but by the end of the night, these'll be littered all over the floor.'

He threw the mask back to the table and prodded an apple.

'Refreshments have been set out, should you require them.' He mimicked the servant. 'Who does he think I am, a fucking grasshopper?'

He pointed at the fruit. 'Don't touch a thing, Dan. You don't know whether it's been laced. There'll be people out there,' he nodded at the door, 'who'll be pleased to see you lose.'

It was the bitterest reminder of the truth. Daniel turned away and shrugged off the cloak that Jen and Pearl had given him earlier. A few days back he would have been glad if they had come with him. Now he was relieved that they were not here.

The cloak was beautifully made: dark blue, cut in the military style and lined with silk the colour of wine. Jen said it was a gift from Octavian and the Brotherhood. She had presented it to him just as he was about to leave. Fastening the clasp at his neck, she'd reached up to stroke his cheek, and whispered, 'I won't say good luck, because you won't need it. We're all so proud of you – no one more than me.'

Pulling her close, he had hidden his shame in her hair. Before he left, Pearl had also hugged him tightly. Even through the thick fabric, he had felt the trembling of her body.

'There's just one more thing.' Melkie stomped over to the table and sat down on one of the spindle-legged chairs. He swatted Rowson's hand from the dish of fruit. 'Didn't you hear me?'

'I thought you just meant it for Dan.' Rowson stepped back, abashed.

Melkie's moustache rippled with disdain. 'A fine second you'll make if you're locked in a privy with your guts falling out.'

Grinning, Musa feigned a punch at Rowson's ample stomach. 'You need to think with your head, not with your belly, my friend.' He turned to Daniel. 'Melkie's right – we can't touch anything here, but I have this ...' Reaching into his coat he produced a small silver flask.

'Brandy. If you need a nip beforehand, I'm happy to oblige,' he turned to Melkie, 'if Mr Trimm agrees.'

'Not for me, not until after.' Melkie sniffed. 'But I don't be-grudge the rest of you. In fact,' he stared up at Daniel, 'it might be just the thing. You've been away from yourself tonight, and for the last few days come to that.' He leaned forward. 'Listen to me. You are the best I've ever put out. I don't say that lightly, but it's the truth. You have nothing to fear from The Bull.'

Daniel looked down at the cloak in his hands. He folded it in-tending to find a space on the rack, but Musa took it from him.

Melkie spoke again. 'And that's the other thing. Daniel's a good enough name, but not for a fighter. I've got a new one for you. Like I said, I've been thinking about it.'

Digging into the folds of his coat once again, he produced a second parcel tied with string.

'Here, try this for size.'

Handing the rolled package to Daniel, he continued. 'What I was thinking, see, was that we needed something strong, but also something that cast a nod to your person. It was my Abigail who came up with it.'

Tugging at the strings, Daniel pulled apart the paper wrapper and unfurled a length of brownish fur.

'What do you think?' Melkie looked proud of himself.

'What is it?' Daniel held up the animal skin. It was nearly as tall as him and appeared to have claws. There was a ruff of thick orange hair where a head might once have been. The smell rising from the pelt was musky and sour.

'That's a lion. Well, it was once, before it got pawned to my friend Jacob Levi. Mrs Trimm has cleaned it up a bit and given it a comb through. "Out of the eater came something to eat, and out of the strong came something sweet."' Melkie nodded approvingly at the pelt. 'Samson's riddle – know it?'

When Daniel didn't answer, he grinned. 'He found bees making their home and their honey in a body of a dead lion. So, I was thinking – or more truthfully my Abi thought – that "The Modern Samson" might be just the thing. Clever girl she is.'

Melkie stood up. 'What I suggest is this – we strip you to the waist and arrange the skin over your shoulder. It's a shame about the head, but I reckon we can do something with the claws. We'll put on a show.'

'*Success demands an element of theatre.*'

Daniel stared at the thing in his hands and Elias's words came back to haunt him. Despite Mrs Trimm's ministrations, it was repulsive. Although he was bitterly aware that he was about to degrade himself tonight, this was too much. A travesty.

'I'm sorry.' He tried to hand the skin back to Melkie. 'I can't.'

Confused, the older man pushed it back at him. 'If you don't like the name Samson, we can just call you The Lion, although to my ear, it don't have the heft.'

'It's not the name.' Frustrated, Daniel carried the tired skin over to the settle and draped it across the back. Turning to Melkie and the others, he shook his head.

'I'm grateful to you, and to Mrs Trimm and Abigail, but this is wrong. I won't wear it.'

There was an ominous silence. Musa and Rowson exchanged wary looks. No one ever defied Melkie.

After a long moment, the older man took out his silver box. Sitting down again, he tipped black snuff onto the back of his hand, raised it to his nose and inhaled. He leaned back, closed his eyes, placed a foot on the edge of the table and crossed the other over it. He reclined in silence in this position for so long that Daniel began to think he might have fallen asleep, but suddenly his eyes flicked open.

'What do you want to be called then?'

Daniel stared despondently at the pelt. There was a dry scuttle from the opposite side of the room and they all watched a mouse zigzag beneath the coats. It disappeared at the end of the row beneath a scarlet coat – part of an army uniform. The gold braid on the sleeves and the shoulders glinted in the candlelight and the starched, brilliantly white cuffs were finished with a black trim and polished buttons.

Daniel pointed to the cloak in Musa's hands. 'I have an idea.'

The corridor was dark. Just ahead, Melkie held the door ajar and surveyed the room beyond through the chink of light. The narrow space where they waited became filled with the scent of the bodies packed in the great hall of Rutland House. The expensive floral colognes that doused the men and the women mingled with the smell of sweat, smoke and wine. There were faint traces of another richer aroma that suggested roasted meat. The Duke had already entertained his guests in high style.

Beneath the braying and laughter, Daniel caught the sound of a flute, a harpsichord and a violin. He was certain that the chattering guests were not paying attention to the musicians.

'How many?' Musa whispered from behind.

'Around two hundred, maybe more.' Melkie moved the door a little. Over his head Daniel caught a glimpse of a huge chandelier. He had never seen so many candles burning together, turning night to day.

'Is Elias here?' He addressed the question to Melkie's back.

'Never!' The old fighter snorted. 'They'll accept his money, but not his person. He might call himself the King of the Rookery but them lot out there are real gentry. He'll be taking an interest, mind. He'll have his spies out, probably among the servants.'

Melkie turned his attention back to the door. 'The square's set up on a platform in the middle. There's a path marked out for us, so we won't have to push our way through. Ah – there he is.' Melkie raised a hand as if to quieten them, although in truth, they were almost silent as they waited for the signal.

The clamour beyond the door began to subside. In a few seconds it was just a murmur. The musicians came to the end of their piece and immediately the babble was replaced by a sense of expectation so palpable that it brushed a finger down Daniel's spine.

From the door Melkie whispered, 'The Duke's on the staircase. He'll bring Safardi out first and then you.' He tapped his nose. 'You're the draw tonight, Dan. Don't forget that. When it's time, I'll call you out and do the introductions.'

In the hall a man started to speak.

'As the owner of several thousand sheep, I must tell you that I treat my agrarian duties with the greatest solemnity. I trust you have been well fed and watered, sheep?'

In answer, a cacophony of bleating and baaing went up before the guests dissolved into sycophantic laughter. Daniel could not see the joke. Surely it was an insult to be compared to a farm animal?

The Duke continued, the drawling words slipping out half-formed as if he could hardly be bothered to finish them. At first, Daniel found it hard to understand what he said, but gradually he became accustomed to the indolent delivery.

'. . . a most extraordinary spectacle. We all know The Bull, his fearsome reputation precedes him, but what of the challenger? Who is he, I wonder?'

'I don't care who he is, sir!' a slurred male voice interrupted. 'As long as he wins me ten thousand guineas, he could be the very devil himself.'

There was an uneasy silence and then the Duke laughed, allowing everyone to share his amusement. Others called out including a woman whose suggestion – 'We have The Bull, could he be The Ram? That would be most appropriate given that we are your flock' – set off more infantile bleating accompanied by lewd suggestions.

Daniel had not known what to expect of society, but it was not this. The men of his regiment had conducted themselves with more dignity. As he waited in the shadows, he was glad to have refused Melkie's fraying lion pelt.

Once the ribaldry stopped, the Duke continued. 'I'll warrant that tonight will be the most excellent beginning to the season that any of us has known. It is my great honour to host this . . .' there was a significant pause that was too long to be an affectation of speech, '. . . *majestic* event.'

There was a collective gasp in the hall and then a fluttering round of applause.

'Fuck me!' Melkie turned from the door. 'The Prince of Wales is out there. Old fatso himself. We're honoured.'

When the applause faded, the Duke concluded, 'And so, I ask you to fill your glasses and take your places around the square. Let battle commence.'

Melkie moved back from the door and allowed Daniel to watch Rafael Safardi stroll to the platform. The man was huge. Naked to the waist, muscles taut as ship ropes pulled from his thick neck and across his back and his chest. A black headdress formed from hide fell to his shoulders. It was topped by two polished horns that curved dangerously to almost meet before his eyes.

As he walked slowly, rolling his shoulders like the creature he was named for, white kerchiefs were thrown into his path, along with scores of crimson roses. It seemed he was already a favourite with many of the women present. Halting beneath the chandelier, The Bull turned to survey the room. For the first time, Daniel caught sight of his face. Dark eyes glinted beneath a jutting forehead. Tonight, the fulsome beard was clipped to display the contours of a strong square jawline. He would have been handsome in a rough-hewn way, were it not for the fact that at some point his large nose had been broken.

Safardi's arrival at the platform was greeted by whoops, cheers and applause. After climbing the steps, he was met by three men. Heads bowed together, they spoke for a moment and then a small man in a neatly curled grey wig and a fine dark blue frock coat led him to the centre of the square. He bowed – presumably to the Duke and his royal guest, although Daniel could not see them – raised Safardi's right hand and began to speak in a heavily accented voice that was surprisingly rich and deep.

'My lords and ladies. It is my greatest pleasure to present to you Senhor Rafael Safardi. My friend has conquered in Portugal, the land of our birth. He has triumphed in Spain, in Holland and in Denmark and most latterly in France. Now he has come to England. Tonight, in London, he will secure his reputation as the greatest fighter of the age. Of any age!

'*Sua majestade, senhor e senhoras*, I give you ... O Touro. The Bull!'

The statement was greeted by a fresh cacophony. Those who supported Safardi began to stamp on the marble floor, mimicking a bull pawing the ground. From his vantage point, Daniel saw that some of them raised their hands to their foreheads and pretended to charge at each other. Wigs toppled and dresses billowed and swung as women capered about on the chequered marble tiles.

His stomach clenched and he turned from the sight.

'And now I ask ...'

The small man's voice rang out again. Surprisingly, it carried over the uproar.

'I ask the challenger to reveal himself. It is time.'

Melkie laid a hand on Daniel's back.

'This is it, lad. I'll go first and call you out.'

He shrugged off the bulky coat and handed it to Rowson. Beneath it, Melkie wore a crisp white shirt and a dark waistcoat studded with gems. Tightening the black ribbon that secured his grey plait, he squared his shoulders and went to the door.

'When I raise this hand ...' he demonstrated, '... you come out. And you two,' he nodded at Musa and Rowson, 'give him some space before you follow.'

'He's at the steps.' Musa turned to Daniel and smiled encouragingly. He opened the door a little wider so that they could hear what was said above the riot that had accompanied Melkie's progress through the great hall.

Daniel had never underestimated Melkie's tales of glory, but until this moment, he hadn't realised the extent of his fame. It had taken several minutes for the old fighter to press through the throng to reach the square, but now the excitement had simmered to a murmur and the crowd was waiting.

'Well, here we are.' Melkie's voice was clear and strong. He spoke as he usually did, not bothering to polish the edges from his London twang.

'A little while earlier I heard His Grace compare you all to his livestock, but unless it was wearing a fucking golden fleece, I don't reckon a sheep could afford to be here.'

From the laughter, it was clear that Melkie could say anything to the adoring crowd. Standing in the passage, Daniel bent his head and listened, dismally, to his mentor.

'Now, I know word's already gone around. Of course it has. You wouldn't be here if it hadn't. But I imagine you're all asking yourselves, "This lad of old Melkie's – what's he like?" Well, I'm standing here to tell you that he's the best and that's God's honest truth. More to the point – it's Melkie Trimm's honest truth. I've trained a hundred men and more, but none of them could hold a candle to him and come away with their chest hair intact. It is my honour and pride to tell you that tonight will be an evening you'll remember for the rest of your lives. Men here will tell their sons about it, and women ... well, let me just say I reckon they'll have a lot to tell their daughters.'

There was a pause and then the moment came.

'He's raised his hand,' Musa relayed to Daniel, before opening the door and stepping aside.

Pushing the beautiful cloak back so that the red lining swept from one shoulder, Daniel adjusted the scarlet military jacket he now wore unfastened beneath it. The light of the great chandelier flooded the passage and his torso shone like bronze.

Melkie's voice came again.

'Your Highness, my lords, my ladies, my gentlemen and everyone and everything in between, I present to you . . . The Soldier.'

Chapter Twenty-nine

When Daniel stepped through the door into the great hall of Rutland House, the sudden silence, heavy with anticipation, unnerved him. Lit by hundreds of candles, the room was hot as a cane field under the midday sun. The sticky air was thick with the stench of bodies, tobacco and wax. Tearing his eyes from the ranks of expectant faces – some masked and some painted – he took a deep breath and looked up. High above, smoke curled beneath a painted dome where fat pink cherubs wrestled with serpents whose golden scales glittered in the light from the magnificent chandelier. The quantity of writhing flesh, both angelic and reptilian, was almost shocking.

'Go,' Musa whispered from behind.

Fixing his eyes on the platform where Melkie waited, Daniel began to walk slowly along the path through the crowd without looking to the left or right. The women's wide skirts – strewn with a multitude of twinkling jewels – rustled on the marble as they turned to look at him. It seemed that thousands of cold sharp eyes assessed him.

After a dozen or so steps, the whispering started. The hissing became a buzz, then a murmur. A man called out, 'Sixty guineas on the blackamoor to win!'

Immediately the clamour began. Although numerous voices continued to shout for The Bull, it was clear that Daniel had many supporters.

'Soldier! Soldier! Soldier!'

A deafening cry went up. The Duke's male servants struggled to keep the path clear as men, but mostly women, jostled to touch him. Flowers and favours fell like snow. The thorny stem of a misjudged rose nicked his right temple, but he didn't falter. Instead, concentrating on Melkie, he blocked his ears to the carnival.

It was only when he reached the steps leading up to the platform that he realised he'd been holding his breath. Turning, he caught sight of Musa and Rowson following several paces behind. Musa grinned encouragingly, raising his eyebrows in acknowledgement of the tumult. Rowson winked.

Daniel's stomach revolted again.

He mounted the steps and immediately Melkie walked towards him. Grasping Daniel's left hand, he held it aloft and proceeded to lead him around the square. The crowd roared its approval. Daniel was uncertain whether it was for him or for the old fighter.

As they walked, Daniel allowed himself to look out into the hall. Beyond the steps a second rectangular platform had been erected. Seated on a large gilded chair at the centre sat a portly young man whose strangely coiffed head appeared to have been squeezed from his braided collar. The man's smooth pink face was almost exactly the same colour as his extravagantly medalled and gem-spangled coat. Daniel imagined that were he able to move – he appeared to be wedged into the chair – he might jingle like a child's toy.

The Prince of Wales was deep in conversation with an older man seated to his right. Unlike his royal guest, the Duke of Calne was dressed in sober grey. The rich sheen of his coat belied the simplicity of its cut while the extraordinary whiteness of the complex stock at his neck declared immense wealth without resorting to vulgarity.

The Duke was a tall, thin-faced man with a sweep of black hair and dark eyes that now, despite the chatter of the Prince, were locked upon Daniel. When the Prince thumped the arms of his throne-like chair in evident pleasure at his own jest, the Duke smiled thinly and turned to the woman seated next to him.

Instantly, Daniel recognised her from Ottobah's description.

The Marquise de Notaille was dressed in a silver gown, the skirts encrusted with sparkling jet and black glass beads sewn in swirls to resemble a star with a twisting, sinuous trail. A second dark comet, formed from more gems, blazed across the peak of her mountainous white wig. The bodice was cut deliberately low to reveal the shape of her breasts and her diamond-draped arms emerged from an explosion of metallic lace at the elbow.

'Her skin is darker than that of any man seated at this table.'

Daniel remembered Ottobah's words as he gazed from the platform. He could not see the woman's face because she wore a moretta, but he was keenly aware of her eyes watching him from beneath the circle of black velvet. Her appraisal was unsettling. Like the Duke, the Marquise was tall and elegant. Straight-backed, poised and imperious, she sat completely still. In her lace-gloved hands she held a fan of black ostrich feathers. The feathers shivered in a breeze Daniel could not detect.

Melkie led Daniel back to the centre of the square where The Bull was now waiting with the small man who had proposed him. They stood so close that Daniel could see the pores on Safardi's flattened nose and the crazing of broken veins around his eyes.

The man was huge. Although Daniel was tall, he could not help but feel intimidated by the fact that the tips of The Bull's horns met just above his own head. Safardi grunted and took a menacing step forward, but his man pulled him back.

'Fucker's smaller without the hat,' Melkie muttered. 'Don't let him get into your head. Own this space.'

Daniel turned away. Pushing back his cloak, he made a sweeping bow to the Prince, the Duke and the Marquise. Then he bowed to his opponent and extended his right hand. The crowd loved this gallantry. There was applause and the chant of 'Soldier! Soldier!' erupted again.

Safardi's heavy-lidded eyes pleated with anger. He swiped Daniel's hand roughly aside. Turning his back, he abandoned his proposer and stalked over to the corner where his seconds waited. Amid the ensuing boos, the small man in the dark blue coat stared frankly at Daniel, clearly evaluating his worth as an opponent. After a moment he leaned forward to whisper into Melkie's ear. Returning his attention to Daniel, he grinned before joining The Bull.

'What did he say?' Daniel watched the man draw Safardi's head low to talk to him.

'He said it's unlucky to shed blood before a fight.' Melkie sniffed and reached up to dab at the tiny cut caused by the thorn. 'Must be some foreign superstition. I've never heard it.' He patted Daniel's arm and guided him to the corner where Musa and Rowson were now waiting.

As they walked, he added, 'He also said you'll be granted five.'

'What does that mean?'

Melkie's moustache rippled. 'He reckons you'll last five rounds.'

Daniel couldn't answer. Removing the cloak and the military jacket he had taken from the rails, he watched Rowson test the golden ropes surrounding the square and considered the awful coincidence.

He had agreed with Elias to fall in the fifth.

The Duke's steward beat a gong once and Daniel moved to the centre of the square. The Bull, however, walked slowly around the edge of the platform, rolling the muscles of his back and scowling at the crowd, which seemed to have taken his opponent to its heart. Without his horned headpiece, Safardi was almost bald, except for a black pigtail at the nape of his neck.

Just before the steward mounted the steps, the Duke's guests had crowded around the platform. Now they were so close that Daniel could see the wax and lead paint melting on the faces of those who did not mask their identity. Their eyes swam with smoke and too much champagne. Trying to ignore the women's lewd comments, he kept his eyes focused on The Bull.

When it came, the first blow was a surprise. Safardi seemed to be trading insults with a particularly vociferous knot of drunken young gentlemen, but then, suddenly, he swung about and landed a blow on Daniel's shoulder. It didn't knock him over, but it forced him to step back. Safardi came at him again, but Daniel parried and struck low with his left, punching The Bull in the stomach. The huge man gasped and staggered back, eyes wide with shock. Daniel went at him again, catching him beneath the chin with a strike that sent him reeling off to the ropes.

'Good lad!' he heard Melkie shout above the baying of the crowd. 'Go after him!'

Following the advantage, Daniel strode across to his opponent, but The Bull dodged to the side, at the same time managing – somehow – to connect his huge right fist to the side of Daniel's head.

Reeling, Daniel stumbled. It was the hardest blow he had ever experienced. The ringing in his left ear muffled the sound in the hall. Shaking his head, he regarded The Bull with a new respect. He knew he could beat him, but this would be a fight like no other. Raising his naked fists, he advanced again, but at the same moment, he remembered what he was about to do.

He was grateful for the sound of the gong.

'He's trying to open this up.' Melkie stared at the seeping cut above Daniel's eye. 'He hopes the blood will blind you. If I was in his corner, I'd say the same.' Rowson handed Melkie a sponge soaked with water and the old fighter dabbed at Daniel's forehead. He squinted at the wound. 'This is nothing, but don't let him come close to it. Understand?'

Daniel nodded mutely.

'Safardi can't deal with a left-hander. That last round was near perfect.' Melkie handed the sponge back to Rowson and set about rubbing a chalk-like paste into the broken skin of Daniel's knuckles. 'You've got him dancing to your tune now. You read him like a book at the end there. I didn't think he'd make it back to the scratch after that last blow you laid on him. When he fell, I thought he was done for in three, but he's made of stone . . .' the old fighter sniffed, 'I'll give him that.'

Acknowledging a signal from the Duke's steward, he crouched on the boards directly in front of Daniel.

'Fuck the fifth, you go back out there and take him in the fourth.'

Knowing that Melkie was right was almost the worst thing of all.

In the fourth round, Daniel proved his superiority again and again, landing blows that surprised even him. Occasionally The Bull retaliated – he managed to knock Daniel to his knees with a powerful, if not entirely ethical, jab to his lower back and one massive clout seemed to have loosened a tooth – but it was clear which of them was in the ascendant. When the gong rang to close the fourth round, the chant of 'Soldier! Soldier! Soldier!' was a bitter reminder of what might have been.

Musa hauled a fresh bucket of water over the ropes while Rowson tended to Daniel's hands. Most of the blood on his knuckles was not his. He knew he should be elated, but he was utterly miserable. He concentrated on the pallid paste, watching his friend massage it into the skin until it almost disappeared.

If he lost the fight, Pearl would be safe. That was everything.

From the corner of his eye, he saw Musa crane over the rope to look out into the crowd.

'Gallantry's all very well – the women lap it up like cream – but don't hold back anymore. It's time.' Melkie's voice seemed to come from somewhere very far away. Impending betrayal took so much space in Daniel's mind now there was little room for anything else.

'Did you hear me?'

Daniel bowed his head.

'Here, take this.' Melkie held a tin mug to his lips. 'There's blood in your mouth, swill it out.'

Taking the mug, he tipped it back and gulped down a couple of mouthfuls, then he did as commanded. The pool of water he spat onto the boards was tinged pink. For a moment, there was a strange tang in the air. The scent of something sour and medicinal filled his nose.

The gong rang out five times. Melkie clapped him on the shoulder. 'Now go and finish him off.'

But as Daniel rose from the stool, the room began to move. Extraordinary colours and lights flickered at the edge of his vision and the square seemed to bulge and distort. Scuffing a forearm before his eyes, he stepped forward, but the ground beneath his booted feet yielded like a sponge.

The Bull was on him before he had even registered the man's approach. A massive strike sent him reeling. Clutching the ropes, he dimly registered a huge shadowy form advancing again. Daniel blinked and tried to focus, but it was too late. Safardi tore him from the ropes and pummelled him repeatedly – in the stomach, in the face, on either side of the head. The man's right fist was like a mallet.

Disoriented, Daniel fell to his knees. Safardi clamped a massive hand over his opponent's stubbled hair and forced his head back. The blow from The Bull's forehead to Daniel's own was as unorthodox as it was effective.

'Get up!' Melkie yelled from the corner. Dazed, Daniel turned to see the old fighter jabbing his balled fist into the palm of his hand. Beside him Musa and Rowson were shouting and shaking their heads. The group split and wavered. Two versions of Melkie Trimm snarled at him while several Musas and Rowsons pointed at the buckets that lined the corner.

The Bull dragged him to his feet and released him. Daniel just about managed to stand. Through a dizzy haze he watched the man perform a victorious march around the square. He gesticulated contemptuously at Daniel and bellowed insults to those who had jeered at him.

Swaying, Daniel vaguely understood that this was the end. He would fail in the fifth round as instructed, but there was no honour in this defeat. Staring out into the crowd beyond the ropes, he saw hundreds of faces twisted with fury and anger. Their admiration had lasted as long as his winning streak.

When the scene blurred, he swiped at the blood clouding his vision and looked again. One of the baying men was familiar. A jolt thrummed through his body as the faces of James Fitzallen swam before his eyes. He would have recognised that man anywhere and at any time.

The effect was immediate. Daniel concentrated and the images coalesced into one. Whatever it was that was happening to him, the sight of that pale triangular face with its aquiline nose and close-set eyes cut a swathe through his confusion. Instantly rage that burned like the heart of a volcano consumed his entire being.

Never, in all his life, had he wanted to commit such violence.

It was, perhaps, unfortunate that when Daniel stepped forward to confront his true enemy, The Bull was in his path. Poor Rafael Safardi had no reason to believe that The Soldier was anything but easy meat now, yet within seconds he lay gasping like a great stranded carp on the wooden boards. The blow that finished him came with such astonishing force that, even many years later, those present swore that they had actually seen The Bull rise several feet into the air before crashing back down to the square.

When Safardi fully understood what had happened, he began to scream in pain and despair. His right arm, twisted awkwardly beneath him, had been broken by the weight of his own body.

Daniel stared at the man at his feet and then he turned his attention back to the crowd, fully intending to take up James Fitzallen and rip every limb from his perfidious body, but before he could go a step further, a cry went up and he was surrounded by a scrabbling mob.

Hoisted to shoulder height, he was carried in triumph around the square while the crowd chanted as one.

'Soldier! Soldier! Soldier! Soldier!'

Chapter Thirty

'It was the water.' Melkie took such a sharp intake of breath that the ends of his moustache quivered. 'I know that smell – dwale. It's an old remedy. My great-uncle Aaron was a medical man – he used poppy and henbane to dull the senses during amputations. It causes hallucinations too.'

He turned to Musa. 'You say you saw the bastard do it?'

Musa nodded. 'Coppin – I'm certain. He was wearing the livery of a servant, but I'd swear it was him. He handed me the second bucket, but it took a moment before I realised who it was and then it was too late.'

Melkie took a drag on his pipe. He said he needed something stronger than snuff after what Daniel had put him through.

'When I find Mr Coppin,' the older man said very slowly and deliberately, 'I'll use his lights to fasten my boots.'

Something in his manner and delivery suggested this was not an exaggeration. Brightening, he clapped Daniel's back for the hundredth time. 'You won, lad, and that's all that matters. I won't pretend it was pretty. That fifth was a shitter, but you still won, despite being drugged to the gills like a dockside whore.' Removing the pipe, he spat on the boards. 'That's an old trick. The fucker.'

Daniel stared down at the glistening black ball of saliva and considered his terrible victory.

After the wild celebrations in the hall, he had been carried to the rectangular platform where the Duke of Calne sat with the Prince of Wales and the Marquise de Notaille. The fat Prince had applauded with great enthusiasm and the Duke had tossed a jingling pouch to Melkie. All the while the lady had retained a perfect stillness. Her stiff silver gown could almost have been carved from ice.

Amid scenes that would have disgraced a party hosted by the Emperor Nero, Daniel, Melkie, Musa and Rowson were then escorted back to the coat room where their evening at Rutland House had begun. Now they were waiting to be formally dismissed.

Daniel's head was muffled by pain and by whatever it was that Coppin had used to drug him. Dwale, was it? No matter the name, he didn't care. His replies to his friends as they dissected the fight were curt and monosyllabic. While Rowson mimicked The Bull's final agony, Melkie gripped Daniel's shoulder and bent low.

'It takes some getting used to,' he said quietly. 'The real thing is completely different to a sparring session and the feelings that come after are sometimes hard. Half of you is still out there ...' he jerked his head to the door, '... the other half is trying to work out what's just happened. I'll say this though, lad, whatever it was you drew on in that last minute, it scared the shit out of me. In all my days, I've never seen anything like it.'

Daniel swallowed hard and didn't look up.

It was obvious now. James Fitzallen hadn't been in the crowd, merely someone who resembled him. The dwale in the water had created an illusion, stirring up echoes from that first time he had been drugged. The sight had obliterated everything in his mind except the desire for revenge. Instead of allowing The Bull to conquer, he had destroyed the man's career and most likely the man himself.

It was a sour irony that in playing such a vicious, envious trick, Coppin had unknowingly achieved exactly what he set out to do. Even though he had won tonight, Daniel had lost. What would Elias do now? More precisely, what would he do to Pearl?

He staggered to his feet. 'We have to go.'

'All in good time.' Melkie sucked on his pipe. 'We're to wait here until fat boy leaves. It's protocol.'

'I have to go now!' Daniel ripped the borrowed military coat from his shoulders and flung it to the floor. Frowning, Musa stooped to retrieve it before hanging it back on the rack. He exchanged an anxious look with Rowson, who shrugged. Behind him the door opened to reveal one of the Duke's male servants.

'You may leave. Your carriages ...' his nose wrinkled, '... are waiting.'

Torches were still burning along Piccadilly. Although most of the fine carriages had departed, the shabby hacks they had arrived in were waiting in the shadows on the far side of the street.

Melkie turned to Daniel. 'You need rest, lad. You've taken a pounding tonight and most likely the dwale will sicken you. Although ...' he grinned, '... I reckon half of London will wake tomorrow with a millstone for a head.'

Ignoring the jest, Daniel walked quickly to the first of the hacks and reached for the leather door handle. Pearl filled his mind. In his clouded, throbbing head, the one thought that had any true form was returning to The Maze and finding her safely asleep – again.

He watched Musa and Rowson clamber into the second hack. They were unusually silent. This should have been a time for triumph but Daniel's dark mood forbade any celebration.

Melkie patted his shoulder. 'In you get then, Dan. If this is how a win takes you, let's hope you never lose, eh?'

Without answering, Daniel stood aside to let Melkie go first. He looked back at Rutland House. Four servants carrying buckets had come out through the doorway to douse the dozen torches lining the steps. Behind them a group of men, stragglers from the evening, emerged drunken and swaying. Their wigs were awry and their coats were buttoned askew. One of them began to sing a bawdy song and the others joined in. Staggering down the dampened steps, they laughed as one of their number missed his footing. Fortified by the Duke's hospitality, he fell without causing great injury to himself while the others jeered.

'Good God! A man might take you for a tumbler,' one of the gentlemen sneered and hiccupped while another tottered unsteadily down to his fallen friend, who now lay curled in the dust of Piccadilly.

'There's a circus camped on the fields at Lincoln's Inn.' He sniggered and continued in a high voice pitched somewhere between the bray of a donkey and the bleat of a goat. 'Perhaps they'll take you on, Winter.'

'One thing is certain,' another of the men chimed in. 'After his losses tonight, our friend will be in need of employment.' Supporting himself on the stone balustrade, the tall thin speaker edged down the steps. The servants had retreated into the shadows where they now watched and waited for the time when they could continue their task unseen and unharried.

When he reached the cobbles where his friend was attempting to rise from the muck, the thin man's face was illuminated by the last of the flickering torches.

James Fitzallen, real and solid as the Prince of Wales, prodded Winter with the toe of an elegant, buckled shoe.

Slamming the coach door, Daniel strode across the street and pulled Fitzallen round to face him.

'You!' The drunken man swayed and blinked. His foxlike face was blunted by intoxication. His eyes seemed both unfocused and untethered in their sockets.

'Look, friends, the blackamoor is here.' He leaned forward and Daniel almost reeled at the blast of wine-soaked breath. Fitzallen plucked at the red-lined cloak.

'It's not often a man is pleased to see a black face, but I am grateful to you.' He grinned. 'Three hundred guineas – that's what I've won tonight.'

Daniel grabbed the loosened stock at Fitzallen's neck and pulled him close.

'Do you know me?'

'Of course I do!' Fitzallen giggled like a maid and feigned a salute. 'You are The Soldier.'

'Look again,' Daniel growled, tightening his grip. 'Who am I?'

Confusion chased fear across Fitzallen's long, pale face. He tried to pull away, but Daniel held so tight that the pin of his stock came loose.

'Your brother Edward was a soldier.' Daniel hissed the words into Fitzallen's face. 'And so was I.'

There was a moment of silence.

'*You.*'

It was as if a veil had been torn from Fitzallen's eyes. The glassy befuddlement caused by the alcohol was instantly replaced by a sharp and cunning comprehension.

'You are a dead man.'

Daniel raised his left fist to strike, but it was caught fast in another's hand. Releasing Fitzallen, he whirled about to find Musa restraining him and Rowson ready to assist. Behind them, Melkie's pipe bowl flared dangerously in the shadows.

Seizing the advantage, Fitzallen backed away and cried out, 'Help! Help here. I have been assaulted!'

His drunken gentlemen companions joined in. One calling loudly for pistols, another for the magistrate. The commotion drew more servants and several late-loitering guests to the doorway.

Musa and Rowson pulled Daniel away. He struggled, but they held him fast.

'Get him inside.' Melkie's voice was hoarse with fury. 'It's the dwale. Must be. That fucker Coppin will pay for this.'

Bundled roughly into the hack, Daniel found himself wedged between Musa and Rowson. Melkie squeezed into the small space too. Now he scowled from the slatted seat directly opposite. Without another word he reached up to knock on the roof. The hack rumbled forward at a pace. Performing a sharp turn, it circled closer to Rutland House before moving swiftly on down Piccadilly.

Through the window Daniel saw two figures emerge from the double doors at the top of the steps. One of them was the Duke of Calne, the other was the Marquise de Notaille. The woman's silver dress shimmered and trembled in the light of the torches that had yet to be extinguished and her long wide shadow fell to the foot of the steps. She had removed her mask.

And Daniel knew her.

PART THREE

A Reckoning

From *The London Courant,*
*16*th *September 1782*

Mister Scribbler's Society Notes

A Moste Notable Victory

London hails a new Champion of the Pugilistic Arts following the extraordinary tournament held at Rutland House in the presence of His Royal Highness, The Prince of Wales. *The Soldier,* for that is the victor's chosen name – and it is surely one that will not easily be forgotten by those present – defeated a certain Rafael Safardi, known across Europe as *The Bull,* in the Moste exhilarating Demonstration of the Noble Sport that this Correspondent has yet been privileged to observe. To describe the Incident of the Contest would be tedious and also illogical given that your Humble Scribe recognised so many of *The London Courant's* gentle Readers amongste those permitted to attende by His Grace, the Duke of Calne. (The latter accompanied, as has become usual, by the Scintillating Lady M ...) It is Delightful, is it not, to Speculate upon the coincidence that the two Moste Colourful additions to our Season should be brought together beneath the famous – some might say Scandalous – painted roof of Rutland House? *The Soldier* was presented for duty by former champion Mister Melkie Trimm, whose reputation needs no recitation here.

Monstrous Discoverie in Hertfordshire

A Calf with Two heads and Six legs has been birthed on a farm near St Albans. It is said that the Monstrous creature is able to feede and walk about while showing little sign of Distress, Confusion or Animosity. The farmer, a Mister Samuel Kitson, is rumoured to have set a highe pryce on the animal's heads in the hope of selling it to a Circus or Carnival.

Failed Bank

It is with regret that we must inform our Readers of the Closure, with immediate effect, of *The Claremount Bank*, 34 Strand. It gives no Pleasure to reporte that Messrs Claremount (father and son) have declared this long-established and widely respected House to be bankrupt. Initial investigations suggest that the Assets of General Depositors have secured a series of irregular investments in Scientificals, most notably the failed Jupiter Aerial Peregrination Company. Readers of *The London Courant* will be Familiar with this company's fraudulent claims as to the possibility of Passenger Flight powered by heated air. Depositors are advised that there is to be a meeting of creditors at 37 Gresham Street at Midday on October 1st.

Feathering Her Neste

Fly to *The Fiery Angel*, Shandois Street, where a delightful fresh-hatched Songbird flourishes in her bower. Newly arrived in London, this Sweete Daughter of Euterpe has already acquired an appealing soubriquet. Your loyal Correspondent intends to hasten to the theatre to sample the song of *The Covent Garden Nightingale*.

Chapter Thirty-one

As the hack clattered along, light from street torches and braziers occasionally illuminated the boxlike interior where the four men were packed tight as a barrel of salt herring.

Daniel stared through the window, but the only thing he saw in the glass was her face. Without the moretta mask, the severe angles of her beauty had been carved into shadows by the guttering light of the torches lining the steps of Rutland House, but there was no doubt that he knew her.

The Marquise de Notaille was Adanna.

In that moment of recognition everything ended, and began again. The distance between them seemed to contract and spin away to a point beyond Piccadilly, beyond London, beyond the world and beyond the universe; locked together they whirled to a place where time and substance had no meaning.

Seated beside the Duke of Calne, sharing the same platform as the Prince of Wales, Adanna had watched him fight.

Or had she?

Was it possible, he wondered, that the drug Coppin had used had caused him to see her? Fitzallen too? The Marquise was real enough, but perhaps the dwale had begun to distort his senses? What if the woman was not Adanna, but a fantasy created by his deepest longings?

Melkie leaned forward.

'It's one thing to fight The Bull, but to take on one of the Duke's guests . . .' He shifted on the seat opposite. 'I had to stop you.'

There was a spark as he lit his pipe.

'I'm putting it down to the dwale, Dan.' He shielded the little flame. 'My great-uncle Aaron told me of a sailor who was given it when his leg was sawn off. Poor bugger thought he had wings. Dragged himself up the ship's rigging, didn't he, and launched himself into the sea. Drowned, naturally.' Melkie sucked and the pottery head of the woman glowed in the darkness. 'Dwale can make a man believe things that aren't possible.'

He was quiet for a moment and then he continued in a more jovial tone designed to lighten the oppressive mood. 'Mind you, before tonight, I wouldn't have believed a Bull could fly. That was a sight we'll never forget, eh, lads?'

Musa nudged Daniel's arm. 'After you hit him, Safardi seemed to hang in the air for a moment before he fell on the scratch. It was incredible. *You* were incredible.'

'He'll never fight again,' Rowson agreed. 'Not after what happened to his arm. Poor bastard.'

He was not revelling in Safardi's misfortune, merely stating a fact. Staring out at the streets beyond the glass, Daniel was dimly aware of his companions' animated discussion of the fight. As they rattled away from the grandeur of Piccadilly, the houses seemed to huddle closer to the hack. The shadows deepened as the roads narrowed into poverty.

His head was heavy and the rocking motion was oddly soothing. He struggled to ward off sleep that was perilously seductive, but the events of the evening began to fray into a dream. Capering nobles became horned creatures swirling beneath a huge chandelier whose glittering branches stretched to meet the edges of a dark and threatening forest. Waiting in the trees . . .

'Hey!' It was Musa who woke him. Bending to the floor of the hack, he handed Daniel something small and hard.

'You dropped this.'

They rounded a corner and light from a brazier glinted on a small golden object. Daniel stared at the arrow-shaped pin that had fastened the wine-stained stock at James Fitzallen's throat. He remembered it now from their first meeting.

He was *not* mistaken.

Clutching the pin so tightly that the point dug into his flesh, Daniel used the pain to sharpen his wits. Everything from the last few hours came flooding back: Melkie's snuff, the tattered lion pelt, a mouse, cherubs writhing with golden snakes, a fat prince in a scarlet coat, a small man in a blue velvet frock coat, a horned headdress, Rafael Safardi crumpled and broken at his feet, the cold, furious eyes of James Fitzallen and, most clearly of all, Adanna shimmering in silver on the steps.

'A dark comet.'

Images crashed like waves spewing jetsam on a beach, but when the torrent receded one thing was left stranded and ominous as whalebones picked clean of flesh. Pearl.

The Mitre Tavern squatted on a corner where Vinegar Yard turned into Crown Alley. Despite its name, the latter was a well-used thoroughfare leading down to Covent Garden. Even at this hour, carriages, hacks and chairs struggled to pass. Humped and crooked, The Mitre was an ancient timber-framed remnant of the days when St Giles was a village on the edge of a marsh. Since then, the establishment had sunk even lower. With its lopsided doors, cracked façade and spavined roof, the tavern was a mirror of its customers, one of whom was pissing against its mottled wall when they drew up.

Although it was late, there were lights behind the small steamy panes of the windows. The raucous sounds from within suggested that Ma Rumney's trade was good.

The hack bounced about as Rowson stepped down first to let
Daniel out. The horse, a mud-spattered grey, tossed its head, whick-
ered and pranced about on the cobbles. Shouting, the driver pulled
at the reins but the creature was skittish, preferring the hay and
comfort of a stable to another tour of the streets.

All Daniel could think about now was Pearl. News of his victory
was bound to have reached Elias – what if he was too late? Climbing
down, he steadied himself against the door before turning towards
the yard where the steps leading to The Maze curled into the ground
beneath the streets and passages of St Giles. The sound of laughter and
song from the tavern was deafening. The singing was coarse – it wasn't
Pearl. Four hours ago, he had left her below in Jen's company with
strict instructions to await his return. For once, he regretted the fact
that they were not working late at The Mitre together. If Pearl had
been surrounded by people tonight, perhaps she would have been safe.

The thought propelled him away from the hack and across the
yard, but he hadn't gone far before his legs buckled beneath him.
Within seconds his friends were at his side.

'Easy there.' Musa hefted him up and supported his right side.
Rowson took his arm.

Daniel struggled to free himself. 'I have to find Pearl.'

'Pearl, is it? Or someone else?' Melkie, who had come to join
them, winked. 'As I said, rest is what you need.' He waggled the
stem of his pipe and nodded at Musa and Rowson. 'Get him back
to his bed. I'll wait here with the hack. I can drop you gentlemen
off wherever suits.' Taking a step closer, he laid a hand on Daniel's
shoulder.

'I don't spend praise like pennies, but I'm proud of you, Dan.
When you wake tomorrow, you'll be the most famous man in
London. It happened for me and let me tell you—'

The end of Melkie's story was interrupted by a loud whistle and
then a yell.

'Fuck me. It's him!'

Over Melkie's shoulder Daniel saw the man who had been re-lieving himself pull hastily at his breeches and yank at one of The Mitre's warped doors to bellow at the revellers inside.

'He's back! Our champion's come home. He's here outside now.'

Swinging about, he swayed drunkenly towards Daniel, who was still propped between his friends. The man made an unsteady bow.

'I wagered a crown on you. And you've paid me back 'ansome. Word on the street is you fought as The Soldier ...' Grinning, he flailed a hand in the direction of his head. 'Let me be the first to salute you. And I won't be the last tonight.' He tapped the side of his strawberry nose and looked back at The Mitre. 'They're already celebrating.'

The tavern door opened and a group of revellers tumbled onto the cobbled yard. When they caught sight of Daniel they started to cheer. A woman leaned out from a window on the upper floor.

'What's going on?' she called.

'He's here.' The drunken man stepped to one side and proudly waved a hand up and down before Daniel as if he owned him. 'Our Soldier's right here.'

As more people emerged from the tavern, Daniel, Musa, Rowson and Melkie backed slowly to a corner. The crowd was good-humoured but dangerously excited. With little to celebrate in their lives, Daniel's success was a respite from hardship. As he watched customers clambering out from the windows on the lowest floor in their eagerness to congratulate him, he understood that his victory was also theirs. But their enthusiasm was hazardous.

'Christ!' Melkie muttered. Swiftly he scanned the yard and pointed to a flat-topped wagon drawn up against the furthest wall. 'Get him up there. If we stay down here, we'll all be asphyxiated by appreciation.'

*

'Soldier! Soldier! Soldier!'

The chanting started again. From the wagon Daniel surveyed the jubilant men, women and children packed into The Mitre's yard. Someone had lit two torches bracketed to the tavern's wall and now a hundred gleeful faces flickered eerily in the firelight. He recognised many of them from the subterranean world of The Maze.

'Can you speak, Dan?' Melkie whispered from the side of his mouth. 'Because I don't reckon we'll be able to get away from here tonight until you do.'

Daniel breathed deeply. The pain from the pin and the chill of the night air had sharpened his mind. Although his body ached, he was now able to think with a lucidity that would have evaded him a quarter of an hour back.

He glanced at Melkie. 'They need to hear me?'

The older man nodded. Still supported by Musa and Rowson who stood on either side of him on the flat deck of the wagon, Daniel rubbed his tattered knuckles. Taking a step forward, he tested his strength and was relieved to find that his legs held.

'We're here if you need us.' Musa clapped his shoulder. 'Just give a sign.'

Daniel threw back the cloak to reveal its red lining and raised a hand to quieten the crowd. At the same moment it began to rain. He was grateful to feel the cool droplets on his face and to taste smoke and iron on his lips as he thought carefully about what he should say. The drunken man had called him 'our Soldier'. He was reminded of Octavian's words on the night when he had first met the Brotherhood.

'*The people of the Rookery need someone to look up to, someone to follow . . . When you conquer The Bull, you will be hailed as a hero.*'

It was a bitter thought. In winning the hearts of many, he was likely to lose the most important thing in his life. The last thing he wanted to do now was address a mob when Pearl's life was in danger. He had to get this over with and find her.

He began to speak, using the voice with which he had once in-spired the men under his command.

'Friends ... My good friends. I thank you.'

Almost immediately the yard fell silent, but the wagon rocked precariously as people surged forward to be as near as possible. Two small boys used the spokes of the massive wheels as ladders to clamber closer to their hero. They could easily have been crushed, but Daniel bent down and scooped one of them up to the safety of his shoulder, while Musa and Rowson hoisted the other between them. The crowd cheered anew at this and it was a moment before he could continue.

'Dear friends and neighbours,' he began again, 'my sister and I have always felt the generous warmth of The Maze. You welcomed us when we had nowhere and now, tonight, I hope that I can begin to repay your kindness. I see that news travels fast in London. You have clearly heard of my victory.'

There was a great cheer and more chants of 'Soldier'. Daniel raised his free hand to quieten them. Responding to something in his bearing and his tone, they obeyed.

'The people of the Rookery need someone to look up to.'

Gazing out over the eager joyful faces clustered around the wagon, he could not deny the truth in Octavian's words. Scanning the crowd, he recognised that these were his people and that The Maze was now his home. For a moment, he felt a deep shame that he had intended to betray their trust.

For Pearl ...

He had to find her and protect her before it was too late. Taking a breath, he continued loudly and firmly.

'But I must tell you that it was not my victory, it was yours.' He looked up at the bedraggled, but delighted urchin on his shoulder. 'Tonight, I fought for all of us – for this boy here and for every one of you. I dedicate my victory to every man, woman and child of The Maze.'

This was greeted by the greatest cheer yet.

'Nicely done.' Melkie's low mutter of approval came from the back of the wagon. 'My wife's a very forgiving woman, but if I don't get home before the sun comes up there'll be cold tongue for breakfast.'

Daniel had never met Mrs Trimm, but he had the distinct impression that she and her husband were well matched. It was, however, not for Melkie's sake that he signed for the crowd to hush once more.

'And now I must beg another kindness of you. The hour is late. I thank you again, but please, allow me – and my good friends here – to get out of the rain, and to our beds.'

This was met by more whoops and calls. On the far side of the yard, The Mitre's door swung open and the substantial silhouette of a woman was framed by the glow from within. She called out in a voice that carried much of Daniel's authority, but none of his grace, 'Leave him be, now. Let him fuck off to his bed and I'll stand a last glass for everyone whose belly can take another.'

Ma Rumney was in a charitable mood. The Soldier's success had increased her night's trade and she could afford to be generous. Light from The Mitre's doorway poured out over the rain-soaked corner where Vinegar Yard met Crown Alley. Three cloaked women turned that corner now; just for a moment, their faces were sharply illuminated. Seeing the crowd, they stopped and huddled together, heads bent close in conversation, but in that brief moment Daniel recognised them.

Setting the boy down, he peered over the heads of the sodden people. What was Pearl doing out so late with Jen and Sally? The relief he felt on seeing her was immediately replaced by a surge of fear that obliterated any lingering effects from the fight. Leaping down from the wagon, he started to force his way across the yard, roughly shrugging off any revellers who tried to catch his arm or impede him.

He was almost at Pearl's side when a huge, plumed carriage, its black lacquer sides slick and shimmering with rainwater, rumbled to a halt in Crown Alley. The vehicle blocked the entrance to Vinegar Yard, casting a shadow that reached the entrance to The Mitre.

A man who had been pulling at Daniel's cloak released him and stepped back. Pointing at the carriage, he turned to shout to the receding crowd.

'Look! He's come himself. The King of the Rookery has come to congratulate his champion.'

Chapter Thirty-two

The carriage was antique in design. With wheels the height of a man and the suggestion of armour in its slab-like sides, there was no grace or beauty in its appearance or proportions. Even the opulent spray of black feathers that sprouted from a gilded coronet on the roof spoke of a sinister purpose. Shivering in the wind and the rain, they whispered of death, not life.

Those who re-emerged from the tavern stayed close to the walls, while those who were still in the yard moved as far from the carriage as they could, allowing it to stand in a semicircle of glistening cobbles. Within seconds, the unbridled joy of Daniel's welcome had been replaced by wary deference. The crowd was silent, every face turned towards the monstrosity that loomed over the yard like a great black catafalque.

In three strides, Daniel closed the gap between himself and Pearl. Gripping her hand, he pulled her roughly away from the carriage and from her friends. She was too surprised to resist.

'Daniel!' Jen hissed at his back. 'What are you doing?'

He turned to glare at her. 'I might ask the same of you.'

Over her shoulder he saw the shining black door of the carriage swing open. A roll of steps fell to the ground. Utterly confused by Daniel's silent determination, Pearl struggled to free herself as he tried to force a way back through the crowd. On the opposite side of the yard an opening led into Lamb Alley and a labyrinth of passages beyond. Escape lay in those dark and twisting lanes.

'Where are we going?' she demanded as he dragged her in his wake.

'There's no time to explain.' He didn't turn to look at her or the carriage.

But it was already too late.

'Where is he? Where is my champion?'

Instantly the people impeding Daniel and Pearl melted away, leaving them completely exposed. The familiar and horribly compelling voice rang out again.

'Ah! I see you. And your sister too.'

With no other option, he turned to face the King of the Rookery.

Flanked by two of his men, Elias now stood beside the carriage. His braided hair fell thick as a horse tail over one shoulder of a long, loose black coat. Embroidered with gold at the cuffs and across the shoulders, it was both martial and decadent. Standing almost a head taller than his guards, his size and his stillness radiated a dreadful power. Even the rain seemed wary of touching him.

Elias's expression was unreadable as his single eye travelled from Daniel to Pearl. He stared at her, raking her body from head to toe before speaking in that deep, plush voice that carried both the rhythm of the Caribbean and the razor of London.

'I have heard that your performance tonight was quite remarkable, Daniel. Or perhaps I should now call you Soldier? You have, most certainly, shown your colours.' He paused. It was only the pulse of a single vein in his corded neck that betrayed him.

'We made a bargain and I will honour it. I have come to *reward* you as I promised.'

'He deserves it!' From the depths of the crowd, a drunk responded with what he imagined to be a statement in support of the King's approval. The man continued in a liquor-slurred voice.

'Most of us wagered on him and he's paid us back double. He's our champion too now. The champion of the Rookery.'

A murmur of agreement rippled around the yard. One of the boys who had clambered onto the cart came running back to Daniel's side. He clutched his leg and stared up him, puppy-like eyes shining with devotion. Spontaneously a ragged cheer went up and then the chanting began again.

'Soldier! Soldier! Soldier!'

Daniel looked up from the boy to Elias. As the sound echoed from the walls, the mask of indifference fell from the man's face. He quickly regained his composure, but the moment had revealed the savage beneath the veneer of the gentleman; the claws sheathed in the velvet.

Far from feeling threatened, Daniel recognised his second triumph of the night. It was a gamble, but he was convinced his instincts were true. Releasing Pearl's hand, he took a step forward and bowed to the King of the Rookery. The crowd stopped chanting and cheered, mistaking the gesture for an act of fidelity.

Straightening up, he stared boldly at Elias. They were a mirror of treachery. There was a twisted irony to the fact that they had *both* been prepared to betray these people, albeit for very different reasons. Daniel was certain that this dual duplicity was not something Elias would wish to expose in so public a space.

Secure in the knowledge that Pearl was safe, for the moment at least, he raised a hand and gestured for the crowd to quieten. When they did, he spoke loudly so that everyone gathered in the rain-spattered yard could hear.

'Tonight, I dedicated my victory to the people of the Rookery. I am proud to be one of their number and honoured to be their champion. That is my reward.'

Now they roared his name. The sound of their favour was louder than ever, leaving Elias in no doubt as to where their loyalties lay. His guards were armed, but they would not be a match for a mob.

The King of the Rookery studied his sodden people and smiled sourly. Stepping closer to Daniel, he clasped his shoulder. An on-looker would have thought it a mark of esteem, but the power of that grip and the pain it caused told the truth. Leaning closer, he bent so that their foreheads touched. The scent of cloves, rum and musk filled the damp night air.

'I will not forget this,' he whispered.

Turning away, he signed for his men to ready the carriage. High on the box and huddled against the rain, the coachman pulled at the reins and the two dark horses in the traces bucked in readiness. Elias strode across the cobbles and entered his carriage without looking back. At the crack of a whip, the monstrous vehicle jerked as the horses took up the strain and then it rolled forward along Crown Alley. When it was gone, a feeble brazier burning across the way seemed to flood the yard with light.

Daniel walked stiffly to the corner and watched Elias carry the darkness away.

'From where I was standing, on the top of that wagon, I didn't see much in the way of congratulation. Quite the opposite in fact.' Melkie stared up at Daniel. 'It's a curious thing when a man pays for someone to be trained by the best in the business and then acts like there's a death in the family when he wins.'

He waited for an answer that didn't come and then he turned to Musa and Rowson who had joined them on the corner of Crown Alley. All three men were soaked to the skin.

'If we stand here much longer, we'll put down roots. We'll leave Daniel to ...' Melkie glanced across at Jen who was deep in conversation with Sally and then at Pearl who was at Daniel's side. Instinctively, he had taken hold of her hand. Her grey street cloak was black with rain. It clung to her like a shroud.

'We'll leave him to his womenfolk,' Melkie concluded.

The yard was almost empty now, although the sounds from The Mitre and the lights at its bleary windows suggested that many intended to celebrate their champion into the night.

'The offer still stands, lads.' Melkie nodded at the hack. 'I'll drop you two off wherever's convenient.' He looked up into Daniel's face. There was shrewd appraisal in the old fighter's eyes.

'Take your time. I won't expect you at the warehouse until you're ready. Rest.'

If only he knew, Daniel thought as he watched Melkie lead Musa and Rowson back across the muddied yard. There was no time to rest, not now. His grip on Pearl's hand tightened. Where would she be safe? Where were the walls strong enough to shield her from Elias's reach? Where was a door strong enough to defend her?

The answer to his questions came so fast it was as if his mind had stored it away against a time of need. A plan unfurled in his mind like a map on a tabletop – the way ahead plotted out like one of the Major's campaigns.

He called out, 'Musa!'

His friend turned and, dropping Pearl's hand, Daniel splashed to his side. They spoke together for a few moments, heads bowed against the rain. Musa nodded, and briefly glanced over Daniel's shoulder at Pearl.

The atmosphere in the brick-lined chamber was not celebratory. Pearl fiddled nervously with the fastenings of her damp cloak while Jen watched Daniel pace from the table to the wall. The tension in the air had sent Sally directly to her own lodgings.

'Where were you earlier?' He watched a single drop of water squeeze through a gap in the bricks and plop to the stones near his bedding. A thin puddle was already spreading along the green-edged wall. It did nothing to dampen his simmering anger.

'I know you weren't here so don't try to pretend you were,' he continued. 'You were out on the streets. I saw you all turn into the yard just before Elias came.'

There was a long silence.

'Well?' He turned. 'Will neither of you answer me?'

Pearl swallowed and stared at her feet. 'I . . . we went out to-night to—'

Before she could finish, Jen ran to him. Taking his face in her hands, she rose to the tips of her muddied toes and kissed him. He tasted gin on her lips.

Releasing him, she twined her fingers with his. 'Everyone down in The Maze was shouting about the fight. They said people were running through the streets calling your name . . . well, your new name, that is. *Soldier.* We couldn't sit down here while all of London was celebrating, so we decided to see for ourselves. We – me and Sally – took Pearl up top to see it all.' She glanced at Pearl. 'That's what we did, isn't it?'

'Yes.' Pearl didn't look up.

'It was a rare night out there on the streets.' Jen spoke so quickly that her words tripped over each other. 'People were shouting about the fight on every corner and toasting your victory. I had a tipple or two myself, I'll freely admit it. But Pearl didn't – if you're worried – even though she could have done.' She paused to draw breath and rattled on, 'But what a thing to remember? It's not often your brother becomes the most famous man in London. It would've been a sin if we hadn't taken her out to see it for herself.'

'You shouldn't have done that.' Daniel wrenched his hands free and tried to subdue his temper. 'It's not safe on the streets.'

Or anywhere.

'Oh, look at your face! Don't be so fierce.' Jen grinned. 'Anyone would think you were fighting us now. I can't believe you'd be-grudge your own sister. She had every right to be out there.'

'*You* had no right to take her out.' He tried to remind himself that Jen had no idea what she'd done, but it was impossible to be reasonable when she had exposed Pearl to such danger.

'I think you'll find that Pearl can make up her own mind about where she wants to be. She's not a child anymore.'

Jen was being playful, but her ill-judged reply added fuel to the bonfire of his fury. Afraid of what he might say, Daniel didn't answer but beneath the fine cloak his heart pounded like a fist. Completely still, his shadow loomed huge on the wall. Even the candle on the table held its breath; the little flame seemed to freeze in the clammy air.

Jen swiped the back of a hand over her damp forehead. Beneath the hood of the cloak, her hair had come loose from its ribbon and lay flat around her face.

'I ... I think I must have toasted your success more times than is good for me.' She took a deep breath and sighed. 'I knew you wouldn't approve, Dan, but it's done now and no harm's come of it. Besides – you won! It's something everyone here wants to be part of. You've seen that for yourself. And the two of us have more reason than most to be happy for you. That's true, isn't it?' she appealed again to Pearl.

Looking up from the stone floor, Pearl nodded. 'We didn't go far, just to ... to—'

'Even the King rode out to see you,' Jen cut in. 'It's not often that bastard Elias comes to The Maze in person like that. You must have won him a fortune tonight. He's a shrivel-hearted whoreson and I wish him nothing but bad luck but – just this once – I'll celebrate with him.'

She started to untie the fastenings of her own cloak. 'The sooner we get out of these wet things the better. We must look like a pair of drowned cats.'

'No.' Daniel stayed her hand. 'Go back to your own room.'

Jen looked up, puzzled. Her skin was damp with rain and the

black with which she'd lined her eyes was beginning to smudge her cheeks. She looked tired and a little worn by the evening. His vision swam. Just for a second, it was Adanna he saw. The austere beauty of her perfectly symmetrical face framed by the coils of a glittering moon-white wig.

He blinked and she was gone.

'I want to hear about the fight from beginning to end.' Jen reached up to stroke the wound on his temple. 'Me and Pearl, we both do.'

He took a step back. 'It's late.' His voice was low and implacable. 'But—'

'Leave us.' There was no room for negotiation in his tone or manner.

'I'll see you later then? Perhaps you'll come along, when ... when?'

His silence on the matter of 'when' quelled her. Shivering in the wet cloak, she spoke more to herself than to Daniel. 'Of course. You should rest now. I heard what Mr Trimm said.' Biting her lower lip, she looked from him to Pearl. 'You should sleep too, birdy, it's been a long night for us all.'

'I think that's best.' Pearl's reply was almost inaudible.

'Very well.' After a long moment of uncomfortable silence, Jen turned and went to the arched doorway. Her hand was on the canvas, but at the last moment she shook her head and twisted about.

'Don't be angry with her. Not tonight. Not when ...' Darting to Daniel's side, she caught him in her arms and kissed him again. Her eyes sought his when he drew away. 'I ... I'm proud of you, Dan. More than I can say. I couldn't leave without telling you that. Promise that tomorrow you'll tell me about it. I want it all – The Bull, the fight, the house, the Duke, his guests. They even say the Prince of Wales was there. I want to know everything – every last detail.'

Daniel's curt nod was both an answer and a dismissal.

Chapter Thirty-three

Jen's abrupt banishment created a chasm that Daniel did not wish to explore and neither, it seemed, did Pearl. The regular plop of water dripping from the curved brick ceiling was the only sound as she peeled the sodden cloak from her shoulders and pretended to tidy their few possessions.

He did not recognise the dress she wore. The hem was muddied and rainwater had soaked high into the fabric, but it was finer than most of her gowns: a dark-sheened blue, square at the neck with ruffles along the bodice and sleeves. It whispered when she moved.

Turning from the shelf where she had stowed their bowls and a half-eaten loaf of bread, Pearl saw his appraisal and flattened a hand at the low-cut neck, a quick self-conscious gesture.

'Sally gave it to me.' She brushed the stiffened fabric of the skirt. 'She's outgrown it, but it fits me well. She said I should wear something special tonight, to ... to celebrate. This dress was a gift, like that.' She pointed at the red-lined cloak that was now folded over a chair. 'It brought you luck, didn't it?'

Glancing at the Brotherhood's gift, Daniel wondered again what Octavian and the others would think of their hero if they knew the truth. Pearl rustled around the squat, bow-legged table and came closer. 'Everyone is talking of the fight. You're famous, brother. What was it like?'

He shook his head. 'Not now.'

'But you won! Surely every moment must be clear in your mind. When I was at . . .' She plucked at the stiff blue satin. 'When I was out on the streets and saw men calling out "Soldier, Soldier", I knew they meant you. I was so proud to be your sister.'

'You shouldn't have been on the streets of London alone.'

'I was with Jen and Sally.' In the candlelight, her eyes gleamed. Daniel recognised that look and the determined set of her pointed chin.

'You mustn't be alone.' He caught her hand. 'Promise me. From now on, whatever happens, you are *never* to be alone, Pearl.'

'You worry too much!' She twisted her lips into a moue of discontent. 'I am a young woman now and quite able to look out for myself.' Infuriatingly it was Jen's voice he heard.

Daniel spent most of the night sitting upright on his bed with his back to the dripping wall. From here he kept watch on Pearl curled beneath blankets in her niche, and on the doorway to their chamber. He did not expect another visit from Elias and his men, but he could not ignore the King's last words to him.

'I will not forget this.'

The fight was over, but the battle lines were now drawn.

His body ached and his knuckles were sore. Without mufflers, the skin had broken across the bones where his bare fists, particularly the left, had connected again and again with the hide of The Bull. That skirmish seemed to have taken place a lifetime ago. Now he had another, more deadly enemy.

His head was remarkably clear as he considered his most urgent strategy. Any lingering effects from Safardi's blows or Coppin's dwale were kept at bay by his determination to take Pearl to a place of safety.

Just before seven when the waker made his final round of The Maze, Daniel roused Pearl and asked her to dress. He told her a friend was coming to see them and urged her to be ready. At first, she was unwilling and more than a little obstinate, but when she learned it was Musa, her attitude softened.

'You mean the younger man who was with you and Mr Trimm, last night?' she asked as she sorted through her small collection of gowns. Like the new dark satin, most of them had been donated by Jen or Sally. 'Is he also a fighter?'

'He is – and a good one.' Daniel watched her select a simple, pale yellow cotton dress that flattered her colouring and her shape.

'She's not a child anymore.'

Jen's words came back to him, but he forced them away. If he had cared to consider the matter – which, as usual, he did not – Daniel might have found that one of the reasons he had asked the young fighter to accompany them that morning relied on the truth of that statement. Musa was a handsome young man.

'He is also a friend,' Daniel continued. 'We have some . . . matters to attend to for Mr Trimm this morning and I don't want to leave you here alone.'

That much, at least, was true, he thought, as he went out into the passage while Pearl washed and dressed. Down the way, a small girl was throwing a ball against the bricks. The dim light of the candles set into the niches along the walls could not disguise her ragged state or her blackened, shoeless feet. When she saw him, she stopped her game and grinned.

'Soldier!' She waved and shouted out his chosen name.

The alarm was raised. In a moment, men, women and children came to the entrances of their lodgings along the crooked passage and began to cheer again. One woman shuffled alongside and grabbed Daniel's hand. She beckoned her thin, grime-encrusted children to join them.

'Here he is, our very own champion. It's not often you'll see his like down here. Why, it's a pleasure to meet you this morning, sir.'

She held his hand and kissed it with scuffed lips. 'My John laid a shilling on you. I'll happily admit it, I wasn't pleased about that, but you made it come good.'

When Musa arrived a little while later, Daniel was completely surrounded.

If Musa had wondered why Daniel was so concerned for the safety of his sister, he found an answer of sorts in the wild, rapturous reception that greeted their progress through The Maze and then along the streets and passages of St Giles.

In truth, Daniel was also astonished – and relieved. His plan had worked better than he had imagined. Elias could not challenge him when he carried the hearts of the people in his pockets. By the time they reached King Street they were followed by a rowdy group of boys who called his fighting name and dared each other to touch him. Disturbed by the racket, pinch-faced shopkeepers rubbed their hands on their aprons and came to their doorways to complain, but they too clapped and shouted with their customers when they recognised 'The Soldier'.

When they reached the edge of Covent Garden they were at the head of a chanting procession. Some of the men, perhaps former soldiers themselves, began a ragged, but hearty rendition of 'We'll Offer No Quarter'. Daniel was glad of it. No one would dare to threaten them in the midst of such an army.

Pearl was clearly delighted by the attention, but also a little startled. He noted the way she huddled closer to Musa when the crowd pressed around them. His strategy was working. She had no idea what was about to happen. Although he felt guilty to use his friend as a distraction, he had no alternative. Pearl was flattered by the company of the good-looking young fighter and Daniel was using that innocent pleasure to ensure her compliance.

Musa signalled to him anxiously and shouted above the noise.

'This is dangerous. Two years ago, Lord Gordon led such a crowd against the papists. It became a riot and the army was sent out.'

'There are only a hundred here with us,' Daniel shouted back.

'And that is enough to alert the militia,' Musa replied.

Daniel looked at the faces around them. The mood was joyful but anarchic. Chaos lurked beneath the merriment. Musa was right to be wary. The streets of London were a tinderbox and he was playing with fire.

It was a relief to reach the mouth of the darkened alleyways leading to The Black Apollo. The narrow, shadowed space could not easily accommodate the crowd. Daniel turned and raised his hand, which set off a new chorus of cheers and shouts.

'Good people, I am overwhelmed by your friendship,' he shouted above the racket.

A man yelled back, 'You're our champion, Soldier – one of our own.'

This elicited more cheers and vigorous shouts of agreement.

Daniel bowed. 'And I am proud to be your humble servant. But . . .' His voice echoed from the walls. There was something in its timbre and gravity that brought a hush to the crowd. 'I must ask you to come no further. These passages are narrow. I would not wish to be the cause of a crush or an accident. A true champion protects his friends. I am touched by your fellowship, but now I beg you to return to your day.'

There was some muttering and then the same man who had called out replied, 'The Soldier is right. It wouldn't do if we trampled the life from his body. To speak plain, it wouldn't do us much good neither. We must bid good day to you, sir, and to your family.'

There were some good-natured calls of agreement followed by reluctant shuffling and a gradual thinning of the crowd. After a minute or two, they were alone.

'Daniel.' Pearl's eyes shone with pride. Glancing at Musa, she grinned shyly. 'Family indeed!'

'Is Mr Richardson here?' He watched Cyrus check the alleyway before closing the sturdy, fortified door.

'He is, sir. You'll find him in the salon by the fire.' The small man regarded the party gathered in the hallway. 'And these people . . .?'

'This is my sister Pearl and this . . .' Daniel indicated Musa, '. . . is a good friend. Please, I must speak to Mr Richardson.'

Cyrus scratched his scalp beneath the powdered wig. 'It's just . . . it's just that young ladies . . .' His eyes went to Pearl. 'Well, it is not something that generally . . .' Shaking his head, he smiled and flicked a gloved hand to indicate acceptance. 'Very well, go on then, but only because she's your sister and it's a slow day.'

He settled back into the padded leather chair at his sentry post by the door and Daniel led the way down the red-painted hall. The scent of good coffee was welcome after the stench of the streets. Moving aside the tapestry curtain at the end of the passage, he allowed Pearl to go first and then Musa.

Cyrus was right. The room was almost empty apart from two men playing chess in a wooden booth and Inigo Richardson who was sitting in a wide, high-backed chair drawn close to the hearth with one of his feet propped on a cushioned stool. His silver hair glowed in the firelight as he studied the newspaper in his hands.

'You two wait there for a moment.' Daniel pointed to a booth some distance from the fire. 'I have something to discuss with Mr Richardson.'

Pearl seemed delighted by the prospect of spending time in the exclusive company of her brother's charming friend, but Musa looked puzzled. Daniel patted his arm.

'I think you'll find my sister easy company. Just for a little while.'

When they were settled – Pearl torn between her curiosity about

The Black Apollo and her pleasure to be alone with Musa – Daniel went over to Richardson.

'The very devil!' The old man laid down his newspaper and smacked his thighs with the palms of his hands. 'Why, I was just reading about you here.' He patted the folded sheet. 'And I was about to send out the boy with a message. The Brotherhood are meeting here the day after tomorrow, Wednesday evening.' He smiled warmly. 'And it's on account of you. There is much to discuss. Sit, sit.'

Wincing as he moved his leg from the stool to make way, he pointed at the chair opposite.

'You are famous, sir, an ornament to The Black Apollo. We will toast your success. Tolly!'

The boy appeared from behind the curtained doorway on the far side of the room and came to stand next to Richardson's chair.

'Brandy, I think. A new bottle and two glasses.' He winked at the boy. 'Not the usual, mind. The best French – from the lower cellar.'

When Tolly was gone, Richardson clapped his large hands and rubbed them together.

'Well, this is quite marvellous. I'd hazard there's a not a man or woman in London who hasn't heard of The Soldier by now. *The London Courant* there,' he nodded at the newspaper, 'is full of your success. It's a rag, mind, but popular. On behalf of the Brotherhood, I congratulate you, Daniel. I may be first to do so, but I won't be the last. Of course, we were in no doubt of your victory, but even so, this is a moment to savour. D'ye hear they're singing songs about you in the taverns?' Richardson leaned forward. 'People are drawing your likeness on the walls. That's a sign if ever there was one.'

Daniel looked away from the man's beaming face and stared into the flames. He wondered if Richardson could see the guilt flickering on his skin. So many secrets – each one binding him so tightly that it felt as if the life was being choked slowly from his body. He hadn't considered the full implications of this moment until now. What should he say? Did he even have the right to ask? He considered the options as his genial host continued to heap praise upon him.

Tolly returned with a tray and set it down on the stool formerly occupied by Richardson's foot.

Grinning, the old man took up a dusty, fat-bellied bottle, peered at the label and turned it towards Daniel.

'This is exceptional.' He grunted as he worked at the cork stopper. 'I never share it with customers. It's for special occasions only. Join me.'

He poured out two glasses and raised his own as a toast, but at the sight of Daniel's expression he frowned. 'Come now. A man cannot celebrate alone.'

Pearl's laughter rang across the room. They turned to see her lean across the table to flick something from Musa's shoulder. The young fighter seemed equally delighted by his companion.

Richardson smiled. 'There's a pretty face.'

Daniel made his decision. 'Sir, I must ask a great favour of you.'

When he had finished, Inigo Richardson was unusually quiet. The old man stared into the flames, turning the brandy glass in his fingers. The fire struck shivering prisms of light from the crystal that danced on the walls. As last he put the glass down and reached beside the chair for his long clay pipe.

'When I married Alys she was already carrying our child and that added to our joy.' He pressed a wodge of tobacco into the pipe bowl. 'But when her time came, it was hard. She tried, God knows she tried, for three days, but the child would not be born. In the end, they said I had to decide – Alys or the babe. A man should not be asked such a thing.' He looked up. Daniel saw tears in his eyes.

'But I made a choice and my dear Alys was saved by it. Our child – a girl she was – died. And afterwards, we were never able to make another. I think of my daughter every day and I weep for her, we both do, but I know I made the right decision. As did you.'

Richardson turned to watch Pearl and Musa for a moment, then he held a taper to the fire and lit the pipe. Settling back into his chair, he nodded.

'There's no shame in putting the thing you love most before everything else. I did the same for Alys and I would have done the same as you if the only family I had in the world was in peril. You did right, Daniel, but all the same, I'm glad it's me you came to as there may be some hotheads who might not agree.'

He sucked on the pipe and stared into the fire.

'The pity of it is that Lady Fortune is a heartless bitch; she always finds a way to make you pay. As for that bastard Elias, he played a false hand, but his time is coming.

'Now . . .' He leaned forward and patted Daniel's knee. 'I'll do two favours for you. First, I won't tell the Brotherhood that you intended to lose the fight, for what would be the point of that?'

He sucked on the pipe and exhaled its aromatic smoke through his nostrils, then he waved the stem in the direction of Pearl and Musa.

'And second, I'll happily take your sister in and keep her safe. I know that Alys will be delighted by her company.'

Chapter Thirty-four

When he returned alone to The Maze, Daniel finally allowed his body and his mind to take the rest he had denied himself. Sleep took him immediately, plunging him into darkness so deep and complete that he did not even dream. At first.

He met her again in the thin place where sleep frays into thought and desire. Her sun-warmed skin was smooth and her body was lean. Her limbs wrapped around him as they lay on a bed of ferns and sweet-scented flowers.

'Daniel?'

Sitting on the stone floor beside the bed, she was silhouetted against the candlelight. He tried to speak, to reach out to her, but just for a moment his body was still trapped by sleep.

'I didn't have the heart to wake you.' She stroked his face gently. The air was filled with the scent of roses.

Something was wrong. *She* was wrong. As his senses returned, a dull persistent pain simmered beneath his skull.

'You need rest, that's what I heard Mr Trimm say. I reckon it's all caught up with you. You've been out for hours. I should know, I've sat here for nearly two of them. It's long past seven now.'

She reached for a candlestick set on the floor beside the bed and raised it.

'A bit more than a scratch . . .' Jen peered at his face, '. . . but it'll heal soon enough. And it's nothing compared to Safardi. They're all talking about it up top.' Her fingers brushed his forehead. 'The air will do it a favour and I've brought something else that will do you good too.'

Leaving the candlestick at his side, she stood and went to the table. There was a rasping sound and a flash as she struck a flint to light another flame. He heard the rustle of paper. 'I thought you'd have an appetite and that you'd be thirsty too so I brought some things. There's porter, bread, cheese, a skirt and gammon pie – that's from Ma Rumney – and some apples from the market. Pearl must have gone out to fetch something too, so we'll have a regular feast when she gets back.'

Pearl.

Daniel looked around the chamber they had shared until a few hours ago. Old patched shawls draped their few sticks of furniture and common weeds drooped in a tin mug on a shelf. For the first time he saw the way that she had tried to make their hovel into a home. Pearl was both horribly missing and painfully present, like the gap left by a drawn tooth.

When she had been informed that she was not leaving The Black Apollo she had treated it as a joke. Sliding a look at Musa, she had grinned and asked him to rescue her. When it became clear, however, that her brother was in earnest, Pearl's good humour vanished. Protesting, she'd beaten her fists on Daniel's chest, before trying to escape along the passage but Cyrus would not open the iron-banded door to release her. Hammering on the wood, she yelled for help and called out to anyone who would listen that her brother was trying to make her a captive. It was a good thing, he decided as he pulled her back along the hallway, that it was a slow day at The Apollo.

Eventually Pearl's furious defiance turned to tears. Exhausted by herself, she curled into a chair and wept. At this point Daniel judged it the right time to explain that he was doing this for her own good. Kneeling, he tried to comfort her.

'It's because of what I did – going out without telling you.' She had looked up at him, crushed and resentful. 'This is a punishment, isn't it?'

In a way it was. But the punishment was all his. For now, he could not bring himself to tell her the truth about Elias and the fight. Explaining the intended betrayal to Richardson had been painful enough.

Fortunately, Alys Richardson had arrived at that moment carrying a tray on which sat a silver spout pot and a small china bowl. Bustling to Pearl's side, she had patted the girl's hand and wiped away her tears before pouring out a measure of rich dark chocolate. Alys Richardson was as plump as her husband and twice as welcoming. Once two bowls of chocolate had been consumed, she gathered the somewhat mollified girl to her straining bodice and whispered about the pretty room she had ready and the jolly time they would have together. This, along with Musa's promise to visit, had gone some way to reconcile Pearl to her prison.

She was protected, but her absence was awful.

Daniel watched Jen move items around on the table and produce more from a rope bag.

'I don't blame you for last night. After the fight you needed time to come back to yourself. I see that now.' She freed a large, crimp-topped pie from brown paper wrapping. 'But I don't expect you to blame me, neither. Your sister badly needs to see there's a world outside these walls. I'm surprised, I won't lie, but I'm glad you've trusted her enough to go out on her own today. Do you have a knife for this pie?'

On her own.

Daniel sat up against the wall. He felt the bricks dig into his back. 'Pearl's not coming back here.'

'What do you mean?' Jen swung about. There was an apple in her hand. 'Where is she?'

'She's safe – *now*. After last night I had to make sure of it. You had no right to take her onto the streets.'

Jen hurled the apple at his head. Missing him, it thumped against the wall and then rolled across the stones to a dark corner. He was glad it wasn't a knife.

'We did no wrong! Where's the harm in taking Pearl out from this ... this ...' She gestured at the stained bricks above her head. '*This!* She's a young woman, Dan, or haven't you noticed? There are better things in life than scrubbing pots at The Mitre and keeping house for your brother – not that I'd call this a house. When I was Pearl's age—'

'I think we both know what you were doing when you were Pearl's age.' He regretted the cheap retort immediately. Jen stared at him and then turned sharply away. She shoved viciously at something on the table and it clattered to the floor.

'That was wrong of me.' Disgusted by himself, he stood and went to her side. 'I didn't mean it.'

'Well, you said it, so you must have thought it.' She squared her shoulders against him.

'Forgive me.' Putting a hand to her arm, Daniel pulled her gently about to face him. Her eyes were glassy, but fierce.

'When I told you about Elias, I didn't think ...' She shook her head. 'I told you so that you'd know the truth. I gave you the chance to end everything between us then because that was the right thing to do. I didn't tell you so that you could hold it against me.'

'I don't.' He pulled her closer. 'I'm sorry. I should never have said that.'

'You did, though.' Despite the tears that threatened to brim over onto her cheeks, she held his gaze.

'I've never told anyone what Elias did to me, not even Jerome, although I suspect he might have guessed.' She swallowed. 'Is that why you sent Pearl away? Because I'm not good enough for her? Not fit to be in her company? I know you want her to be a lady.'

'That's not true, Jen.' He moved his hands to her shoulders and stared into her eyes, willing her to see his contrition. 'Surely you know that?'

'I'm not sure what I know. Since you won that fight you've been a different man. I trusted you, Dan, but it seems you didn't trust *me*.'

'I *do* trust you.' The words sounded hollow, even to Daniel himself. He wrapped his arms about her and whispered into her hair, 'I'm sorry,' repeating the thin apology. 'What I said was wrong. Perhaps it was the fight, or the drug I was given. It must have muddled my wits. I don't know what I'm saying.'

'Drug?'

Jen pulled back. Daniel saw something like hope flicker across her face. Her naked vulnerability was painful. She was usually so self-assured, but his thoughtless words had cut deep. Discovered, she looked quickly away.

'What do you mean, "muddled your wits"?'

It was too easy, but he was grateful to be able to use the dwale to explain, though not excuse, his terrible insult. He even managed to suggest he was fearful that Coppin might still want to take revenge through Pearl.

Another lie. He was building a castle of them.

The truth was that he could not bring himself to tell Jen the real reason for Pearl's confinement because he was ashamed.

When he finished, she was quiet for a moment. Taking his hand, she examined the broken skin across the knuckles. Then she guided the tips of his fingers to the roughened skin of her own palm. 'If you think Pearl's life is hard down here, you might want to consider what it was like for me, all those years,' she said quietly.

'Why do you stay in The Maze?' Daniel lifted her chin. 'Why have you never left?'

She peered into the shadows over his shoulder. Her eyes moved across the wall as if she sought an answer in the cracked bricks and failed plaster.

'There are all sorts of cages, Dan,' she began. 'Some of them grow around you for such an age that you don't even notice until it's too late. Perhaps I've left it too long to know anything different? All I know for sure is that I've made a life for myself here and I have a place. But, Pearl now ...' She paused. 'When I first looked at her – long before you and I became ... well, *before*, I knew I wanted to help her spread her wings and fly free. God knows, it's hard for a woman alone to make her own choices.'

'She's not alone and she's not a woman, she's a child.' Daniel tried to temper his exasperation. 'As for freedom, she's not a prisoner. I've simply taken her somewhere where I know she will be protected. Surely you of all people can understand that?'

'Where is she then?' Jen stared up at him. 'She's my friend, after all. If you truly trust me, like you say you do, then you'll tell me.'

Daniel had always thought of himself as a man of honour, but now, mortified by his earlier blundering insensitivity, he felt tested by the challenge in her eyes. He considered the question and found that there was no great harm in telling her where Pearl was.

'She's at The Black Apollo.' He sighed. 'Mr Richardson and Alys have agreed to look after her until ...'

Until when?

That was a question he could not answer.

'Can I visit her?'

He nodded. 'I'm sure she would be pleased to see you.'

He knew that was true.

Jen's face softened. When she smiled her face had an impish, playful quality that both unbalanced and added to her beauty.

'They're good people.' She nodded and at last Daniel knew they had a truce.

'At least I know Pearl will be happy there,' she continued. 'Alys will be like a second mother to her. I've always thought it a shame they never had children of their own.'

Remembering Richardson's story, Daniel felt a rush of warmth towards the man who was guarding both Pearl and his secret. Jen turned from him and gestured at the food. 'I brought enough for a regiment, not just the three of us. It would be a pity to waste it.'

She went to the table and took up a squat brown bottle. As she worked at the stopper, the thick coils of her hair, caught back with a strip of green satin, shivered down her back. Leaning forward, she swept the ribbon to one side revealing the nape of her neck. The moment had a grace and delicacy that shamed him again.

'There's something else too,' she called back. 'Sally gave me a copy of *The London Courant*. She said, most particularly, to look at Mr Scribbler's Society Notes. I'll fetch it over and we'll read it together.'

'Mr Scribbler – whoever he is – can wait.'

Daniel went to her. Turning her from the table, he kissed her. The taste of her lips and the curve of her body beneath his hands was reassuringly familiar. Losing himself in her copper-flecked hair and her musky floral scent, he reached for the lacings of her dress.

Their passion was a welcome act of oblivion.

Jen was gone by the time the waker made his first rounds of The Maze, but her scent lingered on Daniel's skin and in his bed. The blanket where she had lain beside him remembered her warmth and her shape. Before leaving, as was her habit, she had lit a candle on the table. Another little flame guttered above a tallow stump set into a niche in the wall. He smiled, sat up and rolled the aching muscles of his back and neck.

He was hungry now and grateful for the untouched food from the previous night. A couple of fat-bodied flies buzzed above the table, but undeterred Daniel took up Ma Rumney's pie. Ripping the crust in two, he crammed a mouthful of meat and pastry into his mouth and then he reached for the porter. There was cheese too, he remembered, as he tipped back the bottle and drank. Scanning the table, he wondered if it had fallen to the floor. A wedge of cheddar was there on the stones, along with a furled newspaper, and something that glittered. Frowning, Daniel took up the arrow-headed pin. It was real enough – evidence of his encounter on the steps of Rutland House and proof that he had tackled the man who had worn it. The tiny gems winked in the candlelight as he rolled it between his fingers and thumb.

The stock pin was well crafted and of some value, but the design was commonplace.

Distance replaced his certainty as to the identity of its owner with doubt. Remembering Melkie's story of the unfortunate sailor who thought he could fly, Daniel considered the likelihood that the dwale had tricked him. Perhaps the drug had fed upon his feelings for both Adanna and for James Fitzallen? What if it had dredged those complicated emotions from the place where they were usually guarded and shaped them into phantoms?

Placing the pin on the table, he reached for the rolled copy of *The London Courant*. It was the newspaper that Richardson had set aside yesterday at The Apollo.

'Why, I was just reading about you here.'

Daniel was not vain, but he was curious to know what was written of him.

Kneeling, he flattened the sail-like sheets out on the stones. It was difficult to read the close-packed print in the dimly lit chamber so he took the candle from the table and set it down next to him.

He found himself on page five. Indeed, he was the prime subject of something that called itself:

Mister Scribbler's Society Notes

Beneath the boldly printed words, **A Moste Notable Victory,** Daniel followed a florid account of his success with the tip of a finger.

London hails a new Champion of the Pugilistic Arts following the extraordinary tournament held at Rutland House in the presence of His Royal Highness, The Prince of Wales. *The Soldier,* for that is the victor's chosen name – and it is surely one that will not easily be forgotten by those present – defeated a certain Rafael Safardi, known across Europe as *The Bull,* in the Moste exhilarating Demonstration of the Noble Sport that this Correspondent has yet been privileged to observe. To describe the Incident of the Contest would be tedious and also illogical given that your Humble Scribe recognised so many of *The London Courant*'s gentle Readers amongste those permitted to attende by His Grace, the Duke of Calne. (The latter accompanied, as has become usual, by the Scintillating Lady M...) It is Delightful, is it not, to Speculate upon the coincidence that the two Moste Colourful additions to our Season should be brought together beneath the famous – some might say Scandalous – painted roof of Rutland House? *The Soldier* was presented for duty by former champion Mister Melkie Trimm, whose reputation needs no recitation here.

He read it a second time, noting the reference to the Marquise and to the colour of her skin; *their* skin. Lemuel Darke was right. There was insult here masquerading as admiration.

'... *the scintillating Lady M* ...'

Daniel sat back. Had she been Adanna, or was he mistaken?

Footsteps clattered in the passage beyond the chamber. He looked up as a breathless boy whose clothes appeared to be held together by grime rather than thread tumbled across the threshold. Wiping the back of a hand across his nose, he stared at Daniel as if he might be some class of holy relic.

'You The Soldier?' The question was whispered.

Daniel nodded. The scruffy boy performed a sort of bow and shuffled reverently towards him.

'I was asked to give you this.' From somewhere amid the tatters, he produced a folded note of remarkable whiteness.

Daniel's neck prickled as he stared at the note. Was this a sally from Elias?

'Who gave it to you?'

'A girl up top.' The boy sniffed. 'She was sitting in a fancy coach outside The Mitre and asking for you. She said she had a message to deliver and would I be obliged. I said I knew where to find you and that it would be an honour, sir.' The boy bowed again.

Daniel took the note from his hand. 'Did you recognise her?'

'Never laid eyes on her before. She was like you . . .' the messenger patted his own face, 'but her clothes were fine and she smelled good. Like them lemons in the market.'

Daniel flipped the note over to examine a large red wax seal.

'Did she say anything else?'

The boy nodded. 'No reply is required. She said that her mistress is very sure of the answer.'

The edges of the thick, expensive paper were tinged with gold that caught the candlelight. Daniel tore at the seal and unfolded the note. The message, written in an elegant hand, was brief.

The Marquise de Notaille invites 'The Soldier'
to attend her weekly salon.

Tuesday, September 17th at seven o'clock.

32 Leicester Square

Chapter Thirty-five

This was madness, but he couldn't help himself.

Daniel scowled at the battered face reflected from the shard of mirror propped against the wall. The cut from the thorn was nothing, but the skin beneath his bloodshot right eye was now pouched and swollen. When he put a finger to his cheek, he could feel a tenderness caused by Safardi's last blows.

Stepping back, he took in the length of his person. The black coat, waistcoat and matching breeches were simple but fine. These, along with a plain white stock and buckled shoes, had been provided by Melkie or perhaps – and more likely – by the resourceful Mrs Trimm.

Earlier in the day he had sent a message to the warehouse. In it he described the unexpected invitation to Leicester Square and his need for adequate attire. He had received a prompt answer. Along with a parcel containing the clothing, there was a note in Melkie's surprisingly flamboyant hand.

Make no mistake, lad, they'll all want you now. Happened to me and very fine it was, although I was lucky to have my Hannah to keep me straight. An invitation like that is rare as a frost in hell and it can't hurt your reputation – or <u>mine</u>. Mrs T has her own opinions on the matter, mind, all of them drawn from the scandal sheets. Apparently, those salons are notorious. Half the great ladies of London go to the Marquise

to have their fortunes told while the other half wouldn't be seen in the
same room with her. And she's French.

Something in the heavy pen work of that last line suggested that
although Melkie thought little of his wife's misgivings, the nation-
ality of the lady was enough to damn her. Daniel did not care what
the second-hand gossipmongers said of the Marquise. It was his own
opinion that mattered.

The black coat sat well across his shoulders, unlike the one he
had borrowed and given away. Just a little while ago, Jerome would
have been the first person he would have turned to under such circumstances, but now that was impossible.

Leaning into the mirror again, he avoided his eyes as he tied the
stock in a simple knot. Above the white silk, the darkness of his skin
made his head seem to float untethered from his body. It seemed
appropriate. He was, indeed, losing his mind. A devil was driving
him tonight and he was powerless to resist. There was a challenge
in that message, *'her mistress is very sure of the answer'*, that sounded so
very like Adanna. The girl he had mourned for so long had always
been imperious.

He had to know.

It was a small comfort that Pearl was safe in the care of the
Richardsons. At least he would not have to explain this folly. Behind
his reflection in the glass, the remains of the meal that Jen had intended to share with him were still spread across the table. He had
not seen her since the early hours, long before the arrival of the
invitation. She did not know about the salon and he was uncomfortably glad of it. The smallest voice – so faint that he could almost
shut it out – asked him what he would do if the Marquise really
was Adanna. He tore his eyes from the eviscerated pie and returned
his attention to the stock, which was a little too tight at the throat.

Daniel turned uneasily from the mirror and took up the

invitation. Holding it to the light of the candle, he examined the writing, trying to detect the hand of the girl who had taught him to read and write under the milky light of the Caribbean moon.

Those evenings when he had slipped from the huts and gone to meet Adanna in the forest clearing midway between The Salutation and the quarters of the enslaved had been both thrilling and dangerous. For the first time in a long while he allowed himself to visit the shrine of her memory.

Adanna had been shipped to the Garnett Estate from Dahomey, the land of her birth. From the moment she arrived at the dusty plantation she was different to all the others. Tall and imposing, she radiated a sullen fury that kept everyone – even Daniel at first – at bay.

She was set to work in the boiling house with the children and the younger men and women. Standing mutely beside her during those first days, he showed her how to add the correct amounts of ashes and lime to the raw cane juice before it was heated and ladled by hand into a series of vast metal coppers – reducing at every step until, at last, the syrup-thick mixture was almost crystallised and ready to be sent in clay moulds to the curing house.

When the coppers were bubbling, they could not be left. He and Adanna spent days and nights working side by side. At first, he was scared of this haughty unreachable girl, but one night, exhausted, she had almost fallen asleep on her feet as she stirred the boiling mixture. Her ladle had fallen into the copper and – startled suddenly to her senses – without thinking she had reached down to retrieve it. Daniel had grabbed her hand and pulled her away, not fast enough to prevent a savage burn, but in time to save her from almost certain death. Garnett money would not be wasted to treat the injuries of a slave.

After that moment they became firm friends, and a little while later that friendship deepened.

Daniel became completely besotted by Adanna. He was captivated by her stories, by her grace and by her beauty. In turn, she called him her protector and said that if her father had been alive, he would have made him a great man for saving her life.

Gradually he learned her story. The daughter of a king, she had been taught to speak and to write the language of the Englishmen who traded with her people, the Fon. This was not uncommon for the children of those who dealt with the 'bone men', she explained. Indeed, it was expected for a high-born child to display accomplishments. She told him how her father had loved to display her skills, taking pleasure from the look on the men's pale faces as his clever, beautiful daughter spoke and read aloud to them in their own tongue.

But it was those very skills that undid her. When her people were eventually defeated in battle, Adanna became a valuable trophy. No longer a princess but a prisoner, she was dragged many miles in chains to the slave market on the edge of the sea where she was sold by her people's enemies for a high price. When she spoke to the men who had bought her in their own language, they doubled her price.

Adanna possessed an indefinable quality that separated her from the others on the Garnett Estate. Years later, still haunted by her in his dreams, Daniel recognised that quality as nobility. At fourteen years old, however, he was too infatuated and enmeshed in the coils of first love to examine his feelings.

He was not the only one to notice her. Six months from the day of Adanna's arrival, Mistress Isabella came very early one brilliant blue and gold morning to the workers' quarters. As she sat in her open carriage, the fringe of her white silk parasol trembled in the breeze while Driver Kemp commanded all the young women to stand in a line before her. Without saying a word, she flicked the spiteful silver chains of her tiny jewelled flail at Adanna to indicate her choice. Later that day, Adanna was taken up to The Salutation.

When he received a first secret message from her – carried by Esther the cook who had come down to collect herbs from the shadowed places between the house and the fields – he was elated.

They met at night whenever they could, taking advantage of Kemp's fondness for rum and his man Riley's weakness for women. The risk was great, but so was the reward. Despite the danger, Daniel could not help himself. When he was with Adanna he was blinded by her brilliance and their passion, but when they were apart it was not always easy to block his ears to the things that were said of her.

He could never admit it to his mother or to Jon his brother, but it was true that something in Adanna's manner changed after she went to the Great House. Occasionally she accompanied the mistress when she rode out in her carriage, but she did not smile or acknowledge in any way the people she had lived among. And in the weeks and months that followed, her clothes became very fine for a slave girl, even one who had been taken to work inside. There were whispers about the way she had become plump and plush, while those she had left starved and scavenged.

Their meetings continued in darkness and secrecy. Sometimes, Adanna smuggled books from Sir Oliver's library. It was dangerous, subversive even, for a plantation slave to be able to read, but she told Daniel that one day, when they were both free, it was a skill upon which they would build their future. Under her impatient tuition he mastered his letters with surprising ease and allowed himself to dream of a different life with her.

A year later, when that future together had become imperative, he told her about the plans for rebellion. He told her that at the right time he would send her a sign and that he would come for her so that they could all be together at last.

But he never got the chance.

Daniel crumpled the invitation in his fist. If Adanna had survived that terrible night when the roof of The Salutation had blackened and burned beneath a bloodied sky, where would she have gone?

Lights burned at every window of the pale flat-fronted house. Daniel looked up at the fine symmetrical façade. Two footmen, whose gem-studded livery must surely have cost more than the yearly wage of a working man, flanked the open door. From within, the sound of music and laughter tumbled down the steps.

No. 32 Leicester Square was removed from the Garnett Plantation in every possible way.

He considered the evening ahead. If the Marquise was truly Adanna, then what? Had she recognised him at the fight as he had her, and if so, was this to be a reunion? But what if that final vision from the hack had been an illusion?

The answer lay beyond that door.

He breathed deeply and the sulphurous scent of the street blocked his nose. It was a stench he was familiar with. The Maze was a putrid warren, but even houses as fine as these stood beside gutters clogged with human filth and where the mounded excrement of horses and dogs attracted flies before the pure gatherers came in the night.

A small elegant carriage rolled to a halt before the house. Although it blocked his view, he heard laughter and conversation as its passengers – two women – went to the door. Their voices were brittle as glass and their shrill laughter sprang from the desire to be thought amusing.

Daniel knew he did not belong in this world, and yet he was unable to resist the thought that the girl – now a woman – he had worshipped all his life might be here in London and tantalisingly close.

Straightening the collar of his coat, he stepped forward.

There was a hiss from the shadows. He turned to see a hand beckoning from a darkened alleyway running between two of the houses. Daniel had been expecting something like this. His heart pumped beneath the good linen supplied by Mrs Trimm.

Moving back into the light spilling from the windows behind him, he braced himself for attack. 'If you want me, come out where I can see you. How do I know that you haven't been sent by Elias with half a dozen men at your back?'

'I'm alone.' Hands raised, Sparrow shuffled forward. His oversized coat was bedraggled and stained and several of the brass buttons were missing. As he moved, Daniel saw that he limped, dragging one foot behind him. One of his eyes was swollen, bruised and almost sealed.

Forgetting his fears, he went to take the boy by the arm, but was almost repelled by the stink rising from his coat.

'What happened to you? Who did this?'

'That's easy to guess, I should think. No mystery there.' Sparrow winced. 'He's not happy. And when the temper takes him, he's not kind.' The boy tried to smile. His lips were split and crusted with dried blood. One of his front teeth was missing. Daniel was shocked by the wounds on the boy's face. Those inflicted upon him by Safardi were minor in comparison. 'Elias lost a fortune on you. You weren't supposed to win, were you?'

When Daniel didn't reply, he shrugged. 'It don't matter. I'm glad. It's good to see that bastard suffer – even if he took it out on me. Could have been anyone – I just happened to be handy at the time. Thing is . . .' He paused as another party of guests arrived at the house. Their carriage was accompanied by four link boys whose torches made the classical façades of the houses shiver with light.

'Thing is,' Sparrow began again, 'I've got a message for you.'

'From Elias?'

Sparrow shook his head. 'I'm not going to work for him anymore – not after this. He'll kill me next time most likely and there's no profit in death. No, it's a message from *me*.' Straightening up, he gathered his damp coat around him. 'Elias is making plans for you.

He's had word about your fight – not the one with The Bull, but the other one ... in the street. He's very interested in that gentleman. *Very.*' Repeating the word, the boy fixed Daniel with his good eye. 'As I heard it, there might be two men in London who share a wish to see you brought low.'

Daniel frowned. 'Do you mean James Fitzallen?'

'Probably.' Sparrow shrugged. 'I didn't catch his name properly when I was listening, but I heard something near that. It sounded like Elias was spitting it out.' Concentrating, he repeated the word 'Fitz' several times and seemed satisfied. 'Yes – that would be about right. *Fitzallen.* I'm sure of it. He and that gentleman have arranged to meet up on account of a mutual interest.'

When Daniel looked puzzled, Sparrow tried to wink.

'*You* – you're the mutual interest.'

'Why are you telling me this?'

'Because you could be ... well, I like to think that someone like you might be my f ...' Suddenly self-conscious, the boy stared at his boots where his grimy toes poked through ancient leather. 'Because I like to think you might need a friend like me. And also, because Jen's always been good to me.' He looked up. 'It's mainly on account of her that I thought you should know.'

James Fitzallen *had* been there at the fight. He was not a figment of Daniel's drugged imagination. He twisted about. The windows of 32 Leicester Square glowed in the thickening dark. Was it truly possible, then, that Adanna was waiting for him inside?

Instantly, he was ashamed that his thoughts should run to her, but when he turned back, Sparrow had gone.

Chapter Thirty-six

'You are to wait here.' Halting before a door, the girl turned to stare at him. Her face was pointed with something of a cat in the slant of her wide-set eyes and the pertness of her nose. She was pretty, certainly, although of the variety that did not sit well on an adult. Her skin was a shade lighter than that of her mistress, but where the Marquise was tall, her companion was small and childlike. Daniel could not guess her age, but her slight figure and knowing expression did not match.

Celeste had risen from a gilded chair just inside the hallway when, blinking in the light, he had walked beneath the blazing candle lantern suspended above the octagonal entrance vestibule of 32 Leicester Square. It was clear that she had been expecting him. Dipping into a curtsey, she had introduced herself and then without any further interrogation she had asked him to follow her.

The girl was dressed almost as elegantly as her mistress. The yellow silk of her figured gown whispered as she moved and the red heels of her slippers tapped on the chequered marble floor as she led the way without looking back.

As they mounted the stairs, the sounds of the Marquise's salon – conversation, laughter and the clink of glass – had bubbled from behind a set of highly ornamented double doors on the first landing, but Celeste walked past. Rounding the balcony lined with pastoral landscapes and hazy portraits of fashionably pale and listless women, she had rustled to a second flight of stairs and beckoned him to follow.

As they went higher, the air filled with the fragrance of the voluptuous blooms that spilled from porcelain bowls and vases set at intervals along every wall. Beneath the heady floral scent, Daniel detected a deeper, spiced aroma that reminded him uncomfortably of Elias.

Opening a door, Celeste stood to one side to allow Daniel to enter. 'My mistress will join you soon.'

Confused, he peered over the balcony rail.

'I understood that the invitation was to attend the Marquise's salon. We passed a room on the way here that—'

'I do not ask questions.' Interrupting him, Celeste smiled. The girl's white teeth were small and sharp. 'I simply obey my lady's commands.' Her voice was pleasant and agreeable. French was probably her birth tongue, Daniel thought, detecting a trace in her speech. He did not, however, detect welcome in her eyes. Instead, for a moment, before she turned away to usher him into the room, he thought he saw mockery.

She flicked a tiny, fine-boned hand towards a japanned tray set out on a table beside the fire. 'Refreshment has been provided should you require it.'

The dainty golden clock on the mantel held its breath for a moment and then jingled out a pretty tune to signal the half. Daniel stared at the dial and then at the untouched decanter and glass on the tray. Beside them lay a saucer of wafers arranged into a fan.

From far below the muffled levity of the salon reached the room, but this and the ticking of the clock were his only companions. He had waited for nearly half an hour now. Occasionally he had crossed to the window to watch carriages arrive, but the large pediment above the door and the steps leading to it obscured the view of the Marquise's guests.

The room was square and furnished in the height of fashion. A fire crackled in the hearth and costly wax candles burned in brackets on the walls. Their sweetness mingled pleasantly with the spices Daniel had recognised in the hallway. The scent was stronger here. A heavy day bed lined one powder-blue wall. Its gilded lion's paw feet gave the unsettling impression that it might scuttle to the window, rise up and peer down to the street if he turned his back upon it. Beyond the marble fireplace there was a shuttered escritoire, its parquetry curves ripe with moulded fruit. A bookcase filled the entire wall on the far side of the hearth.

While he waited, Daniel's attention had turned again and again to the portrait above the mantel. The woman who presided over the room wore a closely fitted riding coat over a billowing black skirt. The pale creamy stock at her throat was secured by a large ruby brooch, and a tall hat adorned with a curving red feather emphasised her height and presence. In her gloved right hand she carried a whip. She stood alone beneath the boughs of a storm-lashed tree. The artist had suggested the movement of the branches and the material of her skirt with great economy and skill. The brushwork was free and the application of the paint was both chaotic and bold. Only the face was rendered with precision. Adanna – for it was truly her – surveyed the room from beneath the brim of that striking hat with an unflinching gaze.

The chiming of the clock marked the end of Daniel's patience – he had no intention of waiting here alone for a moment longer. It was insulting to be led to a room and forgotten. Crossing to the door, he tried to open it and was surprised to find that it did not budge. At first, he thought the wood had warped in its frame, but further pulling and shoving revealed that the door was locked from the outside. Celeste had imprisoned him.

Recalling the mockery in her eyes, he wondered if she was playing a trick. If so, it was not amusing. He thought about calling aloud, but wondered if anyone would hear. The Marquise's guests were gathered below and judging by the sounds that reached the room where he now stood, his voice would be unlikely to be heard. He tried the handle again in disbelief.

'I have the key.'

His hand froze.

He turned at the low, liquid voice. Adanna stood before an open door that had been concealed in the bookcase beside the hearth. She glowed in the firelight. Dressed in a wide-skirted gown of golden silk, the rich sheen of the fabric emphasised the gleam of her skin. The front panels of the dress were caught back in complicated loops to reveal a black lace underskirt studded with gems that winked like cats' eyes. As before, a jewel shaped like a twinkling black comet chased across the whiteness of her elegant wig.

Raising the key in a hand gloved in black lace, she smiled; her darkly painted lips parted, revealing a gap between her teeth. 'I must apologise for leaving you here alone for so long.' The door of books swung silently back into place behind her as she continued. 'Now that I am quite ready, we will go down together. My guests have been waiting for some time. They will be impatient.'

Daniel was not prepared for this moment with the woman who had haunted his dreams and so many of his waking hours. Paralysed by a rush of emotion where love, desire, guilt and even fear were impossible to separate, he found he was unable to speak. As she walked towards him, the scent of her perfume – the spice of the islands laced with ambergris and vanilla – was another powerful assault. When she was so close that he could feel the heat of her body, her eyes locked on his. At that moment, he realised with a certainty he would wager his life upon that she *knew* him.

'Adanna.' Daniel managed to stammer out her name, even though his tongue was weighted with lead.

She blinked and her eyes slid away. There was an almost

imperceptible shake of her head before she gestured for him to move aside so that she could fit the key to the lock.

He reached for her arm. 'Adanna. I . . . You and I—'

Immediately she shrugged him away. The movement was so abrupt it was an insult. Stepping back, she smoothed the place where his hand had lain upon the silk of her sleeve as if it might have left a stain.

'Adanna,' he tried again, ashamed at the pleading in his voice.

'You are mistaken, Soldier.' She did not look at him as she fitted the key to the lock. 'My name is Marie-Angélique.' There was a click and she reached for the handle. 'But we will not be so familiar. You will call me *my lady*.'

They walked in silence down the stairs. Utterly confused, Daniel could not find the words, or perhaps the courage, to challenge her. As she went before him, he studied her straight golden back in a misery of incomprehension.

When they reached the broad landing above the hallway where the ornamented double doors led to the room of the assembly, she turned to face him. The jewelled black comet in her wig matched the glint in her eyes as she spoke.

'I must be plain with you, Soldier. You are not present this evening as a guest. You are part of my entertainment.'

Her voice had been smoothed and polished like a stone tumbled in a river and there was an echo of a French accent, but he recognised the richness and depth. Hardly able to take in what she was saying, he stared mutely at her. In the blazing light of the candle chandelier that hung over the hall, she was magnificent. Adanna was tall, but her fashionable wig added to her presence. He was a boy again before her.

'Do you understand me?' she continued. 'It is most important that you do not forget your place. I will introduce you and then you

will be at liberty to walk among my guests. Speak when you are
addressed, but do not initiate conversation. You will not be offered
refreshment.'

'Please.' He tried to catch Adanna's hand again, but withdrew
when he saw her expression. Was that disgust in her beautiful,
glittering eyes? Or fury? Something dangerous crackled between
them. He had the sudden and terrifying sensation that she might
strike out like a viper.

'You . . . you *know* me,' he whispered urgently. 'I am Daniel. You
must remember?'

Ignoring the question, Adanna spun about, her gorgeous golden
gown swirling around her. She signalled with her black feather
fan to a liveried footman standing at the corner of the landing.
Trotting to her side, he reached for the handles of the doors and
flung them open.

Adanna swept ahead and Daniel followed her into a pillared
room filled with women. The excited chatter and laughter stopped
immediately. All eyes turned to the semicircle of steps just inside
the doorway. There were gasps and a fresh flurry of murmurs when
some of the guests caught sight of him standing behind her.

Fluttering her fan, Adanna dipped into the slightest semblance of
a curtsey. Then she snapped the fan shut and beat it three times on
the palm of her outstretched hand.

'I am shamefully late and I must be punished.' Her voice dripped
with honey. Pausing to survey her guests, she tilted her head.
Diamond earrings trembled against the skin of her long neck. 'But
I hope you will forgive me when I bring such a prize.'

She turned to indicate Daniel, commanding him to come forward with a flick of her furled fan.

Numb with bewilderment, he did as she wished. A jolt seemed
to run through the gathering, then some of the women began to
clap, while others called aloud. Their comments were coarse. Daniel

flinched at the attention. The candlelit room was hot and sticky. The stink of champagne and ill-matched colognes was overpowering. It was clear that a great deal of alcohol had been taken while the women waited for their hostess. Their painted mouths were smeared, and beneath daubs of rouge, their cheeks burned, but not with shame.

Adanna's fingers rested lightly on his shoulder. Despite everything, her touch sent an ecstatic shiver through his body. He turned to her, but she was looking out into the room.

'Dear friends,' she began, her mellifluous voice soaring easily above the clamour, 'two days ago it was my great fortune to witness the birth of a champion, and now I wish to share that remarkable opportunity. Knowing that so many of you were unable to be present at Rutland House – ah, men, are they not infuriating creatures? – it is my delight to bring the sensation of our season to my humble salon. I present to you the man of whom we have heard so much. Dear ladies, I offer you ... The Soldier.'

It would have been better, Daniel thought, if the women did not seek his attention, then he would have been able to find a corner from which to watch her. Instead, they swarmed around him, buzzing like wasps drawn to molasses. The younger ones giggled and pushed too close, but their self-conscious excitement was preferable to the interest of the overdressed matrons whose questions were laced with presumption and tooth rot. His skin crawled when they pawed at him, stroking his hand or squeezing his muscles as if he were a prize farmyard animal.

There were two other black men in the room but, as servants, they moved invisibly among the squawking guests carrying trays of glasses and sweetmeats. The women did not acknowledge them and, more painfully, the two men did not acknowledge Daniel.

He tried to be civil even though he wanted to swat the women away and go to Adanna's side, but while they clustered around him, she sat on the far side of the room. Not once did she look in his direction. Instead, she talked with a group of women whose long faces, large jewels and effortfully simple gowns declared the superiority of their breeding. A deck of bright cards was spread across the table before her. Occasionally she gestured at one of the cards and then at one or another of the women whose eyes grew round with excitement.

Stepping to one side so that he could see Adanna more clearly above the feathers adorning the sea of heads between them, he noticed her companion Celeste slip into the room. The girl scanned the scene from the steps at the doorway and then, finding her mistress, she went down to her.

'And is your body as smooth as your face?' A guest whose many chins obscured the pearls at her throat tapped his arm with her fan to regain his attention. 'I've heard that black men are hairless as babes.'

The women around her tittered like girls although the sun had long set on the days of their youth. Reaching up, she brushed stubby gloved fingers across the top of his head. This was as unexpected as it was insulting.

'Why, it's almost like wool!' Snatching back her hand, she snorted. 'I really must feel it properly to be certain.' Freeing the buttons at her wrist, she began to pull frantically at the pink silk of her glove. As she struggled with this trotter, Daniel stepped back, marshalling every remnant of his self-control. If it hadn't been for Adanna, he would have left the room long ago.

'Don't.' He was unable to mask the warning in his voice.

'Why ever not?' The woman was piqued. She turned to her friends. 'I've always wondered what that sort of hair feels like. Richard won't allow us to have a little dark servant in the house, although I want one. He says it's quite wrong, but then he says a lot of things I don't agree with.' There was a determined look in her small, close-set eyes as she returned her attention to Daniel.

'Soldier, bend your head so that we can all touch your hair.'

Freeing her hand from the silk, the woman made to touch him again, but before she could complete her mission, he caught her wrist. The swiftness of this defence was instinctive – Melkie had schooled him well. But the woman was a different kind of opponent.

She stared at his powerful hand around her puffy pink flesh. Affronted and yet quite thrilled to be held in such an intimate manner by the Marquise's muscular attraction, she gazed at the women around her as if to show off a trophy.

'Madam, do not presume . . .' Releasing her, Daniel took a step back. There were marks now on the pillowed flesh where a diamond bracelet had dug a little into the skin beneath his grip.

There were audible gasps and much fluttering of fans.

'Well really!' The woman drew herself to the fullness of her height – which was not a great deal, being equal to her girth – and was about to vent her outrage when she was interrupted.

'My ladies!' A bell-like voice rose over the hubbub. 'My ladies, I must entreat your silence.'

The breathless, flustered group pressed around Daniel quailed at the command and turned to look at their hostess who was now standing at the top of the steps. When Adanna was certain that everyone was paying her attention, she splayed out her fan and fluttered it beneath her chin.

'On the very same evening that our new friend, The Soldier, won a famous victory, a little bird sang for the first time at The Fiery Angel in Covent Garden. I have it on the very best authority that her performance was quite remarkable. Indeed, she was described to me as "exquisite". I simply had to see her for myself, but then I thought how selfish that would be. As you all know, sharing is my greatest pleasure. I make it my business to bring you the most fresh and delectable morsels. And so, tonight, dear ladies, I also present to you the Covent Garden Nightingale.'

With a flick of her wrist, she snapped the fan to a close. It was clearly a signal. At the same moment every candle in the room was extinguished. The women rustled and murmured in surprise and then, very softly, the notes of a violin and a harp began. The tune was sweet but tinged with melancholy. When the melody was established, a young woman started to sing and her voice filled the darkness like a light. The room had been close, but the sound seemed to breathe a welcome coolness to every corner.

Daniel heard little sighs as the guests responded to the beauty of the singer and her song. Gradually servants relit the candles. They began at the back of the room and a soft glow strengthened until, at last, the tall branched candelabra standing each side of the doorway shed a pool of light across the semicircular steps that now acted as a stage.

Dressed in a gown of dark green satin, the woman was partly turned away from him. She was straight-backed, a little above average height with a neatly defined waist. The feathers and ribbons on her headpiece obscured his view of her face as she raised her arms and addressed the final, falling notes of the song to Adanna, who stood a little to the side at the foot of the steps.

When she had finished and the music faded, the singer curtseyed to Adanna and then, bowing her head, she stepped forward into the light. The applause was instant and genuine. She looked up, beaming in bashful delight.

The room seemed to tilt beneath Daniel's feet, the twinkling candles receded to firefly pinpricks and the women clustered around him ceased to exist. In a second, everything faded from his vision, except Pearl standing there alone and painfully exposed.

Adanna beckoned her. As Daniel watched them speak together, his breath came in short ragged bursts that caused actual pain as his throat constricted in horrified fury.

'Another one!' The stout insulting woman pointed her fan at Pearl.

Without warning he was catapulted back to another room in another time when two boorish British soldiers sneered at Pearl and insulted her while she sang in that same pure and crystalline voice.

'I suppose it's only natural that our friend the Marquise should wish to do good by her kind,' the woman squealed on, 'but then she is a titled lady with such high connections that it is impossible to question her choices.' Her tiny eyes disappeared beneath pleats of powdered flesh as she studied Adanna and Pearl. She sniffed. 'Pretty thing, ain't she? For a—'

'Enough, madam! I'll not endure you a moment more.' Daniel pushed past her and strode through the crowd towards Adanna's stage. Every moment of the evening had been torture, but the appearance of Pearl was a final twist of the knife.

Above the drooping feathers and winking jewels, he saw that Celeste was now escorting Pearl back up the steps to the doorway. He followed roughly, oblivious to the tuts and complaints that swelled at his back. Bursting through the doors, he went to the edge of the balustraded landing and looked down.

The two girls had just reached the marble-tiled hallway below.

'Pearl!'

She stopped when he shouted her name and glanced upward. Her hand fluttered to her mouth. Celeste frowned at her and then, puzzled, she stared up at Daniel.

'Stay there.' He rounded the landing, but Pearl turned sharply and broke into a run. Celeste followed her. Instead of crossing the hallway to the main door, the girls darted in the opposite direction. As he thundered down the stairs, Daniel heard the rap of their heels on stone.

'You will wait for me!' His unheeded command rang from the mansion's stonework. On reaching the chequered tiles he doubled back in pursuit and found the entrance to a second minor staircase at the back of the hallway. Forcing a startled servant bearing a tray of split figs aside, he began on the narrow flight of stone steps that spiralled to the lower floor.

When he emerged from the last of the coils he stopped, amazed by what he saw below.

Celeste and Pearl stood at the bottom of the steps flanked by Jen and a woman whose vivid red hair clashed with her scarlet cape. In the dim light, he saw something yellow flitter about the woman's head. Behind them stood an old man with a violin case and another younger man with an Irish harp slung over his shoulder.

There was a moment of silence and then Jen stepped out in front of Pearl – a protective move.

'What are you doing here, Daniel?' Her voice was firm but her fingers gripped the ends of her blue shawl so tightly her knuckle bones shone white through the skin. Her simple dress was a shabby contrast to the golden gown worn by Adanna. The red beads glinting at her throat were paste.

'I might ask the same of you.'

If she heard the danger in his voice, Jen chose to ignore it.

'We have every right. Pearl was invited.'

'As was I.'

'Were you now?' Jen stared up at him. 'Or have you just come to spy on your sister?'

'How dare you.' Fury tightened Daniel's voice to a hiss. 'Who are these others?'

Sliding a curious glance at Jen and then at Pearl, Celeste stepped slowly back and melted into the shadows.

Jen turned to the red-headed woman. 'This lady is Mrs Juno Kelly, proprietress of The Fiery Angel in Shandois Street, and these men ...' she nodded at the musicians, '... are Mr Toby Dilworth and Mr Simon Halse. They accompanied Pearl on her first night at the theatre. And she was such a rare success that she was invited here to sing. A messenger came to The Angel this morning. That's right, isn't it, Mrs Kelly?'

'It is indeed. And it's not a chance you turn down when you're fresh. Tonight could be the making of her.' The red-haired woman took Pearl's hand in her own and smiled up at Daniel. One of her front teeth was gold. 'When word gets about, sir – and it will, mark my words – the *pair* of you will be the talk of London. Such a talented family – Lord! It won't just be London at your feet, it'll be the whole country.'

The fluffy yellow ball that flittered around her head came to rest on her shoulder. Now Daniel saw that it was a canary on a fine gold chain.

'Pearl's been quite safe. You mustn't worry yourself,' the vivid Irishwoman continued. 'We've been waiting with the servants until the time came for us to take her back to The 'Pollo. As I understand it,' she grinned at the musicians, 'our dear girl has made quite an impression tonight.'

'She is not yours!' Daniel roared. Startled, the chained bird twittered and struggled to take flight. Striding down the last of the steps, he wrenched Pearl's hand from the woman's grasp. Pulling her round to face him, he clasped her shoulders and shook her so violently that the glass beads on the green bandeau rattled.

'Why? Why did you do this?'

Pearl gulped and shook her head. 'I did nothing wrong.' Tears began to course down her cheeks, but Daniel was unrelenting. Gripping tighter, he shouted again, flecks of spittle spattering her terrified face.

'Stupid, stupid child. Did you not understand what I told you?'

'What did you tell her?' The drawled question came from the servants' steps.

Daniel turned to see Adanna. Her magnificent dress filled the gloomy space like a sun. She came a little way down and paused just above them.

'You disturb my guests. Your voices can be heard above in the hallway.'

Daniel saw Celeste behind her, glowing in her matching yellow gown like a lesser satellite. The sly, watchful expression in the girl's eyes told him that it was not the sound of their voices that had summoned her mistress.

Jen and Mrs Kelly curtseyed immediately and the musicians bowed, but Daniel continued to hold Pearl fast. Adanna studied the astonished group below her and then she pointed her furled fan at Pearl.

'Who is this girl to you, Soldier?'

'She . . .' Daniel swallowed. 'She is my sister, Pearl.'

Mrs Kelly's bird filled the silence that followed with a burst of song.

Adanna stared at Daniel and then at Pearl. She raised her fan as if she was about to make a remark, but instead she threw it open before her face and turned on the step. She stumbled and then, snapping the fan shut with such force that some of the feathers broke free, she lashed out at Celeste.

'Out of my way.' The girl flattened herself against the wall as her mistress swept upward without another word.

Chapter Thirty-seven

A crescent moon smiled above the rooftops of Leicester Square, but its good humour was not reflected in the puddled street below.

'You lied to me.' Daniel walked swiftly away from Adanna's grand house dragging Pearl, who was torn between protest and gulping sobs, in his wake. Jen ran to keep pace with them, huddling her shawl around her shoulders.

'I did nothing of the sort,' she shouted at his back. 'We were going to take her straight back to The 'Pollo afterwards. You'd never have known about it if you weren't there tonight too.'

'It was a good thing I was,' he snapped angrily. 'You asked me to trust you and yet you did this.' He stopped and turned to look at her. 'How could you, Jen?'

'Quite easily, if you really want to know.' She bent double to catch her breath. 'I went to The Black Apollo this afternoon and I smuggled Pearl out in Betsy's work clothes. Betsy's Mrs Richardson's maid of work. They're the same age and height. Under a cloak you'd never tell them apart.'

It was not the answer to his question and she knew it. Straightening up, she couldn't quite meet his eyes. 'Pearl *had* to be there tonight,' Jen continued. 'It was a fine opportunity. Where's the harm?' She appealed to gaudy Mrs Kelly and the two musicians who had now caught up with them. 'You tell him.'

Mrs Kelly was embarrassed. Puffing beneath her cape, she looked from Jen to Daniel and sucked her cheeks. Nestled on her shoulder, the canary peeked out from beneath the crimson hood, its tiny jet eyes wary but fascinated.

'Well, now,' the older woman began carefully, 'there's no harm in Pearl making a name for herself, but I really thought ...' Shuffling forward, she patted Daniel's arm. 'I thought you knew, sir. That's the truth of it. Ah! There now ...' She craned over his shoulder and raised her arm to attract a hack rounding the corner.

'With your leave, I'll be taking these gentlemen back to their lodgings.' She nodded meaningfully at the shuffling musicians who, like her, seemed very relieved to escape. The hack pulled up alongside and Mrs Kelly let the men go in first. Before joining them, she smiled warmly at Pearl whose face was streaked with tears.

'There now, dry those tears, little bird. You did beautifully tonight. No one can take that from you.' She glanced at Daniel and seemed to be on the verge of addressing further remarks to him, but his expression stopped her. Wrapping the cape around herself, she sent Jen a hard look.

'I'll leave you to make your peace then.'

Once the hack was gone, they stood in an uneasy silence.

It was Pearl who broke it.

'I'm sorry, Daniel. But I was flattered when Jen told me about the invitation. It was such an opportunity that ... Oh, it's no good! You hated me anyway but now ...' Taking a breath, she rallied a little. '*Now* you've shamed me in front of one of the most important women in London. You made me look like a stupid child. I don't think I'll ever be able to—' Breaking off, she turned away and muffled her renewed sobs in the hood of her street cloak. Jen tried to comfort her, but Daniel barred the way.

'Haven't you done enough?'

She glared at him. 'It's not Pearl's fault. Don't blame her. If you're looking for someone to punish, although Christ knows why, it's me.

I went to The Apollo and persuaded her to come tonight. The lady's guests are married to some of the most powerful men in London. It was a chance to show off her talent.'

'She is not a performing dog.' Daniel could hardly bear to speak to Jen, let alone look at her.

'What are *you* then?' Her voice was sharp. 'You were there tonight too.'

Daniel felt blood rush to his face. His mouth was suddenly dry. Why had Adanna invited him, only to insult and ignore him? He swallowed.

'The Marquise was at the fight with the Duke of Calne.'

'Of course she was. It's said they're rarely apart . . .' Jen narrowed her eyes, '. . . among other things.'

'What else is said of her?' The question came out more forcefully – and desperately – than he had intended.

'That she's a courtesan, despite her title. Also, they say she practises magic. According to some, she's a witch.'

'Who are "they"?' To his shame, Daniel found that any crumb of information nourished his obsession. Adanna was like a wound that itched; a scab to be picked at.

'Everyone.' Jen shrugged. 'Sally says it's all anyone talks about at the theatre. She and the Duke come together and sit in his private box. It's said she's bewitched him and wound him round her smallest finger. He's not the only one, mind. Half of London is in her lap. The Lady – if that's what she is – collects novelties. That's her currency: anything new, anything different. Ah . . .' She grinned, almost spitefully. '*That's* why she invited you. This Marquise de whatever wanted to show you off to her friends. You were an entertainment tonight, not a guest. Just like Pearl.' She paused. 'Tell me, Daniel, what did you have to do for your supper?'

The silence between them could have been parted like a curtain.

*

From her bed in the neat attic room above The Black Apollo, Pearl watched Daniel pace the boards. Her eyes were still glassy with tears, but resentment rolled off her like steam from a cauldron. The green satin sleeves of her dress were crumpled where he had gripped her shoulders and the hem was spattered with mud. He couldn't trust himself to speak, not yet. If he unleashed the torrent of his anger upon her now, it would be disastrous.

That fury was not for Pearl alone. Confused and miserable as he was, he understood the bitter truth. Adanna had used the evening to humiliate him. She had cast him to the women assembled in her salon much as a butcher might hurl a bone at a pack of scavenging dogs. It was an act of calculated and deliberate cruelty.

Why?

He paused at the dressing table set beneath a window looking out over the jumbled rooftops of Covent Garden. Was Adanna thinking of him now or was she soundly asleep in her mansion? Perhaps she was with the Duke – wrapped in the fine monogrammed linens of his bed; or his arms?

Were they laughing at him?

Daniel ripped the white stock from his throat and pulled the black coat from his shoulders. He had been a mockery of a gentleman. Staring at the heap of borrowed finery, he remembered that Adanna had worn something similar in the portrait. Had she noted the similarity in their dress, he wondered, as she watched him from the concealed doorway? Had she considered the distance they had come? If she had, then surely she would not have treated him with such heartless spite.

Sweeping a hand across his stubbled head, he turned from the window and stalked back to the locked door. Mr Richardson had been absent when he and Pearl had arrived in the early hours, but Alys had been visibly relieved and overflowing with heartfelt apologies. Through tears of remorse, she told him that after discovering

Jen's deception in the early evening, she had immediately sent Tolly with a message, but by the time the boy arrived at The Maze, Daniel had left for Leicester Square.

He stared at the attic room door and gripped the key in his hand. Pearl would never escape again. Rancid accusations stewed in his mind, each one bobbing to the surface like gristle in a stew smuggled from The Mitre. He was almost certain that the addition of Pearl to Adanna's evening of mortification had been accidental for there was no way she would have known of the connection between them.

But now . . .

He balled his fist around the key. Jen was to blame. If it hadn't been for her and that ridiculous woman with her crimson hair and the canary, Pearl would never have been at 32 Leicester Square. His first instincts were correct. He should never have trusted her.

An hour earlier he had left Jen at the western edge of the square. It was not far to The Black Apollo, just a few streets, but it seemed that Mrs Kelly had commandeered the last of the night hacks. As he dragged Pearl from the scene of her crime, he had heard the tap of Jen's boots as she walked alone in the opposite direction. It was not the act of a gentleman, but Jen had proved herself to be less than a lady. When he thought of her, his anger boiled again. Her deception and Adanna's humiliation entwined like poisonous vines. Tonight, it was difficult to separate the distaff strands of his fury.

He turned from the door. Pearl was watching him. Her eyes glittered like Adanna's diamonds in the light of the single candle Alys Richardson had placed beside her bed.

She pulled at the pins securing the feathered green bandeau to her hair. Tugging it from her head, she threw it to the floor, then, tucking her legs beneath her, she rolled mutely away from him to face the panelled wall.

Daniel realised he had seen the headpiece before. It had lain hidden beneath the sheets of her bed when he had mistaken the rounded hump for a cheese. Jen had claimed it as her own. His temper roiled. They had both been deceiving him for some time. Striding across the chamber, he swept it up and screwed it violently between his fingers until the feathers snapped and the beads scattered across the boards.

'Don't!' Pearl turned at the pattering sound. 'It's not mine. Mrs Kelly lent it to me.'

'And how, exactly, do you know her?' There was a safety, Daniel discovered, in discussing anyone at that moment who was not Adanna or Jen.

'She . . . she owns the theatre where I first sang. It's called The Angel – The Fiery Angel. Sally . . .' Pearl swallowed. 'Sally recommended me. She heard me in The Mitre. She said my voice was too sweet for a tavern and then she and Jen introduced me to Mrs Kelly who gave me a trial. It was only once. Look . . .'

Pearl fumbled with the blankets. Drawing out a sheet torn from a newspaper, she handed it to him. The account of his encounter with Rafael Safardi filled half the page.

He scowled. 'I was there at Rutland House. I do not need reminding.'

Pearl's eyes flashed. 'It's not always about you, Daniel. Look at the bottom – *under* the bit about you. It begins "Feathering her nest".'

He held the paper to the candle flame and began to read.

Fly to The Fiery Angel, Shandois Street, where a delightful fresh-hatched Songbird flourishes in her bower. Newly arrived in London, this Sweete Daughter of Euterpe has already acquired an appealing soubriquet. Your loyal Correspondent intends to hasten to the theatre to sample the song of The Covent Garden Nightingale.

'It was the night of the fight,' Pearl continued as he read the narrow set lines for a second time. 'Jen and Sally persuaded me, although in all honesty, they didn't need to. Mrs Kelly was very encouraging. When I tried for her, she said I had the voice of a songbird. It didn't last very long. I went on between the acts of *The Fortunate Widow* – that's the play Sally was in that night. Jen was there too. And afterwards they brought me back. I was quite safe.'

He remembered seeing the three of them turn the corner into Vinegar Yard, and the sight of Elias's great black carriage looming behind them.

'Safe!' He balled the paper in his fist. 'There is no safety for you – not on the streets and especially not in a theatre.' He spat out the last word with particular venom, adding, 'Sally – I might have known.'

'She is respectable.' Pearl straightened her back. There was an achingly familiar defiance in her manner as she continued. 'She and Jen are my friends. They thought it was wrong of you to lock me away. As did I.' Her eyes gleamed angrily. 'As for Mrs Kelly, she has treated me with nothing but kindness. She even paid me.' Rifling under the blankets again, she produced a tiny embroidered pouch and emptied its contents into her hand. Coins shone on her palm.

'Six shillings.' She looked up. 'I didn't know how to tell you, but look. It's more than I've ever brought back and you've never ...' She faltered. 'This can feed us and I can save more when I sing—'

'You will not perform again.' Daniel's growl stopped her. 'I never thought that you could lie to me, Pearl, but this ...' He threw the screw of newsprint into a corner. 'You are all liars. You, Jen, Sally, Ada—'

Swallowing the name, he turned away to avoid looking at Pearl. 'You deceived me. You all have.'

He thought of Adanna's cruelty again. Even now he couldn't help himself.

'I didn't. If you hadn't been there tonight, you would never have known,' Pearl replied. 'And even if you found out, it would have been long after I was safely back here. That was always the plan.

Mrs Kelly said it was a great opportunity to be heard by the best in society. We decided that the thing to do was—'

'We?' Daniel thumped the panelled wall and the door shook in its frame.

'Yes, *we*.' Pearl's voice was firm now. 'Jen, Sally and I. *We* decided together that I should accept the invitation. Sally couldn't be there tonight, she's on stage, but Mrs Kelly offered to come with me herself, which was an honour.'

'There is nothing honourable in what you did.' He turned. 'How could you perform for those women?'

Pearl stared at him. 'You were there too.'

When he didn't reply, she pushed the coins carefully back into the tiny pouch. Rising, she placed it on the dressing table. 'I did not lie to you, Daniel – neither did Jen. We simply did not tell you.' She paused. 'If it was such a terrible thing to do, why did you attend the salon?'

There were many answers to that question, but none he could give her. He looked down at the boards where green tufts from the broken plumes danced in a draught from the gap beneath the door. He thought of the damaged feathers that twirled in the air when Adanna snapped shut her fan.

'What did she say to you, the Marquise? I saw her speaking to you just before you left with her companion.'

'That girl Celeste, you mean?' Pearl wrinkled her nose. 'Pah! She behaved as if she owned the house. She was insulting when she took me up to the salon, but the Marquise was very gentle. She told me that the reports had not done justice to my talent. She said . . .' Pearl frowned. 'She said something very odd. She asked me my age and when I told her, she said that when she was fifteen the world turned beneath her feet. Did she speak to you?'

'Not beyond instructing me as to my behaviour.' Exhausted and defeated, Daniel sat on the end of the bed. 'I was there as entertainment. I should not have gone.'

Even now he wondered if that was true.

'Jen was right then.' Pearl bent to collect the scattered beads. As he watched her gather them into her palm, he remembered again that day in New York when she had sung in the Fitzallens' house, her hair bound beneath a simple white turban. Then she had been a girl, but tonight he had seen her, for the first time, as a young woman. The moment had pierced his heart. She reached for a feather mangled by his anger.

'Why did you wear that thing, Pearl?'

'The bandeau?' She looked up, puzzled. 'Mrs Kelly said my hair was too difficult to dress.' Returning to her task she bent forward and added quietly, 'It was pretty.'

Stung by the reminder of the women at Adanna's salon, Daniel whispered, 'But you are beautiful.'

Shaking his head in wonder, he rose, gathered her into his arms and hugged her.

'I'm not angry, but you must stay here, Pearl. Please.'

'Why?'

Her question was muffled by his shirt. Drawing back, he looked into her eyes. The young woman who stared back at him deserved the truth – some of it at least.

While Daniel told her about the fight and his intended betrayal of the Brotherhood, Pearl sat very still, but when he explained exactly why he feared for her safety he saw a vein throb in the delicate skin of her throat.

After he finished, she was silent for a long time.

'Elias is truly a monster and that man ... Vincent Carney.' Pearl linked her hands tightly in her lap. 'The thought of him watching me is ...' Unable to continue, she shuddered. 'Now I understand why I am here. But for how long?'

'That I can't tell you. But I will think of something.' Wishing he had a better answer, Daniel laid a hand over hers. 'But now I hope you understand. Promise me that you won't leave again until I come for you.'

After a moment she nodded and looked at him directly.

'I would have done the same if I were you, brother.'

It was an absolution.

A little while later, just before he left The Black Apollo, Daniel pressed the key to the door into her hand as a gesture of trust.

Chapter Thirty-eight

When Daniel returned alone to The Maze, Jen was waiting in his chamber. There were purple shadows beneath her eyes and her hair was lank and dull. Ignoring her, he went to the table and set down a paper-wrapped bundle. A baker had forced a warm loaf fresh from the oven into his hands as he'd walked back along Little White Lion Street. The early morning sun had gilded the passages and his long shadow had stretched ahead of him as St Giles woke to a new day. Richardson was right. It had been odd to pass the crude images of The Soldier daubed on so many walls. The grateful baker had trebled his wager.

'Pearl has a beautiful voice. It would be a shame to hide it.' Jen spoke to his back. 'She could do much better for herself, just as you have.'

Daniel stared at the tabletop where a small black beetle was edging towards the bread.

'You didn't even think to ask me.' His voice was flat.

'No . . . well, that's to say yes, we did.' She paused. 'We *did* consider telling you, but we knew what you'd say. Pearl always reckoned it was out of the ordinary for you to allow her to go to work at The Mitre with me, but a theatre? Now that would be another matter completely.'

'But you still did it.' He crushed the beetle beneath his thumb and turned to her. 'You went ahead behind my back.'

Jen plucked at her drab brown dress. 'It was a game at first. A bit of fun. But when Mrs Kelly took a proper shine to her—'

'You lied,' Daniel interrupted. 'You encouraged Pearl to perform, you took her to a public place where God alone knows what might have happened to her and then you deceived me about the invitation to sing for Ada— for the Marquise.'

Twisting the cloth between her fingers, Jen shook her head.

'It wasn't like that.'

'What was it like then?'

'It was . . . a chance. Who knows where it might lead? Some of the finest women in London were there last night.'

'The finest women?' He spat out the words. 'I've seen whores at the docks with better manners.'

'You were there too. Why was it so wrong for Pearl? That's a ripe contradiction. It's fine for a man to do what he likes, but not for a woman. The old story – is that how it goes?' Retreating from the brink of another battle, Jen raised her hands as a truce. 'I know, Dan. I know why you were there. We all have to make our way in the world and take advantage of anything that comes our way. Mrs Kelly says—'

He cut her off. 'I don't care what that woman says. I never want to hear her name again.'

'Listen to me, Dan.' Moving closer, she tried to catch his arm but he shrugged her off. The scent of her cologne was cheap and the string of red glass beads at her throat looked chipped and tawdry.

In some part of his mind that he did not wish to visit, Daniel knew that his behaviour was unnecessarily harsh, irrational even, but at that moment the woman standing before him was a vessel for his anger. And she was not Adanna.

'Why are you here, Jen?' The brutal question was almost an insult.

'Because I wanted to set things straight between us.' Her eyes glittered in the candlelight. 'I thought that today you might . . . you might understand. Truly we did nothing very bad, Dan. You must see that?'

In answer, he went to the doorway and pulled at the canvas.

'Leave.'

Daniel could hardly taste the bread. Chalk had been added to the mixture with a heavy hand and the texture and flavour were stony. He tore off another chunk and forced it into his mouth. Even though the question of Pearl's safety was settled again, for the moment at least, there were other matters that were not so easy to lock away.

The candle flame jittered in the brass lantern on the table beside the bread, throwing his shadow to the bricks. The shape was very like one of the images he'd seen daubed on the walls of St Giles.

'OWR HERO – THE SOLJER', someone had illiterately proclaimed in sloping blue paint.

He was not a hero. He was a man who was haunted by the past, by the present and by the future.

It was only now as he chewed the dry, unyielding bread that he remembered Sparrow's warning.

'As I heard it, there might be two men in London who share a wish to see you brought low.'

At the time, he had been so consumed by Adanna the only thing that had registered was a dreadful hope. If he had truly seen James Fitzallen that night, perhaps he might not be mistaken about the Marquise?

Disgusted to find that even now she took precedence, he ripped another jagged chunk from the loaf. Something dead with many legs was baked into the dough. Immediately what remained of his appetite vanished. He swiped the baker's gift from the table and it bounced on the stones before rolling into the shadows. A sudden dry-footed scuttle from the corner indicated it had not gone to waste.

Daniel cradled his forehead in his hands. If Sparrow was right then his enemies in the highest and lowest of places had found a common interest, but what did that mean? When he tried to find the quick intelligence that had served him as a soldier, all he found was her. Even now, she crowded every other thought from his mind.

Why, after all that had passed between them, had she refused to acknowledge him? Why had she treated him with such callous contempt? And why had she lied? No matter what she called herself now, Marie-Angélique, Marquise de Notaille *was* Adanna.

He turned to his bed where the clothes he had worn to her salon lay crumpled on the coarse blankets. He hadn't slept for hours now, but the whirl of his thoughts wouldn't allow him to rest. He wondered again what Adanna had made of the plain black frock coat Mrs Trimm had chosen for him.

It came to him then that there was one place where he could empty his head.

The young man sprawled at Daniel's feet raised a hand in submission. He pulled himself together and stumbled to the bench along the wall. Melkie glanced at the defeated fighter who was now slumped forward, dazed by the speed and ferocity of Daniel's attack. The bowl of the pipe glowed ominously.

'I thought I told you to stay away. A week at least. Win or lose, a man needs time to align the humours after a fight.' Removing the pipe, he jabbed the end at Daniel's chest. 'And that applies to you more than most, considering what happened at Rutland House.'

Daniel surveyed the warehouse.

'Is Coppin here?'

There were around a dozen men present today. When he had arrived unexpectedly, they had cheered so loudly that the pigeons roosting in the rafters had taken flight. Now the birds were gathered together on a beam above the doorway.

'What d'yer take me for, a lily of the field?' Melkie snorted. 'A few of the boys visited Mr Coppin's favourite hostelry. When he recovers, I very much doubt that he'll show his face – what's left of it – within a hundred miles of London. It's not Coppin I'm worried about, it's you. Why are you here?'

In answer, Daniel went over to the young fighter he had trounced. Crouching beside him, he rested a muffled hand on his shoulder. 'I'm sorry. Did I hurt you?'

'Nothing that won't heal.' The lad's lower lip was split. He grinned painfully. 'It'll be something, though, when I tell my girl that The Soldier did this to me. You done me a favour, I reckon.'

He laughed and, despite himself, Daniel joined in. 'Tell her from me,' he said as he stood up, 'that you gave me a hard time.'

Returning to Melkie, he shook his head. 'I just wanted to practise, but once we started, I couldn't hold back. It was wrong of me.' He swiped the sweat from his forehead. 'You asked why I was here. The truth is, I had to *do* something and I . . . I had nowhere else to go.'

Melkie sniffed. 'You shouldn't be here at all. I've been told, in a very direct manner, that I'm not to admit you.'

'Told by who?'

'Elias – well, one of his *gentlemen*.' Melkie spat onto the boards. 'But as I see it, if he's not paying me to train you, I can do what I want.' He stared up at Daniel. 'And what I want to do is see you win again and again. It'd be a crime to hide a talent like yours. In a week or so I'll be happy to see you back. Challenges for you have been flying in and out of here like those fucking rats with wings.' He pointed his pipe at the beam where the pigeons still huddled together.

'In the meantime, Dan, I'd thank you not to take out whatever it is that's eating you up on another man. It's not the way. You've got to control the anger, not let it control you. I thought I'd taught you that.' The extravagant moustache rippled. 'You look like a banker who's just found a pile of horse shit locked in his safe. What's troubling you?'

'Nothing.' Daniel began to unwind the cloth from his knuckles. 'You're right. It's too soon.'

'Musa told me about your sister.' Melkie let that hang between them.

'Pearl is staying with friends, just for a few days.'

'That's not quite how I heard it.' A ring of smoke rose into the air. 'Musa didn't think she was too keen on the idea.'

Daniel threw the rag to the boards. 'I told you, she's with friends.'

'If you say so.' There was a long silence. 'If you ever need help then all you have to do is ask.'

When Daniel didn't reply, Melkie changed tack.

'Those items of clothing Mrs Trimm sent over – fit you, did they? She's got an eye for the male physique, my Hannah.'

The last thing Daniel wanted to be reminded of was Adanna's salon, but Melkie continued nostalgically.

'How did it go off then? Did the fine ladies take to you? I remember what it was like. They couldn't get enough of me. Throwing all sorts my way, they were. Of course, I was a married man even then, but I imagine you can take your pick. Mind you . . .' he smiled as he tapped the bowl of his pipe on the side of his boot to empty its ashy contents onto the boards, '. . . as I recall you've already got yourself a nice girl. Now, what I recommend you do with yourself is—'

Daniel never learned what Melkie was about to propose. There was a shout from the entrance to the warehouse and they turned to see Sparrow held between two of the fighters. He waved at Daniel and struggled to free himself.

'Who, or more to the point, *what* is that?' Melkie pointed at the ragged visitor with the stem of his pipe.

*

'Wait. Slow down.' Daniel pushed the mug of watered beer across Melkie's desk. 'Start at the beginning.'

Sparrow hunched forward in his tattered coat. It had experienced a notable fall from grace since Daniel had first met its owner. He guessed the boy had been sleeping in it. Sparrow's face was grey with street dust and the wounds inflicted by Elias were still crusted with blood.

He took a swig from the mug and eyed the bun that Melkie had produced from a drawer in his desk. It was dry and probably two days old, but from the way the boy looked at it, it could have been a towering dessert set before the Prince of Wales.

'I've been at a loose end since ... since ... you know.' He nodded at Daniel and tapped the cheek below his swollen left eye. 'I want you to know I've stuck to my word. I'll never work for him again.'

'Who does he mean?' Melkie turned in his chair.

'Elias.' Daniel replied.

Melkie took a sharp breath. 'And it was Elias who did that?' He asked, pointing at the boy's injured face. 'Fucker! He pushed the bun closer to Sparrow.

'Is this about James Fitzallen?' Daniel frowned. 'The man you told me about last night. You said you'd overheard Elias talking about him.'

Sparrow shook his head. 'It's not that. Like I said, I'm not going near Elias again. I've already told you everything I heard. Was it useful?'

He rested a hand palm up on the table and flicked a hopeful look at it. ''Cos, if it was ...'

Daniel stared at the boy's mutilated hand. Although it was long healed, the ragged stump of the smallest finger was evidence of Elias's savage temper. For all his sheen of civility, the man was a monster, just as Pearl said.

Sparrow waggled his remaining digits hopefully, but when the expected coin was not forthcoming, he folded his arms.

'A man's got to make a living somehow. That's why I'm here. First off, I don't want you to think bad of me.'

His eyes returned to the bun. Although he didn't reach out, the force of his gaze could have drawn it towards him.

'Go on,' Daniel encouraged. 'I won't think badly of you.'

The boy scratched his matted head. 'It's like this, seeing as I don't have much in the way of work, I've been looking for fresh opportunities to be of assistance. Now that you're a person of standing, I thought I might be useful to you. Last night, after you came out of that fine house in Leicester Square, I watched you all talking and then I went after you when you and Pearl went off down to the Garden.'

'You followed us.' Daniel raised an eyebrow.

'In a way, I suppose I did,' Sparrow agreed. 'But it was on my own account, sir. I wasn't spying, not like that girl. Like you and me, she is.' Sparrow pointed at Daniel's face. 'Small with sharp features and a tongue to match. I only found that out later.'

'You're not making sense.' Daniel glanced at Melkie. 'Tell us exactly what happened.'

Sparrow took a breath. 'Well, at first, I was going to follow Jen when she walked off on her own. As it was so late, I thought she might 'preciate company. But then I saw the other girl creep out of the house you'd gone to. She was dressed in a street cloak with the hood drawn up and she lingered in the shadows by the railings like she didn't want to be noticed. I could tell she was watching you – I know that game – so I thought I should take note of what she was doing. You and Pearl started off and she took after you, following every turn you made in the lanes.

'When you went into The 'Pollo she stood outside and tried to make out what it was on account of it not being signed in the usual manner. I watched her all the while from behind a corner, but she knew I was there. When she came back up the alley, she pounced on me like a cat and wanted to know why I was following her. She gave me a right ear-lashing, then she pinched me and pulled at my coat. I lost some more of the buttons then. Quite wiry she is, for all that she's so little.'

'What did you say?' Daniel felt Melkie's eyes on him. It was hardly surprising – first Musa's mysterious visit to The Black Apollo, and now this.

Sparrow took another swig of beer. 'I told her she was mistaken. I wasn't following her at all. I said I was carrying an important message for you. It was the only thing I could think of at the time. Then again, it is – was – mostly what I did for Elias, so it came very natural to mind. The girl said that if I was telling the truth then I'd know what the place you'd gone into was. She started to pinch me again to get me to talk, but she took off smart when a group of apprentice boys came down the alley.'

Sparrow wiped the cuff of his sleeve over his nose. 'But it turns out that one of us *was* carrying a message after all.' He produced a folded letter sealed with a blob of red wax from the depths of his coat. Pushing it across the table to Daniel, he reached, at last, for the bun.

'She should have been more careful of her person when she was setting about me.' Sparrow spoke with his mouth full. 'While she was at it, I took the liberty of examining her pockets to see if there was anything worth taking. There was no coin, but I found that. I'm not too good with my letters, but I reckon it's for you.'

Daniel stared at the familiar curlicued handwriting on the crisp white paper. Adanna had written:

For The Soldier.

Chapter Thirty-nine

The seal had been broken. Daniel had seen enough intercepted messages from his days in the army to know when someone had opened and resealed a letter. There was a slight ridge across the wax where it had been pressed together and heated again. When he held it to the light, he could see the faint pattern left by the tips of someone's fingers. But that didn't matter. What concerned him most was Adanna's message. The invitation was clear and signed with the truth.

I will be at home and alone this evening.
A

She was a lodestone. He could no more resist the force of her summons than he could prevent the sun from rising. Standing outside the mansion in Leicester Square dressed once again in the good sober clothing provided by Mrs Trimm, Daniel composed his thoughts and his person with difficulty. A carriage accompanied by two trotting link boys rolled past and a dog barked and limped from the shadows in pursuit. The creature, a mangy thing, gave up after a moment or two and sat in the road panting and scratching at its flank where jutting ribs measured many months of hunger.

Daniel pitied the animal. London was cruel to those who fell from her favour. He returned his gaze to the house and remembered his last visit. Tonight, the windows were dim, but lamps glowed either side of the entrance and there was a soft gleam from behind the shutters of the second floor.

Swiping the remnants of Maze dust from the sleeves of the black frock coat, he went to the steps. He paused, wondering if this was the right entrance to use. In answer, the door above swung open and a footman came out. He stared at Daniel from beneath the billowing roll of his wig without comment and then he beckoned him inside. After securing the door, the man pointed to the staircase. His powdered face was a perfect blank, but it was clear that his arrival was expected.

Several candles fluttered in sconces on the wall, but the shadowy hallway was very different to the night of Daniel's last visit. Except for the ticking of a clock, Adanna's house was silent. He turned back to the footman to find that his unasked question was answered by a flick of a hand towards the curving marble stairs.

The grand first landing, where the ornamented doors led into the salon, was almost in darkness. The gloom was barely alleviated by two small candles burning in an ornate sconce at the foot of the next flight of stairs. Gripping the rail, Daniel looked up. It seemed to be lighter above. Hearing a door open, he continued upward, and when he reached the landing he saw Adanna's companion Celeste walking ahead of him. She turned at the sound of his footsteps and the contents of the silver tray in her hands rattled.

'You!' The girl was evidently surprised. Composing herself, she held his gaze boldly and smiled, revealing her sharp little teeth.

'My lady is expecting you.'

'Is she?' Daniel stepped closer. His shadow towered above hers on the wall. 'But are *you*?'

Celeste's eyes hardened. 'I do not understand.'

'Oh, I think you do.' He took Adanna's note from a pocket. 'I believe this was intended for me, but you did not deliver it to my hand. In addition . . .' he turned the seal to face her, 'when I received it, this was broken and repaired. The message had been read. Do you know who might have done that?'

Celeste took a step back. The decanter on the tray jiggled against the glasses. 'I would never presume to do such a thing. It is the private correspondence of my mistress. I was set upon by a ruffian before I was able to deliver it to you.' Her smile did not match the hostility in her eyes. 'As I told you, it was stolen from me. *Comprenez-vous?*'

'Did you tell your mistress about the theft?'

'I did not think . . . It was not necessary to . . .' Her eyes slid away.

'I see.' Daniel nodded. 'You did not think it was *necessary* to tell her, did you? If you have read this message – and I think you have – then you will know that I had a choice in the matter. If I did not come, the Marquise would never know the true reason why.'

'Yet here you are, all the same.' The girl's tilted eyes did not leave his. Daniel had met many cunning wretches. Their guilt was often masked by a layer of bravado. He moved closer.

'I wonder what she will say if I tell her what you did.'

Celeste seemed to consider her position and pursed her lips. 'Very well, I admit that I did not tell her that it was stolen. But what about the boy who took it? What if he broke the seal, not me?' She looked down at the tray. After a long moment she spoke again. 'Please don't tell her. She will be *furieuse.*' It was odd to hear the pleading tone in her small voice.

When he didn't answer she looked up, the flint in her eyes replaced by uncertainty. 'You are here. Nothing is lost to you. The mistress is in her receiving room. I took you there before on the night of the salon. Follow me.'

She was about to move away, but Daniel gripped her shoulder. 'Wait! Why were you following me yesterday?'

The girl flinched at the touch. She stared at his hand on the sprigged cotton of her dress and then she looked up, smiling with a sweetness that belied the triumphant scorn in her answer. 'Because I wished to deliver my mistress's message directly into your hands, sir. Now, if you will come this way.'

The girl opened the door and stooped to take up the tray. Leading the way, she indicated that he should follow. The room was in darkness apart from a fire spitting in the hearth beneath the portrait.

'Your guest is here, my lady.' The girl went to a buffet along the wall furthest from the fire. Setting the tray down, she lit two candles and turned. 'And I have brought refreshment.'

'Leave us.'

Celeste curtseyed in the direction of the voice and went back to the door. It creaked as she pulled it open, but Adanna spoke again.

'We are not to be disturbed. No one is to be admitted to the house tonight.'

'But ma'am . . .' Celeste hovered half in and half out of the doorway. She looked at Daniel. '*Que dois-je dire si le duc vient ce soir?*'

There was a tut. '*Dis-lui que je dors, mais que demain j'attends sa compagnie avec impatience.*'

Daniel recognised the language as French, but not the meaning of the words.

'*Oui, madame.*' The girl curtseyed again in the direction of her mistress's voice. She shot a sly and superior look at Daniel and closed the door behind her.

'Come closer. Let me see you.' The deep silky voice came from one of two high-backed chairs set before the fire. Taking a breath to steady himself, he went to the hearth and turned. Adanna was curled in the depths of the larger chair, the folds of her Chinese silk wrapper gown massed around her like the petals of some hothouse bloom. There was a shameless abundance to the fabric that contrived to protect her modesty while revealing her form. Her hair was bound by cloth matched to the gown. At her side on a low table, playing cards, all face down, had been arranged in the shape of a fan. Next to them, there was a narrow black box inlaid with scrolls of mother of pearl.

She smiled.

'Daniel.'

He was amazed at his body's response to the sound of his name on her lips.

She pointed to the chair opposite her own. Despite the freedom of her dress, she wore fine black lace gloves, golden rings drawn over the mesh.

'I was not certain you would come.'

'I . . . I was not certain myself,' Daniel lied. He shook his head. 'You invited me to your salon and yet . . .' He was unable to continue. The firelight glowed in her eyes and he found he could not look away or trust himself to speak. Reaching out, he caught her hand and was shocked as a wave of prickling energy overwhelmed him.

'Is it truly you?'

Freeing herself, she pointed again at the chair. 'There is so much to say, I hardly know where to begin.'

His hand still burning from her touch, he sat down and watched her select two of the playing cards from the table. Without looking at them, she passed them to him.

'Perhaps my friends will tell us.' She pointed at the cards. 'It is a skill I learned long ago and it has served me well. Indulge me. What do you hold?'

Bewildered, Daniel studied the painted images in his hand. One showed a man and a woman standing beneath a tree. In the branches a hidden cherub took aim at the man with a bow and arrow. On the other card a naked child pointed at a smiling sun.

'Let me see.'

He held them to the light of the fire. Adanna smiled. 'Of course.

They never fail me.' Unfurling, she tapped the card with the man and woman. 'These are the lovers. And this . . .' she took the card with the sun from his hand, '. . . is the card of joy . . . and of birth.'

Flames danced in her eyes. 'Tell me, Daniel. Tell me everything that has happened to you . . . and to our daughter since the night when The Salutation burned to the ground.'

Breathing deeply, he stared at her and then at the cards in her hand. At first, he was silent. The past had been locked away for so long that it was almost impossible to free it. Truth was heavy, strange and unfamiliar on his tongue, but when he began to speak at last, it was a relief to release the secret he had guarded for sixteen years.

Adanna stared into the fire. 'The Maroons were waiting at the bay?'

Daniel nodded. 'They kept their side of the bargain. They took us by water to the south of the island and then we travelled inland to the mountains. We, Pearl and I, lived there among them for many years. We were free, but freedom has a cost.'

'How did you pay for your rescue?' She continued to look into the flames.

'Some of the men had taken things of value from The Salutation. There was enough.'

Firelight gilded Adanna's forehead and slanting cheekbones.

'There was nothing left at the house after the slaves came, Daniel.'

Even though it was long ago, a grisly image rose in his mind. A head rolled from a hessian bag and a man stooped to tear jewels from a dead woman's ears. He reached for Adanna's hand once more, but she would not allow him to take it.

'It was terrible for us all,' he said quietly. 'But they were not slaves, Adanna, they were good men and women whose lives had been made a hell. They were your friends, your people.'

She did not answer. The fire popped and golden embers spurted into the throat of the chimney.

'Continue.' She waved a lace-clad hand. A large diamond set into a gold ring captured the flickering light. He felt the insult but was strangely compelled to obey.

'Afterwards, life in the mountains was difficult,' he began. 'The Maroons were fair, but strict because their survival depended on it. We moved camp often to evade detection. At first, I was thankful for freedom, but as the months passed and then years, I became haunted by the fact that we were still trapped on the island and in constant danger of discovery. I could not bear the thought that Pearl might be captured and returned to a place like the Garnett Estate. She believed that I was her brother because that was what we – my mother, Jon and I – had told her. We kept your secret, always. And eventually there was no point in telling her . . .' He saw Adanna close her eyes and stumbled.

'It's a long story, I'll try to be brief. I was sent by the Maroons to do business with a smuggler who worked from one of the hidden bays. I knew he traded across the islands and that he had contacts in the ports of America. I asked him if I could join his crew and he agreed. That night I carried Pearl to his ship among the sacks of stolen sugar he had bartered for arms and I hid her on board. When he sailed next day, I went too. It was a risk, but I had to take it. And we were fortunate – his men were good to me and to Pearl when they found her. Several of them had taken a similar route and were inclined to sympathy. One of them told me that the British army was willing to recruit men like me and pay them. That became my goal. It was hard, especially for Pearl who was still young. I dressed her as a boy and kept her close and eventually I worked a sea passage for us both to Boston where I enlisted.'

Adanna listened intently to Daniel's account of his days in the army. She did not speak or move as he described his friend.

'The Major was a good man. There were many who were not, but Edward trusted me, he gave me responsibility and the chance to prove myself. He and Elizabeth, Mrs Fitzallen, were childless. She made a favourite of Pearl and when—'

'She made my daughter a pet!'

Daniel was surprised at the venom in Adanna's voice. It was the first time she had interrupted his story. Frowning, he shook his head. 'I would not be here if it were not for them.'

'And look at you now.' She smiled. 'Fitzallen – it is a familiar name. My friend the Duke of Calne has a wide circle. There is one among them . . .' She shifted in the chair and the gorgeous wrapper fell open a little more. 'John? No, James. James Fitzallen.'

Daniel sat forward. 'He is the brother of my friend. He was at Rutland House on the night of the fight.'

Adanna nodded. 'As I said, he is an acquaintance of the Duke.'

'But he is not a friend to me or to Pearl.' He scowled. 'James Fitzallen is the cause of our misfortune.'

It was painful to recount the humiliations of his life since he had arrived in London, but Daniel told her almost everything. He did not leave Jen from his story, but through a reticence he could not entirely explain, her presence was reduced. When he spoke of her, the stock at his neck seemed to tighten a little. He loosened it.

He noticed that whenever he mentioned Pearl, Adanna looked away or shielded her face with her long gloved fingers. He could not begin to fathom her feelings or their complexity. In truth, she had never been a mother to their child. When Adanna was taken up to the Great House, a baby was already growing within her. As the weeks and then the months passed, she dressed with care to disguise her perilous condition. She was young, tall and slim and she carried with little sign or difficulty, but if Lady Isabella had found out that her clever companion was with child, the punishment would have been cruel, fatal even. On the night that Pearl was born in darkness and secrecy, it was his own mother who carried the tiny mewing girl from the woodland clearing. And from that day it was his mother who cared for her and claimed her as her own.

They sat in silence for a while. Outside, a carriage rumbled on the rutted street and a dog barked. Adanna stared at the card in her hand and traced the outline of the child pointing at the sun with the tip of a finger. Setting it down, she rose and went to the buffet. Daniel heard the rustle of silk and the clink of glass as she poured wine from the decanter.

Returning to the fire, she handed him a glass and raised her own in a toast.

'We have come very far.'

He mirrored the gesture and lifted the wine to his lips.

'Poor, poor Daniel.' He froze at the malice in her voice. Staring over the rim of his glass, he felt again the crackle of something deadly leap between them.

'Adanna, I—'

'Silence! You have said enough.' The blaze in her eyes now did not come from the fire, but from within.

'Did you ever think of me? Did you ever consider what happened when those men and women ripped The Salutation apart that day?' Without giving him the space to reply, she continued ferociously. 'I cursed you then, Daniel Garnett, just as I have cursed you every day since. You promised to send word. You promised to protect me, but you saved yourself. You took my child and you left me to die.'

Stunned, he opened his mouth, but words did not come.

'I . . . I've thought of you every day,' he managed at last. 'I went to find you that night but the house was alight, burning so fiercely it lit up the sky. I watched it collapse on the hillside and I thought it was too late. They all said . . .' It was pathetic – the bleat of a boy. 'Please, Adanna,' he tried again. 'I thought you were dead.'

'I might as well have been.' She gazed at her portrait above the hearth. 'But as you see, I am very much alive. Let me tell you what happened after you abandoned me to the savages and to the flames and then we can decide who has had the worst of it.'

Chapter Forty

'First, we heard the drumming, then we saw the lights in the wood. Only I knew what it meant because you had warned me. They were all distracted, not yet frightened because they didn't understand, but *I* did. I went to Lady Isabella's room and I took as many of her jewels and trinkets as I could push into the bodice of my dress and then I went down and onto the veranda. There were men on the lawn already, most of them carrying torches. They called for the master and the mistress, but when they wouldn't come out, they began to march on the house. I looked for your face among them but you were not there and I became frightened. The only safe place I could think of was the wash house. I ran there and buried myself beneath piles of stinking linens. I heard it all – the screams, the shouts, the timbers cracking as the house collapsed, the gunshot when the militia came. I breathed ash and smoke, but I didn't move until I was certain it was over. And then I ran.'

She stared into the depths of her wine.

'It took me two days to reach Kingston. Mostly I walked at night because it was not safe to be seen on the roads, but it was easier to lose myself in the town. No one thinks to stop a servant girl carrying a bundle as long as her head is lowered in deference. I considered my options and I went to a whorehouse near the harbour – don't look so shocked, Daniel! The mother was happy to take me in without question. I was young and beautiful and men pay well for fresh meat.

The English are happy to buy the company of a warm brown whore when their pink wives turn cold. I was popular and I earned good coin. When I was not called upon, I sewed the jewels I had taken into the hem of my skirt and I planned a different future.

'One of my regular customers was a Creole trader. He was an ugly man, squat with bowed legs – we called him The Frog – but he had a small boat and trafficked goods between the islands and the coast of America. When he wasn't grunting on top of me, I listened to his tales of New Orleans – all the women in the whorehouse harboured a fancy to go there – and I saw what I should do. I offered to pay him if he would take me and he agreed.

'I was not a fool. I only gave him Isabella's ruby necklace when my feet were aboard his boat. We sailed at night and as I watched the lights of Kingston grow smaller and fainter I spat into the black sea and vowed that I would never return.

'On the third day we struck anchor in the tiny bay of an island so small it probably does not appear on any map. There was another ship waiting for us – an old brigantine – and I discovered that my Creole had made another bargain. I was a fool after all. He sold me to the pirate captain for the entertainment of his crew. A woman is a rare commodity on such a vessel. You will not be able to imagine my treatment by those men. I had worked as a harbourside whore, but on that ship, I discovered the depths to which a man – or woman – may fall.'

Adanna took a sip of wine. Daniel wanted to say something. Anything. He leaned forward, about to speak, but she raised her hand to stop him. Twisting the stem of the glass, she took a larger gulp and continued.

'You might say it was fortunate that the captain developed a partiality for me. Or you might say that I made certain he did so; after all, it is better to serve the Devil than his demons. I pretended to return his affection and soon he was the only man I serviced, but all the while I waited. One night, after the taking of a Spanish barque loaded with brandy and wine, my chance came. I moved while the men were drunk on liquor and victory. I stole from the captain's bed and went to the hold where I lit several small fires. Then, taking whatever I could find without drawing attention to myself, I climbed along the rope from the stern to the bumboat. I cut it free, and as I bobbed away on the black water, I watched the sails of that old brigantine burn and the spars tumble into the sea. Finally, when I could no longer hear the screams of the men, I lay down and slept.

'I do not know how long I floated in that little boat. Truly, I had thought that death was preferable to my life on the ship, but as the hot days passed and the water and the wine I had taken ran out, I questioned my decision. When fishermen found me, my skin was cracked and my tongue so dry and swollen that, at first, they could not force the smallest drop of water into my mouth.

'Fate has a strange way of tricking us, Daniel.' Cupping the glass, Adanna stared at him. 'Those fishermen took me to New Orleans. They also took almost everything of value I possessed. I was not in a condition to resist when, believing me dead, they searched me and found the last of Isabella's jewels sewn into the hem of my skirt.'

She stood again. Taking Daniel's glass along with her own, she went to the buffet and refilled them.

'And so, I was forced to begin again.' She sat, curling her long legs beneath her.

'Freedom has a cost, as you rightly observed. I was not a stranger to whoring and it was the profession to which I returned, but I was not careful enough and once again I found myself with child. Given my circumstances, I could not allow it to be born. When I rid myself of it, using the methods and herbs recommended by women who had been similarly afflicted, I also rid myself of the chance of ever carrying a child again.'

Adanna frowned and swirled the wine in her glass. 'I had already given birth to a live baby. Who could know that such a small unformed thing could be so bloody and so difficult to bear?'

Daniel flinched at the coolness in her voice. Her story was terrible, and yet she told it with the equanimity of a woman giving orders to her dressmaker. He stared into his own glass and found that he did not want to drink.

'At least in New Orleans I found myself among equals.' Adanna did not share Daniel's scruples. She took a mouthful of wine and settled back luxuriously. 'When my looks and my strength recovered, I went to a famous madame – from Brittany – whose clients were mostly French. Louise was an old woman by then and no longer active, but she chose her birds with great care. She chose me and gave me a new name. Soon I was her favourite and also the favourite of her most wealthy clients.' Adanna smiled and turned to tap the cards at her side. 'She taught me many things, among them the art of divination. Men are such fools – how they loved to hear of their glorious futures.

'One of those fools was an old man with property in both America and in France, the land of his birth. He was a widower and his three sons had died in infancy. I believe he was once considered something of a rake. Certainly, the freedoms and particularities offered by the houses of New Orleans were more to his taste than those of his French estate, which he had not visited for many years. He was already quite ancient when we were first introduced. I noticed how his mind wandered as freely as his hands and, immediately, I saw my future . . .' Adanna gazed at the portrait above the hearth and raised her glass, '. . . and his.

'The Marquis de Notaille – last of a long and noble line – died six months after our wedding, but before he expired I made very certain that, should such a sadness come to pass, his estates and titles should pass to me quite legally and without challenge.'

She turned to Daniel and grinned broadly, revealing the gap between her teeth that had always charmed him. Seeing the look on his face, she laughed.

'And so, you see, I really am a Marquise – I am a titled lady, but I am like no other lady in this city. When I met the Duke of Calne in Naples last summer, I told his fortune too.'

'Surely you cannot mean to m ...' Daniel struggled to say the word, although her meaning with regard to the old French aristocrat had been clear.

Adanna smiled. 'I mean to marry him, if that is what you are trying to say? I believe he will ask me. His delight is to shock. When you are as rich as he, nothing can harm you – not even the greatest scandal.' She raised an eyebrow. 'Now, what do you think of my story? Who has suffered most?'

When he didn't answer she turned to the table and flicked open the ebony-inlaid box beside the cards.

'Do you remember this trinket? It is the only thing I took from The Salutation that the fishermen didn't find.' She took out a thin golden object and shook it. A score of fine silver chains studded with jewels shivered in the light of the fire. It was the flail that had once belonged to Isabella Garnett.

Adanna laid the chains across the palm of her hand and stroked them. 'Over the years, I have discovered that men enjoy the scratch of my cat. They like to be punished for their misdeeds.'

Rising from the chair, she allowed the Chinese wrapper to slip from her body. She was magnificent and terrible as she came slowly towards him, the firelight mapping continents in the dips and curves of her smooth naked flesh. Daniel turned away, but her scented fingers stroked the side of his face before sliding beneath the loosened stock to his neck and then to his shoulder.

Her caress was shamefully irresistible. Within seconds his body was her captive.

Chapter Forty-one

A shaft of sunlight from the half-opened shutter woke him. Daniel groaned in the tumbled sheets, uncertain of where he was. A moment later, memories and images of the previous night flooded his mind and he turned to Adanna.

She was not there.

Instead, a leather pouch sat in the dip of her pillow. He pulled it towards him. The chink of coins told of the contents, but when he opened the strings there was also a fold of paper tucked inside. Opening it, he saw what she had written.

For your services

The words stung like the bloody stripes left by the flail on his back. He was dismissed and this was her final cruelty. She had used him, as so many men had used her. Appalled, he threw the pouch to the floor where it rested next to his crumpled shirt.

Last night, consumed by an overwhelming passion where lust, guilt and horror were so entwined he could not pick them apart, he had lost his mind. Their lovemaking had been wild and vicious, and although he had responded to her touch and to the shockingly familiar contours of her lips and body, he had known that this was an ending, not a beginning.

He blinked at the shutters. From the angle of the light, the sun had long risen and judging from the chill of the linens beside him, so had Adanna. Rising from the vast and richly draped bed, Daniel collected his clothes from the floor. The only furniture in the elegant yellow-painted room was a bed. There did not even seem to be a way out.

He looked for the hidden entrance leading through to the room where they had first met and could not, immediately, see a doorway. After pulling on his breeches, shirt and waistcoat he went to the wall and traced a faint rectangular outline in the panelling. There was something else too – a small hole. He put his eye to it and saw most of the room beyond. The thought of her watching him that first night as he waited in such hope and trepidation was like another smarting blow from her tiny gilded whip.

He ran his fingertips along the almost invisible outline of the door and pushed at a raised area in the painted wood. Immediately the panel swung silently open and Daniel saw that the spy hole was placed in a gap between two books. He wondered who else Adanna had watched from her bedchamber. The thought was unnerving. Flooded by a sudden, almost suffocating need to be out of that room, out of that house and as far from her as possible, Daniel retrieved his shoes and coat from the floorboards and went to the hidden door.

Despite its size, the house was completely silent. Servants did not scurry across the marble hallway below or chatter on the landings above. The air itself was inert. He went quickly down the stairs and was surprised to find the wigged servant who admitted him the night before still at his post. Without looking at him and without saying a word, the powdered man opened the door, releasing Daniel to the street like a used strumpet.

He stared at the knotted wood of the table. These natural defects were joined by a multitude of stains that told of many years of use. It was before midday and the old tavern at the end of a passage off

Maiden Lane was quiet. That suited him well, as did his seat in a gloomy wooden booth at the rear of the room.

Daniel had not known what he expected from a reunion with Adanna, but he had not imagined the overriding emotion to be shame.

He felt sullied from the night – sullied by her and by his inability to resist her even though by the time she had reached the end of her tale, he no longer recognised her. Of course, the years had changed her, they were both altered, but the girl he had loved and mourned had vanished. Now he wondered if she had ever existed.

It was not the fact that Adanna had worked as a whore – for how else was she to have lived? It was her corruption. Her life had been hard, terrible even, he could not disagree, but the blood in her veins had turned to poison. It was a difficult thing to consider, but had he always been blind to her ruthless self-regard? Last night she had spoken of murder as if it were as easy and natural as applying carmine to her lips.

The only thing he had taken from her chamber was the curt, contemptuous message. Pulling it from the pocket of his coat, he studied her chillingly formal hand. Years ago, his mother had told him of enchanters who cast spirits from the bodies of the possessed. Staring at the calculated insult written on the square of paper, he understood that the night had been an exorcism. The link between them was broken.

He tore the paper into tiny pieces and brushed it furiously to the sawdust. A small dog that had been snuffling beneath the tables rushed eagerly to his side hoping for scraps, but after lingering for a moment, it ambled away, tail drooping in disappointment.

Daniel took a swig from a tankard and returned to his study of the whorls in the wood. They looked back accusingly. Swallowing, he raised his eyes to the cracked plaster ceiling where low-slung beams bowed from the weight of the floors above pressed upon him. The ale tasted of vinegar. It had been cut.

The bitterness reminded him uncomfortably of Jen that day in The Dolphin. He saw now, only too clearly, that his infatuation had been the reason for at least some part of his harshness towards her. From the moment Adanna had reappeared in his life, he had pushed Jen from him.

'Is that why you sent Pearl away? Because I'm not good enough for her? Not fit to be in her company? I know you want her to be a lady.'

The stale beer soured in his mouth as he recognised the grain of truth in Jen's accusation. He had, indeed, been blinded by Adanna's status and apparent nobility and had compared them. How could he have been so wrong?

They were different in every way possible, but Adanna was the unworthy one.

Not once had she asked about her daughter, at least not in the way of a mother. There was no reason now to tell their child the truth. It was better to let her continue to think of him as a brother; the alternative was too difficult to contemplate.

He was thankful for his daughter's sweetness. Before he had left her at The Black Apollo for a second time, Pearl had insisted on giving him part of her earnings. He had been unwilling to take her money, but she would not be refused. However, it seemed that he did not need it. When he had tried to pay for the jug of ale that now sat before him, the landlord of The White Lion had patted his hand and leaned across the sticky counter.

'You don't need that here.' The man had winked conspiratorially. 'The only payment I'd ask, if you're inclined, is to come here again so that I might tell my customers of The Soldier's patronage.'

Daniel had never felt less like a hero. Plucking at the collar of his second borrowed coat, he raised the tankard and sank further into gloom. He was so engrossed in his dismal thoughts that it was some time before he realised that the booth behind him had become occupied. He heard a man's deep low voice.

'In these last days the decline has been rapid. He cannot last much longer.'

'I can give him something for the pain,' another man answered, 'but there's little more I can do. Last night I thought the effort might kill him. That or disappointment.'

Daniel sat up with a jolt. He recognised the accent and the solemn tone of the speaker. The second voice belonged to Jerome. He listened to the men continue their discussion and realised with a sense of foreboding that they were discussing Octavian. Rising from his bench in the booth, he went to them. Lemuel Darke was seated opposite Jerome, who looked up in surprise.

'Daniel!' He moved his spectacles to the bridge of his nose and eyed him coldly. 'Where were you last night?'

At first Daniel thought that Jerome meant the visit to Adanna and was, in some way, mocking him. Then, with another swoop of shame, he realised what Jerome meant. The previous evening, he was supposed to have attended a meeting of the Brotherhood. Richardson had told him of it when he had first taken Pearl to The Black Apollo. There was nothing he could say. Ashamed, he shook his head. 'I ... I can offer no excuse.'

'No, for indeed there is none.' Jerome could barely conceal his hostility. 'You allowed a man so near to death that it whispers in his ear to wait for you for three hours in a hard chair when he should have been in his bed.'

'You were the cause of our gathering,' Darke agreed. 'You were the reason Octavian waited so long.'

Daniel remembered Richardson's excitement when he had told him of the meeting.

'And it's on account of you. There is much to discuss.'

He stared grimly at the sawdust while Jerome continued.

'Octavian said you would come. He said he was sure of you, but at last he was disappointed, as were we all.'

'I am sorry.' Daniel looked up. 'Last night I was . . .' Guilt made a hostage of his words. He took a breath. 'It will never happen again.'

Jerome snorted. 'Octavian is so frail I am not sure he will move from his bed *again*. What were you doing last night that was more important than our cause?'

'Nothing.' As Daniel replied, it was an obscure comfort to know that he spoke the truth. 'Nothing,' he repeated more firmly. 'Please, what can I do to make amends?'

The men exchanged a significant look and then Darke pointed to the seat opposite his own. When Daniel sat down, the journalist looked around to check that he was not overheard. Leaning forward, he spoke in a voice husky with tobacco. 'You can lead them. Octavian believes the time has come.'

'I have no wish to be a new King of the Rookery.' Daniel looked at the men's grave faces. 'I will stand by your side, but I—'

'They need a leader!' Darke interrupted, the planes and angles of his lean face were sharpened by the lantern above them. 'They will follow you, Daniel. There's never been anyone before who could unite the Rookery as you could.' He turned to Jerome, who still smouldered in the depths of the booth. 'What did you tell Octavian last night?'

'I merely repeated what is common knowledge.' Jerome pushed his wine glass back and forth across the tabletop like a chess piece. 'I told him of the way the crowd followed you through the streets two days back. They called your name and sang songs in your honour. Octavian believes that we must strike at Elias now, while you have their love.'

'Believe me, I have more reason than most to see Elias gone, but . . .' Daniel swallowed. 'I am not the man you think I am.'

'It doesn't matter what I think.' Jerome glanced at Darke. 'We are going to Octavian now. If he is alive after his exertions . . .' he allowed the accusation to sink in, '. . . I have medicine to ease his pain.' Licked by the lantern light, the gilded lenses of his spectacles obscured his eyes. They sat in silence for a moment and then he shrugged. 'Perhaps, if you were to come with us it would rouse his spirits. If he is able, he will persuade you.'

The space that Octavian shared with Marcus was cramped as a nutshell. The cellar was beneath an old house whose upper floors appeared to be divided into several dwellings along with a second-hand bookshop at street level. The narrow lane where this building was crushed between others of similar dubious appearance was situated where Covent Garden frayed into St Giles.

Jerome and Darke had led Daniel along a side passage into a muddy yard. At the back of the building, a flight of narrow steps led down to an arched doorway that opened into a tiny room crammed with books and papers. The place was warmed by a meagre corner fire that choked out smoke. It was lit by this unsatisfactory hearth and by the jaundiced glow of a single candle lantern strung from a beam.

After admitting them, Marcus secured the door and pointed dolefully to what appeared to be a bundle of cloth in a battered wing chair pulled close to the sputtering fire. With his broad shoulders hunched beneath the press of the wooden ceiling, he seemed to fill most of the space.

Jerome knelt beside the chair and whispered, 'Octavian.'

Daniel saw the bundle shiver. A small hand crept through the cloth and reached towards the apothecary.

'I confess I am pleased to see you.' The cracked voice was almost unrecognisable.

'I have brought something as I promised.' Jerome dipped into a pocket and produced a green glass phial. 'Four drops in wine or small beer will ease the pain. Twice a day should be sufficient, but if . . . if necessary, you may take another drop on the tongue.' He turned to Marcus. 'Did you hear that?'

The large man nodded.

'You are a good friend to me, Jerome.' Octavian coughed. Daniel could not decide whether the benefit of the fire outweighed the effect of the smoke in this tiny space. His own eyes stung from the fumes.

'I have brought other friends.' Jerome folded the bottle into twig-like fingers. 'Here is Lemuel come to see how you fare today, and also Daniel come to apologise.' He glanced sourly at Daniel, who stood at the door. The damp cellar was too cramped with people and paper for him to have moved any closer. Darke had taken up a space beneath a low arch beyond the hearth. He stooped to fit himself beneath the bricks.

Jerome continued. 'If our company is too much to bear you have only to say.'

'Daniel?' The bundle began to unfurl. In a moment, Octavian's head emerged. Dry grey skin, pulled taut across the bones of his skull. 'Where is he?'

Moving carefully, Jerome allowed Daniel to take his place.

'I am here.' He tried to disguise his shock at the man's decline. 'I am sorry that you waited for me last night. I know that I am the cause of your pain and discomfort.'

'The cause of my pain and discomfort is disease.' Octavian's eyes retained the brightness of a bird. 'I am glad to see you now.' He looked over Daniel's shoulder at his other visitors. 'Have you told him?'

'He is yet to be persuaded.' Folding his arms, Darke leaned back uncomfortably in his niche. 'I'm just a hack but you're the orator, Octavian. Speak to him.'

'You honour me.' The sick man smiled. 'Before I do so, if you would be so good, my dear friend . . .' He held up the phial and Marcus reached over Daniel's head for it. Taking a bottle from the side of the hearth, he poured wine into a small tin mug and then he carefully added four drops of Jerome's tincture.

'Will it make me sleep?' Octavian stared at the mug.

'No.' Jerome sat on a stack of books. 'Not this first time. It may, eventually, have a cumulative effect, but for now you will find that the sharpness of the pain is blunted, not your thoughts.'

Octavian nodded. 'That is good, for I need my wits to make my case.'

Daniel shifted aside as Marcus crouched to hold the mug to Octavian's lips. He was moved as much by the tenderness between them as by the awful certainty that they would soon be parted.

Octavian flinched. 'This is bitter stuff, apothecary. You must learn to sugar your pills.'

'With or without sweetness, the result is the same.' Jerome smiled sadly. 'Besides, sugar is costly, as we all know.'

'As we know and value your honesty.' Daniel saw a look pass between them and understood that Jerome had not hidden the truth from his patient. When Marcus had helped Octavian to finish the wine, he allowed Daniel to take his place once more. Fixing him with sharp eyes, Octavian tilted his head.

'Darke calls me an orator, but I have not the time or the energy for artful construction. Listen to the words of a dying man. The Brotherhood has many aims, but if I can leave this world knowing that we have begun to make the Rookery a better place, my passage will be easy. It can do our cause no good when every day so many of our people are perceived as the lowest in London. It must—'

Wracked by a sudden coughing fit, Octavian broke off. There was an unmistakable rattle as he gasped and struggled to breathe. His hand flailed desperately as if trying to clutch the air. Without knowing what to do, Daniel caught hold and held tightly.

Gradually the spasm subsided and Octavian was able to continue.

'In the years of Elias's rule, the Rookery has become a place of desolation – a byword for all that is low, vicious and worthless. Our wretched brothers and sisters cannot escape the reputation their king has forced upon them.'

He spoke slowly and carefully. Although his voice was firmer now, Daniel could hear the effort it cost him.

'Oh, I have had such ambitions.' The sick man smiled grimly. 'I do not expect change to come on the swift wings of an eagle. It will come slowly, for that is the nature of things, but the reign of Elias must end and that ending will be a beginning. Milton tells us that Satan's greatest sin – and his tragedy – is that he allowed himself to sink into despair. Hope – that is the saviour, Daniel, and you will be the hope of the Rookery. *You* will be a beginning.'

'But I . . . I do not see how . . .' Daniel turned to appeal to Jerome and to Darke, but their eyes were fixed on Octavian, who seemed to rally. The tiny man gathered his fragile body and sat straighter.

'The people of the Rookery are like children. They need, for want of a better word, a father. Elias will fall, of that I have no doubt, but there will always be someone waiting to fill his place. What if it were to be someone worse? The Brotherhood is agreed. It would be better to replace him with a man who shares our vision. A good man who can advance our cause. The Rookery does not need another king, but it does need a hero. The people will follow you.'

His eyes burned. 'Lead the rebellion. That is what we ask of you.' He gripped Daniel's hand with a force that seemed extraordinary for one so frail. 'It is what *I* ask of you.'

Daniel did not get a chance to reply. Someone hammered so heavily on the door that the wooden bolts juddered in the staples. Above the pounding came the sound of voices.

'Who's there?' Darke shouted out.

'Sparrow and Jen.'

'Are you alone?'

The answer to Darke's question was the rattle of the door. 'For

Christ's sake, open up,' Jen called urgently. 'It's just the two of us and no one else.'

Marcus looked questioningly at Octavian, who nodded. When he unbolted the door, the pair tumbled across the threshold.

'Mr Meriday said you'd likely be here, Lemuel.' Panting, Jen steadied herself against the door jamb. The hem of her dress was sodden and her loose wet hair fell in knots that clung to her face.

'They've been taken by the runners – all of them.' She could barely get the words out. 'They came an hour back. Mr Meriday saw it all.'

She broke off to gulp down air and Sparrow continued. 'It was lucky he wasn't inside when it happened, although he almost was. He said you'd know what to do, Mr Darke.'

'Not so fast.' Darke frowned at Jerome. 'What has happened? Who has been taken, where?'

'There was a raid on The 'Pollo, that's what.' Bending double, Sparrow shook his head and gestured to Jen to finish for him.

'They took everyone,' she gasped. 'Mr Richardson, his wife, Cyrus, Tolly and the other wait boys and anyone else who happened to be inside at the time.'

'Everyone?' Books toppled as Daniel rose from Octavian's side. Jen froze in the doorway. Avoiding his eyes, she nodded. 'Mr Meriday saw it all. He said they had wagons waiting. Anyone who was there at The Apollo just before noon was dragged outside, loaded up and carted off.'

Now she looked at Daniel.

'You took her back there.' It was not quite a question, but Daniel nodded mutely, barely able to comprehend the enormity of her words.

'Christ!' Jen swept damp hair from her eyes. 'Then Pearl will have been taken to Bow Street with the rest of them.'

Chapter Forty-two

It was raining heavily by the time they reached Bow Street. Jen and Sparrow were barely able to keep pace with Darke, Daniel and Jerome as they pounded through Covent Garden, but now they all huddled together beneath the bulging awning of a rag shop.

Bow Street was almost as poor and disreputable as St Giles. Daniel was surprised to see that several of the houses standing so close to the bastion of the law were brothels where painted, semi-clothed women beckoned from doorways or called from the open windows.

The magistrates' court and offices were housed in an old flat-fronted building much like all the others in the street. It was only the barred windows that marked its purpose. A row of flattened narrow arches, iron-barred like the windows above, but without glass, ran along the wall at street level. When carriages passed, filthy slurry washed up against the wall and slopped into those dark cavities. Daniel struggled with the thought of Pearl captive and terrified in one of those dank spaces. He turned to Darke, who had led the way.

'What can we do?'

'Not *we*, my friend. Wait here and I'll go inside.' Darke pointed at steps leading to a wide metal door. 'I've attended court many times and written about the cases that come before the magistrates. I'm familiar with some of them and several of the runners too. I've even helped them in the past.'

'I'll come with you.' Hunched against the rain, Daniel started for the steps but Darke caught his arm.

'I'll go alone. It will be best that way. If we all go together, we could be mistaken for a mob.'

'Lemuel is right,' Jerome nodded. 'The riots of 1780 made them wary. The building was not greatly fortified before then, but now ...' He glanced at the barred windows and removed his spectacles to wipe them on the sleeve of his coat. 'It would not help our friends if we were to be arrested too.'

'But we have done nothing wrong,' Daniel protested.

'And neither have they.' Darke stared at him. 'You still have much to learn about London.'

'Go and find out, Lemuel. We'll wait here.' Jen's hair was plastered to her head and the blue fabric of her plain dress was blackened by water. Clasping her bedraggled shawl around her shoulders, she glanced at Daniel and then looked quickly away. 'Let him go alone. It's for the best.' There was a tearing sound. Suddenly water that was caught in the bulge of the awning gushed through a rip in the canvas, soaking them all anew.

'We could wait in The Globe.' Sparrow pointed hopefully to a tavern further along the street. 'At least we'd be dry.'

The Globe was narrow, beamed and uneven like an old ship. On account of the rain, business was brisk. The aroma of damp wool, unwashed bodies, rough alcohol and cheap tobacco was not a happy blend.

Daniel moved the tankard from hand to hand across the tabletop. He was in no mood to drink. When he thought of Pearl something in his chest tightened like a fist. He knew that Darke was right, but waiting while another went into battle did not come easily.

'He can't be much longer, now.' Jen addressed herself to Jerome. Since taking seats at a narrow table near the bowed window overlooking the street, she and Daniel had not spoken a word to each other. It would have been impossible for the apothecary not to notice the tension between them. He pushed at his spectacles and twisted about to peer through the fugged glass. Beyond the window the rain fell like a veil.

'Perhaps the fact Lemuel has not returned is a good thing?' He turned back. 'I would be more dismayed if he had come to the door half an hour ago.'

'That's true enough,' Sparrow said with a nod. 'If anyone can find out what's happened, Mr Darke can. He's smooth as an otter when he wants to be. They say he was a spy once.'

'As *I* heard it, he was an actor.' Jen frowned. 'But then, he's never spoken of the past.'

'Perhaps it is not something he wishes to discuss.' Jerome took a swig of porter. 'We must be content that Lemuel is our friend, for I would not want him as an enemy.'

When Daniel considered this, he found that he agreed. Darke was the most mysterious and enigmatic member of the Brotherhood. When he joined them, he seemed to be visiting from a different world.

They looked up as the door swung open, but Darke was not among the three dripping men who pushed through the steaming crowd to the counter.

'What I don't understand,' Jerome said, staring grimly into his tankard, 'is what Pearl was doing there.'

'If I hadn't persuaded her to sing for Mrs Kelly, her brother wouldn't have locked her away at The Apollo.' Jen reached for her gin. 'It's bad enough that Mr Richardson, his wife and everyone else was taken ...' she gulped down a mouthful, 'but to think that she was there too.'

Hearing the catch in her voice, Daniel looked up to see tears streaking down her cheeks. Jen jabbed at the glass, slopping gin across the tabletop. She stared furiously at the spilled liquor. 'It's the foulest drop of Old Tom I've had in a long time. Bleedin' muck. It's been cut more times than a bolt of Spitalfields silk.'

Daniel knew that she was probably right about the gin, but quite wrong about everything else. As he watched her shiver in her damp dress and shawl, dabbing miserably at the spilled gin, the guilt he had experienced since waking in Adanna's chamber came flooding back, drowning him in an ocean of culpability.

'*I* am to blame, not you.' He reached for her hand. Jen flinched at his unexpected touch, but then she looked up. The hurt in her eyes stung him. Unable to hold her gaze, he stared at the tabletop. How many lies and half-told stories had led to this miserable moment?

Seeing no point in further secrecy when it had cost him so dear, he began to tell them about Elias, his threats and the real reason he had taken Pearl to The Black Apollo. In his heart, he knew it was the reason for the raid.

'I can see why you might come to that conclusion, but Elias is not one to court the attention of the law. This is too public even for him,' Jerome said, frowning. 'The Black Apollo is a particular enterprise, but it is long-established, respected even, and Inigo Richardson is well liked. The King of the Rookery would find it difficult to persuade a magistrate to act on his behalf.'

'You're wrong. This *is* the work of Elias.' Daniel thumped the table. 'He said he would make me pay for what I did and now he has. Pearl is—' He stopped himself from revealing the final truth. 'My sister is all I have. I would rather he had come for me than for her, but he's clever. According to Melkie, all fighters have a weak spot that can be exploited. She is mine. Elias warned me what would happen if I failed him. The irony is that when I took Pearl to The Apollo, I thought she would be safe. I was a fool.'

'You're no fool.' Jen shook her head. Circling a fingertip in the spilled gin, she continued in a low voice. 'I see it now. In your place I'd have feared for her safety too. And I can see why it fired you against me. You did the right thing.' She looked up. 'I just wish you'd told me. Surely you could have trusted me, Dan?'

The accusation in her eyes cut deep as a surgeon's blade.

Jerome peered across the table. The lines between his brows deepened. 'I am sorry you felt unable to tell any of us.'

Daniel wilted under the apothecary's penetrating gaze. He was ashamed to have been so willing to betray the Brotherhood. It chipped at the very core of his being. He had always seen himself as a man of honour, but London had stripped that last dignity from him, along with everything else.

'The bonds of family are the tightest of all.' Jerome's words brought a little comfort. The brown eyes behind the panes were suddenly sharp. 'There is no shame in wanting to protect your . . . sister.'

'But how did he know Pearl was there?' Sparrow looked from face to face and held up his hands. 'I didn't tell him, if that's what you're thinking.'

'You're not the only bird in his pocket, Sparrow.' Jen shrugged. 'We all know Elias has spies everywhere.'

'But it's a peculiar thing,' Sparrow piped up again, 'that The 'Pollo should be raided now, when no one's ever taken against its existence – 'cept the 'prentice boys, that is, and as I hear it, it's well guarded against them. Taking everything on the balance, I'm inclined to agree with you, sir.' He nodded at Daniel. 'This has the mark of Elias all over it.'

'Look!' Jen pointed to the door. 'Lemuel's back.'

As the journalist came towards them, the smile on his face was a welcome sight.

Daniel stood up. 'Pearl. Is she . . . Where is she?'

'All in good time.' In his long black coat, Darke loomed over the table like a cormorant. He swept up Daniel's tankard and emptied it in a few deep gulps.

'Talking to an idiot is always thirsty work,' he said with a grin, 'but I have news. Yesterday, a charge was laid against Richardson regarding the legal status of the liquor sold on his premises. It was alleged that he traded with dealers without paying duties to His Majesty's Board of Excise. The Black Apollo was also reported as a bawdy house.'

'But there are a thousand such houses in London!' Jen was incandescent. 'In this very street, there are women touting for trade from every third doorway right under their noses.'

'Indeed,' Darke agreed. 'But the excise matter was the more serious crime and certainly the cause of the raid. I believe the charge of irregularity was a spiteful addition. However . . .' he paused for effect, '. . . in a few moments I expect our friend Inigo Richardson, Cyrus and the boys in his employ to walk through that door.' He pointed to the entrance. 'And soon Alys and Pearl will join us too. All charges have been dropped.'

Daniel experienced a dizzying sense of relief.

'Well, this is excellent news!' Jerome rose to shake Darke's hand. 'How, Lemuel? How did you manage it?'

'More easily than I thought possible.' His eyes glinted. 'As I said, in a professional capacity I know my way around Bow Street. When I went in, I looked – as is my habit – at the day posts listing the cases, the charges and the magistrate presiding. Sir Sampson Wright is away. In his absence, his cases are to be heard by others. I saw that Inigo was due to come before Henry Dixon. This was my first stroke of fortune, because I know Henry Dixon.' He arched a brow. 'Well, that is to say, I know *of* Henry Dixon. Most particularly of his connection to a notorious molly house in Moorfields known as Mother Peg's.

'My second stroke of fortune was to talk to one of the runners of my acquaintance and to discover that Mr Dixon was at that very moment in court, but likely to leave within the hour. I loitered in the hallway and when Mr Dixon appeared on the stairs I was waiting. He was almost at the door and just at my side when I bent to whisper in his ear.

'"Mother Peg is missing her Little Lily." That was all I needed to say. He stared up at me, gaping like a landed codfish, and then I asked, most politely and reasonably, if he could spare a moment of his time to talk to me in private. It was an offer he could not refuse. Our brief conversation, in Wright's panelled office, beneath a portrait of the King, was most fruitful.'

'You blackmailed him!' Jen clapped her hands.

'Blackmail is an ugly word, Iphigenia.' Darke tilted his head. 'I make no judgement on how a man might seek entertainment, but there are others, including Mr Dixon's wife and wealthy father-in-law, who would not be so indifferent. I merely presented him with some alternatives and invited him to make an informed choice. He chose well. And he ordered the duty constable to give me these.' He held up a note and a ring of keys and patted Daniel's shoulder. 'This should unlock Mrs Richardson and your sister. Follow me.'

The innkeeper asked no questions when Darke presented the constable's note. After examining the signature and following the three lines of writing with the tip of a tobacco-stained finger, the man nodded. Taking a lantern from the shelf behind him, he lit the gristle of wax inside and pointed to an arched doorway at the furthest end of the tavern. Beyond it, a short flight of wooden steps led to a dim passage so cramped that even a boy like Sparrow would have had to bend to navigate it.

'The cellars beneath The Globe have been used as cells for many years. It's a convenient arrangement. Watch out for the beam.' Darke dipped his head even lower. 'Usually, men and women awaiting trial are separated. My garrulous runner told me that the women taken from The Apollo are here.' Halting at a grilled archway in the bumpy stone wall, he set the largest key on the ring into an ancient lock. There was a grating noise as the metal gate swung open to reveal a flight of stone steps. The scent of earth and fouled water filled Daniel's nose. The thought of Pearl held in such a dismal place, even for a short time, was appalling. The fist in his chest pummelled again.

'I'll go first.' Darke held up a lantern. 'There are three passages at the bottom, we're to take the one on the left.' He began to descend and Daniel followed.

'Do you know who made the allegations against Richardson?' He spoke to Darke's back.

'I asked my tame runner that very question. There was nothing on the charge sheet or in the notes, which is irregular.' The deep voice echoed in the confined space. 'From my experience it's likely to be a rival. The Apollo is successful. Richardson is a wealthy man. That and the colour of his skin are enough to provoke jealousy.' Darke turned and the lantern light brought an eerie intensity to his face. 'It's more than jealousy. There are people in this city who despise us. If Richardson had been found guilty, he would, in all likelihood, have been shipped across the Atlantic to a plantation despite the fact that generations of his family have lived in London for many more years than that of the King.' He paused. 'Alys and your sister would not have escaped that fate.'

Daniel remembered that day at the London docks. Six chained men, filthy and defeated, had stumbled from the quayside onto a gangplank leading up to a black hulk. The dreadful silence had been broken by a weeping woman clutching a child to her breast and calling to her man.

He reached for Darke's arm. 'Thank you. I cannot begin to repay you for what you have done today.'

'But you can, Daniel.' The journalist stared up at him. 'Octavian has told you what to do.'

Swinging the lantern around, Darke continued down the stairs. At the bottom, they went to the left and found themselves in a second passage lined with low-arched doors. Water puddled the stones at their feet and the lantern made little impression on the blackness ahead. Disturbed by their arrival, something squealed and scurried away.

'Pearl,' Daniel called out. When there was no answer, he called again. There was a shuffling in the darkness.

'Who . . . who's there?' It was a woman's voice.'

Darke raised the lantern. 'It's Lemuel, ma'am. Come to free you.'

'Oh, thank God! Did you hear that, lamb?' The woman, who Daniel now recognised as Alys Richardson, spoke again. 'Is Inigo with you?'

'He is free and he will be waiting above with the others.' Darke held the ring of keys to the lantern and selected one. As they walked, the lantern showed crude chalk numbers marked on the doors of the cells. The further they went, the more the fetid stench strengthened as if the Thames and all its swilling evils were confined here together. Darke's coat trailed in liquid filth when he halted to fit the key to a lock.

The door swung inward, revealing a cramped and stinking hole. In the feeble light Daniel saw two shapes huddled together on a pile of sacking humped against a glistening wall. Alys Richardson pulled her cowering companion close and whispered, 'There, lamb, it's over now. Our friends have come to take us home.'

Bending, he went inside, knelt at Pearl's feet and took her icy hands in his.

'I'm here.' He kissed the top of her head. 'I'm so sorry. Forgive me.' Cupping her chin gently, he tipped her face upward.

The girl blinked and shrank from his gaze. She was delicate and pretty, but she was not Pearl.

'Where is she?' He turned frantically. Lemuel was helping Alys to her feet. 'Where is Pearl?' He shouted her name so loudly that it echoed from the stones. Alys steadied herself against Darke and reached out to the frightened girl.

'You're safe now, Betsy. You come with us. We'll have you back with your mother in no time.' Staring warily at Daniel, the girl took Alys's hand and rose from the sacking.

'Where is Pearl?' he demanded again. 'Why is she not here with you?'

Alys pulled the shivering maid to her breast and comforted her. 'There now. It's over.' Looking at Daniel, she seemed confused. 'Is she not with the men?'

His face gave the answer.

'I'm sorry.' Alys shook her head slowly. 'We fought to stay together when they came upstairs, but they took your sister from us. If she's not with Inigo and the others, I don't know where she is.'

Chapter Forty-three

Inigo Richardson held his wife as if he would never let her go again, and when he finally did, he enfolded Cyrus, Tolly and the three other wait boys who had been taken into custody in a bear-like embrace, his plump cheeks streaked by tears.

Daniel loitered on the edge of the group torn between envy and despair.

'I am sorry.' He turned at the sound of Jerome's voice. The apothecary had come to stand next to him. Daniel swallowed the painful lump in his throat. 'I am glad that Richardson and the others are free, but it is hard to watch when . . .'

'When Pearl is not among them?'

Daniel nodded. It was bitter to see Alys comfort the girl he had found in the cell. Jerome followed his gaze.

'Betsy cleans for the Richardsons twice a week. She is a sweet mouse. It must have been terrifying for her.'

'And what of Pearl?' Daniel demanded, his voice choked. 'What can it be like for her, wherever she is?'

'If there is anything to be known, Lemuel will find it. I am truly sorry, Daniel. We have not been friends these last weeks, but I would not wish the loss of a child on my greatest enemy.'

In the silence that followed this simple statement of fact, Daniel stared at the boards and considered several replies. At last, without looking up, he spoke quietly.

'How long have you known?'

'The love of a parent for a child cannot be mistaken. I've seen it often enough in my work. I suspected it for a while – I've watched you with her and I've seen a bond that goes beyond the concern of a brother. But it was when you told me earlier that you were willing to lose the fight for the sake of Pearl that I knew I was right. And besides . . .' Jerome smiled sadly, '. . . she looks so very like you, and acts like you too. She has your spirit.'

'She means everything to me.' Daniel looked up, careless now of the tears brimming in his eyes. Jerome nodded and tactfully returned his attention to the group celebrating freedom.

'It is not my secret to share, but does anyone else know the truth?'

'No one, not even Jen.' Daniel watched her rub a smut from Tolly's nose. She ruffled the lad's hair before bending to talk to another of Richardson's boys. As if aware of his scrutiny, she glanced over at him. She pulled self-consciously at her shawl but then she straightened up and came to them.

She looked back at the Richardsons. 'It must be hard to see this, when Pearl is still missing.' Reaching out, she caught Daniel's hand. Surprised and grateful, he gripped her tightly. Jen stared at their hands linked together and looked up.

'I'll do anything to help her, Dan.'

'As will we all.' Jerome pointed to the door. 'Lemuel has returned. Let us hope he has the information you need.'

'There is nothing in the register or the notes of the arrest. I saw it myself – the others are listed, even the four customers taken, but there is no mention of your sister.' Darke's face was grim. 'It's as if she was never there.'

'I took her to The Black Apollo myself. She can't have vanished.' Daniel slammed a clenched fist into the palm of his hand. He would have punched his way through a brick wall if it meant he could find Pearl on the other side.

'I'm afraid you're wrong. People disappear from the streets of this city every day.' Darke glanced at Jerome. 'Our people in particular.'

'Who would gain most from taking her? That's where we must apply ourselves.' Jerome clasped Daniel's shoulder. 'I believe you now. This is the work of Elias. This is his revenge. Does he know that she is—' He stopped himself. Removing his spectacles, he busied himself with an imagined smudge on the glass. Before anyone could interrogate his question, Richardson joined them and unexpectedly folded Daniel in his arms.

'I'm sorry, lad, sorrier than I can tell you.' Releasing him, Richardson stepped back, fresh tears glassing his eyes. 'I cannot forgive myself. I gave you my word that your sister would be safe and yet—'

'What happened, exactly, when the runners came?' Daniel's interruption was terse. The older man's apology was heartfelt, but he needed something more useful than regret.

'I'll admit it took us by surprise. They hammered on the door demanding that we open up to them, and as a law-abiding man, I did so, for I have nothing to hide. But they swarmed inside like a pack of dogs, turning the tables and breaking the chairs. They took everyone they found. Alys was upstairs with Pearl and little Betsy. They dragged them down to be carted off with the rest of us. Two covered wagons and a large black carriage were waiting at the end of the passage. The last thing I saw after they forced me up inside was my Alys swatting a man who'd made too free with her person. "That's my girl," I called out, but she didn't hear me. And then it was too late. They pulled down the flaps and the wagon rolled off.'

'And my sister? Did you see what happened to her?'

Richardson shook his head. 'I thought she was with Alys and Betsy. It was Cyrus who saw her loaded into the carriage.' He turned to call to the doorman. 'Cyrus, come here. Our friend has a question for you.'

The doorman of The Black Apollo was dishevelled but none the worse for his treatment. Despite his small stature, Daniel recognised something of Melkie in his pugnacious stance and muscular build. He could see why Richardson employed him.

Pushing at his damp lopsided wig, Cyrus nodded. 'I saw her dragged over to the carriage. Mrs Richardson tried to keep Pearl with her, but the men were very determined to part them. Your sister put up quite a fight, sir.'

Daniel took little comfort from the thought of her resistance. If anything, it made it worse. He tried to think clearly.

'Were the men who took her runners like the rest?'

'They all looked very alike, sir. It happened so fast and the alley-ways were dark. It was raining then too. There was so much uproar and commotion that I didn't think to look for a distinction between them. I'm sorry.'

'The carriage, then – was it marked?'

Cyrus shook his head. 'Not that I saw.'

'Was it the one belonging to Elias?'

This question came from Sparrow who had slipped to Daniel's side.

'I don't know.' The doorman's reply was doleful. 'As I said, it was chaos.'

'It's not your fault, Cyrus.' Jerome turned to Darke. 'Is there any way we can find out more?'

'If Pearl was taken by the runners, then perhaps, but there is something odd here. Why would she be separated from the other women? Why her?'

'I do remember something.' Cyrus pulled off his sodden wig and wrung it between his fingers. The chalky powder became a pallid paste on his skin. 'Not something about the raid, but something about Pearl. Something odd, just as you say, Mr Darke. Yesterday Ephra Sall came to The Black Apollo. He's never been before. I was surprised, but I didn't turn him away as he has a right to entry, despite his master's reputation. Tolly said he went to every public room as if he were looking for someone and then he tried to go upstairs to your private rooms, Mr Richardson. That was when Tolly came to fetch me. I asked Ephra what he was about and said he was hoping for a glimpse of a nightingale.'

'He meant Pearl!' Jen gasped. 'That was the name Mister Scribbler gave her.'

Jerome scowled. 'That man is as repulsive as his master. What did you tell him, Cyrus?'

'Nothing. I told him that if he wasn't prepared to produce a coin, he should leave. And he did.'

Ephra.

The distinctive name was familiar. Daniel tried to remember where he had heard it before but it shivered at the edge of his memory like a fish slipping from a net.

'What would Carney's apprentice want with Pearl?' Sparrow's question landed that herring.

With a shudder, Daniel recalled the scrawny printer's straggling red hair, his pocked and pallid face and, most horribly, his bony, ink-stained fingers. And he remembered Elias's warning:

'My tame printer has taken quite a liking to your sister.'

Chapter Forty-four

Vincent Carney's shop in Goat Alley looked much like any other in the squalid backstreets of St Giles. Housed in an ancient building with flaking plaster and a jettied overhang that shadowed the puddled cobbles, its purpose was not immediately obvious. Yet when Daniel glanced up at the rusted metal sign suspended beneath one of the beams jutting out over the passage, he could not mistake the unsubtle advertisement.

The bracket to which the dripping sign was attached was shaped like a phallus, complete with tarnished brass balls, and the plate swinging below was generously curved at the lowest edge to mimic a woman's breasts. The name 'Carney' had once been inscribed in gold paint across the metal, but the only letters retaining a vestige of legibility were the 'C' and the 'n'.

He turned to the others. 'Jerome, Lemuel. I'd be grateful of your company. But you should wait outside, Jen. Sparrow, you'll be happy to stand with her, won't you?'

'Of course.' The boy straightened in the folds of his coat. 'And if anyone happens to come along while you're ... doing business inside, then we can alert you, sir.'

Sparrow had accompanied them from The Globe. He was like a small stray dog that, having decided on a master – in this case Daniel – would not be deterred from following the object of its devotion.

'I'm coming with you,' Jen bridled. 'I'll be more use in there than out here. I've had dealings with Carney before.'

'You don't understand.' Daniel kept his voice low. 'We may have to use force.'

'I can look after myself. I've done so for years.'

Daniel rested a hand on her shoulder. 'I would not put another I care for at risk.'

Jen stared up at him. She seemed about to say something, but instead she rubbed the rain from her eyes with the corners of her shawl. After a moment, she nodded. 'Very well. I'll wait outside with Sparrow. Remember what I said about Carney – his tongue's as slippery as an eel.' She shivered. 'They say he keeps the girls in the cellar. Whatever he says, that's where she'll be.'

A bell jangled as Daniel opened the door. The rectangular space smelled of old paper, mustiness and mice, and lurking beneath there was something unpleasantly meaty – a combination of sweat and unwashed bodies. The panelled walls were lined with prints. Piles of large leather-bound books and folios cluttered the surfaces of the four tables set out either side of the room. At the far end, a sickly lantern was suspended over a long wooden counter.

'With you in a moment.' The reedy voice came from behind a patterned curtain drawn beyond the counter. 'Feel free to acquaint yourself with my stock. For the true connoisseur, I direct you to the table on the left of the door. Fresh from France – very rare. A most exquisitely detailed set and exceedingly natural in every way. Best I've had in a while.'

Daniel scowled at Jerome and then at Darke. The journalist put a finger to his lips. They gazed in silence at the prints arranged on the walls. Vincent Carney's stock-in-trade was obscenity calculated to titillate the basest appetites. Rendered in crude but effective lines, the images left little to the imagination – if a mind were capable of conjuring such depravity. Many of the women in these scenes were black, their naked skin cross-hatched and shadowed with a care and particular attention to detail that seemed obsessive.

'Her skin would produce very well on the plates.'

Daniel shuddered at the memory of Elias's words. The thought that Pearl should be anywhere near this man made his stomach pitch. Footsteps sounded from behind the curtain and Vincent Carney stepped into his shop. He smiled, exposing his atrocious teeth, and spoke in that broken wheedling voice.

'Now, gents. How may I help you this afternoon?'

Removing a pair of heavily framed spectacles that magnified his eyes to an extraordinary degree, he blinked, peered at his customers and recognised them.

'Ephra!' Carney called and turned, but Darke moved quickly. Vaulting over the counter, he ripped the curtain aside and went into the back of Carney's premises. Daniel heard scuffling and then Darke reappeared, dragging Ephra Sall by the ear. Carney's apprentice was, if anything, a more repellent specimen than his master. He was short and thin but an incongruously fleshy belly, revealed by the open shirt, hung over the top of his breeches. His face was blunted by a patchy beard where the remnants of food were caught in the bristles near his mouth. The young man's small black eyes darted about the room. Daniel was reminded of a cornered rat.

'I ain't done nothing. Let me go. You tell 'em, Carney.' Ephra spat out the words in a coarse London accent. 'I never touched her.'

'Shut your trap,' Carney hissed.

'Where is she?' Daniel spread his palms on the counter and leaned closer. Vincent Carney was a tall man, but he was thin as a pole. He shrank back, intimidated by his interrogator.

'I don't know who you mean.' He glanced angrily at Ephra, who was cowed and wriggling in Darke's fierce grip.

'I've come for my sister, Pearl.' Daniel jerked his head at Ephra.

'I know this man went to The Black Apollo looking for her. Where is she?'

Carney pushed at his lank red hair. It was so spare that beneath the lamp his scalp shone through like bone. He smiled. 'How should I know?'

Shooting out an arm with a speed that Melkie would have been glad to see, Daniel caught the printer by the throat and pushed him against the wall to the side of the counter. He was repulsed by the feeling of the man's Adam's apple bobbing above the skin of his hand and by the damp, gritty quality of the flesh beneath his fingers.

'Then why did your apprentice just tell us that he never touched her? Who did he mean, if not Pearl?'

Carney writhed against the panel. His yellowed, bloodshot eyes began to water. 'Let me go. She's not here.' He managed to choke out the words.

Daniel was aware of a movement at his side. Something flashed in the lamplight. He was amazed to see Jerome point a small blade at Carney.

'Go and look for her, brother. We'll wait here.' The weapon did not waver in Jerome's steady hand. 'Vincent Carney won't move an inch. I promise.'

Daniel found many things in the sordid, windowless room beyond Vincent Carney's shop where the sour smell mingled with something metallic. Three presses stood primed and rows of fresh prints – the ink still wet on the page – were pegged like washing beneath the beamed ceiling. A heap of stained rags was mounded in one corner and in the other a trap door stood open revealing a flight of steps. He went to the opening and called Pearl's name but the only answer from below was the ticking of clawed feet.

In the cellar – a long low, lamplit space that went further than the shop above – Daniel found stained mattresses and racks of outlandish

clothes that served no purpose other than to demean the models in
the prints he had seen above. Whips, chains and an assortment of
items associated with the pleasure of pain hung from the walls and
leather dildos were arranged in order of size on a shelf along the back
wall. At the foot of one of the mattresses, an easel, legs splayed like
a foal, suggested that this was a place of artistic endeavour.

Apart from spiders and a scab-backed rat, which scuttled to the
shelter of a crack in the stone walls, there was no other living thing
in Carney's cellar. Daniel returned to the shop above, distraught
and disgusted.

'I told you,' Carney hissed at him as he emerged through the
curtain. 'She's not here.'

Daniel confirmed this with a brief, bitter nod at both Jerome
and Darke.

'Then where is she?' Darke twisted Ephra's ear and the short man
squealed in pain.

'It won't do any good to hurt him.' Carney stared dispassionately
at his apprentice. 'Ephra doesn't know any more than me.'

'Then why did he go to The Black Apollo? He's never been there
before.' Jerome kept the knife level with Carney's throat.

'I'm sure you'd know all about that, Saint Apothecary, what with
it being something of a private club. What is it you call yourselves?'
Carney pretended to consider his own question. 'Ah yes, I have it.
The Brotherhood of Crows.' His laugh was a thin wheezing sound.
'Brotherhood of Shit Sacks is more like it.'

Daniel resisted the impulse to take a swipe at the man's head.
Carney's neck was so long and thin that a well-landed blow could
break it in two.

'Answer the question,' he growled. 'Why did Ephra go there
looking for my sister?'

'Elias said she was lodged at The Apollo and I wanted to make
sure of my prize. I wouldn't be let in, but I knew he would be.'

Carney waved an ink-stained hand at his apprentice. 'That was a mistake. The trouble with Ephra is that he's got suet for brains. He drew attention to himself, when all I told him to do was observe.' He scratched under the collar of his shirt and Daniel saw tiny black things crawling amid the wiry ginger hairs. 'Promised her by the King himself I was, in payment for my special attention to his particular interests. Elias told me to expect your sister as a guest – said he had some business in hand on the matter and that she was coming my way – that was the general gist of it.' He smirked. 'I reckon I'm as disappointed as you, Soldier. I'd made *so many* plans to welcome your nightingale into my bower, but that's not going to happen now, is it?'

'What do you mean?' Daniel moved closer, crushing the thickened lenses of Carney's extraordinary spectacles beneath his boots.

'I mean, not after the raid on The Apollo this morning. I heard all about it from one of Elias's men – a regular customer. He came here in the early afternoon full of himself and his master, but what I care about is what I'm owed. Wherever she is, she's not coming to me, as I was promised. The King of the Rookery has played me a false hand.' A malicious grin crept across Carney's pitted face. 'Perhaps he caught a proper look at her and decided to keep her for himself? He likes them young, just ask your friend with the curls and the sweet bubbies.' He made a crude gesture mimicking the shape of a woman. 'That little whore knows all about Elias's taste for virgins.'

The blow that sent Vincent Carney crashing through the curtain and into the room beyond his shop was as swift as it was certain. Daniel moved to finish the job he'd begun, but Jerome held him back.

'Leave him. He is the very least of our concerns now.' He slipped the unexpected knife back into his sleeve. 'If Pearl is not here, where is she?'

'I fear that Carney may have answered that question.' Darke

released Ephra, who scurried away into the back of the shop, and turned to Daniel who was staring at the shabby, half-torn curtain as if the swirling Indian pattern might hold some hidden clue.

'What now?'

There was a long silence before Daniel answered.

'Octavian has told me what to do.'

Chapter Forty-five

'Well, this is quite a gathering.'

Melkie studied the crowd assembling on the floor of his warehouse. It was late and the cavernous space was lit by candles balanced on every beam and housed in every crevice. Huddled together above the doorway, the pigeons watched the unusual proceedings below with an air of affront.

'If I'd known, I would have got Mrs Trimm to provide refreshment.' He pushed a plug of tobacco into the bowl of his pipe and took out his silver tinderbox.

'May a man ask, in advance, what the fuck's going on?'

'That will soon become clear.' Daniel raised a hand to welcome Ottobah, who had just arrived. He watched him go to join Colly Meriday. The bluff ostler had been the first to answer Darke's message.

An extraordinary meeting of the Brotherhood of Crows had been convened at short notice. After the events of the day, Daniel had chosen the warehouse as the venue. The Richardsons had suffered enough already and it would not be wise to draw further attention to The Black Apollo.

From Melkie's side, he watched the men he knew greet each other and he saw several others with whom he was not familiar deep in conversation. He was surprised to see two black women in the hall, but then he remembered that at the first meeting he had attended he had learned that the Brotherhood included sisters.

Darke had warned that it would be impossible for everyone to attend, but Daniel was glad to see that so many had responded to the call. Alongside them, Musa, Rowson and a dozen fighters he knew and trusted were also present. After consulting Melkie, he had asked them to stay beyond the sessions of the day and he was touched that they had agreed without question.

Scanning the warehouse now, he saw Jen talking to Musa. They stood in a corner a little distant from the others. From the stricken look on his young friend's face, he guessed that she had just told him about Pearl. For the hundredth time, he tried, unsuccessfully, to banish the images that flooded his mind. Clarity, that was what he needed now.

Clenching his fist so tight that his nails dug crescents in the skin of his palms, he turned back to Melkie. 'Do you remember telling me that if I ever needed help, all I had to do was ask?'

'I didn't know it was going to be a tea party.' Melkie clenched the pipe between his lips and applied a lighted taper to the bowl. 'But I have a strong premonition it won't be.'

Jerome appeared at Daniel's side. 'We should begin. Darke thinks it unlikely now that more will be able to attend.' But as he spoke, Inigo Richardson entered through the arched door.

'I am amazed to see him after all that has happened today.' Jerome waved and beckoned him over.

Daniel shook Richardson's hand warmly. 'I would not have blamed you if you had stayed with Alys tonight, sir.'

'Nonsense. I have a duty to you and to your sister. I trust this . . .' Richardson gestured around at the warehouse, '. . . is for her?'

'Partly.' Daniel nodded grimly. 'And for Octavian.'

'Poor man. It will not be long now, but that will be a kindness.' He glanced at Jerome, who did not disagree.

'Now, what of Pearl? I understand you went to Carney's shop this afternoon when you left The Globe in such a hurry, but she wasn't there.' Richardson's statement of fact gouged like a knife in an open wound. 'Did that sly bastard tell you where she is?'

Daniel shook his head. 'But I think he gave us enough information to work that out. It's why I have asked everyone to come here tonight.'

'But the place was a debtor's prison. It is built like a fortress, and besides, Elias is always guarded. His men are armed,' Jerome appealed to the gathering. 'We cannot hope to succeed. I am as eager as every person here to see an end to this monster, but this would be madness.'

He looked up at Daniel, who had taken the high ground on Melkie's desk to make his address to the gathering.

'I am sorry. I know how much she means to you, but your plan will not work. It will not free the people of the Rookery and it will not free your . . . sister.'

Darke folded his arms. 'How else do you suggest we take him? The people of St Giles will follow Daniel. They are ready. There has never been a better opportunity. Octavian would say this too, if he were here. Even though I write for a living, I lack his powers of persuasion, but I will say this: if we do not strike now when The Soldier could attract a thousand souls to his side, then when?'

This was greeted by murmurs of agreement, but many people looked uncertain.

Colly Meriday stepped forward. 'I am a blunt man, as many of you know. This is a brave plan and Daniel would be just the man to lead a mob against the King of the Rookery but it is doomed, as our good apothecary says. What of the militia? Those who survive their guns will be thrown without trial into the deepest cells and never seen again. In the trade we have a saying about lame horses: shoot them dead before they suffer.' He raised his broad flat hands. 'I'm sorry.'

Ottobah patted Meriday's shoulder. The gesture was the final nail in the coffin of Daniel's campaign. The war was lost before it had even begun. The warehouse fell silent. Even Melkie stared at his fine Spanish boots.

Jerome was right. The house of Elias was an impregnable bastion. The iron bars that had once held prisoners captive now acted as a defence against the world, while the miserable courtyard in which it stood was a trap. Anyone who gathered there would be a target for Elias's men and for the guns of the London militia who would surely assemble to quell rebellion.

It didn't matter how many were prepared to follow him. It would be a suicidal mission and one of the first victims would most certainly be Pearl. Daniel swallowed the ball of lead in his throat, along with the bitter truth. He should have seen it from the start – at the very least before he'd stood on Melkie's desk and asked the Brotherhood to rouse the Rookery to follow him to certain death. They called him The Soldier, but this would have been a tactical error with the gravest consequences. Love and desperation had clouded his mind to reality.

He stared down at the floor where the chalked lines of the day's practice squares were scuffed and broken by a hundred pairs of feet.

The terrain was against him.

In America, the Patriots had succeeded because they knew how to use the land, while the Redcoats still fought as if they were on a battlefield in Europe. Again and again, Major Fitzallen had warned that they failed because they did exactly what their enemy expected. There were always Patriot spies within their own camp, and when they fed back information, their commanders must have laughed at the stupidity of the British, fighting an old war in a new world.

Daniel frowned. Even now, Edward Fitzallen's warning rang true. Elias was prepared and equipped for an assault from outside – the attack he expected – but what if it came from within?

Galvanised with fresh inspiration, he looked up. 'Jerome is right. Even if we could raise a mob to storm his fortress, the cost would be too great. I would not lead people to certain death. But what if there's another way?'

He jumped down from the desk. Scooping up a chalk stick from the floor, he knelt to map out a rough plan on the wooden boards, marking the enclosed courtyard, the passages leading to it and the shape of the former prison itself.

'I need your knowledge.' He stood up. 'You have all lived in this city for many years longer than me. Tell me about this building – its history.'

'It was a private debtors' prison when my father was born.' Richardson tried to examine Daniel's plan, but his portly stature prevented him from bending. Instead, he squinted at the chalk marks. 'And many years before that, in the days when my grandfather's great-grandfather worked as a cloth merchant, I believe it was a convent. It's very old. Once it was surrounded by fields, but now it's surrounded by a thicket of brick.'

'Do you know what's here?' Daniel pointed to the space at the back of the building on his plan.

'More of the same.' Richardson shrugged. 'Elias knew what he was doing when he set himself up there. As our friend Jerome says, it's a fortress. The only way in and out is through that courtyard. Not that anyone ever sees him leave, mind.'

Daniel's head shot up. 'How can that be? I saw him myself at the gathering beneath the church. And he came in his carriage to Vinegar Yard.'

'That was either theatre or a threat. You must have angered him a great deal, Daniel, to have lured him out like that. It's rare that he's seen on the streets.' Jerome knelt to stare at the chalk marks. 'He uses the old passages. The Maze is not the only network beneath St Giles. Elias uses ways known only to him and his most trusted men. For all his power, he is frightened that one day someone will find a way to him. He is not the King of the Rookery, he is the King of Rats.'

'I know a way, sir.' Daniel looked up at Sparrow's voice. He hadn't noticed him earlier, but, obviously, he'd been there all along. Insinuating himself between them, the boy took the chalk from Daniel's hand and drew a large ring in the middle of the courtyard.

'There.' He sat back on his heels and nodded, evidently pleased with himself.

'What's that?' Daniel stared at the circle, unable to work out Sparrow's intention.

'It's a way in.' The boy handed him the chalk. 'When Elias beat me that last time, they all thought I was dead. On that point, I wasn't too certain me'self. That's when I heard him talking about that other man, the one who knows you.'

'Fitzallen?'

Sparrow nodded. 'That's the one. After Elias had finished his ranting, he told his men to take me away. Two of them carried me down to the cellars. Deep down there's a stone room with a channel of water running through it. One of the old rivers, I reckon. They threw me in, thinking that the water would flush me down to the Thames and that would be the last they'd see of me. But they were wrong. I wasn't dead and the water was so cold it brought me back. It carried me away, just as they hoped, and all things considered, I probably would have drowned before I reached the river. Truthfully, I thought I *was* dying when I looked up at a round patch of light. I imagined it might be an angel coming to fetch me, but then I realised I was at the bottom of the well in his courtyard. And what's more, there were iron bars set into the walls of it all the way to the top.'

Daniel looked at the solemn faces. 'It must be tonight. Why wait a moment longer? If we can enter through the well, as Sparrow suggests, we'll have the advantage.'

Jen stepped forward to address the gathering. 'You need rest. We all do. It's late. Surely it would be better to do this tomorrow?'

'And what of Pearl?' Daniel appealed to Jerome and Darke. 'You both heard what Carney said. To think of her trapped in that place with that devil is—' He stopped, unable to give form to his hideous fears. 'I say we go tonight.'

Darke nodded. 'I'll go there gladly for the sake of your sister, Daniel, but this will be our chance to end Elias. I must make that clear to everyone present.' His gaunt face was more sombre than ever as he looked at the people around him. 'If you come with us, there will be bloodshed.'

'That must be understood.' Daniel nodded. 'As Octavian said, the reign of Elias must end, but that ending will be a beginning. Who is in agreement?'

After a moment, Colly Meriday raised his hand; so did Ottobah and most of the others.

'I need a dozen men at most, less probably,' Daniel said, trying to convince them. 'If we move swiftly, we can overpower anyone inside Elias's fortress before they are even aware of us.' He turned to Richardson. 'I'm afraid those men must be younger.'

The proprietor of The Black Apollo patted his stomach. 'My days of crawling through sewers are long gone.'

Jerome prevaricated. 'There is still the watch to consider. A group of armed black men, moving through St Giles at such a time ...' He glanced at Daniel. 'The journey across the Atlantic in the hold of a Guineaman is terrible enough, but the fate that would await us on the other side—'

'Are you saying we should do nothing?' Daniel rounded on him.

'I am no coward.' Jerome blinked behind the panes of his spectacles. 'I am merely saying that we should think this through.'

'We have thought long enough.' Darke glared at the hesitant apothecary. 'Now is the time for deeds.'

'I have some information that may help.' Ottobah stepped forward. His clothes were immaculate as usual, but the light of the candles drew out the colours of the paint spots in his hair.

'Tonight, most of fashionable London will be attending the Drury. Mrs Siddons is to make her return to the stage. My employer and most of his aristocratic clients will certainly be there. Afterwards, the Prince of Wales is holding a ball in the lady's honour.'

'How does this help us?' Daniel frowned.

'The Prince is ever-conscious of his safety.' Ottobah smiled. 'As cowards always are. Revolution is in the air. He has ordered the runners to patrol the streets within the vicinity of his presence. Tonight, they will be concentrated at the furthest end of Covent Garden. There is no better night for a group of armed men to move, unnoticed, through the alleyways and passages of St Giles.' He glanced at Jerome. 'Especially if those men are black.'

'They won't all be.' Rowson stood forward. 'I'll come with you, Dan. Someone has to keep an eye on this one.' Grinning, he nudged Musa's arm. 'I'm sure there are other fighters here who'd say the same.'

Immediately more hands rose.

'I won't stop anyone from going.' Melkie sucked on his pipe. 'If I was a younger man, this is a fight I'd be spoiling for too. It's about time someone knocked that fucker from St Giles to St Petersburg.' He exhaled a stream of smoke. 'Or to the gates of St Peter himself – if you're that way inclined.'

At last, Daniel was flooded with a sense of gratitude and hope.

'Who is with me?'

He was elated to see agreement ripple through the gathering. Taking a breath, he bowed his head and whispered a thank you to a God he wasn't sure he believed in.

'Will you need arms?' The question came from Meriday. Surprised, Daniel looked up.

'I can give you two brace of pistols. They're often needed in the livery trade, especially at night. Can you use them?'

Glancing at Darke, Daniel nodded. Overhead, the steady patter of rain that had sounded on the warehouse roof throughout the meeting turned to a sudden, bludgeoning assault. Candles balanced on one of the beams were extinguished by a leak. It was a timely warning.

Daniel turned to Sparrow. 'How far is the passage from the bottom of the well to the cellars?'

'I don't remember it too clear.' The boy wiped his nose with the back of a hand. 'It can't be more than forty feet at the most, maybe not even that.'

Daniel studied the resolute faces of his volunteers. 'How many of you can swim?'

Fewer hands rose at this question. It made his final decision easier.

'Very well, then.' He bent to take up the chalk again. 'This is how we'll proceed.'

He began to draw the layout of the interior of Elias's bastion on the boards of the warehouse.

Jen sank to the boards next to him. Taking the chalk from his fingers, she drew a room beyond the octagonal chamber.

Without looking up, she twisted the red glass beads at her throat and whispered, 'This is where he sleeps.'

Chapter Forty-six

It was past midnight and the alleyways of Covent Garden and St Giles were eerily quiet. Even the whores had given up touting for trade, and they never shut up shop when there was likelihood of passing coin. Most of the street braziers had been doused by the rain and the few that survived in the deluge spluttered feebly. The rain, the lateness of the hour and perhaps Mrs Siddons had conspired to give them an advantage.

Daniel led the small group into the narrowing warren of dripping passages. The darkness suited their purpose. Flattening themselves to the crumbling walls, they moved swiftly, alert to every sound and movement. Occasionally they encountered a rolling drunk or a lone horse and rider. Just once, a small carriage scraped the walls as they concealed themselves in an alleyway, but they could not have designed a better night for the purpose.

Including Daniel, there were six in the party. The ability to swim, or lack of it, had decided the matter. Ottobah and several of Melkie's fighters had accepted, reluctantly, that this was not a mission they could join. Now he was followed by Darke, Musa, Rowson, Sparrow and Jerome.

Despite his earlier hesitation, Jerome had insisted that he should come. Daniel had been surprised but grateful. The knife the mild apothecary kept in his sleeve – apparently a surgeon's tool carried for protection when visiting patients late at night – hinted at a hidden, steelier part of his character. As for Sparrow, it had been impossible to deter him. Daniel knew that even if he ordered the boy to stay with Melkie, Jen and the others at the warehouse, he would not have obeyed. Besides, his knowledge was useful – as were the remaining buttons from his stinking coat.

Before they left, Jen had come to Daniel's side. He was kneeling on the boards studying his plan and hoping his memory of the place was true. Sparrow had added to this diagram, drawing an outline of the cellar with the water channel and further marks indicating the subterranean chambers beyond.

'Daniel, listen to me, it's important. I have to—' Bending close, she had rested a hand on his shoulder, but Melkie interrupted them. Thrusting a package into Daniel's hands, the old pugilist had pointed to the doorway.

'Meriday's boy just delivered these. Use them well.'

Although the package was wrapped in oilskin, Daniel recognised the shape of the pistols beneath the waterproof wrapping. That was the moment when the danger ahead became real. He had looked up, but Jen was no longer there. He caught sight of her over in a corner talking to Sparrow, their heads bent close together.

There hadn't been time to say farewell.

The four wrapped pistols were now in a leather bag over his shoulder; he felt the weight of them as he walked. Similar bags were slung across the backs of the others. Some contained clothing sealed tight in oilskin, while others concealed useful tools and items more deadly than dry shirts and breeches.

The moon and stars were shrouded by rainclouds, but even so a thinning in the darkness suggested that the opening to the courtyard was just ahead.

'Sparrow!' Daniel whispered and motioned for the boy to come closer. 'Which side of the well has rungs?'

'The side nearest to us.' He adjusted the collar of the jacket donated by Melkie to replace the voluminous coat. 'That's lucky, I reckon?'

'And how much space is there at the bottom – can we all go down at once?'

'It's tight down there, I won't lie. Maybe two at a time would fit. The thing is—' They froze as a patch of condensed shadow slipped past them. The cat paused to look back and its eyes caught the only light in the alleyway. Sparrow continued in a hushed voice. 'The thing is, the channel leading from the well into the cellar is narrow. It'll take just one at a time. It spills out of the wall opposite the rungs. It's arched at the top – you'll feel it if there's too much water down there. Hold your breath, dive under, kick your feet and swim fast, that's the way.'

'You are telling the truth, you *can* swim, Sparrow, can't you?' Daniel could not see the boy, but he felt his indignation.

'I've been thrown in the Thames more times than I care to remember, sir. If I couldn't swim then I wouldn't be standing here now.'

As Sparrow suggested, they went in pairs; Darke and Sparrow went first. The night swallowed them whole as they slipped from the mouth of the alleyway and into the courtyard. Apart from the patter of crumbling stone, barely distinguishable from the rain, there was hardly a sound as they climbed over the edge of the well.

They waited and counted. There were no lights visible at the barred windows of Elias's fortress, but the tiniest sliver of yellow indicated the grille in the fortified door and the presence of a watchman behind it.

When the sign they had agreed for trouble or danger – the mew of a cat – did not come, Daniel sent out the next pair, Musa and Rowson. After counting to one hundred again, he exhaled and realised that he had been holding his breath.

He turned to Jerome.

'Ready?'

'Almost.' Removing his spectacles, Jerome pushed them deep inside his shirt. 'I won't need these in the dark.'

This small, reliably sensible gesture magnified the immensity of what they were about to do. Jerome had been Daniel's first real friend in London. He didn't know if the rift between them could ever mend entirely, but when they had spoken frankly about Pearl earlier that day, he had felt something change.

'I am glad to have you with me tonight, Jerome.' He kept his voice low.

There was no answer, but after a moment Daniel felt the weight of the apothecary's hand on his shoulder. 'I am ready, brother.'

Bent low and careful to silence their footsteps, they crept from the passage to the lip of the well. Jerome scrambled over first. His descent on the iron rungs echoed from below, but the noise was contained. Daniel followed.

As he swung down to the first of the rungs, he looked up. Rain fell on his face as, just for the briefest moment, a crescent moon scythed through the clouds. It was a good omen. A lifetime ago on the cane fields of the Garnett Estate, his mother had taught him to wish on a waxing moon. He did so and felt her blessing with him.

'*Think of the future, not the past.*'

Fleetingly, he felt the presence and strength of another.

The stinking water at the bottom of the well was ice cold with a scum-frothed greasiness. It had been a long time since anyone had drunk from here and lived to drink again.

As the others had done before him, Daniel slipped off his coat. Unhindered by sodden cloth, it would be easier to swim. As he freed himself, he took care to keep hold of the bag knowing that the weight of the pistols would drag it to the bottom. Releasing the coat into the fetid water, he called softly to Jerome. He could not see him, but he could hear him splashing nearby.

'I'm here.' The answer echoed off the rounded stone wall. 'When you step off the ladder, Daniel, go straight across. The entrance is about six inches below the surface.'

He heard Jerome take a huge gulp of air and then the splash of water against stone as he dived. Alone, Daniel looked up again, but the moon was gone. He waited a moment to give his friend a start and then, filling his lungs, he plunged beneath the scum.

Moving against the flow was more difficult than he had expected. The walls of the coffin-like channel were slippery with moss, or something more unpleasant, and it was difficult and disgusting to push upon them to make headway. At last, just when he felt his lungs might burst, Daniel was aware that the space around him had widened and that something glowed in the darkness. Pushing upward, his head broke through the water and he breathed again. Never had foul air tasted so sweet.

Darke reached out to haul him from the channel. In the light of a single candle – several had been packed into the bags – he saw that the others had begun to change into the dry clothes they had carried with them. This practical suggestion had been Jen's, who pointed out that a group of sopping men would leave a trail any fool might follow.

Without a word, Darke handed him a sealed package. Daniel stripped and dried himself as best he could and then he pulled on the dry shirt and breeches. The fabric was dark – the men would be shadows. He left his boots in a corner of the dank stone-lined cellar, just as the others had done. It was better to tread lightly in the house of the enemy.

Taking up the leather bag he had carried through the channel, he took out another package wrapped in oilskin. In silence Jerome handed him his knife to slit it open. Inside, Meriday's pistols – their purpose belied by their neat size and the pretty scrolls engraved on the handles – glinted in the candlelight.

Daniel handed one to Darke, who pushed it into the top of his breeches, and the others to Rowson and Musa, who stared at the pistol with a fascinated horror. The young man tried the weight of it in his hand and then he followed Darke's lead.

From his manner, Daniel suspected that Darke had more than a passing acquaintance with firearms, but he wondered about the fighters – a brief demonstration at the warehouse was the total of their experience. If it came to it, he hoped that would be enough.

Sparrow's eyes were fixed on the pistol in Daniel's hand.

'It's real then, ain't it?' he whispered.

Daniel nodded. 'A single bullet. But it should be enough.'

The boy shook his head. 'No. I mean this.' He gestured to the vaulted ceiling overhead. 'All this. We're really going to do it, aren't we?'

Just an hour earlier, Daniel had felt something very similar when he'd taken delivery of Meriday's package.

'Yes.' Reaching out, he clasped the boy's shoulder. 'Yes, we are.'

A flight of narrow stone steps led up from the cellars to an arched door that opened to a small, high-ceilinged room. In the fluttering light of Daniel's candle, the fretted stonework fanning above them looked like the bones of giant hands knotted in prayer. The room was bare apart from a large and ancient wooden chest pushed to the wall.

Sparrow pointed to a small door.

'There's a passage through there leading to the hallway.' He kept his voice to a whisper. 'Most usually, at night the door is watched by Tasker. He was at sea before he came here. They say he was a pirate. Whatever he was, he's a brute. He's not tall, but he's wide and he's strong.'

Unconsciously Sparrow touched the back of his head and Daniel knew immediately who he meant. When he had first been summoned by Elias, the bald head of the watchman guarding the door had been covered by a tattoo of the sun, its rays stretching down to a thickened pink neck.

Daniel put a hand to Sparrow's shoulder.

'Are you ready?'

The boy nodded.

The candle flickered wildly. Daniel couldn't tell if it was caught by a draught, or if it jittered in Sparrow's nervous fingers. From the half-open door at the back of the cavernous hallway, he watched the boy walk slowly and silently. Not expecting to repel enemies from within, the watchman's attention was focused entirely on his post. A single candle burned in a silver wall sconce next to the door. Its little flame was steady.

When Sparrow was within five yards of the door Tasker moved. The boy froze, but the watchman merely grunted and scratched at the cleft of his bottom. Although he was squat and bow-legged, he was a muscular and dangerous mastiff.

Sparrow looked back just once, before stepping forward again.

'Mr Tasker,' he whispered, loud enough to be heard.

The man spun about. Sparrow held the candle away so that his face was partly shadowed.

'I hear you fuck pigs, sir.'

The man scowled. 'Who are you?'

'Wouldn't you like to know, fat arse.'

Spinning about, Sparrow pelted to the back of the hall and Tasker gave chase. Daniel couldn't help smiling. His assessment had proved correct – Elias had not chosen the watchman for his brains.

It was over very quickly. When Tasker blundered through the doorway leading to the passage, Daniel was ready. He brought the butt of Meriday's pistol down on the back of the man's head and he sank to his knees dazed by the blow. Daniel hammered again, finding his mark at the very centre of the sun tattoo. Tasker groaned and toppled forward. He moaned on the stones and then he was still.

'Is he dead?' Sparrow crept back and raised the candle.

Daniel shook his head. 'But he won't trouble us tonight.'

He listened for a moment to make certain that the scuffle had not raised the alarm and then he beckoned to Darke and Jerome, who dragged Tasker back to the room with the vaulted ceiling. The others were ready with rope and cloth. Within a couple of minutes, Elias's watchman was bound, gagged and shut in the chest.

Musa pushed his fingers through his damp hair. 'That was easy enough.' He grinned, but Daniel shook his head.

'That was nothing.'

When they reached the first landing there was a faint glow above. They waited for their eyes to adapt to the gloom and then they took up their agreed positions. From consultation with Sparrow and from previous experience, Daniel knew there were likely to be at least four guards on duty – two on the next level and two more outside Elias's chamber. He reached into the pocket of his breeches.

Buttons from Sparrow's discarded coat gleamed faintly in his palm. He hurled them up the staircase and they clinked and jinked as they tumbled all the way down again.

Musa and Darke crouched behind the heavy balustrade of the landing while Daniel, Jerome, Sparrow and Rowson pressed themselves into the deep shadows at the turn of the stair where a great carved newel post rose like the prow of a ship.

After a moment, the boards creaked above as someone moved to the top of the staircase. Daniel threw a second handful of buttons. They bounced and jingled on the wood and the guard pursued the sound. From the light that swung on the stairs, sending his giant shadow to the wall, he was obviously carrying a lantern.

When he reached the lowest step, he paused and the light pooled about him. Noticing the brass buttons scattered across the boards, he bent forward to scoop them up, mistaking them for coins. Before he realised the truth, Darke pounced. Yanking back the man's head, he slit his throat with a single swipe of a blade. Musa swooped for the lantern, catching it before it fell.

As blood gurgled from the gaping hole, the man flailed, but he couldn't make a sound. His eyes rolled in their sockets and his hands grasped at nothing as if he were trying to catch hold of the air he needed to live. It was over in a minute.

Musa stared at the body. 'I've never ... *never* ...' The whisper died on his lips.

'Then you are lucky,' Darke said with a shrug. 'Remember what these men have done,' he murmured, 'and then you might find an appetite for the work.'

'You coming back tonight, Barley?' The question came from above.

Musa extinguished the lantern. At Daniel's signal they shrank back into the shadows as he hurled the last of Sparrow's buttons at the stairs. Once again, they clattered and jangled on the wood like shillings.

'For fuck's sake. It's the middle of the night.' There was a pause. 'Is that a whore you got down there in the dark? Poll, is it? Like last week? Keep her warm, I'll have a taste of that too.'

The stairs creaked as the second guard descended. When he reached the landing, he turned and stumbled over the body, falling flat at Darke's feet. He struggled more than his colleague when the knife slit his throat, but the end was the same.

Jerome stared at the dead men and then he knelt to close their eyes.

Glancing up at Darke, he whispered, 'My knife, Lemuel.'

The journalist wiped the blade clean on the dead man's breeches and handed it to him.

Every sturdy metal door on the floors they had cleared was locked. Even if Pearl was held captive in one of the old debtors' cells, Daniel could not call out for fear of discovery.

He sat on one of the seats recently warmed by the guards and stared at the table between them. Light from a single candle danced on the men's heavy pistols, two glasses and a pitcher of wine. He took one pistol for himself and handed the other, without comment, to Darke.

'What next?' Rowson spoke a little too loudly. Musa nudged him and placed a finger to his lips. Although they were trained fighters, the pair were far from their usual sphere of competence. Even so, Daniel was glad of their muscular enthusiasm.

Darke pointed at the stairs and Daniel nodded. Before they could reach the chamber of the King of the Rookery, they would have to deal with at least two more guards above. He considered using the button trick again. Would lightning strike twice? Major Fitzallen had been a fine strategist, but he'd never underestimated the role that luck played in a campaign.

'*Never push Fortune beyond the limits of her patience.*'

Remembering that advice now, Daniel slipped the buttons he'd collected back into his pocket.

Fortune clearly appreciated his respect. Fresh creaking of boards sounded from above as booted feet stomped across the upper landing. A voice slurred, 'Fetch another bottle while you're at it.'

'Wine or brandy? There's rum in the cellar.' The reply was also thickened by drink.

While the guards debated, Daniel motioned his men to return to the floor below. They did so quickly, their bare feet hardly making a sound as they descended.

The guard was clearly surprised to find the post below his own deserted. He called the dead men's names, and when there was no reply, he took up the candle and came slowly down the stairs, pistol held ready. Catching sight of a pair of feet, he raised his candle to reveal the rest of the body to which they were attached. Instantly he whirled about, the flame guttering wildly. The light fell upon Sparrow's face as he crouched in the space just behind the carved newel post.

Terrified, the boy raised his hands. Huge with fear, his eyes glittered eerily in the light.

'Duppy!' Aghast, the man stepped back. He warded Sparrow off with the candle. 'But you're dead. I saw to it myself. Get away from me, you—'

His words were stopped, not by a knife, but by the pistol Daniel held to his back.

'Give me your gun,' he hissed into the guard's ear. 'There are many of us and one of you. If you call out or try to run, I will shoot.'

The guard did as he was told. Handing his pistol to Daniel, he swallowed and nodded. 'What do you want?' His breath smelled of brandy.

'How many guards are up there? Whisper it.'

'Just one now. There were four of us on duty tonight.'

'Good.' Daniel jabbed his own pistol again. 'Call your friend down. If you give the slightest indication that there's anything wrong, I will kill you.'

With the muzzle of a pistol held to his spine, the guard – who had truly believed himself to be haunted by the ghost of a boy he had murdered – could hardly refuse his commission.

Once they had removed the incriminating bodies, he called up to his colleague and managed to lure him down the staircase to the deserted hallway.

'Over here,' he called from the shadows as the drunken man

staggered down the last flight of steps. 'I've got rum. The best from the stores, and there's more where it came from.'

It was easy to overpower him in the dark.

Hands bound and their mouths stuffed with their own woollen socks, Elias's men were forced to shuffle down to the cellar at gunpoint. The others waited in the hallway while Daniel and Darke bound the guards' feet and roped them together before leaving them without light in a corner of the dank chamber where they had abandoned their shoes.

When they went back up the stone steps, Daniel locked the door into the vaulted room and then, to make certain, they all dragged the chest in which Tasker lay silent across it. Moving soundlessly back to the hallway, they gathered at the foot of the great wooden staircase. There was a faint glow high above. Glancing at Darke, Daniel raised his hand to signal the final advance.

Chapter Forty-seven

The door to Elias's room was closed. Daniel stared along the uppermost landing where more candles, eaten down by the night, fluttered in silver scallop-shaped brackets along the panelled wall. Darke and Jerome were with him. The others, including Sparrow, waited on the floor below. Daniel was surprised by Sparrow's acceptance of this demotion, but then he remembered what Elias had done to the boy and thought he understood.

Now, all Elias's guards had been replaced by Daniel's men.

Raising the pistol in his left hand, he padded softly on the boards. The air was filled with the scent of spices. It was similar to the fragrance of Adanna. She had intoxicated him, for a while, but here an acrid musk-laden tang beneath the opulence whispered of rot.

Daniel halted at the door and listened. The room beyond was silent. Motioning for the others to be ready, he twisted the metal handle. There was a tiny squeak of protest as he pushed the door ajar. He paused, alert to the smallest sign of alarm from within.

When nothing stirred, he pushed again and the door swung open. Levelling the pistol, he edged forward, every muscle primed for attack.

Two candles guttered on Elias's mahogany desk. The strange unpleasant scent in the gallery was leavened now by good tobacco and rum. As before, books and papers crowded the desk, paintings lined the walls and rich thick rugs were strewn across the boards.

There was no sign of Elias or of Pearl. Or of Infanta! How could he have forgotten her? Cursing himself. Daniel turned swiftly and was relieved to see that an extravagant quantity of midnight blue velvet had been drawn over the animal's cage.

'She will not disturb us now. She has learned the consequences of disobedience.'

Recalling Elias's words, he gave silent thanks for the man's tyranny.

Despite his bare feet, he was also grateful for the muffling effect of the Turkish rugs as he led the men into the room. He saw their surprise at the luxury and splendour. So far, their encounter with the house of Elias had revealed it to be a spartan, functional space, closer to a barracks than a palace. They had not realised that beyond the door of the upper gallery he lived like a prince.

Under the black-eyed gaze of the sitters in the many portraits leaning from the walls, Daniel turned to examine the octagonal chamber. More elaborate stonework fanned across the ceiling high overhead. Where the walls were not covered by books or paintings, stone niches suggested the ghosts of windows. Daniel remembered Richardson saying that many years back the building had been a convent. Now its purpose was far from holy.

Firelight gleamed on the golden figures inscribed across the red lacquer screen at the furthest curve of the chamber. Behind it, Daniel saw a heavy curtain drawn across another tall arch.

This is where he sleeps.

Raising the pistol again, he pointed the way.

Beyond the curtain there was another short passage. Soft light from a candle lantern overhead fell upon wall paintings whose detail had long faded into the crumbling plaster. Daniel went first, careful not to make a sound, miming to the others to be careful of their tread on the dusty stone.

The passage opened directly into a square stone room with a heavily beamed ceiling. The walls were blind, the only light coming from an open fire that crackled in an ancient hearth that stretched along the entire length of one wall. It was so tall and set so deep into the stones that four men could have stood beneath it. A cluster of bottles and upturned glasses were ranged before it. There were three exhausted candles before the hearth too, nearly burned to stumps in their fine silver sticks.

The air was threaded with rum, cloves and something musky and sour.

A vast canopied bed dominated the room. Draped with crimson velvet curtains that pooled onto the floor at each corner, it seemed to float on an ocean of blood. As Daniel's eyes grew accustomed to the firelight, he saw that the bed was occupied. A muscular back striped by long-healed scars curved towards him.

Motioning for the others to follow, he moved closer – holding the pistol steady. Now he could see the mane spread across the pillow and the golden chains around the man's neck.

Elias's arm was thrown across another mound beneath the velvet.

Daniel's throat constricted at the sight of black hair lost in the whiteness of rumpled linen. Aware of a change in the atmosphere, the girl shifted. Turning her head a little, she stared out from the depths of the monstrous bed. She was younger than Pearl and she was white. Her eyes were swollen with tears and her lips and cheeks were bruised.

Torn between relief and disgust, he put his finger to his lips. The girl blinked and her eyes went to Jerome, who had come to Daniel's side. He felt his friend flinch.

If it hadn't been for Pearl, Daniel would most willingly have shot a bullet into Elias's head at that moment, but as he considered what to do there was a ticking, scratching sound from the furthest shadows.

With a yowl, Infanta leapt onto the bed. Eyes narrowed and tail flicking, she stood over her master, a low growl rumbling in her throat. The effect was immediate. Alerted by his final and most faithful guard, Elias rolled in the sheets. Grabbing the girl, he sat up abruptly, forcing her roughly in front of him. Her tiny body was hardly a shield, but the pistol he aimed to her head was a strong defence.

'Make a move and I will shoot.' He jabbed the muzzle into the side of the child's temple and she gasped at the sudden pain.

Infanta wrinkled her nose and drew back her black lips, revealing long yellow incisors. She hissed and her striped tail battered furiously against the velvet curtain.

Elias's strange single eye burned brighter and more savage than those of his pet. Moving to a kneeling position, he sat back on his heels. Corded with muscle, his arm was still wrapped around the girl's body.

'Guards!'

The girl squirmed and Elias gripped tighter.

'Guards!' he called again angrily and loudly. Daniel caught a flicker of unease in his eye when no one answered.

He kept his own pistol level.

'No one is coming. We have dealt with your men, all of them.' Daniel's voice hardened. 'Where is she?'

A sly smile pulled at the corner of Elias's mouth. 'Who?'

'You have no time left for games.' Daniel indicated the men around him. 'Where is my sister? I know she's here.'

'Do you now? And who told you that?' Even now when he was cornered, his rich rolling voice dripped with condescension. Instead of vulnerability, his naked body rippled with menace.

Infanta jumped down from the bed and began to prowl back and forth along its length. Loyal to her master, she patrolled the space that divided him from his enemies.

'Vincent Carney told us she was here,' Jerome answered. 'He had no reason to lie. Indeed, it was *you* who lied to him. You took Pearl after the raid on The Apollo.'

Elias laughed. 'You're wrong, apothecary. Search every room and every corner, but you'll not find her. If you don't believe me, go seek her. I have nothing to hide. I look forward to hearing you admit your error.'

'We've made no error coming here.' Darke raised his pistol. 'This ends tonight. Your time is over.'

Elias held his gaze. 'If you do not leave now, I will kill her.' The girl began to cry. Infanta snarled at the high-pitched wail of fear.

'Judith here is nothing to me, other than a toy, but I know that there is not one among you, not even you, Darke,' he smiled at the glowering journalist, 'who could watch me blow her brains against the wall. And I will, you all know that.'

Following this statement of simple and awful truth, the ticking of Infanta's claws and the crackle of the fire were the only sounds in the room.

'It seems we have reached a stalemate.' Elias studied Daniel's face. 'I warned you that the cost of defiance would be a dear one. The very *dearest one*. Your sister is gone and you will never find her. That is the price you will pay every day for the rest of your life. The pain of it will eat into your heart.'

Daniel salvaged a sliver of hope. 'Then you know where she is?' He took a step closer, but Elias twisted the pistol into the skin of the girl's temple.

'Stay where you are. Your nightingale has flown. I have no idea where she is now. You may threaten me all you like, but I cannot tell you where she is because I do not know. That was not my part of the bargain.' Still clutching the girl, he leaned forward. 'She may even be dead by now.' His eye glowed with malice. 'Tell me, Soldier, who has lost and who has won?'

There was a rattling sound. Immediately Infanta ran to the hearth where scores of tiny glinting objects pattered against the stones. A true cat, she chased the little red beads with her great paws, twisting and pouncing as they skittered across the floor. Absorbed in her game, she didn't notice when her flicking tail knocked over a dying candle and two of the bottles, sending them spinning and leaking across the floor.

'You!' Elias scowled from the crimson depths of his great bed. 'You brought the whore with you.'

Daniel was momentarily confused. Turning, he was shocked to see Jen framed in the arched doorway, a tiny silver pistol trembling in her hand.

Something shimmered and moved on the fringe of Daniel's vision. The smell of brandy filled his nose. Tearing his eyes from Jen, he saw blue sparks dancing across a puddle of liquor spilled from the fallen bottles. The alcohol slipped along a shallow groove in the stones. Almost immediately, the brandy and with it the flames that skipped on its surface reached the crimson fabric of the bed hangings spread out across the floor.

The velvet was old and dry and the dye used to colour it was incendiary. In a moment, the heaped cloth blazed and a filigree of spitting golden tendrils burned swiftly upward into the drapery surrounding one corner of the bed. Smoke began to rise as the fire consumed everything at speed.

Terrified, Infanta cowered by the hearth. Open-mouthed, she paced a tight circle of fear and confusion and then, unable to cross the barrier of flames, she crouched and leapt, landing heavily in the midst of the bed where she yowled and thrashed her tail from side to side.

The yowling turned to a screech of pain. Although Daniel could not see clearly through the thickening smoke, he could not mistake the stench of burning fur.

'No ... NO! Come here, girl.' For the first time, he heard fear in Elias's voice and was suddenly quite certain that Infanta was the only thing the man cared about. The huge canopy was alight now and the velvet hangings at every corner were columns of fire. The windowless room was a tinderbox, filling with whirling, glowing cinders. Choking, Daniel covered his nose and mouth.

'Christ! The girl!' Before he could stop her, Jen darted past him. Gathering her skirts, she leapt over the blue flames and disappeared into the billowing smoke.

Something moved in the heart of the burning bed. Framed amid the fiery hangings, Daniel glimpsed Elias, who now held the frantic cheetah in his arms. Infanta writhed and tried to scratch and bite him, but he held tight. With difficulty, the huge man moved to the edge intending to escape the inferno, but Darke levelled his pistol, forcing him back.

'As I told you. This ends tonight. Go to hell, Elias.'

The last Daniel saw of the King of the Rookery was his petrified expression as he looked up at the roaring, spitting canopy of his bed. There was a groaning sound and then a huge and final snap as it split in two, collapsing in a heap of fire.

Rooted to the spot, Daniel stared at the shuddering mass of flame. Muffling his face in his shirt, Jerome pointed to the passage. 'We must get out.' He spluttered out the words as thick black smoke constellated with smouldering ash swirled around them.

'No!' Daniel buried his face in the crook of his arm. Oblivious to the flames that licked at his feet and his shirt, he sprinted around the conflagration.

Jen and the naked sobbing girl were crouched against the wall on the furthest side of the heaving bonfire of Elias's bed. Although Jen was trying to shield her, the skin of the girl's arms and back was already livid and scorched by the flames.

'Take her!' Jen shouted above the roar of the fire. 'I can't carry her.'

Daniel scooped up the child and huddled her to his chest. Coughing, Jen rose and together they pelted back through tongues of flame to the doorway. Behind them, there was a deafening rumble as the ancient timber ceiling of Elias's bedchamber caved in. A final piercing shriek of agony confirmed that Infanta had been reunited with her master.

Black smoke pursued them as they raced from the burning chamber. Clutching the girl tight against him, Daniel paused to let Jen go first and then they followed the others down the galleried stairs.

At the bottom in the hallway, Rowson wrenched open the door, releasing them all into the courtyard. In the sharp dawn air, the girl's whole body began to shiver violently. Daniel had seen men terribly injured in battle who reacted in the same way. It was shock rather than fear that caused them to tremble.

Handing the child to Musa, he paused by the well and stripped off his shirt to cover her scorched flesh. Jen struggled to remove her petticoat.

'Those burns need cooling.' Her voice was hoarse from the smoke as she peered over the edge of the well. 'But the water's too deep to reach.'

Daniel stared at her. 'How are you even here?'

Instead of answering, Jen handed her petticoat to Jerome. 'She'll be all right, won't she?'

Jerome didn't answer.

As they wrapped the child, a great cracking sound split the air. Daniel looked up to see flames spurting from the broken roof of Elias's fortress. Silhouetted against the brightening sky, ancient timbers jutted upward through the blaze like the ribs of some huge and hideous creature. The groans as the wood charred and buckled sounded like the death rattle of a monster.

Chapter Forty-eight

By the time Daniel beat on the doors to Melkie's warehouse, early morning sunlight was already gilding the puddles in the rutted streets. The rain had cleared and the fierce enamelled blue of the sky promised a day of sparkling clarity.

'It's Daniel,' he called and hammered again. 'Let us in!'

After a moment the door opened to reveal Melkie and several of the others who had stayed behind. They were armed and wary, but with one look at the exhausted faces of the returned they stood aside.

Daniel staggered forward and laid the girl on the wooden floor. The shivering had stopped but now she did not move or make a sound.

'Water, someone, quickly!' Sinking to her knees, Jen laid a hand on the child bundled in her petticoat and Daniel's shirt. 'I should have got to her sooner.'

He crouched down beside them, horribly aware of the acrid scent of burned hair and flesh. The skin of his own left arm was pink and raw where he had shielded the girl from the worst of the flames as they raced from the burning chamber. Jen was remarkably un-scathed, although the scorched material of her gown revealed how close she'd been to peril. He laid his hand over hers.

'You might still have saved her life, Jen. What made you do it? How did you even get inside?'

Eyes fixed on the girl, she drew a deep breath. 'I had to be there, surely you can understand that, Dan? I *had* to see him die with my own eyes or I'd never believe it.'

The girl moaned. Her eyelids fluttered, but then she was still and silent once again.

'This is my fault.' Jen sat back on her heels and dashed at the tears coursing down her smut-stained cheeks. 'Just before you went off, I arranged it with Sparrow that I'd follow and, then, if he got the chance, he'd let me in. He was good as his word. When I came up to the others on the landing, they tried to stop me, but it was no use. In the end Musa gave me his fire piece – he insisted on it ...' Reaching into the folds of her dress, Jen produced the small silver pistol that had trembled in her hand. She laid it on the boards between them.

'I knew where to go. I followed you all up to Elias's room. I heard everything as I stood there in the passage wracking my brains what to do. And then it came to me. Sparrow told me what you'd done with his old brass buttons and I thought I could use that trick again with my beads. I reckoned if I could distract Elias, just a for second, then I might be the one to blow his brains out. God knows I wanted to. But instead, I started that fire. And now, because of me, this poor mite looks likely to ... Oh God!' Jen broke off. 'Pearl – she wasn't there, was she?'

Before Daniel could answer, Jerome was with them. He carried a large jug and rolls of material were slung over his shoulder.

'We must wrap her in clean damp cloth.' Pushing at his spectacles – a remarkable survivor of the night – he knelt and carefully freed the child from the linens. Suddenly she shrieked in pain because the fabric had stuck in places to the burns. Jerome's face was grim as he worked. 'I'm sorry, Judith, but this will make it better.' He began to press newly dampened fabric around her and Jen set about soaking more strips in water from the jug.

It was typical of Jerome that he should remember the girl's name.

Daniel could not bear to watch. Rising, he walked to the warehouse wall and rested his pounding head against the wooden panel.

'Your sister is gone and you will never find her. That is the price you will pay every day for the rest of your life. The pain of it will eat into your heart.'

Elias taunted him from the hell he had most surely gone to.

It was wrong – terrible even – he knew, but part of him hated Judith for not being Pearl. Running from the burning chamber, he'd even tried to convince himself that it was his daughter he held tight in his arms.

'I'm sorry about Pearl.'

Melkie's voice was carefully bland. 'Musa just told me what happened. I'm not usually lost when it comes to words, but I don't know what to say to make it right.' He felt the old fighter's hand on his back. 'I'm proud of you, lad. Proud of the lot of you. Today you cut a canker from the heart of London and that's something.'

Daniel turned. 'It's nothing. Without Pearl I am nothing ...' Unable to continue, he looked away from Melkie's dreadful sympathy.

Over by the door the men he had led to Elias's fortress talked to those left behind. Darke was deep in conversation with Ottobah and Meriday, who often glanced sadly at Daniel. Richardson and the female members of the Brotherhood stood together, their heads bent close in murmured conversation. Rowson spoke quietly to a group of Melkie's fighters. Musa sat alone on a bench and stared at the boards.

They should have been celebrating the death of a tyrant but Daniel's loss had turned their moment of triumph to a sombre reckoning. As he watched, Darke turned to him. The journalist's grave, angular face was resolute. He raised the tin mug in his hand and then he bowed. The men with him copied the toast and the gesture.

Daniel did not respond. Clenching his scorched hands, he looked away. He did not want to be a king; he wanted to be a father.

'Sir. Can I have a moment?'

'Not now.' Daniel didn't even look at the boy, but Sparrow was insistent.

'It's just there's someone asking to see you.'

Daniel turned to him, his voice clogged by anger and misery. 'I do not wish to see anyone. Leave me.'

'Well, the thing is ...' Sparrow stood his ground, '... I reckon you *will* want to talk to her. It's that girl who set upon me in the alley near The 'Pollo a few days back. She's waiting outside and she reckons she knows where your sister is.'

Celeste squinted in the shaft of sunlight that sliced along the passage beside the warehouse. Shielding her eyes, she stepped back and stared at Daniel. The tips of her soiled yellow shoes were visible beneath the muddied hem of her cloak and her hair had come free from the pins that held it from her face. In the sharp clear light, he realised she was older than he had first thought. There was nothing childlike about the look in her eyes.

The day's business down by the river was rumbling into life. Wagons and carriers already filled the streets. They pressed themselves against a wall as a cart loaded with barrels lumbered up from the quayside.

'How did you find me?' Daniel could not quieten the warning voice in his head. Celeste had never been a friend to him.

'Easily enough. I went to The Maze at first light. A woman told me I was most likely to find you here. You do not seem to visit many other places in London.' She grinned slyly. 'Apart from Leicester Square, *n'est pas?*'

He ignored the jibe.

'You've come about Pearl?' The flutter of hope beneath his ribs was almost as unbearable as the pain of her loss.

She nodded. 'I know where she is. Well, not *exactement*, but I know where she is going.'

Daniel's neck prickled. He was elated by this news, but also wary. There had always been something spiteful, menacing even, in Celeste's manner.

'Why should I trust you? Or your mistress?'

Her pointed face hardened. 'I have no loyalty to her, quite the opposite in fact.' The trace of a French accent heightened the furious disdain in her reply. 'Last night my lady told me that my services were no longer required. She ordered me to leave her house and she gave me this.' She produced a small clinking pouch and emptied the coins to the stones. 'I cannot live on twenty shillings and no reference. What is to become of me now?'

Daniel resisted the urge to pull the young woman towards him and squeeze her throat until he had the full story. 'It is Pearl that concerns me. Where is she?'

'She is with my mistress. Last night my lady sent her apologies to the Duke and did not accompany him to the playhouse or to the *gras* Prince's party for Madame Siddons.' She smiled. 'You English treat actresses in such a strange way; they are fallen or risen, with nothing in between.'

'I am not interested in Mrs Siddons,' Daniel said through clenched teeth. 'Tell me about Pearl.'

'I am, if you only would be courteous enough to listen.' Her manner was obnoxious, but he had no choice. She studied him from beneath the lashes of her slanted eyes and her gaze flicked across his naked chest. If she was hoping to play the coquette, her efforts were wasted. After a moment she continued.

'They left from Leicester Square in the early hours of this morning.'

'Pearl was at Adanna's house?' Daniel used the name without thinking.

'If you mean the house of my mistress Marie-Angélique, Marquise de Notaille, then yes, your ... *sister* was there, briefly. When she arrived she was very lively. My mistress ordered that she be drugged to quieten her. There are many places in that house where a person might spy. My mistress has found it very useful to watch and to listen, and so have I.' Now she stared directly up at Daniel. 'My lady does not know that I have discovered all her secrets.'

'I am sick of games,' he growled. 'Tell me exactly what happened.'

'It is very tedious,' Celeste said with a pout. 'But I see I must speak as if to *un niais*. Your Pearl was brought to my lady yesterday afternoon by a man of her acquaintance, a friend of the Duke. His name is James Fitzallen. I know this, because when you stayed for one night at Leicester Square and shared the bed of my mistress, she rose very early and went to him. I have a *bon ami* among the footmen. He told me where the coachmen took her that morning and he also told me that James Fitzallen's carriage came to the house yesterday with your ... *sister*, is it?' Celeste raised a brow. '*With your sister.* And now my mistress is taking her to France. It is very simple, not a game at all.'

'If she turned you from her house last night, how do you know where she has gone?'

Celeste folded her arms beneath her cloak. 'In the service of my mistress I have learned that information can be useful. Four hours ago, I watched from the shadows of the square and saw one of the footmen carry your sister to the carriage. The Marquise was already waiting inside. I watched the carriage roll away and I wondered where they were going. *Alors*, I went back to the kitchens where I knew I would find my friend. He knew of my dismissal and he gave me sympathy, dry bread and cold meat.' She pulled a face of disgust. 'But he told me that the Marquise had gone to her estate in France and that she had taken her new girl with her. He was sorry for me. He said it was wrong that I should be replaced after so many years of good service, but ...' Celeste fluttered her fingers before her face, '... this happens to us, does it not? When we are children they want us as little pets, but when we grow older, they cast us aside.

'Oh! I nearly forgot.' She clapped a hand to her lips. 'There is this also.' She dug into the pocket of her cloak and produced two tiny figures made of straw and wool. One of them was clothed in something approximating to a uniform; the other, small and delicate, wore a green dress and matching head band. The larger of the two dolls was pierced in the area of the heart by a large rusted nail.

Celeste held it out to Daniel. 'I believe this is supposed to be you. The Marquise makes many such things. She once told me of an old French woman in New Orleans who tutored her in the art of magic.' She dangled the hideous doll before him. 'They think us so very ... *naive*, do they not? And yet their own superstitions ...' She shrugged. *'Alors.* If she collected any of your hair – or perhaps your blood ...' her hard little eyes met his meaningfully, '... after the night you spent with her then it will be woven into this poppet. There is also one made to resemble the Duke, which she keeps in her jewel box. It does not have a nail. My mistress has bound her own hair around its eyes.'

Daniel stared at the loathsome object. 'Why are you showing me this?'

For all her studied insouciance, Celeste could not mask the hatred in her voice or in her face.

'I am telling you about Pearl because I know it will bring my former mistress grief. I have nothing now, but I will expect a reward for my help. If you leave soon, you may even catch them on the Dover Road.' She cocked her head to one side. 'Of course, my footman friend was quite wrong about Pearl. My lady would not make her daughter a servant. I think that is right, *n'est pas?'*

Chapter Forty-nine

It was nine o'clock when they crossed the river into Southwark. The Thames was smooth and almost blue beneath the sky. The water sparkled in the morning sun and gulls swooped low over the water.

As they rode towards Greenwich, the buildings thinned to clusters of hamlets, fields and farms. Beyond Blackheath, the tree-lined country roads became a quagmire of ruts and puddles. Daniel took comfort from the knowledge that a heavy-laden carriage would find it hard to travel at speed with mud sucking at its wheels.

In contrast, their mounts were swift and sure-footed. He was grateful for Colly Meriday's offer of his fastest livery horses and was glad of the companions who had agreed to ride at his side. Although Ottobah was not a swimmer, he was clearly a skilled and elegant horseman. And, once again, Lemuel Darke revealed himself to be a keeper of secrets. He rode the bay Meriday had matched to his lanky frame with the confidence and ease borne of long practice.

The muscular grey that Meriday had paired with Daniel was a reminder of his days in the army. The creature was intelligent, responding to his lightest commands with agility and speed. If the purpose of the expedition had not been so grave, he would have enjoyed this echo of an earlier life.

His mood lifted even more when they rode through an orchard just below the treacherous wooded rise of Shooters Hill – where

Darke cautioned them to be wary of footpads – and passed a line of carriages slowed by the state of the road. Clogged with mud and buried to the axles, the wheels could hardly turn. Adanna had several hours' start on them, but the sight increased Daniel's confidence that they could catch her.

The clothes they wore now were borrowed from Meriday's men. Darke wore a long coat, much in his typical style, Ottobah had accepted a close-fitting grey jacket and Daniel wore a black coat that, unusually, fitted him well. Darke also wore a wide-brimmed hat. As he rode, he had the swagger of a bandit.

When the sun was overhead, they halted in a coppice on a rise just outside Dartford to share the provisions assembled by Melkie. Until this point Daniel had not even thought about rest, still less food, but now when Ottobah unwrapped a large meat pie and tore it into three he devoured the pastry and its dripping load in seconds.

There was no time to dismount. They passed the food and the flask of ale from hand to hand in silence. Brushing the last crumbs from the pommel of his saddle, Darke pointed to the river that twisted like a silver snake in the distance.

'The road is old. It follows the Thames for some way but diverts when the land flattens into the marshes. The lady won't have gone far. We'll catch her before the day is out.'

The glade was bathed in soft golden light as their horses cropped at tufts of grass and birds chattered overhead. Ottobah glanced up into the dappled branches and shook his head. 'By the time the sun sets on this day, Octavian will no longer be of this world. There is little more Jerome can do for him now.'

The message had come just after Daniel's meeting with Celeste. A boy whose family shared rooms in the building where Octavian and Marcus lived had been sent to look for Jerome. Relieved at finally finding him, he had begged the apothecary to come back and soothe the frail man's pain. Jerome was still tending to Judith at the time, but Jen had persuaded him to go, promising to take his place at the girl's side.

'Will he be able to help him?'

Darke nodded slowly in answer to Daniel's question. 'Our friend is a man of compassion. He will not see another suffer. I know he will tell Octavian of our victory last night, and that will ease him to his rest.'

Ottobah leaned across from his horse to clap Daniel's back. 'You did a great thing, my friend. If he is called today, Octavian will die knowing his final wish has been fulfilled.'

Daniel looked away. At last, he had begun to appreciate the significance of what they had done. The death of Elias changed everything, but without Pearl his world was meaningless.

It was Darke who intercepted his thoughts. 'What I don't understand is why the woman, the Marquise, has taken her. What would a girl like Pearl be to her?' He pushed back the brim of his hat and studied Daniel with keen black eyes. 'Or perhaps it is *you* that concerns her?'

The question fell like a stone into a moment of silence creating rippling questions. The chatter of the birds seemed to cease as Daniel sought a reply.

'It's a long story, too long for now. When this is over, I will explain.' His horse threw up its head and began to pace on the turf. 'It began when we were both little more than children.'

'You knew her?' Darke's question was even, but he did not seem surprised.

Daniel nodded. 'Many years ago, yes. But now I wonder if I ever truly did.'

'Life changes us all. It's the lesson we must learn to survive.' Darke reached into the leather bag at his side. He tossed small red apples to his companions. 'In my experience, women are subtle and more intelligent than most men. That makes your former ... *friend* a formidable enemy.'

Pulling on the reins of his horse, he spurred it to a trot and then a canter. 'There cannot be many carriages on the Dover Road this day as fine as the one belonging to the Marquise de Notaille,' he called back. 'Come, let's find your sister.'

Beyond the spare village of Northfleet the land thinned into a tufted marsh, just as Darke had said. The horses made light work of it, their hooves sending clods of mud up into the air. When the route curved away from the course of the river it continued on a raised bank of earth through a series of sluice-channelled fields. Occasionally they thundered past a farm or a barn, but this was a poor wet place where the living was hard.

According to the last milestone they had passed they were three miles from Rochester when Daniel caught the glint of afternoon sun on a vehicle a little distance ahead. The brilliant blue lacquer and gilded decoration was unmistakable. It was the fine carriage Celeste had described.

He signed to the others to slow.

'She's there,' he pointed. 'Darke, I need you to ... persuade the driver to pull up, and Ottobah, you and I will hold the footmen when he does. They'll be armed but we'll have the advantage. Once we have her stalled ...' He faltered at a sudden surge of emotion. 'Once we have her stalled, I'll take back Pearl.'

Darke pulled the silver pistol from his belt and glanced at Ottobah. 'Do you know how to use a firearm, painter?'

Ottobah nodded grimly. 'But I would prefer not to.'

It happened fast. When Darke's huge bay horse halted some way in front of the shimmering carriage, he caused it to rear beneath him. At the same time, he fired a single shot into the air. Immediately the glossy black pair in the traces bucked and skitted. Without any option the driver pulled the carriage to a halt. Frightened, he laid down his whip and the reins and raised his hands.

Daniel could not blame him. In his flying coat and wide hat, Darke was magnificent and terrifying – a highwayman come to life from a lurid engraving.

He and Ottobah spurred their horses forward and called out. The two footmen at the back of the carriage turned at the shouts.

'Drop your weapons.' Daniel held the pistol steady. 'You won't be harmed if you all do as we ask.'

Two small pistols fell to the mud and the driver threw aside his whip. A moment later another gun, presumably the driver's, fell to the muddied road.

Daniel spoke quietly to Ottobah. 'Do you know what to do?'

The young man nodded. 'I have them. Go. Take her back.'

Daniel dismounted and went to the carriage door. The letter N was painted on the brilliant blue lacquer in bold scrolling gold. Violet curtains were drawn at the windows.

'Adanna,' he called out. 'I know you have Pearl. Release her and then you can go on your way.'

When there was no reply, he tried again. 'I offer my word. Give her up and you will not be harmed.'

The silence that followed made up his mind. Striding to the carriage, he pulled at the looped handle of plaited leather. When the door did not budge, he took a step back and shot the lock. It swung open on well-oiled hinges, but steps did not rattle down to the ruts.

Brandishing the pistol before him, he leapt. The carriage rocked as he steadied himself against the door frame. The enclosed space was suffocated by Adanna's presence; filled with her will, fugged by her scent and crammed with the tumbled folds of her midnight blue travelling cape. In the deep purple shadows cast by the shrouded windows, he could not see her face, but he saw the gleam of metal.

Daniel gripped the frame of the carriage door and levelled his own weapon. From the corner of an eye, he saw a long fur-covered mound on the seat opposite Adanna. Beneath it, Pearl lay drugged and senseless, just as Celeste had told him.

'Leave us or I will shoot you.' The voice from the velvet shadows was savage. The aristocratic veneer had been stripped away to reveal that most deadly and irrational of creatures – a cornered animal.

Daniel stared at the tiny silver pistol in Adanna's hand and made a swift calculation.

Slowly he lowered his own weapon. 'The game is lost. I have two armed men outside. Your driver and footmen have cast down their arms. I do not believe that you will shoot me, but if you do my friends will kill you.'

'Then what if I kill her?' She moved the pistol towards Pearl.

'That is an empty threat.'

'Are you so sure?' She spat out the reply. 'You know what I am capable of.'

'I do,' he agreed, evenly. 'You murder to take what you want – and you want Pearl. That is why I know your threat is hollow. If our daughter meant so little to you, you would not have gone to such trouble to take her from me. And you will not kill me. From what I know of you now, Adanna, I cannot believe you would sacrifice yourself.'

'And what of her sacrifice?' Adanna shifted on the seat. Now he saw her wide black eyes and the austere beauty of her face. 'If you truly love Pearl, give her to me. In France, she will be enrolled in a convent school where she will live among the daughters of the aristocracy. I will return to London and I will accept the Duke's offer of marriage. There will be no issue of that union. One day, Pearl will inherit two great estates and two ancient titles. What can you give her in comparison?'

'Love.' The simple answer contained all the riches of his heart. 'The love I have given her since the day she was born.'

Adanna smiled spitefully. 'But your love has been built upon a lie, Daniel. I will tell her the truth – how you broke your promises and abandoned me to die – and in time I will make her love me. I will give her everything; wealth and opportunities she could never know with you. One day she will make a brilliant marriage, perhaps a match greater than my own.'

'How little you know her.' He was repulsed by this grotesque version of Pearl's future. 'You cannot buy her. She is old enough and wise enough to make her own choices.'

Shamed by the irony, he stopped. They were fighting over a child who was no longer theirs to command. It had been a shock to see Pearl as a young woman on the night of the salon. Since then, no matter how hard he had tried to ignore it, he had understood the truth. Neither of them had a right to possess her, not anymore. It was a lesson Adanna had not yet learned.

'How can she make a choice when she does not know me, Daniel? You denied me that chance – the chance to be a mother – when you left me to burn to death beneath the roof of The Salutation.'

This was a twisted version of the past, yet even now, Adanna's words and the rhythm of her speech compelled him. What if she was right ... what if?

He fought against the sinuous poison of her tongue.

'You are wrong. I was forced to make a choice that day and it has haunted me ever since. I loved you, but I truly believed that you had died. From then on, Pearl became the centre of my life. I made a vow that you would live on through her.'

Adanna laughed. 'How convenient. You used her to assuage your guilt.'

Pearl stirred a little beneath the furs. Daniel was suddenly uneasy. He glanced at the mounded form on the seat.

'Can she hear us? What did you give her before you left London?'

'A strong tincture of poppy. She is lost to the world now. We will be at sea when she wakes fully and then it will be too late.' Adanna paused. '"Live on through her." How pathetic you are. I am insulted that you imagine the life you have given her would be sufficient for me.' She leaned forward. 'Go back to your little world, your little victories and your little life, Daniel Garnett, and leave Pearl to me before it is too late. You have powerful enemies. How do you think I managed to take her?'

'I do not think it, I *know*. You went to James Fitzallen. He signed a warrant for the raid on The Black Apollo, but Pearl was not taken with the others, she was taken to you.'

'My, my. Perhaps a treacherous little bird has spoken in your ear?'

When Daniel did not answer, Adanna shrugged. 'It is no matter how you found out. My good friend Mr Fitzallen assures me that your prospects are bleak. He mentioned someone called Elias who will make very certain of that. Soon, Daniel, you will be brought so low that you will beg to be taken back to Jamaica and to the cane fields. How could I allow Pearl to suffer with you? If you truly love our daughter, as you say you do, let her go.'

'And what if I say no?' Pearl's voice was shockingly like Adanna's.

Unravelling herself from the furs, she suddenly lashed out and managed to swipe the tiny pistol from her mother's hand. The weapon fell to the floor of the carriage and scudded towards his feet.

'Take it, Daniel!' Pearl kicked viciously at Adanna as she bent to retrieve the pistol. The carriage began to sway and rocked on its springs at the skirmish within. Adanna scrabbled to catch the sliding weapon, but the stiff material of her voluminous travelling cape hindered her movement. The ivory-handled pistol skittered past Daniel and out through the open door.

Hissing and baring her teeth, Adanna scrambled back on the seat, clawing the buttoned leather with her gloved fingers. She had nothing left to play but her fury.

'She is mine.'

Daniel shook his head. 'She is not yours to take; she is not even mine. Pearl is her own person. It has taken me a long time to learn that.' He did not look away from Adanna, but he was aware of Pearl turning to him.

'Does she know the truth, Daniel?' Adanna's eyes flashed. Her voice was slippery with menace.

'I know love.' Pearl spoke clearly and firmly. 'And that is truth enough.'

Before Adanna or Daniel could reply to their child, there was a great thump on the side of the carriage.

'What's happening in there? Do you require our services, Daniel?'

Darke's question suggested a way to be rid of the Marquise de Notaille forever.

Daniel glanced out of the window. Pearl was safe with Darke and Ottobah. They stood together beneath a tree some distance from Adanna's carriage and waited.

The two footmen and the driver had been sent packing on foot along the Dover Road. By the time they reached Rochester and raised the alarm, Daniel knew that he and the others would be long gone. He was unarmed now, but he had a weapon more deadly than bullets to deploy. He turned his attention back to Adanna.

'Do you understand that this is the end? You have lost her forever. Not that you ever possessed her.'

'Come with me.' Her eyes were lost in a band of shadow, but her voice was softly beguiling. 'We can live as a family in France.'

There was a rustling sound and her hand crept from the cloak. She rested her gloved fingers on his knee; the large diamond of the ring she wore over the lace seemed to pulse in the light.

'I have always loved you, Daniel, surely you know that? I was angry, but now ... don't you see? Now we can live together, just as we planned all those years ago. I was wrong to take Pearl from you, but Lady Fate has shown me the way. This can be our new beginning.'

He shifted to see her more clearly. In the violet depths, Adanna had never looked more beautiful or more dangerous. Despite the honeyed words, her rage hung between them heavier than her fragrance.

'We both know that is a lie.' He held her eyes. 'Is it truly Pearl you want, or revenge?'

Adanna snatched back her hand. A moment later she wrenched the ring from her finger and worked at the lace of her glove to reveal flesh that was scarred by labour. Daniel remembered the ugly burns that, even now, crimped and withered the flesh of her thumb and index finger. They were the result of that fateful day – so long ago – in the boiling house of the Garnett Plantation. The day that had led, eventually, to Pearl's birth.

'Is this what you want for her, for our daughter?' Adanna raised her hand to the light. 'No one, not even the Duke himself, has seen this. It is not the hand of a lady. Give me Pearl and I will make her a great lady.'

'I cannot. She has made her choice.'

'Then what of me?' There was an ocean of venom in her voice. 'You gave me no choice that day when The Salutation burned to the ground. You owe me dearly, Daniel.'

He stared at her roughened, damaged hand and tried to remember the girl he thought he had known. She was not the woman before him now.

Experiencing a rush of pity that every version of Adanna would despise, he hardened his heart and gestured to the window.

'We spoke of choices. Let me offer you one. Today you have met two of my friends. Mr Cugoano is employed by the artist Richard Cosway, I think you know him? I understand he has been commissioned by the Duke of Calne to paint you.'

She didn't answer.

'Mr Cugoano is a talented artist in his own right,' Daniel continued. 'Cosway relies on his skills for portions of his larger paintings – those on classical themes.'

Adanna sat back. 'He is just another servant.'

'Then perhaps my other companion will interest you more.' Daniel smiled. 'Mr Lemuel Darke is a journalist – he has many friends and connections. His pen is free and he writes for a number of publications, from the popular sheets to the newspapers read by the highest in the land.' He paused. 'I am prepared to let you continue to France and to your estates. But hear me, if you ever return, I will make very sure that an account of your life, just as you told it to me, is printed in every newspaper in London. My talented friend Mr Cugoano will produce a series of illustrations to accompany that lurid tale. Those illustrations will be made into prints. The rise of the Marquise de Notaille is a lively story, I think even you will agree? The circulation will be huge.'

'You lie.' For the first time, Adanna sounded unsure.

Daniel shook his head. 'I wonder how your aristocratic friends would react to a woman who, by her own account, was not only a whore and a murderer, but also a witch?' He reached into his pocket and threw the poppets given to him by Celeste to the floor of the coach. 'I also have your figure of the Duke of Calne.'

This was a lie, but he knew it would cut. She stared at the figures as he continued.

'In London most people are not so superstitious as to believe in witchcraft, but they despise tricksters, frauds and cheats. You will be notorious, Adanna. You will be shunned and then it is likely that you will be arrested. They say a woman cannot survive a year in Newgate Prison, that's if you're lucky and they do not execute you.'

He leaned forward. 'Or perhaps, as I believe is more common for those like us, you may be sent back to the islands.'

Adanna turned her face to the curtained window.

'There is one more thing,' he continued. 'I understand that through your late husband you have become the owner of a cotton plantation in the vicinity of New Orleans. If you do not free your workers and send word to *The London Courant* that you have done so, your story *will* be told.'

She did not look at him or say another word as he dismounted from her shining blue carriage.

Pearl sat before Daniel on the grey horse. He tightened his arms around her and inhaled the scent of her skin and her hair. It was late afternoon and the sun was low over the road, sinking into bands of pink and gold. It would be a glorious evening.

The horse lengthened its stride, breaking from a brisk trot to an easy rolling canter. Following a dozen yards behind, Darke and Ottobah quickened the pace of their own mounts. Daniel heard them talking and knew that he was the subject of their murmured speculation. Not that it mattered. Pearl twisted to look back at the stranded carriage. Now it was no more than a dot on the road behind them, although occasionally the setting sun sparked flashes from the gilded paintwork.

Abandoned, Adanna sat alone in the cage of her life.

Turning back, Pearl sat upright in the saddle, her eyes on the road ahead. 'That woman is not my mother.' Her voice was firm. 'But you have always, *always* been my father.'

Chapter Fifty

Octavian was buried on a day when the sun shone through the rain. The place chosen was on the eastern side of St Giles Churchyard where a fig tree grew. It was not the finest corner and he would not spend eternity surrounded by once-wealthy bones, but every morning he would be among the first to greet a new day.

So many people had gathered at the graveside to pay their respects that a passer-by might have thought that one of London's great men was being laid to rest. In that, they would not have been mistaken. A less charitable onlooker might also have speculated at the number of black mourners assembled in such a notable public space.

Inigo Richardson and Colly Meriday had paid for Octavian's coffin, for his burial plot and for the services of the rector. When the ground settled, they promised that they would also pay for the inscription and erection of a stone. Daniel suspected that these kindnesses would matter little to the man they honoured. His was a rational modern mind. If there was a place for God within it, that deity would not care for ritual.

Marcus stood on the far side of the pit. Tears tumbled from his eyes as he watched half of his soul lowered gently into the earth. Darke comforted him when he let out a great howl of anguish. It was the first time Daniel had heard a sound from his lips.

He looked down into the grave. Marcus's pain was raw and dreadful to see, but so was the tiny coffin already spattered by mud and crumbling earth. Only now did he fully appreciate the void that Octavian would leave in the hearts, but especially the minds, of all those present.

'We must support him.' Jerome stood at Daniel's side. 'Octavian was his world. Without him, Marcus will be a lost child.'

A brisk wind snatched at the rector's stole and surplice as he finished his brief monotonous eulogy. It was a bitter irony that of all those present he had the slightest connection to or appreciation of the man he laid to rest. Stooping to take up a handful of earth, he gabbled the formula and opened his hand above the coffin. The pattering sound on the wood below was lost in the rain.

Daniel glanced across to where Pearl stood with Jen, Sally and Mrs Kelly. Chained to her wrist, the woman's canary was the only bright thing at the graveside. As was the custom, the women stood apart, their covered heads bowed. When the sun broke through the clouds, raindrops scattered like jewels from the skirts of their black dresses.

In the week since her rescue, Pearl and Daniel had become closer than ever. He had told her about her mother and about their days together at the Garnett Plantation, but he had been careful to paint a picture where there was light along with darkness. He knew he could never tell his daughter the whole story. It was better to let her think that Adanna's actions had been prompted by love, however warped and twisted.

Discovering the truth of their relationship had released them both. Now they were completely open with each other. Pearl was determined to continue as a singer and he knew better than to stand in her way. She was also, after all, Adanna's child.

His daughter raised her head. Black wisps of hair escaped from the close-fitting lace cap that framed her delicate face. She was, truly, a beautiful young woman.

Beside her, Jen stooped to take up a handful of earth. Snatched by the wind, the ribbons of her black bonnet whipped around her. When she straightened up, he saw that her face was streaked with tears along with rain. The chill of the day had brightened her eyes and her cheeks.

Jerome made a small gesture to indicate her. 'I think something broke between you, but it can be mended. It should be.'

Daniel glanced at his friend and then at Jen.

'Iphigenia loves you.' Jerome removed his spectacles to wipe them on the sleeve of his best coat. 'If you can't see that then I can give you nothing to improve your vision.' He smiled sadly. 'I was afflicted too, but she was never for me.'

Jen stepped forward to release the handful of soil. She was less than five feet away and when she looked up from the grave their eyes met. Daniel tilted his head towards her and brought a hand to his heart.

She replied with a nod and the smallest of smiles, then she too dipped her head before turning away.

He had been a fool. He knew that now. The brief blazing madness of his reunion with Adanna had been lust, not love. They shared a past but not a future.

He watched Jen rejoin the women. Chased by the wind, the first fallen leaves of autumn scuttled at the hem of her gown.

In the last few days, she had given him and Pearl the space to renavigate their lives, but they too had met and spoken frankly. If anything, honesty had made their bond stronger than ever. When he told Jen the truth about Pearl, she had been delighted.

Concluding the business of death, the rector snapped shut the Bible. Without offering further words of consolation, he turned back to the church where dry clothes and desiccated books offered the comforting reassurance of familiarity.

They stood in silence for a minute or two and then Richardson cleared his throat.

'Octavian was frail, but his body held a mighty soul. His loss touches us all. If you wish to raise a glass in his name, you are all most welcome to come with me now. Many of you already know The Black Apollo, and for those that don't, it will be my pleasure to introduce you to a place where Octavian found friendship and respect.'

Jerome and Daniel were among the last to leave. From the corner of an eye, he saw two sextons lurking behind a box tomb, their shovels propped against it. Over by the rail, a fresh mound of earth topped by a bright posy marked the spot where Judith, the girl he had found with Elias, had been buried two days back. The child had never recovered from those dreadful burns.

Daniel and Jen had lain flowers on her little grave before the service today.

'Come.' Jerome patted his shoulder. 'We'll go to The Apollo. I know that Darke wishes to speak to you.'

'Sir.' Sparrow insinuated himself between them. 'I have something.'

Dressed in a new dark coat that fitted his skinny frame, the boy looked a good deal cleaner and smarter than Daniel had ever seen him. This was due to Melkie, who had agreed to take him on at the warehouse as an errand boy. Daniel suspected the gruff old fighter had detected an echo of himself in the scrappy lad and even felt something approaching affection for him, even though he would never admit it.

Sparrow reached into the coat and produced a tattered object resembling a dead crow.

'I took this, when we was running away from the fire.' He thrust it into Daniel's hands. For a moment he didn't recognise what it was, but then he realised he held the crown of black feathers.

Sparrow pointed to the symbol of Elias's rule. 'I thought it might be useful, in the days to come. Or perhaps as a souvenir?'

Daniel stared at the crown. The wind ruffled the feathers and a sudden shaft of sunlight brought out the rich sheen of purple, green and blue in the barbs. It was almost beautiful. Twisting it between his fingers, he slowly ripped the thing apart, allowing the broken feathers to drift across the churchyard like black snow.

He watched them tumble and spin away and then he stepped to the lip of the open grave.

Bowing his head, Daniel made a promise. 'No one will wear it again, Octavian.'

'In conclusion, I ask you all now to toast a good man and a good friend. Octavian, may you rest in peace.'

Richardson wiped the back of his hand over his cheeks and turned to his wife, who was similarly moved. 'And now, Alys and I welcome you all and urge you to enjoy our hospitality. Let us all speak of our friend, and perhaps on this day new friendships will be made. I know that would please him greatly.'

Darke stood at the back of the room with Daniel and Jerome. He nodded approvingly. 'Inigo is a bluff man but his heart is as big as his fortune. And this …' he studied his glass of brandy, '… is the finest I've had in a long time.'

Daniel had never seen so many people in The Black Apollo. The mourners who had gathered in the churchyard had been joined by many others. For the first time, there were also white men and women in the coffee house. Jerome explained that they were citizens sympathetic to the aims of the Brotherhood. There were familiar faces too. Deep in conversation, Ottobah and Meriday stood by the hearth. A long black case was tucked beneath Ottobah's arm.

Fittingly, along with sadness, there was good humour and bright conversation. Over in the corner Mrs Kelly was frantically trying to call her bird down from a chandelier. The canary had escaped and now it watched her with an air of insolent amusement. Jen, Pearl and

Sally – hardly recognisable today in her plain black gown – struggled to contain their laughter.

'I have something for us.' Darke set down his glass and reached into his coat. 'It's from Octavian – a message from beyond the grave if you like, although it is something he gave me some time ago. Here, you should open it.'

Daniel took the sealed letter. It was addressed to *The Brotherhood of Crows*. Before the final days of his illness, Octavian's writing had been firm and elegant.

'What is it?' he questioned Darke and then Jerome.

'A last bequest.' Darke tipped back his glass. 'Open it.'

Frowning, Daniel tore at the seal. A single sheet of paper fell to the boards.

Bending to retrieve it, he saw that he held a banker's promissory note instructing the proprietors of '*Messrs Goudge & Carstang of Cheapside*' to pay the bearer '*whosoever he may be*' the sum of five thousand guineas. The signature beneath this message was unreadable.

Puzzled, Daniel looked up. 'What is this?'

'The future.' Darke grinned. 'Octavian took a great risk when he duped Elias into signing it. He gambled on the fact that the King of the Rookery could not read. His only regret was that it was a trick he could, in safety, play only once. Elias had secret accounts all over the city. He was a man of great wealth, and that,' he indicated the note, 'is the sum of one of them. If we use it well, we can strengthen the work of the Brotherhood. He told me to give it to you when he . . . was gone.'

Daniel looked at Elias's ugly scratch mark. 'Why me? Surely this is for us all?'

Jerome nodded. 'It is, indeed, for all,' he said. 'We must also consider the Rookery. Some of this money can pay for medicine, for food and for representation. It is Octavian's gift and his message to you.'

'I won't be their king.' Daniel handed the note back to Darke. 'I've made that plain. I told Octavian that.'

'There will be no coronation.' Darke smiled. 'Listen to me. You are a man they admire. One of their own. Octavian's fear was that Elias would be replaced by someone worse, but we can make sure that doesn't happen.' He glanced at Jerome, who smiled encouragingly. 'Tomorrow night, there will be a gathering in the great crypt. I will send out the word when I leave here. From now on, there will not be a King of the Rookery, but there will be a council. Octavian's wish, and ours, is that you, Daniel, will be its leader.'

The plaintive notes of a violin prevented him from saying any more. The Black Apollo fell silent as, accompanied by Ottobah, Pearl began to sing a lament. Her clear, soaring voice touched the soul of everyone present.

Celeste pushed through the last of the mourners. There were too many glasses on the tray in her hands and when Meriday turned and accidentally jolted her arm several crashed to the floor. Her small mouth knotted itself to a pouch of discontent as she bent to collect the jagged shards. It had been good of Richardson to employ her. A woman in her position would have found it difficult to find work outside a brothel or, worse, on the streets, but Daniel knew her current role was not what she wanted. Adanna had probably been a cruel mistress, but in her employ Celeste had enjoyed a life and status that was far more to her liking. He did not trust the woman, but if it hadn't been for her, he was certain that he would have lost Pearl forever.

'Let me help.' He bent down beside her and picked up the larger pieces of broken glass that had shattered beneath a table. She did not thank him when he dropped them on her tray; instead, she tossed him a surly look and sashayed away.

There was still a great deal of glass scattered on the boards, most of it too small to tackle without injury, but there was also a discarded newspaper – *The London Courant* – fallen to the floor. Daniel reached for it, intending to scoop the glistening shards together. He was about to roll it up to suit his purpose when his eye fell upon a familiar name in the article beneath his thumb. Flattening out the sheet on the table, he began to read.

The Audentior, Naval Frigate, expected Pool of London

Caught in a tempeste off the Cape of Good Hope in June, His Majesty's Vessel was Separated from its convoy. Such was the Damage inflicted by the Storm, that there was no Option other than to return to London. While making this journey, The *Audentior* was attacked off the Guinea Coast by French Corsairs – the very Scourge of the Seas. Despite the Condition of his vessel and the tryals recently experienced by his crewe, Captain Stephen Benson successfully repelled this Assault, leaving the richly laden Corsair *Capricorne* in a more parlous state than that of his own command. On his return, it is expected that Captain Benson will be decorated for his Resolute Action, which not only saved the lives of many, but captured a significant prize in the name of His Majesty.

Daniel read it again, and then one more time to be sure there was no mistake. The man who had witnessed the last will of Major Edward Fitzallen was returning to London. Captain Benson had always been a man of honour, but now no one would question the word of a hero.

'Think of the future, not the past.'

Daniel heard Jon's words as clearly as if his brother stood beside him.

Acknowledgements

Like many of the best stories, the book you have just finished began life on a rainy night in the back of a London black taxi cab. Steeped in 'the Knowledge'*, a driver recounted the tale of the many formerly enslaved men who had come to London in search of freedom after fighting for the British in the American War of Independence. As he carried his fascinated passenger past St Giles' Church, the driver remarked that these men were known as 'The Blackbirds of St Giles' – and his words struck a chord.

Through the magic of osmosis – that being the gradual passing of this intriguing historical nugget from person to person - the 'Blackbirds' finally nested in the mind of our indefatigable agent Eugenie Furniss. It was she who brought us together and asked if we might write a novel based on the idea that 18th-century London had a hidden black history.

Although we had never worked together before, Eugenie rightly suspected that we would hit it off and that our different interests and

---

* The Knowledge of London, also known as 'the Knowledge', began in 1865. It is the arduous process by which someone hoping to become a licensed cabbie still learns the streets of London, committing to memory thousands of routes and thousands of buildings and landmarks, along with points of interest and history. Having completed 'the Knowledge' two of Kate's late uncles were London Black Cab drivers

skills would make for a good mix. One of us (Marcia Hutchinson) is a former lawyer with a forensic interest in Black history and the other (Kate Griffin) is a former journalist, with a passion for London.

Marcia is the daughter of Jamaican migrants to the UK who were part of 'the Windrush generation'. Between 1948 and 1971 half a million Black men, women and children arrived from the Caribbean lured by the promise of opportunities – promises that were not met. The boat that brought the first of these hopeful people across the Atlantic was called *HMT Empire Windrush*.

Kate was born in London within the sound of the famous Bow Bells of St Mary-Le-Bow, Cheapside, which makes her a true cockney. Her family, which includes immigrant Irish ancestry, has lived in London for generations.

Writing together as Lila Cain, we felt we could bring our unique perspectives to *Blackbirds*. And so, armed with little more than the words 'Blackbirds of St Giles', we began to research.

The story that emerged was one of poverty and sadness.

There were indeed hundreds of Black men, women and children living in the notorious rookery of St Giles in the late-18th century. In a haunting echo of *Windrush*, many of the men – after escaping enslavement – had fought legitimately for the Crown in the American War of Independence and had been promised a bright, free future, only to find themselves destitute when they finally came to England.

For outcasts there was nowhere further to fall than the rookeries of Georgian London. These nests of thieves and paupers were feared and despised and the St Giles Rookery was probably the most infamous pit of disease, degradation and despair. Its inhabitants *were* known as 'blackbirds', but this was most probably an allusion to the place's dangerous reputation. The St Giles Rookery was also known as 'The Holy Land' for the large number of Catholic Irish who sheltered there. In addition, it was a refuge to destitute Scots driven south by the Highland Clearances and countless others who, utterly impoverished, had nowhere else to go. The real 'blackbirds' were diverse, but they were united by the fact that they were viewed as the dregs of society. Their lives were bleak.

As we began to plan and write this story, we knew that we wanted to add hope to the darkness. We started by creating the central characters – which was great fun over several weeks and many glasses of wine – and found ourselves passionately interested in their lives and their personalities. Soon these characters developed a life of their own. Pearl, in particular, told us exactly what she wanted to do! When we came to developing the plot, we were so completely invested we knew that could not allow Daniel, Pearl and their friends and allies to fail.

At the outset of our writing partnership, we discovered a mutual love of *Bridgerton*, a historical TV series that is ground-breaking and important in so many ways. But where *Bridgerton* is a glorious fantasy, we wanted *The Blackbirds of St Giles* to be founded more squarely in gritty reality.

We have taken liberties, but the historical background to the book you've just read is largely accurate. And yes! We are quite aware that in some ways our story is also a caprice, but it is one that is based on truth. We knew this was important and sensitive ground and we wanted to do our characters and the very real people they might have been full justice. While writing, we continually asked ourselves the question, 'what if?' and that led us down some unexpected but logical pathways.

Estimates vary, but it is thought that during the 18th century over 20,000 Black people were living in Britain, mainly in ports and cities such as London. For centuries there had been a Black presence – we make this clear with characters such as coffee house owner Inigo Richardson – but in the 18th century there was a notable spike in the Black population. In the main, this was a consequence of the slave trade, but equally, many people were domestic servants, seamen or soldiers. Some notable Black people of this period achieved fame as musicians, writers, thinkers and businessmen, and we wanted to celebrate them.

Ottobah Cugoano – imagined here as a member of the Brotherhood of Crows – was a significant figure in the abolitionist movement. Born in West Africa, he was sold into slavery at the age of thirteen. In 1772 he was purchased in Grenada by a merchant who took him to England where he learned to read and write. After emancipation he worked for artists Richard and Maria Cosway, becoming acquainted with several prominent British political and cultural figures.

However, no matter their social rank, during this period Black men, women and children would all have been cruelly aware of difference and alienation. Whatever their background, most would have experienced prejudice and oppression.

In terms of our writing partnership, we have learned so much from each other along the way. We have argued, sulked, listened, laughed and celebrated together. As well as this book, our partnership has produced a firm and lasting friendship. We hope we have created a rich, absorbing, almost Dickensian historical adventure, but one where Black characters are right at the centre of the stage and at the heart of the action

Together as Lila Cain we would like to thank Clare Hey, our superb editor at Simon & Schuster, and everyone in the team there who has helped to bring our story to the page with such care and enthusiasm. A huge thank you also to Louise Davies and Tamsin Shelton who guided us through the edit process with great skill. We would also like to thank our wonderful agent Eugenie Furniss, without whom this book would never have happened, and most particularly the late Ileen Maisel – a glorious force of nature – who took that fateful taxi ride past St Giles' Church. We hope we have done justice to the hidden aspect of London's story that fired her imagination.

Marcia would also like to thank: Peter Kalu and all the writers at Commonword in Manchester whose workshops helped her to hone her craft. Russ Litten, whose encouragement helped her believe in herself. Her daughter Lila, who has championed her writing for years, mega writing buddies Dipika Mummery and Clare Ramsaran and lockdown (and lifelong) writing friend Mo Pickering-Symes and finally, The Musketeers – Ekua Bayunu and Amna Abdullatif – who kept her body and soul together over some tumultuous years.

Kate would like to thank *so many* people that it's impossible to list them all here. She hopes they know who they are. Special shoutouts to old friends Leah, Lisa, Frances, Debbie and Antony who have always encouraged and believed in her; to writing friends, especially Essie, Sean, AJ, Anna, Antonia, Miranda and the fabuloussssssss 'Nest of Vipers' (the most supportive and friendly group of authors), to the St Albans massive, and finally, most especially, to Stephen, her incredibly kind and long-suffering husband.

Together we are proud of our Blackbirds and hope they fly.

Lila Cain
5th March 2024